Evenings on Dark Island

A novel by

Rhett DeVane and Larry Rock

All rights reserved. No part of this book shall be reproduced or transmitted in any form or by any means, electronic, mechanical, magnetic, photographic including photocopying, recording or by any information storage and retrieval system, without prior written permission of the publisher. No patent liability is assumed with respect to the use of the information contained herein. Although every precaution has been taken in the preparation of this book, the publisher and author assume no responsibility for errors or omissions. Neither is any liability assumed for damages resulting from the use of the information contained herein.

Copyright © 2010 by Rhett DeVane & Larry Rock
Cover photograph by Rhett DeVane
www.rhettdevane.com
The phrase "*Boogity, boogity, boogity. Let's go racin', boys!*" was used with the expressed written permission of Darrell Waltrip.

ISBN 0-7414-5931-0

Printed in the United States of America

This is a work of fiction. Names, characters, places, and incidents either are the product of the author's imagination or are used fictitiously. Any resemblance to actual events or locales or persons, living or dead, is entirely coincidental.

Published April 2010

INFINITY PUBLISHING
1094 New DeHaven Street, Suite 100
West Conshohocken, PA 19428-2713
Toll-free (877) BUY BOOK
Local Phone (610) 941-9999
Fax (610) 941-9959
Info@buybooksontheweb.com
www.buybooksontheweb.com

Dedication from Rhett DeVane:

This book is dedicated to three of my core family
who no longer grace this earth plane:
my father, mother, and sister.
And to my brother who still does, thank goodness.
Mom, Dad, and Sis, this is only the beginning.
Hope y'all are laughing and cheering from where you sit.
Bubba, I know you are!

Dedication from Larry Rock:

This book is dedicated to my girlfriend,
who also happens to be my wife.
And, to the wren that lives in my garden. You inspire me.
You are one of the smallest birds out there,
yet your song and bravado are as loud and as boisterous as
the hawk's. May no one ever tell you your actual size.

A special thank-you:

- To Grayal Farr for his archeological knowledge.

- To Andy and Sandy Mohney for the "crash course" on all things NASCAR.

- To Darin Jones for his help with NASCAR contact information.

- To Donna, Hannah, and Susan—the ladies of the WWW critique group—for your support, patience, and advice.

- To all the coworkers, friends, and family members who have tolerated Rhett and Larry as they created the world of Dark Island.

Chapter 1

Saturday evening: late.

Rattmelia Japonica: crown jewel of the Dark Island inner garden. The bloom, perfect in its total essence of *ratness.*

R. B. "Arby" Brown leaned close and touched the plant with the tentative caress of a lover.

"You are lovely."

In profile, the flower appeared mundane; just another southern Camellia on a nondescript evergreen woody shrub. The direct view shocked the eyes. Rosy petals fanned out around a tight center-pointed bud, with two wiry clusters of yellow stamens at nine and three o'clock and a matched set of small round protrusions set like beady eyes at twelve o'clock. The visage of a rat; not unlike the reflection Arby faced every day when he chanced to pass a mirror. The Camellia's scent added the finishing touch; the fetid odor of blended garbage too long in the steaming Florida heat. As with the gardener's other hybrids, the plant's behavior deviated from its nature. Most of the Camellia species bloomed in the winter months. This one favored the heat and humidity.

A smooth male voice caused the master gardener to jerk upright.

"You have outdone yourself, Arby."

Five years, he had worked for Vincent Raynaud Bedsloe III, and he still couldn't get accustomed to the man's strange ability to materialize from thin air.

"Thank you, Sir. She *is* magnificent."

His employer stepped from the shadows and stood beside him. Other than the quirky habit of dressing in 1950's movie star attire, Vincent would pass as just another forty-year-old wealthy playboy. The man had more silk smoking jackets than Hugh Heffner.

Not that Arby leaned toward admiring his fellow males, but it was not hard to see why the Hollywood types who frequented The Spa at Dark Island gravitated to his boss. Vincent possessed classic good looks and breeding: dark hair and eyes, a slender build, impeccable grooming and manners, and the ability to converse intelligently on any subject. Long-legged women fawned at his feet and he could have his pick, if his tastes ran to that sort of thing.

Arby was one of the select few who knew: Vincent's passions ran in a different vein. Literally.

A gentle land breeze disturbed the Spanish moss draped like mourning shrouds in the live oak branches overhead. This time of night, no spa patrons wandered the extensive formal gardens in search of titillation. The last formal dinner of the week had passed, and they were either satiated and asleep, or packing for the next day's departure.

"Of course," Vincent said, "these might not be the favorites of our guests."

Vincent's nose twitched. One problem with preternatural senses: odors detectable by normal human olfactory devices became almost intolerable. Over time, he had learned to filter out the background tang of the coastal marshes: a blend of brine, decaying plant and animal matter, and the occasional exhaust perfume of a passing motorboat engine.

"Not to worry," Arby said. "You and I are the only ones allowed into the garden's inner sanctum."

Vincent nodded. "I detect something else." He lifted his head slightly. "Have you been using chemicals again, Arby? You know I detest the smell."

Arby thought for a moment before answering. "Has to be the willow water." He pointed to the greenhouse. "I collect young willow branches and cut them into pieces. It takes three or four small branches to make a gallon. I add the pieces to water and simmer over very low heat for ten to twelve hours. Very important: it cannot boil. After, I let it cool and bottle it up. Oh, and I always label it so that no one drinks it by accident. It is somewhat toxic to humans."

"Fascinating." Vincent nodded. "And you use this how?"

Vincent directed his full attention to his gardener and Arby soaked it in like a warm milk bath. Never in his miserable existence had anyone cared enough to make small talk, much less look him directly in the face. Through a series of jobs, he had kept his face concealed with masks and, lately, a beekeeper's mesh hat. The only profession where his rat-like features and small stature had not only come in handy, but also advantageous, was his last: attorney.

"I put cuttings in a glass or jar and cover the ends with the willow water overnight. The tonic contains a hormone that helps plants root."

"Your talents were wasted in the legal arena," Vincent said. "Though I am pleased to have an overseer who can take care of business, too."

Thanks to his association with Vincent Bedsloe, Arby left it all behind: The stares. The whispers. A childhood where his peers called him *Rat Boy*. Now as overseer, gardener, and chief gourmet cook for The Spa at Dark Island, he was free. The small number of legal dealings on occasion, he gladly provided at no charge.

Vincent removed a small glass vial from his jacket. He held it to the dim light. A dark liquid inside seemed to emit its own eerie luminescence. "Add a couple of drops of this. The plants will surely flourish."

"I'd rather save that for the patrons," Arby said. "No telling what it would do to my plants. They might start to think I look like something they'd like to chew on."

"Good point." He slipped the vial back into its pocket.

"Something I want to address—after the weekend's festivities—it has been another long and dry spring, now well into summer. We've had very scant rain. We really should consider a series of controlled burns, Sir. The underbrush is like tinder."

Vincent's nose wrinkled. "I dislike the way the land looks after one of those, Arby. And the smell! The patrons won't abide it, nor can I."

"Fire is actually therapeutic for a southern forest. If we start in the late fall when most of the vegetation becomes dormant, we should be able to complete the acreage before the end of the year. By next spring, the green shoots will appear. Nature has a marvelous way of reinventing herself."

"What of the mansion grounds? Your gardens? The houses?"

"One of the first things I ordered when you and I first affiliated was a wide plowed firebreak around the spa grounds. The gardens are amply irrigated. No worries there."

Vincent thought of the pungent smoke. His sensitive nose twitched. "I think I shall put that off for a bit, Arby."

"I advise against procrastination, Sir. Unless we start to have an abundance of rainfall, or a tropical system pushes in moisture from the Gulf of Mexico, this will be the third year of extended drought."

"Point taken, Arby. I will consider it. No promises."

Vincent's shoulders squared; a gesture his overseer recognized. The discussion was over. No use flogging a dead rat.

"Ah, and one more I must show off..." Arby moved to an ornate iron arbor and waved his arm like Vanna White revealing a letter on *Wheel of Fortune*. "My latest darling—*Mousezilla Passionata*."

The vine—pointed leaves with a series of spinney lavender blossoms—grew in a thick interwoven thatch around the metal rungs. A proliferation of dinner plate-sized flowers, suspended from stubby thick stems, jockeyed for space.

Vincent leaned toward one of the blooms, then looked to the gardener with one raised eyebrow. "Odd. No foul scent."

As if on cue, the flower quivered, made a watery noise, and shot out a spray of mucous. A green glob clung to the tip of Vincent's nose.

"Nice." Vincent snapped a fresh linen handkerchief from his pocket and wiped the smear of plant slime from his face.

Arby stifled a laugh. One thing Vincent Bedsloe could not abide; anyone laughing at him. "I like to think of myself as multifaceted, Sir."

Vincent's lip curled in disgust. He discarded the hankie in a nearby refuse container. "You are that, my friend."

"I am surprised to find you out here," Vincent said. "With all the general bedlam with the impending Blue Blood Ball."

Arby sucked in a lungful of air and blew it out slowly. The annual Blue Blood Ball to benefit the American Hemophiliac Association loomed. Just five days left to corral all the different suppliers, caterers, technicians, and security officers. So many details.

"I had to take a break, even for just a few stolen moments with my children." He fondled the softball-sized red bloom of a blood lily. "It relaxes me. Greatly."

"It will come together beautifully, as always, Arby. I have the ultimate faith in your abilities."

"I sometimes wonder if we should have spa patrons here at the same time," Arby said. "Perhaps it would be better to have the week vacant."

Vincent shook his head. "You know that would not be feasible. This week is booked well in advance. Plus, the chosen four pay double the normal fee, just to stay here during the gala."

"I suppose a few more thousand in addition to the required donations from the gala attendees…"

Vincent rested a hand on his gardener's shoulder. "All for a good cause. I simply can't abide the idea of all of those hemophiliacs bleeding out." He tsked. "Such a waste of precious liquids."

Arby hesitated for a moment before broaching a touchy subject. "If only I could have a bit of the blood distillate…I would have much more energy."

"Now, Arby. We have gone over this so many times it bores me. The consequences far outweigh the benefits. Don't you agree?"

Arby's shoulders slumped. "I suppose."

Vincent studied his friend and employee. "I don't know what long-term effects the distillate has on humans." He chuffed. "Not like we can request FDA trials. Could cause liver damage. Kidney failure. Who knows?"

"I could always…turn."

Vincent's features darkened. How could a mere human—much less a rat-faced one—truly grasp the concept of eternity? A life separate, devoid. An image of the only human he had ever loved flashed into his mind and he shoved it down before the emotions swept across his sore heart. *Julio*. The one person who had known him. Accepted him. Taught him to accept himself. But that was before everything changed and life—or what Vincent considered the opposite of life—forced him to reinvent himself.

Vincent felt the blood tears gathering in his eyes and willed them away. "After all you know and all you've witnessed. Do you really want to become like me. Like—?"

Arby threw up a hand. "Stop! Don't say her name!"

Vincent nodded. "We will discuss this later. I promise. After the gala. If you still feel strongly about it. Passionate about it." He gave a dismissive wave.

Arby swatted a fat mosquito. The insect was full of blood. "I hate these little blood-suckers!" He closed his eyes and sighed. "Sorry, boss. I didn't mean to—"

"No harm, Arby. I know they annoy you. Fortunately, my altered chemistry turns them away. Still, one has to admire their beauty and design. Such efficient little creatures. Such kindred spirits."

Arby hesitated a moment. "I do think it might be wise to contract someone to spray before the gala. I know our main tent is always air-conditioned, thus less of a chance for the mosquitoes worrying the guests, but they are in harm's way when they venture to the restrooms or into the moon garden."

"Absolutely not! I abhor the smell of the chemicals, for one thing. For another—how could I live with myself if I was responsible for the slaughter of these little innocents? No pesticides. I'm shocked you would even consider it, Arby, with your love of everything green and natural."

"It was not for me, Sir. Really. Would you consider citronella candles, perhaps? Their scent is effective. They are natural. Not deadly, and no lingering effects."

The Master of Dark Island nodded. "It could work. I'll figure a way to blend it into the decorating scheme." He patted his overseer on the shoulder. "Consider it done."

Arby motioned to the plants surrounding the inner garden. A line of foul-scented flowers—hybrid dahlias, blooming vines, Black-eyed Susans, and an assortment of perennials and annuals—stood sentinel. A small area held a mixture of culinary and medicinal herbs. And, hidden cleverly in a thicket of cane, a healthy stand of marijuana.

"You wonder why I breed my hybrids so carefully?" Arby asked. "The mosquitoes and biting flies generally keep their distance. This is the only place on the grounds where I can find peace without hosing down with repellant." Arby took a deep inhalation and smiled. "I love the way they smell. So unpretentious. So real."

"If it keeps you safe and happy, I can learn to appreciate the...bouquet." Vincent smiled. "I don't think I'll work them into the gala floral arrangements, though. It takes a certain tolerance to appreciate their...unusual aroma. We'll stick with the citronella candles. No offense intended."

"None taken. What of this week's patrons?" Arby asked.

Sunday: the changing of the gilded, privileged few at The Spa at Dark Island. The name itself, deceptive. Dark Island wasn't an island; more of a peninsula-like spit of land connected to the mainland by a narrow concrete bridge and security gate, private and secluded—a feat in itself in Florida. The section of the Gulf Coast was one of the few areas not infested by the typical mouse-hat-wearing tourists. No sugary beaches lined the periphery, only knee-deep mud flats. No hotels or restaurants for miles. Nothing but oak and pine hammocks. A perfect spot for millionaires to retreat and renew, unnoticed.

The moneyed class came for the high-end spa treatments: Dead Sea salt rubs. Hot stone and exotic oil massages. Mud baths. Seaweed facials. A few metaphysical rituals thrown in as accents.

The most important—though none knew just how important—the daily B-12 injections, laced with just enough of Arby's special distillate. Liver spots disappeared overnight. Lines faded. Gray and thinning hair grew plush and dark. Posture improved. Energy returned. All the subtle and not-so-subtle signs of aging receded. Guaranteed to last for one year before creeping back to vex the host. A sure guarantee of return clients.

The magic was in the blood distillate, Arby knew. People were infinitely gullible. Rub some slimy goop on their skin, feed them a diet of rabbit food, put them through a workout twice a day, smudge their rooms with burning sage, hang crystals around their necks, and stick them with needles. Anything to court youth. All good, but not what caused the miraculous transformation.

The return? A couple of pints of fresh human blood they would never miss. Oh, and fifty-thousand dollars for the week. This particular week—a hundred thousand. Chump change.

They came, too, for Vincent Bedsloe.

The mystique surrounding the reclusive man had grown to legendary proportions. The extravagant dinner parties. The midnight walks in the gardens, escorted by the attentive host. All of the special touches that only a former party and event planner could muster. The desserts—especially Arby's special herb-laced brownies—drew raves, even from the anorexic runway models.

"Are you going to The Dark this year?" they whispered over cocktails.

The Spa at Dark Island. One must *be* somebody. Somebody with enough money and clout to wrangle an invitation. Somebody insecure enough to come back year after year.

Vincent pulled a Cuban cigar from the smoking jacket. He ran his finger over the foil band, admiring the miniature artwork. So detailed! He slipped off the band and put it in his pocket: one more for his notebook. For many years, he had kept the cigar bands jumbled in a brandy snifter in the media room. Now, he organized his favorites in a handmade leather binder, complete with a commentary and points in his personal rating system. Julio had loved the cigars from his motherland. As with so many things from a dead and derailed past, they provided a thin tether for Vincent; a gossamer string tied to Cuba and one of its magnificent native sons.

Arby watched as his boss went through the ritual of sniffing, snipping the tip, and lighting: an exercise taking a good couple of minutes to complete.

Vincent drew in a puff and released a cloud of smoke and relished the moment. Yet another worldly pleasure that could no longer worry his health.

"Barbie left the list before she retired for the day," Vincent said. "Four, this week. Three are repeats—a starlet, a male actor past his prime, and a senator's wife. The other woman, I don't recognize. The daughter of a Texas oil baron, from her application." Vincent considered. "Ever notice how many patrons we get from California? Did they pass a law that it's illegal to look over twenty-five out there?"

"Hollywood." Arby snorted. "Enough said."

Vincent laughed. The sound: rich, throaty, and sexual. Arby wasn't gay, but the sound still made his knees weak. His boss's features morphed to concern. "I've had the oddest feelings of unrest. I hope they aren't on target."

Arby flinched. Vincent's premonitions were historically correct. What would it be this time?

"You don't suppose the one whose name shan't be uttered and her stable of miscreants are getting ready to descend, do you?" Arby deadheaded a hybrid black rose bud. The pungent odor of garlic stung his nose. For certain, no one would ever make a fancy potpourri from its dried petals. Though he didn't grow actual garlic—Vincent deplored the plant—the rose with its heady bouquet was allowed. "I just hate it when that woman comes. Not to dis' your blood sire, boss, but she is entirely disruptive."

Vincent nodded. "When Emmaraud and Jimmy Rob go on one of their trumped-up redneck rampages…"

Arby nodded. "God help us. It took me two days to clean up their blood-drunken mess last time she was here."

Emmaraud Bonneville.

Just thinking his blood sire's name raised the fine hairs at the base of Vincent's neck. Why the hell couldn't he have had one of her wildly handsome male consorts as his creator? Instead, he was stuck for eternity with a centuries-old female who acted like a sex-crazed teen. When she and Jimmy Rob Jones partied, a few locals went missing, and it was up to him and Arby to sweep up the dirt and hide the lifeless husks.

Why had Emmaraud chosen a middle-aged gay man? Simple. The fashion at the time amongst the female moneyed jet-setters: a gay best friend. Emmaraud played with the idea of being a Fag Hag. Liked it. Decided she wanted her own gay boy best friend for all eternity. Turned her vamp eyes toward the man in charge of catering the Miami Beach party she was attending at the time.

Vincent woke up on Dark Island inside a mansion with a terrible hangover and a matching set of holes in his neck. His old life dashed to dust. Julio; a bittersweet memory.

The rest was history.

"Let's not mention her name again," Arby said. "Lest we call her forth. The woman has an uncanny ability to tune in…" He swept one hand through the air. "…from whatever European villa she's infesting at the time."

Vincent took a long drag from the Cuban cigar. The fragrant smoke calmed him. "Five years, Arby. Next month. Who would have ever dreamed that your little idea would take off? And in a downward economy, it still flourishes."

Arby snipped a handful of marijuana leaves to add to the batch of brownies he would later bake. Best to have them fresh for the incoming clients. A plate would await them on the side garden patio; a nice way to start their week. A good buzz made them appreciate the grand kick-off dinner later in the evening.

"Never discount the value of vanity, Sir. That, and greed, keep the world turning."

"Coming as it does from an attorney, I take that comment as truth." Vincent touched a dahlia blossom and a sticky white slime oozed onto his hand. The skin erupted immediately with blisters, then returned to normal just as quickly. "You've been crossbreeding with poison ivy again, haven't you?"

"More than one way to keep people away from my private garden, Sir."

Chapter 2

Sunday afternoon

DEA agent Reanita Geneva Register hit the Dark Island limousine's intercom button. "How much longer until we get to this place?"

The driver's voice: "About fifteen minutes, Ma'am."

She leaned back in the plush leather seat and sighed.

"I'd rather be captured by some third-world government and water-boarded for classified information, than be in Florida in July," she said aloud to no one.

If a promotion didn't come from this assignment, it never would.

As soon as she had stepped from the plane in Gainesville, her hair had soaked up moisture and flattened like a skull cap. The antiperspirant slathered beneath her armpits had lost its punch, judging from the whiff of foul sweat she got whenever she shifted positions.

Damned lucky, that's what the agency was. To have her as an agent. None of the others in her particular division—the boys—were as ruthless and single-minded. Not one ounce of extra fat stippled her body. Intense daily workouts kept it tight and perfect. Men ogled. Until they saw her face. Certainly, she never had to worry about sexual harassment.

I just saved my DNA for brains instead of wasting it on looks, she thought. *Any woman can get by on appearances. It takes someone like me to excel in other ways.*

She smoothed the designer dress. Garish, tropical colors in a print that could wake the dead. Not her usual style of government-drab. Whoever had done the shopping had a strange idea of how an oil baron's daughter from Texas dressed. The three Louis Vuitton suitcases were no doubt filled with flimsy, flashy outfits in god-awful shades. Lacy underwear in scarlet and black. Shoes worth more than her paycheck. And bathing suits. Her stomach churned at the thought of a bikini. Or, a thong.

"Oh, crap!"

She'd just have to wear the damn thing. At least no one on Dark Island would know her or ever see her again. As soon as she discovered the culprits behind the alleged midnight drug deliveries, she could go home to D.C. and forget the whole ordeal.

She stared from the limo's tinted windows. For the past twenty minutes, the scenery had not changed: miles and miles of spindly pines and scrub oaks dotted with an occasional farmhouse or trailer. How did people live out here? It was barely mid-morning, and the heat rose in shivery waves from the asphalt. Sure, it was hot in D.C at times, but nothing like the devil's cloak hanging over the Deep South. Since the edge of Gainesville, the only sign of life had been a small clutch of skinny cows clustered beneath the shade of a live oak. Oh, and five goats.

The limousine turned onto yet another narrow road and accelerated. The vehicle had a GPS mounted on the dash, though the taciturn driver didn't seem to need it. Good thing. Reanita prided herself on a keen sense of direction, but she had lost track after the ninth turn. Other than once in Nevada, this was the nearest to the middle of nowhere she had ever found herself. Surely, there wasn't a Starbucks or McDonald's for miles. The only thing she knew for certain; they were now heading due east. The coast had to be near.

A few minutes passed before a small bridge appeared in the distance like a mirage of a desert oasis.

The Spa at Dark Island, a small sign read. *Visitors allowed by pass only.* The Spa's logo—the same one as on the limousine's doors—was centered above the printing.

The driver slowed and stopped the vehicle. Reanita watched him get out, walk to a covered console, and punch a series of numbers into a keypad. The ornate security gate jerked once and swung open.

After a few turns through a thick cypress swamp, they passed a large sign with a color version of the Spa at Dark Island's logo. The background—shadowy in tonal gray, black, and white—showed a moonlit coastal scene, the water and shore framed by the tall dark silhouettes of cypress trees. The thing that caught Reanita's eye was the ancient symbol in the middle, a stylized rendering of a phoenix in the yellow, orange, and deep reds of fire, its wings outstretched toward the heavens. Understated white block printing curved at the periphery read: The Spa at Dark Island. Below the sign, plantings of annuals mirrored the brilliant sunset shades.

If the filigree on the gate and the elaborate sign were any indication, the house and grounds would be spectacular.

"I don't care if this place looks like the freakin' Taj Mahal," Reanita mumbled. "It better have a killer air conditioning system."

****

Reanita's first thought upon entering the massive antebellum-styled mansion: *Money. Lots of it. Either old and dirty, or new and dirty.*

The young blond woman seated behind a rosewood Louis XV desk glanced up. "Welcome to The Spa at Dark Island, Miss Register. I trust you had a pleasant trip?"

Reanita recognized the antique desk from her preparatory cram-course—*Obnoxious Wealth 101.* If first impressions held true, the piece wasn't a reproduction and was worth more than her gross salary for at least ten years.

"Yeah." Reanita did her best to fall into the role of a spoiled oil baron's daughter. "Whatever."

The limo driver appeared in her wake with two of the three bulging suitcases. Reanita marveled at the excess. When she traveled, a duffle bag normally sufficed—just a change of underwear, fresh shirt, and meager toiletries. Oil baron daughters obviously required more accoutrements. She hoped all of the shoes weren't spiked heels like the ones currently torturing her feet.

The receptionist's nametag read *Barbie*. The ubiquitous Dark Island logo appeared in miniature beside the script.

You've got to be kidding me, Reanita thought. *Barbie? For real?*

Reanita immediately sized her up. Surgically enhanced boobs—at least a D cup. Body—clearly no more than a size zero, the bitch. Collagen-pumped lips. Why the hell did women do that? It reminded Reanita of a baboon's ass. Perfectly curled to be bed-head-messy blonde hair. Reanita checked for dark roots. Either little Miss Barbie was a true blonde, or she got paid enough to keep up with the required stylist's time.

Baby blue eyes. Of course. If they landed in the same category of the rest of the woman, they weren't the original equipment's shade either. Tomorrow, she might be a green-eyed beauty.

Perfect teeth. Some orthodontist had made a fortune. Looked as if she had at least eight incisors, with one of those smiles that stretched back to the wisdom teeth. And so damned white the glare could blind.

Best to lay off the bleaching gel, sister, Reanita mused, *before you flay them down to the nerves.*

Either way—enhanced or not—the woman was stunning. Reanita hated her right off.

"We have refreshments in the atrium, if you wish," Barbie said. "I'll have your luggage sent to your suite."

"I could use a drink." Reanita shoved the oversized Balenciaga handbag toward the limo driver.

Barbie's pasted-on smile didn't waver when she exchanged glances with the second employee. "I'll show you the way. The other guests have already arrived. I can make introductions."

Had to give her credit. She was well-trained enough not to let her disgust over Reanita's bat-like features cast a shadow across her own.

Reanita trailed behind Barbie. The Italian-tiled hallway leading to the atrium gleamed in the ambient light of massive floor-to-ceiling windows. The heels of the DEA agent's Prada snakeskin sling-backs and Barbie's black mules tapped a matching staccato rhythm. Ahead, an arched threshold opened to a glass-domed room filled with a jungle of palms, orchids, and exotic plants.

When she and Barbie entered, three people stopped their conversation to stare long enough to register the intruders.

Barbie made introductions before leaving the room. The three spa patrons—her companions for the week—made the briefest of eye contact before finding something else, anything else, to focus on.

It's going to be a long week, the agent thought.

Reanita bit into a moist brownie and almost moaned aloud. By the time she had wolfed down the third chocolate confection and two glasses of clearly expensive champagne, her mood had brightened.

****

Vincent preened in front of a full-length mirror. *Yet another vampire falsehood,* he thought, *the whole no-reflection issue.*

A normal mirror sent back his image, though slightly distorted as if focused through rippling water. Most of his blood kin shunned mirrors, but not for the reasons provided in the lore. They didn't look good in them. Above all, vampires were terribly vain.

Enter technology. The emergence of digital imaging. Nothing money and a little ingenuity wouldn't provide. Vincent possessed the prototype of the first *Monster Mirror*, as he had dubbed it. Within a few months, copies hung in the lairs of vampires in every corner of the world. Emmaraud even had a compact size she always carried in whatever designer purse she possessed at the moment. It took a keen eye to discern the split-second delay between a movement and what the mirror portrayed; long enough for the imbedded camera to record the scene and send it to a mini-processor that spit it back as a crisp reflected image. Soon, the holographic imager Vincent had ordered would take the mirror's place in his affections. To be able to see one's full image in 3-D without turning this way and that: a wonder of modern invention!

Authors and Hollywood never got the details correct. He read all of the books from Bram Stoker's masterful original to Anne Rice's novels and the *Twilight* series. Vincent delighted in the 1872 gothic tale *Carmilla* by J. Sheridan Le Fanu—the first depiction of vampires as romantic and sensual beings, rather than horrific monsters. He watched *First Blood* on HBO. Laughed at the vampiric cartoon character Butters on *Southpark*. His DVD library spanned three long shelves with every vintage vampire movie every filmed. Posters from popular films hung on the media room's walls. His favorite: Frank Langella's depiction from the 1979 *Dracula* movie. Without a doubt—no putdown to Brad Pitt—Mr. Langella's handsome and enigmatic figure proved the most erotic and romantic. He had lost count of how many times he viewed the video.

If Frank Langella ever visited Dark Island, Vincent would be hard-pressed to obey one of his strictest rules: never, ever bite a patron. It was bad for business.

Wooden stakes through the heart. Silver bullets. Withering from the sunlight. Clever little pop-out canine teeth. Crosses held at arm's length. All the sleeping-in-caskets crap. Amusing. But, wrong, wrong, wrong.

Especially the part about sure-fire methods to extinguish the Brothers and Sisters of the Blood.

"They can't kill one of us," he said to his image. "Hell, we can't even kill ourselves."

Hard to kill something undead.

Of the other blood kin he knew—mostly Emmaraud's clutch of flighty friends—most would give up eternity with no qualms. All fought the boredom of life without end. A few—he had heard—starved themselves into a kind of suspended state. Withered to a husk, they lay buried in forgotten crypts beneath ancient buildings or in uncharted subterranean enclaves. After millennia, they still existed. Stuporous, hungry beings with no peace in sight.

Vincent understood, deeply, the quest for something to make the days meaningful. Vampires reminded him of spoiled rich kids with unlimited toys and amusements. Always looking for something new to engage their passions. Anything to stave off the desperation of a hollow non-life that could never be fully lived.

Some days, he would shove a wooden stake into his own black heart so he never again had to hear the disharmonious strains of *Happy Birthday* and, Lucifer forbid, *Jingle Bells*.

Endless years of holiday ceremonies stretched out like a parched Death Valley highway with no gas stations or tree-strewn watering holes in sight. Vincent was only sixty in vamp years—a baby in their realm—and he had already grown weary of his preternatural place in the natural world.

Humans were the only things he found the least bit interesting. But not to feed upon. Bad taste, to play with one's food.

Vincent tucked a silk handkerchief into the burgundy smoking jacket and ran his long fingers through his thick black hair. How would he look, now, if he were still human? He did the math.

"Forty when I was made in the early 1950s. It's now…" He paused. "I'd probably be dead. No, I *would* be dead." *And Julio is already dead*, the annoying inner voice reminded him.

He ran a hand down to his flat stomach. Beneath the jacket, his abdominal muscles rippled in a washboard pattern. Each night, he joined the patrons in the gym and went through the motions of a thorough workout. Not necessary. He could swill beer and eat Twinkies and take-out pepperoni pizza for a year and not gain a pound.

"Given I could actually eat," he pondered aloud.

Food. God, how he missed the taste of food, more than a lover's touch. Filet mignon. Lobster dripping in drawn butter. Marinara sauce. Chocolate!

He closed his eyes and sighed.

A memory of the party—the last one he had catered—replayed in his mind. Table after table of succulent appetizers and decadent desserts; all presented in colorful, enticing displays. Presentation was everything. A tower of prime rib on a rotating spit. Oysters on the half shell, their moisture glistening in the candlelight. Prawns wrapped in thick slabs of bacon.

Vincent had watched a woman glide from one gastronomic creation to the next—sniffing, touching, devouring with her eyes, yet never tasting. He passed it off as just another wafer-thin heiress with no wiggle room in her Wranglers.

Emmaraud. The vixen who had turned his life into separate historical sections. B.E.—before Emmaraud. And

A.E.—after Emmaraud. The woman who did what no other woman could do: steal him from Julio.

Vincent's eyes flew open. "Stop! Stop thinking of her!"

He turned from the digital mirror, grabbed the detailed patron information print-out, and left his private quarters.

The evening was young. He was very old. And the patrons—his only salvation—awaited.

****

James Robert Jones—Jimmy Rob—used his preternatural night vision to navigate the narrow path leading to the coast. Modified to battery power, the knobby-tired ATV made little noise. Perfect for his purposes.

He stopped shy of a small inlet and shut off the electric motor. The whine of mosquitoes and June bugs: a sound he used to love. Now, his hearing caused the noise to blare.

To distract his mind, Jimmy Rob ran through a directory of his passions: hot rod cars, blood mixed with booze of any kind, poker, and the queen of his nightmares, Emmaraud Bonneville. Just thinking of the spider-legged woman made his cold blood even colder. The fact he couldn't just have her anytime he pleased made him lust for her even more. What had it been now, ten months or longer? Hard to keep up with the passage of time when he didn't have to punch a clock and the days blended together like the sludge pouring from his oil pan.

Jimmy Rob thought he had seen just about everything a female could offer. And then some. That was before Emmaraud. Sex with her made human copulating look like a ladies' prayer meeting. Good thing he could heal quickly. When Emmaraud turned it on, stuff got broken, scratched, and clean near cut off.

He loved the fact she had the same last name as an automobile. That, and the famous racecar track, the Bonneville Salt Flats, eighty-eight miles west of Salt Lake City, Utah, on I-80. He couldn't have asked for more.

Just thinking about the annual speed trials made Jimmy Rob tingle with a bad case of *salt fever*, a term reserved for race addicts who descended on the Flats every August. Bonneville Land Speed Racing: a unique sport of wild-eyed people who drove hot rods, roadsters, belly tankers, lakesters, motorcycles, streamliners, and diesel trucks to *shoot the salt*. Folks came from all over the world for the weeklong event.

Jimmy Rob's mouth watered. He could just see Emmaraud on his arm as they walked through the pits, checked out the vehicles, and swapped slang with the owners and drivers. If he could interest Emmaraud in NASCAR, maybe she would catch salt fever and take off to Utah with him. It was all about speed. One thing Emmaraud Bonneville lusted after was speed.

God, he loved that woman! Or the closest thing he had ever felt to love.

He focused on the distant putt-putt of a small outboard engine. Right on time.

In a few minutes, an aluminum Jon boat sluiced to shore. The sole occupant used an oar to push through the thick mud until the nose of the small craft rested on a clutch of dead grass.

"Jones?" A voice called out. "You here, boy?"

Jimmy Rob appeared at the bow.

"Jee-zus Kee-rist! You scairt the life out of me!"

"Keep your voice down." Jimmy Rob said.

The man huffed, then hawked up a gob of mucus and sent it flying into the water.

"Like anyone is going to be anywhere near here, this time of night."

"You got my square grouper?" Jimmy Rob chuckled at the colloquial reference to the bales of marijuana often found bobbing in the Florida waters where they had been cast overboard in haste by law enforcement-pursued drug runners.

The man whipped a small tarpaulin aside. "Right chere. Jamaica's finest. Got my money, my cash, my do-re-mi?"

Jimmy Rob dug in his jeans pocket. "Don't I always?" He handed over a roll of cash. "Hope this is as good as the last."

"Make you see drooling bats hanging from the ceiling. No shittin' ya."

The man pulled out a small flashlight and checked the pay-off. Jimmy Rob cut into one of the burlap-wrapped bales and took a sniff. Pure skank: The scent alone could give a mortal man the munchies for a week.

Jimmy Rob lifted one of the bales. "Get off your sorry ass and help me load this."

With the strength his vamp blood provided, Jimmy Rob Jones could've easily hoisted all four of the bales with one finger. Best not to show off in front of the warm-bloods. People tended to talk. Then, he'd have to kill him. That wouldn't be in his, or the man's, best interests. Good dope dealers willing to deliver were hard to come by.

"You seem like a man what appreciates a good smoke." The skipper loaded the last bale on the ATV's rear rack.

Jimmy Rob used a set of bungee cords to secure the load. "I do, for dang sure."

Most of the product, he would trade for car parts. The other, he'd sell on the side for money to spend on pool games and Saturday night wagers. Maybe some new NASCAR gear.

Jimmy Rob clapped a meaty hand on the man's shoulder, careful to use a fraction of his strength. No need to have the ole boy end up in the hospital with a compound fracture or a dislocation.

"Makes for a real fine living." Jimmy Rob pulled out a second smaller roll of cash and handed it over. "I almost forgot. Here's a little tip. I realize I'm a little out of your way."

The dealer and the doper. One headed toward the Gulf Stream. The other toward an Airstream. Dark Island stood sentinel, the silent partner.

Chapter 3

Sunday evening

The last fingers of sunset filtered through silhouettes of live oaks as Vincent descended the mansion's central curved staircase. He never failed to feel like Scarlet O'Hare sweeping from the second floor to the first; all he needed was a hoop shirt and a mile of crinolines. Better yet, a flowing black, red silk-lined cape draped over a tux—more his style. Like the one hanging in one of his closets, custom made for the Blue Blood Ball. To the well-heeled patrons who would gladly shell out the hefty required donation, Vincent's attire would smack of his famed eccentric nature; part of the party's theme. Other than Halloween, the gala was the one time Vincent could dress in full Hollywood vampire drag.

From the bottom of the stairway, he paused to sense the latest group of spa patrons. Good. All were seated at the expansive table, hopped up on Arby's herbal brownies and alcoholic libations.

The room with its twenty-foot gilded ceiling and velvet-draped windows would kick off the decadence of the spa week. The candlelight reflecting from a row of gold-framed digital mirrors and polished mahogany. The best china— High Point Platinum pattern with the Dark Island logo, created exclusively by Pikard—rows of silverware, linen napkins, and delicate crystal goblets. The aptly-lighted centerpiece, made entirely from plants and flowers grown on the grounds, adding just the right splash of color. Tonight, the floral arrangement was a blend of white and purple blooms chosen to coordinate with his silk smoking jacket.

A subtle layer of blended scents drifted from the mansion's gourmet kitchen. Vincent had reviewed the menu earlier, and now tried to pick out the various aromas. The chilled soup: butternut squash. Followed by a salad of lacy mixed spring greens and grape tomatoes with Arby's special parmesan vinaigrette dressing. The main course, highlighting the fresh seafood delivered daily to the Island, was Florida grouper topped with sun-dried tomatoes, spinach and goat cheese. Warm rosemary-laced bread with soft sweet cream butter. Two sides: roasted new potatoes and a seasoned blend of grilled red bell peppers, yellow squash and zucchini. Lime sorbet to cleanse the palate. Then to the desserts, the most talked-about portion of any Dark Island dinner: dark chocolate torte with raspberries and a warm white chocolate drizzle, or Key Lime Cheesecake so wonderfully tart it made a human's mouth pucker.

No one would ever say that Vincent Bedsloe III couldn't throw a dinner party.

The Master of Dark Island stood at the formal dining room threshold, purposely still until first one, then all of the seated guests noticed and fell silent. He didn't need the digital mirrors to tell him he commanded the room. The youngest patron—a beautiful starlet named Patrice Palmer—gasped and emitted a low sexual moan. The rest stared.

Vincent made a quick mental note: *Limit the alone time with Ms. Palmer. Remember last year when she stripped naked in the moonlit garden and tried her best to part my clothes from me as well?*

Humans had such a thing for dark and mysterious. Had his hair not been lustrous and black, he would've had to dye it.

"Good evening," he said as he flowed into the room, resting a hand briefly on each patron's shoulder, greeting them with a warm smile, before taking his seat at the head of the table.

Three of the patrons held the *glamour:* a faint shimmer from the blood distillate deep in their cells. The fourth, a slender bat-faced woman, did not.

"Vincent, my boy," the other male at the table said, "Good to see you again."

The Dark Island host nodded. "As with you, Thomas."

An efficient server poured wine, delivering a special non-alcoholic blood version to Vincent. To anyone, the liquid held the appearance of a rich Bordeaux. Though he would not dine with his guests—yet another of his fabled quirks—it was another thing to not share in a good glass of vino. The private vintage, Arby kept locked away in a separate storage cellar and labeled in satire as *Blue Blood Bordeaux.*

"I brought a little gift," the man continued, "A box of those Camacho Triple Maduro cigars you like so much."

"Ah, yes! How thoughtful of you, Thomas. You and I shall have to retire to the smoking parlor one evening this week. I have a couple you might like to try as well."

Vincent scanned the actor's glamour and recalled the taste of his blood, with the faint flavor of underlying health issues and prescription medications. High blood pressure. Acid reflux. Prostrate issues. A miasma of vitamins and herbal supplements. Mixed with caffeine, nicotine, and metabolized alcohol. And the sugary taste reminiscent of rotting plums. Too much sweetness. Perhaps, he had not allowed Thomas' vintage sufficient breathing time before he tasted. He made a mental note to check closely to make sure the sugary undercurrent wasn't a fault of the technique. Vincent wondered if the aging character actor—a man who claimed to be early in his sixties but was seventy-six—had taken the Spa nutritionist's suggestions the past year. Soon,

Vincent would know if Thomas had inched further toward full-blown diabetes.

The blood also held a hint of the owner's emotional state.

Thomas Tilton: sadness left over from four divorces, estranged children, and little real affection. Above all, fear and desperation from a long career dotted with supporting roles and the fading chances for an older male actor to achieve real fame.

Vincent turned his attention to the middle-aged woman with stylish short brown hair seated beside Thomas. "Julia. I am so pleased you came back to be with us. How is the Senator?"

Julia glanced away just long enough for Vincent to know: trouble in political paradise. She would never publicly admit it, but Julia Holt hated Washington and the constant pandering. Hated her life. Hated herself. Hated her husband and his jackal friends. The glamour told Vincent all of this and more: she hadn't had sex in months. For all of her pasted-on happiness—her civic face—Julia Holt was desperately unhappy and ripe for an affair. Judging from the furtive eye contact between her and Thomas, it might just happen this week.

One of the staff's many mottos for the exclusive nature of the spa popped into Vincent's mind: *What happens at The Dark stays in the dark.*

Julia's blood: a blend of Oxycontin, vitamins, antidepressants and a hint of basil.

Pity, Vincent mused, *she is the kind of woman who oozes maternal love, yet she can't have children.* The blood distillate might repair certain things, but it couldn't fix a diseased—now surgically erased—womb. Had the cancer returned? Had it spread? Vincent reminded himself to check her blood for hints of the markers.

"Senator Holt is in Costa Rica at the moment." Julia took a small sip of wine. "My husband is on the foreign affairs committee, you recall. Plus, he is up for reelection."

Politics: the only section of human affairs that left Vincent completely dry. Why anyone wasted precious time on all of the soap-opera wrangling was beyond him.

He nodded and turned his head to the view the other side of the table. "Miss Patrice. You are stunning, as always."

The starlet blushed. Vincent could smell the vanity from a mile away. Her glamour held little except vapid self-absorption. Her blood: a watery mixture of just about everything found in a health food store. And two aneurisms deep inside her head close to the brainstem. One day, she would flame out in a quick burst of headache pain. Unlike Thomas, Patrice Palmer would probably not have to concern herself with being a has-been.

"Thank you, Vincent." Patrice batted thick eyelashes his way. Her long hair hinted of extensive hours in the stylist's chair. At least five shades of blonde and light brown highlights caught the candlelight's glow.

"I am awaiting your next movie," The Master of Dark Island said.

The starlet sat a little straighter in her Chippendale chair. "It's a dark comedy. About a woman vampire who only bites rich and powerful men. I got the lead. You know, vampires are hot right now."

If he didn't stop her, he and the guests would be held captive for hours. Still, the idea of a new vampire video caught his attention.

"I must hear the details, my dear. Save them for just me, will you?"

The vixen actor tilted her head and offered him her best seductive smile. "I'll do that."

Vincent forced himself to hold eye contact with the bat-faced young woman seated next to Patrice. When he first met Arby, he doubted anyone on the planet could be as misfortunate in the looks department. He was wrong. Hopefully, wealth somehow compensated for what nature had cruelly denied.

"Miss Register. This is your first time with us."

"Skip the Miss and call me Rea. Everyone does."

"Rea, I trust the staff has seen to your initial requirements?"

She smirked. "Sure. But my cell phone won't work. I don't have even one freakin' bar."

Vincent nodded. "A common problem, I'm afraid. We are far from a tower here on Dark Island. Sometimes, my overseer tells me, one can get a faint signal at certain spots on the coast line."

Reanita frowned. The oil baron's daughter might be okay with this, but the DEA agent wasn't. How the hell was she supposed to report any illegal activities? By smoke signal? Why they hadn't provided a satellite-linked phone was beyond her. Budget cuts, no doubt. They had spent a fortune to get her here. That and a sat phone could possibly raise a red flag.

"We have land lines for your convenience, Rea. Though, we encourage our guests to disconnect from the outside world, at least for their time here."

She couldn't help but notice how the handsome host held her gaze. In spite of herself, Reanita warmed to the enigmatic man.

"I will be happy to review our small list of rules with you, since the others have vacationed with us before. Perhaps, a stroll through the night gardens after dinner?"

Reanita nodded.

Vincent's gaze roamed to take in the other guests. "Just to review for those of you who have not been here the week before one of our galas—you might notice activity during certain hours of the day and evening, particularly after Tuesday. We instruct the workers to stay only on the south lawn, as this is where the party tents, lighting, and other preparations take place. No worries for any of our guests, though. The pool, tennis courts, trails, and gardens are all at your disposal. We do ask that you not venture past the mansion grounds at night, though. There are things in the swamps that are...unkind."

The Master of Dark Island clasped his hands together. "Enough of that. Your pleasure is in our hands. Enjoy!"

Patrice Palmer shot a hot look across the table toward Vincent. Thomas and Julia appraised each other. Reanita turned her attention to the fragrant soup that had appeared like magic in front of her.

From behind the kitchen door, Arby caught his first glance of Reanita Register and fell hopelessly in love.

It was going to be an interesting week.

****

Well past midnight, Vincent escorted Reanita to small formal garden at the rear of the main house. Julia and Thomas still held court in the media room, flirting over cordials and enough snippets of each other's lives to gain the intimacy required for a few minor marital indiscretions. Patrice—begging off immediately after dinner—sat, wreathed in a fog of sandalwood incense, in a cross-legged lotus yoga pose in front of the floor-to-ceiling digital mirrors in a quiet meditation room off the workout suite.

The day help had left the Island, leaving only a skeletal staff to tend to the needs of the Spa patrons. A separate building, shielded from view by a thick cane break, held the quarters for the permanent staffers: a massage therapist and her family, two housekeepers, and one of the personal trainers and her gardener husband. The only person allowed to stay in the main house—other than the patrons—was Arby. His suite occupied the same wing as his master's.

Reanita lifted her face to the slight land breeze. The temperature had dropped to the low eighties, a welcomed break from the midday heat. She noticed a large box-like shape overhead and pointed to the night sky. "What's that? Looks like some kind of tree house."

Vincent followed the direction of her gesture. "That is one of six bat houses spotted around the island. My caretaker has a particular affinity for the little creatures."

Reanita shivered and wrapped her arms around her chest. "Ew!"

Vincent wondered if the woman had ever seen a close-up picture of a bat. If she had, she might have felt a certain kinship, given her facial features.

"You should be glad the bats are here, Rea. They consume up to three times their body weight in insects every night. Dark Island would be torturous for you, otherwise, with the mosquito population left unchecked. Much of the land is swampy. A perfect breeding ground, especially when we have an abundance of rain."

"Oh." She considered. Her exposure to nature was as limited as she could possibly manage. "Why is it up so high? It looks like some kind of apartment on stilts."

"To house a bat, one must build where they prefer to flourish." He motioned to the sky. In a few days, and just in time for the Blue Blood Ball, the moon would be delightfully full. "Watch. You can see them darting about. Hunting."

"I noticed them as soon as we came outside. I thought they might be some kind of really fast birds...owls...or, something."

Vincent subdued the amused smile threatening his cool lips. Wealthy city folk: They were so amusing when they ventured into the natural world. Just wait until the woman got a load of the freakishly large cockroaches so fond of the Florida underbrush. Or the banana spiders that spun huge magical webs to catch the morning dew and anything unfortunate enough to touch their sticky handiwork.

How ironic, that she would be afraid of bugs and bats. On Dark Island, so many other things, unnatural things, waited and watched.

"While owls do hunt at night—and we have several species—the night skies of the Island belong to the stalkers of the darkness. The bats."

"Sounds all so...Count Dracula-ish." Reanita laughed.

Vincent's sensitive ears echoed. It would be best for his sanity's sake not to say anything vaguely amusing in the woman's presence. Reanita's laugh was the screeching of a boat's metal flanks against dock pilings. It felt so good when it finally stopped.

They walked on a winding slate pathway lit by solar landscape fixtures. Arby's *moon garden* closed around them. The intoxicating sweet scent of the Nicotiana—a night-flowering plant, a variety with large white trumpet-shaped blooms—filtered through the air. A few steps deeper into the garden, Vincent's nose detected the aroma of Lady of the Night; a heady blend reminiscent of jasmine, with undertones of cloves, oriental five-spice and cinnamon. Shortly after sunset, the Lady of the Night flowers' aroma went from zero to full power. The three to five-inch orchid-like white blooms bobbed like ghosts above the dark foliage.

His pants brushed against the lacy fronds of lavender and rosemary, herbs added to the moon garden for their scents. Several grasses either lined the pathways or provided a framework for the plantings. Aztec variegated lirope, white-flowering muhly grass and clumps of white fountain grass with its soft wispy plumes. Adding a tall backdrop, Gold Band pampas grass rustled in the night breeze, mixed with stands of Golden Goddess bamboo. With the low solar lighting and the reflection from the moonbeams, the effect was mystical, other-worldly.

Vincent admired the intent behind the seemingly random design. Many of the plants, shrubs, and trees had been chosen for their pristine white blooms, their flowers catching and reflecting the soft ethereal glow of the moon. The garden path was lined with smooth white pebbles that shimmered in the lunar illumination and helped to light the way. During the Blue Blood Ball, the moon garden was always a favorite of couples slipping away for a few moments of lusty fondling.

Reanita glanced around the moon garden; the most serene place she had ever been. "You must have a huge staff to keep up with all of this—the house, the grounds."

"A good many. Mostly day workers. As to the gardens, others might do the grunt work, but one man, my overseer, runs the show."

Reanita's mind raced. Who better to grill than the help? They were always in the background and witnessed everything. Even the things not sanctioned by God and the Law.

"This man—this overseer—he lives somewhere off-Island?"

"So many questions." Vincent held Reanita's elbow and guided her back through the maze of hedges toward the mansion. "You need not concern yourself with details, Rea. Leave that to us."

The chill of Vincent's fingers shocked Reanita for a moment until a wave of attraction took over. Blood flushed her cheeks. She stuffed the unusual feelings and forced her mind and mouth to work. "I'd like to meet him."

Vincent halted. "Why?"

Reanita shrugged. "I like gardens. Maybe I want to start one."

Vincent chuckled softly, thinking of the absurd nature of her previous questions. "Oh, come now. Why would someone of your standing dirty her delicate hands? I'm sure your father would pay for a top-notch gardener to fulfill your wishes."

Right. Reanita thought. *If you knew my father, you'd know the man wouldn't buy me anything, unless it was another round of rot-gut whiskey.*

"Of course he would. But sometimes I wish I had a hobby of my own."

From his vantage point—hidden behind the thick trunk of a mature Southern magnolia tree, Arby watched his master and the newbie spa patron. A tall clump of ginger to his right sent out a peachy aroma that tickled his nose.

A network of mulch-paved service paths paralleled the slate walkways throughout the estate's extensive gardens, used by Arby and the grunts in order to stay out of sight of guests and still perform the myriad of duties required by the grounds. Now, the paths provided a way to spy on the loveliest creature he had ever seen.

Arby watched Reanita's movements. How the flowing evening gown with the billowy sleeves swayed like moth wings when she moved her arms. Ethereal beauty—the way the moon light dusted her profile. Arby knew he was looking at the one woman he would never tire of: His soul mate.

When Reanita laughed, Arby felt his heart flutter. The sound: Celestial. Bold.

Reanita leaned into Vincent and gave him a sappy, lovesick smile. God, why did all the females react the same way to the monster? Did he give off some weird pheromone? What?

Arby sighed. *He's not your type, my love. Trust me. Number one, his door hinge doesn't swing that way. Number two, he's far from the settling-down, guy-next-door fellow.*

When the two turned back toward the mansion, Arby caught sight of Reanita's pale bat-like features. She smiled and jabbered like a love-sick teen queen to her escort and host.

He had to have her.

Chapter 4

Monday morning: the wee hours

Vincent stepped from the shadows into a pool of fluorescent light. A matched set of motion-activated security floods scanned his movements and spewed additional illumination in two 190° arcs.

Good thing Jimmy Rob doesn't pay his own utility bill, he thought.

Every time he had to confront his blood child—the aftermath of one of Emmaraud's dares—Vincent cringed. The man, vampire or not, was a cretin.

The outside lighting fixtures highlighted the redneck's humble abode: an aging, weathered aluminum Airstream camper, set on an irregular series of concrete blocks. Automotive cast-offs dotted the weedy half-acre lot like ugly yard chickens. If there had been any other feasible way to watch over the man, some plan to keep him from completely destroying the fringe white trash population of central Florida, Vincent would have never moved him to the back of the Dark Island property.

The whole thing was Emmaraud's fault.

"You are some whacked vamp," Emmaraud—then, in her retro Cher look-alike phase—had glanced at Vincent in disgust. "I don't think I have ever known you to pull a direct feed. Not even a sip! When I was a newbie back in Egypt, I didn't have a choice. I had to feed off humans. You, you are so damned spoiled. Synthetic blood. Blood you import from Cuba packed in dry ice." She paused. "Suppose it's partially my fault. I never pushed you years ago. Brought you cadaver blood. Rejects from the blood bank in Miami. You never had to work for your meals. You are a blight! You are a sham of a vamp, Vincent!"

The words stung: like having your birth mother call you out for wetting the bed.

"I can do a direct feed. I simply chose not to."

Emmaraud had stopped the metallic black convertible BMW 6 Series—650 CIC— in the middle of a narrow back road. Nothing for miles except mosquitoes and snakes and a whole lot of dark.

"Right. I'll make you a promise, Vincent. If you bite the next human we see, I will leave Dark Island for a full year. Dare you!"

A year without Emmaraud and her coven of misfits. He cringed at the thought of them—even now—running amok on the island, scaring the guests and wildlife. Vincent hesitated for a moment. "Game on. Next one we see, I bite."

In a couple of miles, a clearing. A concrete block building painted dark green. Neon signs expounding several brands of cheap beer. A few spent cars and trucks in the dirt and gravel parking lot.

"There." Emmaraud pointed. "Next one that stumbles out."

Vincent swallowed the rush of blood bile threatening to erupt from his midsection.

She parked the Beemer in the deep shadows. They waited.

The front door banged open. Three people emerged. A man and a woman, arm-in-arm, supported each other to a mud-pocked pick-up truck. The other, a stocky male who could barely walk, lurched toward a vintage muscle car and fumbled for his keys.

Emmaraud tapped a painted talon on the steering wheel. "Well?"

Vincent took a deep breath. At least the victim was male. And, he shortly discovered, surprisingly feisty for one so inebriated. Even with Vincent's preternatural strength, it took two tries to bring him down. The vamp subdued the last of the man's will to fight with the first bite, draining him nearly dry.

Emmaraud stood beside him. "Shit, Vincent. You didn't have to kill the guy."

"I...I didn't mean to." He stared down at the immobile body and strained to pick up any signs of life. "His heart is still beating. He's not dead!" Vincent looked to Emmaraud. "What'll I do?"

"Two choices. Either I help you dump the body—'cause he *is* going to die pretty soon. Or...you turn him."

One thing Vincent could not bear for eternity: being a murderer. He was a lot of things, but not that.

"Nick your wrist," she said. "Drop a little blood into his mouth. That will revive him enough to get him back to the Island. I'll show you what to do from there." Emmaraud shook her head and walked back to the BMW. "Don't you dare get blood in my car, either!" she called over her shoulder. "You know I always get the cream interior."

Right, Vincent thought as he picked the comatose man up and threw him across one shoulder. *Perfect for an impulsive vampire like Emmaraud. A shade that would show body fluids.*

Jimmy Rob the redneck man died that night. Jimmy Rob the redneck vampire was born. Vincent became a blood sire to his worst nightmare, short of Emmaraud.

At least, he didn't have to deal with her for a year. Small consolation. Jimmy Rob was his biggest mistake, and he just had to live with it.

For eternity.

A low, wet snarl snapped Vincent to the present. A chain rattled like cemetery bones. "Why a vampire requires a watchdog is a mystery," he mumbled, making a wide arc around the salivating, butt-ugly pit bull.

A voice called out: "Precious? Precious? What you see, gal?"

Jimmy Rob stood with a wrench in one hand. "Oh, it's just you. Thought I smelled something foul."

"Nice. Very nice, James. Could you, perhaps, show me just the slightest modicum of respect due to your blood sire?"

The redneck hawked up a wad of blood laced with phlegm and shot it expertly. It landed at Vincent's feet. "I'll tell you what I used to tell my mama. I didn't ask to be borned. Not to her, and, sure as shit-fire, not to no faggot vampire."

"I do *so* look forward to our little father-son talks."

"What made you lower yourself to drop by? I already told that rat-faced servant of yours that I'd take a look at the limo tomorrow night. God, you got four others. If one ain't purring like a got-damned kitten, you freak out."

Vincent held up a hand. "Easy. Easy. I didn't come to berate you about the limos—though, it is your job to keep them operating at peak efficiency."

The redneck vampire huffed and spun around. Vincent trailed behind him toward the only part of Jimmy Rob's domain he deemed important enough to keep immaculate: the garage.

"I'd offer you a cup of coffee, but I can't drink it anymore. Oh, I suppose you can't either." Jimmy Rob cackled at his attempt at humor. "What the hell do you want? I'm kind of busy right now. I'm getting ready to drop the rebuilt engine into this GTO."

The thought of sipping coffee or anything else with the likes of Jimmy Rob appalled Vincent. The cretin had no feeling for the finer things of life...or death.

Grease. The fumes of gasoline and solvents. Rubber. Car exhaust: The perfume of a redneck.

Vincent slipped a scented linen handkerchief from his pocket and held it to his nose. The smell of lavender masked the automotive odors to a certain degree.

Jimmy Rob stared at his blood sire. "Jee-zus."

Vincent's eyes scanned the shiny inventory of a long workbench with its obligatory pegboard. He took note of the tools: wrenches, screwdrivers, whatever that thing was, hammers, pliers. All neatly hung.

That there is Jimmy Rob's altar. Vincent's mind used his best southern slang drawl for the thought. The handkerchief hid the smirk toying with his lips.

His gaze continued to survey the room. Diamond-plate steel cabinets covered the north wall, presumably storage for all the *engine stuff* Jimmy Rob kept buying.

The Dark Island Master's mind wandered. *How can he afford all of this equipment? Plus the junkers in the yard awaiting restoration?* A new automotive carcass seemed to have erupted from the overgrown grass every time Vincent visited.

Attention to the south wall revealed matching black pearl Sears Craftsman AXS multi-level toolboxes with neon-blue LED task lighting in the drawers. Lit up like Vegas without the showgirls. Vincent spotted a digital message center with date, time, and temperature information. One contained a built-in CD player, spewing out some God-awful song about a bird flying free.

The illuminated toolboxes' drawers stood open like jeweler's cases. Socket sets, impact wrenches, timing lights, gear pullers, assorted hammers and mallets, pull bars, plus wrenches of all kind: all sorted into separate compartments.

Vincent noticed one particular drawer lined in shiny navy velvet like a tiny casket for its occupants, a series of torque wrenches. From his viewpoint, Vincent could see the polished sheen and doubted a speck of dust or oil was allowed to remain long on the tools.

The rest of the wall contained a large, bulbous fire engine-red air compressor and an assortment of hydraulic, engine, and transmission jacks. A chain hoist on a track divided the ceiling. A spotless motor dangled like bait to a fish over the maws of an awaiting automobile. The only attempt at decoration—other than a Hoochie-Mama calendar—was a massive mounted fish. Arby took a closer look at the redneck's newest artwork—a huge wide-mouth striped bass somehow affixed to an electric guitar. What the heck? Seemed a bit out of place with all of the equipment, but who was Vincent to judge low-rent art sensibilities?

How the state-of-the-art garage existed in the train wreck-landscaped home site was beyond Vincent.

"You having some kind of space-out attack, or whut?" Jimmy Rob shot his blood sire an annoyed frown.

Vincent snapped to attention. "I came to ask…would you be so kind as to stay away from the gala this year? I hate to keep you—you of such careful breeding—away from such a desirable social event. But I must insist. You tend to upset my guests."

Jimmy Rob picked up a second wrench and juggled both in the air. He snatched a third and kept all three moving as he talked. "Freakin' good, ain't I? I should go on Letterman."

"We'll just give him a buzz."

Jimmy Rob caught the wrenches in one hand as easily as snagging three suspended Q-tips from the air. "Don't worry your pretty little head. I won't even be around. That hoity-toity group you hang with bores the crap outta me. They walk around in all their fancy gowns and suits, acting like their shit don't stink." He dropped the wrenches onto a workbench and picked up a tin of Red Man chewing tobacco soaked in a base of beef blood. "Nope, you can have your little gala. This good ole boy is gonna be in Daytona! Whoo-weee!"

"Daytona?"

"It's Fourth of July." When Vincent failed to react, Jimmy Rob continued, "The Freakin' Coke Zero 400 at

Daytona! Just one of the biggest damn NASCAR races ever!"

Vincent tilted his head.

Jimmy Rob pushed a thick plug of tobacco into his cheek. "NASCAR...you know, fast cars going 'round and 'round? Lots of wrecks? Plenty of partying? My main man Dale Jr.? Number 88?" Jimmy Rob spoke slowly, enunciating each word as if he was dealing with a slow toddler.

Vincent grimaced. "I am familiar with the sport."

"My point, girly-man—I won't even be here for your little *swa-ray*. I managed to score some last-minute tickets to the big dance at Daytona. Now if you will excuse me, I have important work to do."

Vincent stood for a moment before turning to leave.

"Hey, you heard anything from Emmaraud?" Jimmy Rob called out. His head was buried in the automotive bowels of the GTO.

Vincent whipped around. "Why do you ask?"

Jimmy Rob's head peered over the hood. "Just wonderin'...I got an extra ticket to the 400."

"You know as much as I, when it comes to her." Vincent glanced around the clearing, half expecting his blood sire to materialize.

"I called her cell phone number. Just went to voicemail. I hate talking to a damned machine."

"Funny. You spend all of your free time with machines. One would think you would be enamored."

The redneck vampire's brow creased. "I don't know what the hell you are talkin' about, half the time. Wish you'd speak plain English, you fruit."

Vincent felt the enamel on his teeth crumble to pearl-dust. Good thing it would grow back. Otherwise, he would surely put some lucky dentist's kids through college. "She never announces her visits. Not to me. Not to you. Not to anyone."

Jimmy Rob directed his attention to the engine. "She shows up, you tell her to come see me."

"I will be pleased to send her your way, I assure you."

Vincent stepped away from the lights lining Jimmy Rob's lair and stopped for a few moments to watch the fireflies' glowing green dance at the edge of the tree line. He smiled. So much beauty was missed by those doomed to haunt the daylight hours.

****

Reanita drifted inside a marshmallow: Soft. Silken. Suspended on a cloud. Womb-like. Supported in places she didn't know she needed support.

Angel-song filled the air around her—and a weird tapping.

Tapping? What's in a cloud, to tap on? Her dream-fogged brain pondered on the feasibility of doors or any surfaces hard enough to facilitate such a noise.

Whatever it was, the annoying clamor continued. Got louder. More staccato and insistent.

A perky female voice accompanied the tapping: "Miss Register! Good morning! Miss Register! Time to rise and shine!"

Reanita drew her awareness to the feel of her skin against the sheets—luxurious Egyptian cotton with an absurdly-high thread count—and forced her eyes to open to slits. At first, she thought she had died and ascended to some sort of high-end heaven. She peered around the room in the early dawn filtered light—surreal, how the hazy sunbeams reminded her of a breakfast food commercial. Dark furniture—the pieces matching. Original framed watercolors. Fresh flowers in a Waterford vase. No clutter. No gun on the bedside table. Not her bedroom; for sure, not in her neighborhood.

She rolled from bed and fell onto all fours. Whatever party she had busted the previous evening must've been a lark. She managed to pull herself to her feet.

"I'm coming, for God's sake. I'm coming."

Reanita turned the brass knob and opened the door. She blinked to clear her vision. Sandra Bullock stood on the opposite side.

"Good morning, Miss Register. Time for the Dark Island W B B—the Walk Before Breakfast."

No, not Sandra Bullock, but a dead ringer for the actor in a skin-tight pink, coordinated workout set.

"Wha...what time is it?" Reanita glanced at her bare wrist and frowned. Her trusty Timex normally never left her body. She even showered wearing it.

The mission's details came rushing forward in a flash. She shifted from confused DEA agent to pampered heiress.

"It's six o-clock. Time to rock and roll!" The slender brunette did a little step in time.

"And, you are?"

"Stefanie—with an *f*."

Reanita scraped a hand through her hair. "Okay, Stefanie with an *f*, why are you bothering me this early?"

"Didn't you read your customized Dark Island itinerary, hmm? It was included in your admission packet."

A low thrum cranked up behind Reanita's temples. If she didn't get some aspirin soon, the headache would move in, bring friends and build a school.

"I have an itinerary?"

"I'm the a.m. trainer. We value structure here at the Spa. Every morning, we take a mile power walk. Gets the old blood pumping." Stefanie with an *f* smiled. A row of perfect white teeth glowed. "Regard for your spirit, regard for your body, means regard for yourself!"

Reanita fought the urge to snarl. Where was this chick's cheerleader outfit?

If Stefanie with an *f* was any indication, the week was going to be one long Dark Island motto. Maybe she should write them down. Give her something to amuse the boys with, later on.

Where is my gun? Reanita thought. *I can take this bitch out and get back to dreamland in about two seconds...*

Stefanie with an *f* held up one finger as if she had just hit pay dirt in the inspiration department. "Tell you what—since you aren't quite dressed, I'll just round up the other guests. We'll meet you in ten minutes in the main entrance hall on the first floor."

Without waiting for an answer, Stefanie with an *f* spun around and loped down the hall. A slipstream of some kind of fresh linen body spray followed.

Reanita stumbled into the bathroom, splashed water on her face, and downed three aspirin with a tall glass of water.

"No more champagne for you, old girl," she said to the mirror.

Something about the reflection bothered her. Her movements seemed a little—off. If she didn't know better, she would swear she had been drugged.

She rummaged in one of the suitcases and pulled out a skimpy jogging outfit: Mint green mini-shorts and a moisture-wicking tank top printed with a series of cutesy running stick figures. The thin stripe across the top of the ankle socks matched the shade perfectly, as did the hair band. She slipped her feet into new running shoes and marveled at the cushiony insoles. Hers back at home had seen so many miles of pavement and abuse, the arch support had flattened out.

No way could she take her revolver. There wasn't enough excess material to hide a case of lip balm, much less a gun. Hopefully Stefanie with an *f* would take the group on some kind of paved track and not into the backwoods.

As she made her way down the east wing hall to the elevators, Reanita worried about something Stefanie with an *f* had mentioned—somewhere, mixed in with all the enthusiasm and marketing. The a.m. trainer? That meant there had to be a p.m. trainer as well.

Reanita groaned.

Chapter 5

Vincent settled onto the massage table and allowed his body to sink into its thick cushion. The twice-weekly hour and a half session with Dark Island's therapist Raven was one of the few times he allowed himself to completely relax.

Through the inner sanctum's soundproofed walls, he could still pick up the muffled sounds of the mansion coming to life: Angelina's musical laughter as her floured hands expertly pinched off hunks of dough for sticky buns. Maria and Elena—the Cuban housekeepers—chattering in soft Spanish as they cleaned the patrons' rooms. The whine of Arby's voice, instructing the day garden staffers. Barbie's heels tapping across the Italian tiles. Stella the palmist and psychic singing along with an Elvis tune. The feral cats meowing at the kitchen door, waiting for Angelina to share scraps and an occasional bowl of cream. One of the personal trainers—he focused to pick up the voice and smiled, ah yes, Stefanie with an *f*—corralling the half-asleep patrons for the morning stroll around the grounds.

If he wished, he could stretch his senses outward to hear the early morning birdsong, the cardinals, wrens, and chickadees fighting for territory at the feeders, the crickets singing lullabies in the parts of Dark Island that rarely saw light, the mating bellow of a bull alligator. Even farther, an occasional whoosh of a car ten miles away on a lonely county road.

Some days, Vincent fought *not* to hear the world.

A soft tap at the door: "Mister Vincent?"

"Come in."

A petite Hispanic woman entered.

"Good morning, Sir."

Raven slipped around the room in the semi-darkness, turning on the CD player and readying the tray of oils and emollients. Vincent studied the young woman. Barely five feet tall with creamy brown skin and thick long black hair gathered loosely into a bun at the nape. No makeup. Her natural beauty needed no unnatural aid. A faint scent of patchouli reminded him of the '60s era.

Arby had chosen well. Raven—not her given name—had come to Dark Island five years back as part of the original team of laborers hired to bring the gardens back from ruin. His overseer had immediately noticed the young woman's strength and willingness to please, and suggested sending her to Gainesville to learn massage therapy. Her husband Hector—now foreman of grounds staff—proved to be just as loyal and dedicated. The couple lived on-Island in a modest ranch-styled house. With few expenses, they were able to send the majority of their ample paychecks back home to a small village in Mexico. No amount of migrant labor could have provided the luxuries Hector and Raven earned. Their gratitude made them two of the Island's most devoted and trusted employees.

"Classical this morning?" she asked. "Or would you prefer piano? I have a new CD of a wonderful fingerstyle guitarist from North Carolina—?"

"The guitar. I am a bit burned out on classical."

For the first few minutes, Vincent chatted with the therapist. So early in the week, very little of importance entered the conversation. Later, after Raven had a chance to work on the patrons, she might provide tidbits of information gleaned during the sessions—mostly personal snippets

Vincent used to gain insight and provide a more personalized regime.

"And how is our baby girl?" Vincent said. "I haven't asked after her for a few days."

Raven used herbal-based oil, designed by Arby to provide the perfect amount of lubrication and to react later with the tanning bed's UV light to turn Vincent's pale skin a nice shade of brown. Arby dubbed the concoction *Vamp Tan in a Can.*

"Christina took her first steps yesterday. Hector and I were thrilled." Raven chuckled softly. "Only now, I must make sure there is nothing she can reach that will harm her. She is so inquisitive, that one."

Yet another thing to worry over. A child on the Dark Island grounds. Not for himself—he would throw himself into the fire before he would harm an innocent. But he couldn't say as much for some of the low-life vamps Emmaraud brought around. To them, a human baby would be as enticing as Kobe beef, and much too succulent to ignore.

Vincent forced the worry from his mind and allowed his senses to focus on Raven's talented hands. To look at the woman, one might think her incapable of deep tissue work, but Raven could lower the automatic table and use her body weight, elbows, and forearms to their best advantage.

For a few moments, Raven spoke in soft tones of her child. Vincent felt the warmth of maternal love wash over his sore spirit. He barely recalled his own mother, and what he did was not laced with fondness. His childhood had been spent with a series of nannies or farmed out to one boarding school or another.

Raven's hands slid down his back in a stroke called *effleurage,* a slow and deliberate motion intended to evenly spread the oil and warm the muscles and skin before deeper work.

Touch: one thing he missed about being a human, almost as much as the enjoyment of food.

Other than Raven, no one touched Vincent Bedsloe III.

"You are very tense this morning." Her expert hands probed the tops of his shoulders.

"Not surprising, Raven. It all kicks up a few notches, starting today. I have to review the party tent placement with Arby later this morning. Since we have two hundred guests confirmed—our largest amount ever for this event, even given the current economy— I've had to modify the size of the main tent this year. Arby has to meet with the suppliers. I have an elaborate decorating scheme, and it is imperative for the groundwork to be properly in place. People think a large event just happens. Throw up some decorations—like a kid's birthday party—a few hours ahead of time, and add food and drinks. It's not like that at all. So many details. So many details."

"If I might suggest, Sir. This is your time to release your tension. If you allow your body to relax, you will be more effective later."

He sighed. "Of course you are correct. Consider it done."

For the next hour and a half, Raven provided a cocoon of tactile sensations. Sensual, yet not sexual. Respectful. Honest.

When she silently left the room, Vincent remained on the massage table for a few minutes, relishing the tingly afterglow. He stood and walked to the tanning bed, stopping briefly to apply the herbal oil to his private parts, the places even his trusted massage therapist didn't venture.

Vincent smiled at the thought of leaving the bronzing oil off for a couple of weeks. He would be the only one to see the comical results: his privates, contrasted by the surrounding deep tropical tan, glowing as if caught in the limo's high beams.

****

Reanita schlepped behind the walking group. Though she prided herself in her general fitness—she could keep up with the best of the men on a ten-mile obstacle course—the little *WBB,* as Stefanie with an *f* kept calling it, was kicking her butt.

"Hey, Rea!" the trainer dropped back to check in with the slacker taking up the rear. "You okay?"

"Peachy. Just f-ing peachy."

Reanita frowned. How were the others coping? The movie star and his senator's-wife concubine-to-be seemed to be lost in their own little world; matching strides with their heads tilted together in some kind of obviously arousing conversation. Little Miss Starlet was tuned into her I-Pod with a loopy grin smeared across her painted lips.

A line of sweat dripped down Reanita's brows and stung her eyes. A second river of perspiration formed a clammy reservoir at the base of her sports bra.

"I know the humidity can get to you," Stefanie with an *f* said. "You'll grow accustomed to it. It really bothered me at first when we—my husband Scotty and I—moved down from Pennsylvania."

Reanita perked up at the mention of the north. "God. How do you stand it?"

"I like the heat, actually. It is so freakin' cold in the winter where I'm from. Down here, I don't have to deal with shoveling snow or driving on ice. It's a trade-off."

The trainer unfastened a spray bottle from the carabineer clipped to her shorts and misted her arms and legs as she continued to walk. Reanita inadvertently inhaled a large whiff and sneezed.

"Oops! Sorry!" the trainer held the bottle up. "All natural. Repels the bugs. If I didn't hose down, I would be one huge red fester. The mosquitoes love me. Must be the sweet blood."

"Got to be it. I notice they're not bothering any of the rest of us."

"Hey, as long as I am around, you have no worries. I'm, like, the perfect person to invite to a picnic. Better than one of those pest strip things. They flock to me."

The trail curved through a stand of saw palmetto bushes. Stefanie with an *f* called out, "Hey, you guys? Remember to watch where you step. The rattlers love to hang out in this section of the Island."

Reanita's eyes grew round. "Rattlers?"

The trainer waved a hand through the air. "Oh, not to worry. We make plenty of noise. The snakes generally keep their distance, or slither off. They are more frightened of us than we are of them."

"I doubt that."

"The moccasins are another story. They can be pretty aggressive."

"Moccasins?"

"Uh-huh. The pygmy rattlers can be a little testy, too."

Reanita scanned the trail around her and slowed her pace. "Pygmy rattlers?"

"They are small snakes, compared to the others. Their bite generally won't kill you, but make you really sore. Sometimes, maybe even loose a digit."

The trainer continued her diatribe as she walked.

"Then, there are the coral snakes. Don't see them very often. They're really pretty and colorful, but really deadly. They kind of chew to inject venom instead of bite. A lot of people get them confused with King snakes. King snakes aren't poisonous, but they have the same stripes and colors as the coral snakes. They have this little ditty down here to help us tell them apart. Red touch black, friendly jack. Red touch yellow, kill a fellow. Has to do with the sequence of the color bands, you see?"

Reanita's eyes darted from her feet to the surrounding woods.

"Don't worry. Really. We've only had one person bitten in the two years I have been on the Island, and that was a grounds worker. Though, it was kind of odd where the bite marks were." Stefanie with an *f* shrugged. "Ah, well. You just have to be aware of your surroundings."

"Snakes have their place in the ecosystem," the trainer added. "I particularly like the oak snakes because they eat cockroaches."

"That would endear them to anyone," Reanita agreed.

"The Florida roaches are freakin' huge! They call them palmetto bugs, but they're just roaches on steroids. And they fly! One hit me right between the eyes just last night as I stepped out of the mansion. I promise you, the sucker was three inches long! I make my husband Scotty kill them. They make this awful kind of wet crunchy noise when they pop. It makes my skin crawl."

The trail turned toward the coastline. Soon, stands of tall grass appeared on either side. Reanita noticed several areas where the vegetation appeared to have been beaten down. "Why did you do that?"

The trainer shook her head. "We didn't. The gators did."

Reanita swallowed around the lump forming in her throat. "Gators?"

Stefanie with an *f* nodded. "They hang out in the grass. We have some huge ones—over seven feet from nose to tail."

The trainer took note of the patron's stricken expression. "Oh, I've scared you. I'm sorry. My husband often tells me I say too much. It's just that I find all this Florida stuff so interesting. I have books on the native snakes, birds, all of that. If you see a gator, he or she generally won't bother you. Unless she is near her nest. Then, it might be a different story. Gators can run pretty fast."

"Um...as in, how fast?"

"I read where they have been clocked at twelve miles an hour. Isn't that crazy?"

Reanita felt her sweat turn cold. "Oh yeah. Crazy."

"They can only get up that kind of speed in a straight line, though, and for short distances. They are more like sprinters than marathon runners. Just remember...if one takes off after you, all you have to do is zigzag. They have to stop to change directions."

Zigzag. I can do zigzag. Reanita reassured herself. *Just think about dodging gun fire.*

The coastline—a long muddy beach—appeared. Reanita noted two wooden docks and remembered she was supposed to be researching illegal smuggling activities instead of taking a nature course. A small tin-roofed shack stood on the shore.

"What's that?"

Stefanie with an *f* paused before answering. "Just the Island landing."

"So, do a lot of boats come in here?"

"A few."

For all of her nature babbling, the trainer seemed instantly reticent.

"So, do the patrons come in by boat sometimes?" Reanita asked.

"Mostly supplies. Fresh seafood."

Stefanie with an *f* increased her pace and caught up with the rest of the patrons.

Obviously, Reanita had entered a no-talk zone.

"Breakfast will be waiting when we get back!" the trainer called over her shoulder as she picked up the pace. "Let's turn it on for the last quarter mile. Showers, then Angelina's hot cross buns, everyone!"

The trail entered the edge of the formal gardens near a two-acre vegetable patch. The bushes rustled and a young man carrying a rifle stepped out. Reanita instinctively dropped to a crouch and pawed her waist for the weapon that should have been there.

"God, Scotty!" Stefanie with an *f* stood with her hands propped on her hips. "How many times have I told you not to do that! It scares the patrons."

He offered a sheepish grin and lowered the weapon. Reanita now noticed it was merely a pellet rifle. The young man favored the Looney Tunes Elmer Fudd character with a non-seasonal plaid hunting cap, complete with ear-warming flaps.

He held a finger to his lips. "Be vewy, vewy quiet. I'm hunting wabbits."

Stefanie with an *f* laughed and kissed her husband on the cheek. "I know, hon. I know." She turned to the rest of the group. "My husband, Scotty. He's mostly harmless."

Patrice plucked one of the I-Pod's ear buds out. "You kill them?"

He shook his head. "Ah, no. Just ping them on their little cottontails, enough to scare them from the garden. They eat everything. The boss insists that we not use any repellants or traps. The whole humane, green thing."

Snakes. Gators. Kamikaze roaches. Now, junior Rambo. Reanita wondered if a raise and a promotion wouldn't be in order when the assignment was all over.

Chapter 6

Monday night

Arby's night vision had always been excellent. His earliest memories—even as a toddler—revolved around nocturnal wanderings. He could slip past the snoring *nanny-de-jour* and out of the nursery on silent mouse-feet, and spend blissful hours roaming the darkness. The night world held great magic: fireflies blipping signals in neon green, shuffling creatures making their rounds, the whoosh of the avian hunter overhead. Arby felt then, and now: his true power rested in darkness.

Imagine how much more I could see if only I could have The Blood, he thought.

What if he could somehow convince Vincent to share? Even a touch of the distillate might make a difference. He thought of the main advantages, other than the obvious. For a gardener, the idea of an eternity to create new subspecies loomed huge. To affect small changes in biology took several growing seasons, if it could be accomplished at all.

The possibilities caused his heart to race in ways that years of finagling legal mitigations never could. Endless time? Day upon day to experiment? To actually see a tree he had planted reach full maturity. To witness the rare bloom of a century plant. Better yet, to successfully cultivate the Titan Arum, also called the *corpse flower*, of which few had ever bloomed in captivity. When one of the alien-appearing plants produced the phallic deep burgundy flower that stood taller than a human, visitors came for hundreds of miles to witness it and gag on its putrid odor, a combination of sulfurous compounds with the fitting names of *cadaverene* and *putrescine*. To Arby, the foul-scented plant was a thing of beauty he had only seen online. As an eternal being, Arby might produce his own Titan Arum. The thought brought a flush of near-sexual excitement.

Arby picked a familiar path toward one of the Island's many hidden coves. The commercial docks served for produce and household supply deliveries, and several local fishermen stopped at Dark Island to offer the best of their fresh catch before taking the remainder to the ports further south. The water route proved the most useful for such a disconnected haven as The Dark. Land deliveries took several days longer, and the large trucks buckled the asphalt and put unnecessary wear on the Island's only bridge. The rare times Arby conceded and allowed the heavy transport vehicles across the narrow bridge were for the three annual special events held on-Island: the upcoming Blue Blood Ball, the Dead of Winter event in late January, and—Vincent's favorite—the All-Hallowed-Eve's party at the end of October.

For the past couple of weeks, extra provisions had arrived every couple of days. Vincent's supply of special decorations. Exotic spices. Vintage wine and champagnes. Recently delivered: The largest fresh Gulf shrimp, oysters, and scallops. Prime Reserve beef sirloin came from Omaha, packed in dry ice. Crates of local fresh tomatoes, lettuce, cucumbers, and vegetables were brought ashore. Between meeting with suppliers, caterers, and PSG—the Event Production Company out of Tallahassee—Arby made numerous day and night runs to the docks to meet boats, or to the main gate to direct the delivery trucks to the service road rear entrance of the mansion.

Tonight, he waited at the private beach. Not a commercial shipment, this one. Vincent Bedsloe III had a wicked taste for Cuban—and not the sandwiches, but Cuban blood smuggled to supplement the small samples provided by Dark Island patrons. No harm came to Castro's willing donors; each compensated well for a pint or two. Officials pocketed payoffs and turned a blind eye. Everyone profited. Plus, with the blood came Vincent's fresh supply of hand-rolled Cuban cigars.

Periodically, Arby's boss would become overly bored with the normal stew of spa patrons and dream up an impromptu affair to liven things up. Arby recalled one just the spring past: a small party of select garden aficionados, given in his honor. No one—not even Arby's kin—had ever made a fuss over his birthday on April Fool's Day. Seemed that birthing a rat-faced boy had been the joke of all times on his parents. And certainly, after he was orphaned, no one paid attention to the rat-boy's special day. Vincent had touched Arby in ways no human ever had, just by recognizing the fact that he had been born. The tour included the formal master gardens and a talk on exotic ground covers as well as a peek at the inner sanctum hybrids (sans the well-concealed hemp plants) for a handful of special guests.

It had been one of the highlights of his adult life; better than falling in love and having it returned, which he had never experienced. His peers ogled over his special breed of annuals and perennials, remarking on the distinct odors and odd colorations, begging him for clippings. Though the visitors never saw his face, Arby felt the satisfaction of showing that splendor could come from such a gardener as himself; a person shunned for his lack of physical beauty.

Clearly, if he had eternity to market his careful work to the special few, a flourishing business would follow. *Never underestimate people's taste for the weird.* Arby smiled at his cleverness. The statement could be his personal motto.

Bushes swished behind him. He stopped and scanned the woods. The crickets were still singing: a good sign. He waited for a moment. An opossum trundled from the palmettos, sniffed in his direction, and continued on his way. Arby smiled. To most people, 'possums were nasty little creatures with unattractive features, overgrown rats that ate carrion and snarled with rows of pointy teeth. All true. Arby loved them.

Jumpy; the pressures of the upcoming gala were making him jumpy.

Arby shrugged off the feeling of unease and continued to walk. Who in their right mind would be out in the swamps of Dark Island at this time of night? Vincent, perhaps. The vamp loved to take long evening strolls. But his boss would announce himself and walk alongside for a bit, as he had on many occasions.

The swampy land gave way to soft sand. The smell of mud and sea salt. The gentle lap of the tide. The skitter of tiny crabs. A partial moon granting enough light for dim shadows.

Arby waited.

When he saw the green bow beam of a small boat, he turned on his hand-held flood light and motioned the skipper to shore. The skipper spoke a blend of broken English and Spanish. Arby handed a thick envelope over, then helped the man to unload three Styrofoam containers into an over-sized cooler inside a small shed on shore. He slipped a small box of the cherished cigars under one arm. The skipper used an oar to push away from the mud, then lowered the outboard motor into the water when he gained sufficient depth. Arby waited until he could no longer see the boat's running lights in the distance before he padlocked the door on the sturdy wooden hut. In a couple of hours, he would return with one of the Dark Island electric carts and transfer the Cuban Delivery to the industrial freezers in Vincent's private suite.

As he turned toward the mansion, he couldn't shake the feeling that someone—or something—watched his movements from the dark.

****

Reanita observed the furtive exchange from behind a clump of palmettos. To keep her mind from the slithery noises around her, she hummed a nursery rhyme in her head. She could just feel all of the snakes Stefanie with an *f* had described, curling around her feet, waiting for the wrong sudden move to sink their venomous fangs into soft skin. She would die a slow and painful death, swelling with poison in the Florida swamps.

She shuddered.

The two men she watched—one she had followed from the mansion and one from the boat—carried some kind of boxes to a little building. This time of night with so much clandestine flair—?

Paydirt!

She salivated at the thought of looking inside one of the containers. Had to be drugs or some other type of contraband. Else, why all the work to keep it undercover?

She focused on the smaller of the two men; the one she had tailed from the grounds. Even in the dim moonlight, she could tell he wore some kind of protective gear—a HAZMAT suit? What kind of whacked-out stuff were these folks dealing?

Reanita's skin prickled with the pinch of mosquito bites. Though she wore long pants and a shirt with sleeves, the little blood-suckers still found exposed tissue to inject. No way could she risk spraying down with some of Stefanie with an *f*'s special repellant. The scent carried.

The boat pushed away. The little man watched for a moment and turned in her direction. She watched him stuff a small oblong box beneath one arm. Reanita scrambled to her feet and tried to move as rapidly and stealthily as possible toward the mansion. She made a quick mental note of the shed's position.

****

When Arby entered the edge of the formal gardens, he heard a soft *whump,* as if a large overripe melon had hit the soft dirt.

"Anyone there?" he called out.

A low feminine moan answered. Arby rushed toward the noise. He recognized the woman in an instant, though she lay in a rumpled clump at the base of a native hydrangea bush. "Miss Register!"

Reanita held her right foot and cursed.

"What are you doing out here in the dark?"

Reanita struggled to her knees. Arby held out a hand to assist her.

"Crap. I think I've sprained my ankle."

"Oh, dear." Arby guided one of her arms over his shoulders and helped her to stand. "I think you might've fallen prey to an armadillo's foul doings. The little buggers dig holes everywhere. That's why it is unwise to venture from the lighted pathways."

Her ankle throbbed with a beat of its own. "I...I thought I saw a deer, or something—"

"Most likely. They do tend to move around and feed when the moon is near to full. Still, I must insist that you not wander by yourself in the future. It's not safe."

Reanita noticed the little man's clothing: a full light-colored jumpsuit and a bee-keeper's hat. His facial features were obscured by the netting. Not the HAZMAT suit she had originally thought. Still, odd.

Arby nodded toward the mansion. "Let's get you inside. I'll have Vincent take a look at your ankle. If need be, we can make arrangements to drive you into Gainesville for an x-ray tomorrow morning."

"I can put weight on it. Really, I don't think it's broken."

No doctors. Absolutely no doctors! Her mind raced. *Too many questions. And I'd be the laughing stock of the department. 'Hey, we sent the bat-faced girl to Florida and she had to slink home with her tail between her legs because she sprained her poor little ankle!'*

Arby said. "Got to follow the I-C-E routine. Ice, compress, elevate."

"Wait. Who are you?"

"Nobody really. Just the groundskeeper."

The pain made her more irritable than the collection of bug bites. "Do you have a *name*?"

He hesitated. "Arby." His skin tingled where Reanita's body touched his. He pushed down a longing so fierce, it constricted his throat.

Inside the mansion, Arby helped her to a small couch in the patron's living room. He gathered pillows and gently propped up her legs. "There. Don't move. I'll be right back with assistance."

The beekeeper's mask did not come off, even inside. Reanita wondered about it briefly, between pounding spasms of her abused ankle.

Arby located Vincent in the study, puffing a Fuente Opus X. The master gardener stopped short, forgetting the reason for his mission when he heard his employer's jovial laughter. Vincent seldom succumbed to overt mirth.

"Sir?"

"Oh. Arby." Vincent grinned. "I was just thinking about the tidbit I stumbled upon just this morning on *Wikipedia.* Aren't computers just the best thing ever? Did you know, before the Industrial Revolution, tuberculosis was sometimes regarded as vampirism?"

"No, Sir."

"Seems when one member of the family turned up with the symptoms and others became infected and lost their health, it was believed to be a result of the original TB victim being a vampire and preying on them. The symptoms of TB—red swollen eyes, sensitivity to light, pale skin, low body heat, coughing blood—were the same ones associated with vampires. Of course, early in the twentieth century, TB was rumored to have masturbation as its cause." Vincent chucked again. "Imagine. Most of the adolescent males would be thrown into TB sanitariums if that was the belief now, and we didn't have the relief provided by modern pharmaceuticals."

Arby smiled. "Bizarre, what one can find on the Internet. I recently located a variety of camellia named *Blood of China*. Not with my interesting aroma or traits to be sure, but it might make an interesting addition to the general gardens."

Vincent stepped up to the digital mirror above the hearth and studied his computerized reflection. "I don't have red eyes, do I, Arby?"

The caretaker shook his head. "Only upon occasion when you overindulge a bit in a particular blood vintage. Otherwise, no."

"Then, I suppose I look just like any other human who's gone on a bender. No harm there."

Arby jerked. "Oh. I completely forgot why I sought you out! Miss Register seems to have suffered an injury. I found her deep in the gardens."

"What was she doing out there?" Vincent asked. "The guests are warned against such behavior. What if she had stumbled onto Jimmy Rob's land? He has little restraint."

"I don't know, Sir. She says she was following a deer."

"Hmm." He extinguished the cigar. "I'll see to her ankle. Tonight, we can wrap it and have her apply ice. The distillate will take care of the healing. Make sure she gets her treatment first thing tomorrow."

Arby thought of his role. For the first time, he felt a twinge of guilt at what he would do to Reanita Register on her second day on Dark Island.

Later—long after the night sounds of the mansion died down and Reanita retired to her suite—Arby walked to the adjunct greenhouse behind his inner garden. The spot seemed sacred: the one place he could remove his bee hat and feel secure, though he kept it handy on a special hook just inside the door. Three other hothouses were situated in an area reserved for grounds maintenance; the home for the regular plants. This one, half the size of the others, belonged to the caretaker. Arby had one of the two padlock keys; the second, ferreted away in Vincent's private quarters.

The master gardener stood just inside the entrance to the arboretum and immediately felt his blood pressure lower. More than any other place he had lived in his miserable childhood, this spot was *home*. The place of his heart. He thought of it at all times and anxiously awaited the stolen moments he spent in its green womb, almost like a drug addict anticipating the needle prick.

There will be no judgment here, he thought.

The plants—his children—accepted him as he was and returned his love equally with amazing flora. *Talk to your plants,* the so-called experts advised. *The idiots.*

"What a medieval, moronic cliché. Plants don't have ears. They sense. They feel their environment." He snorted. "How ironic. Everything else in this tourist-infested state is running around with an *extra* set of ears, but not my plants."

Arby ran his fingers through the lacy fronds of a maidenhair fern.

"I am so dependent on all of you to give me life, yet you all are dependent on me for your survival."

He proceeded down the rows of plants, letting them brush against him, allowing their auras to blend with his. In a few moments, he set about his scheduled task: preparing flats of *crossandra infundibuliformis* for a new mass planting near the entrance of the grounds. The hardy fledgling annuals with their showy spikes of apricot-colored flowers would be ready in a few days for their new home.

"Go out and show 'em your glory," he relayed telepathically.

Rows of developing hybrid plants crowded every shelf and hung in pots from the overhead pipe beams. A mister watering system kept the air humid. Drops of moisture dripped from the tips of the leaves and plopped on his nose and eyelashes.

A single blossom on one of the larger Camellias caught his eye. Reanita and her sprained ankle faded from his mind. He rushed to the far corner of the greenhouse and bent down. Seeing the hybrid plant's first bloom was like witnessing the birth of a child—his child. The root stock of an ordinary pink Camellia grafted with *Rattmelia Japonica;* the plant had produced a rare bloom—a pink, white, and red-striped flower with the distinctive rat-like features at the center. Eye candy. He leaned closer and sniffed. The bouquet reminded him of overripe bananas with a faint sulfurous undertone.

"You are more beautiful than your parents," he whispered.

What to name her?—he already considered the plant female. Arby thought of the one thing he cherished. The one thing he loved more than anything on the earth. And in such a short time.

"*Reanita Japonica.*" He nodded. Smiled.

A fitting tribute to his one true love, whether he could ever have her or not.

****

Vincent stood in the midst of the Dark Island swamp, his L.L. Bean hiking boots mired in the mud. Even in the driest of years, this part of the Dark retained small areas of moisture. Whenever he felt unsettled, as he had in the past few days, the vampire visited the spot.

His spot. Only his.

The silent ghosts of the Native Americans who once communed with the alligators and snakes kept him company. He sat down on the bent trunk of one of the few hardwood trees in the acreage. *Water-finder* trees—what his resident horticulturist called the unnaturally-shaped hardwoods. Arby had provided a fanciful story of how a sapling might develop at such a strange inverted-Z shape, reminiscent of a garden bench. In the fable, the bent trunk pointed in the direction of fresh drinking water and had been human hand-trained in such a way to provide a signal to the native people.

Vincent liked the legend—fabricated, or not. The Bedsloe family lineage reportedly included one ancestor with Indian bloodlines. By Vincent's calculations, he would be one-sixty-fourth Native American.

The vamp blood had probably long since gobbled up any connection. Still, Vincent chose to harbor the idea that some small part of his core, some clutch of hidden cells, contained the indigenous blue prints.

It might explain how the only son of wealth could have such intense amour for the woods. In his childhood in upstate New York, the forest behind the family's massive house had provided a respite from the cloistered world of beautiful moneyed people. Most of the time when he escaped into the forest, no one bothered to question or come looking.

He thought about Arby. The poor rat-faced man. Was he as fond of the woods for the same reasons as his employer? Did he escape teasing and bullying by seeking the forest's solace? Arby's caretakers—the overseer had mentioned being orphaned at an early age—certainly never worried about the child roaming in the deep woods. The local fauna would likely suffer greater trauma from encountering such a rat-faced human.

Vincent took a deep breath. Beneath the heady scent of decaying layers of vegetation, he detected the faint scent of a passing skunk, the spoor of countless rodents and small mammals, and the ever-present tang of the nearby Gulf.

The background song of the swamp filled the air—the insistent whine of hungry mosquitoes. The insects lit on Vincent's skin long enough to figure out that he would provide no nourishment. One poised on his hand and he held it up to study it closer. His preternatural night vision showed the creature in intimate detail.

"You are such an efficient little hunter," he said in a low voice. "Through the ages. Through wars, famine, drought—you survive."

Not unlike vampires.

In the extended dry season—more common than ever in Florida with the earth changes no one seemed to take seriously—the mosquito and her kin would hunker down in the vegetation, shutting down their metabolism until conditions proved once again favorable. They often traveled miles for a meal, and Vincent had read on one Internet site, how salt marsh mosquitoes had been trapped fifty miles from where they started. Amazing.

He sensed that the creature on his hand was a female. Recently fed and sluggish. Females could take in more than their weight in a full blood meal. Vincent admired the trait. The little insect could do something he couldn't do.

The mosquito lifted off and disappeared into the darkness, a stalker with a buzzing alarm system.

"Good thing I don't whine when I'm hungry." Vincent smiled, thinking of the startled expressions of the humans on Dark Island, when their benefactor circled their warm bodies with a warning cry. No, he would take his nourishment otherwise.

He spotted a small cluster of greenery growing from a rotting tree trunk and leaned down to study the leaves.

"Look at what I have found," he said. "A blood fern."

Vincent gathered several spires into a silk pouch for Arby. The gardener would be pleased. The nondescript ferns were generally difficult to locate and only sprouted when conditions were perfect. Small spore sacks the color of dried blood on the backside of the leaves provided a powerful sedative used in one of the caretaker's special herbal teas. Other than the handful of Creek Indians in the Florida panhandle who had reportedly used the rare fern for a type of spiritual quest, few knew of the plant's well-guarded potential. Good thing. If discovered by the drug companies, it would be sought out in the swamps of the Deep South and harvested to extinction. Another magical hidden thing, best kept secret.

For a few moments, Vincent Bedsloe shook loose the aura of impending doom that had settled onto his shoulders like an undead monster's cape.

Chapter 7

Tuesday morning

Every time she moved, Reanita's ankle let her know how unhappy it was. Sleep had been impossible and she felt like death not even warmed over. The swelling had subsided a little, but the flesh had turned from an angry red to dark purple. No doubt, it would be one of those deep bruises that morphed through every color in the spectrum before it finally returned to a normal flesh tone, days later.

How the pluperfect hell was she supposed to do her job if she had to hobble?

"You've worked with worse, Reanita," she coached herself. "Remember the time you fell headfirst into the prickly pear cactus in Utah?"

Plus, she had been shot. Twice.

A sprained ankle wasn't going to slow her down. Much. Nothing was wrong with her mouth or inquisitive brain. Until she could navigate the grounds again, she would just have to settle for rattling the cages of the employees and patrons until something shook loose.

A tap sounded. Reanita rolled over and stared at the door.

"Ree-ah?" a voice called out in a high-pitched, two-note song.

"Stefanie with an *eh-uff?*" She answered in the same sing-song, only sarcastic.

God help, surely the trainer didn't expect her to tramp through the woods with an ankle the size of a softball. Did she?

"Let yourself in. I can't come to you at the moment."

The a.m. trainer opened the door a crack and stuck her head inside. "I heard about your little boo-boo. No worries. We'll miss you on the WBB, our little Walk Before Breakfast, but there are lots of other upper body routines we can do after breakfast."

The woman was a freak about fitness. If her husband proved as thorough with his job, there wouldn't be a rabbit left on Dark Island.

"We'll see."

"I'll have Barbie send up a set of crutches…or, would you prefer a wheelchair?"

"No. No wheelchair. I'm not an invalid. The crutches will do fine."

Stefanie with an *f* nodded. "I spoke with Raven. She wants to get you into the therapy room. She works wonders with lymphatic draining. Something about the way she does this special massage to help the swelling and toxins to subside."

Reanita raked her hand through her hair. A layer of sweat and dirt from the previous evening's activities held the locks together like syrup. A shower would be nice. And challenging.

"I'll be down in time for breakfast," Reanita said. "You and the others have a great little walk."

The door closed. Peace. Blessed peace. If only she had some pain medication to squelch the pounding radiating up her leg, life would be good.

Reanita heard the others march down the hall: Stefanie with an *f*'s high-pitched encouragement, the actor's baritone, the starlet's attempt at early-morning sultry, the senator's wife's well-modulated voice.

She rolled over and closed her eyes. The snakes, roaches, and gators would have to do without her this morning. Hal-a-freakin'-loo-yah.

A couple of hours later, a soft tap at the door awakened her for the second time in one morning.

"What? What!"

The door opened a crack. "Miss Register, I bring for you, your breakfast on a tray." The voice, unsure of the language, musical with a strong Hispanic accent.

Reanita sat up and plumped the pillows behind her. "That'd be good, since I really don't feel much like walking. Come on in."

Had to give it to the place as far as service went. For the hefty sticker price of a week's indulgence, Reanita figured they should chew the food for her, too.

"*Señor* Arby make special eggs for you." The dark-haired young woman said. She settled a white lacquered bed tray across Reanita's lap and offered a crisp linen napkin. "He say is good for your foot, for you to eat good breakfast."

*Arby...Arby...*Reanita's mind searched for the face to go with the name. *Ah, yes. The little man in the beekeeper suit.* "He cooks?"

"Jes. *Señor* Arby very good."

Reanita nodded. *Talented guy. Smuggler. Grounds-keeper. Cook. No telling what roles the man played on the Island.*

The server uncovered warmed plates. One, filled with sour cream biscuits and blueberry muffins, orange blossom honey and softened butter, and the other with a two-egg omelet and three strips of crisp country bacon. An insulated pitcher held fresh coffee.

"Jew want I bring orange juice?" the server asked.

"No. This is more than I will ever eat. Thank you."

"Okey-dokey." The woman smiled, obviously pleased with herself for mixing in a bit of slang with her hesitant English. "I come for plate later."

In a week, she would be back to flaccid breakfast burritos and stale coffee. Might as well make the best of the current situation.

Reanita dug into the omelet. The first bite nearly made her eyes cross with pleasure. "God, that is so good…"

The eggs were chiffon-light, filled with a mixture of spinach, artichoke hearts, sun-dried tomatoes and cream cheese. Perfectly seasoned.

By the time Reanita finished, the tray held nothing but crumb-strewn plates.

She grabbed the pair of crutches someone had surreptitiously delivered to the room and managed to navigate to the bathroom and into the shower. The hot water felt heavenly on her scalp and shoulders, but made her ankle throb like rats doing a disco.

Getting clean took twice as long. Dressing provided another challenge. Something loose would be best. Nothing binding, or even touching, her ankle. She donned the thick white logo-emblazed robe and crutched to the bureau where all of the designer clothing lay folded neatly in the long drawers. After several attempts to balance and riffle through the contents, she opted to lean the crutches to one side and teeter on her good foot.

A tap sounded at the door.

She resisted the urge to yell out: *Grand Freakin' Central Station! Step aboard and bring your friends!*

"Might as well come in," she said, then beneath her breath, "Everyone else has."

A slender woman stepped into the suite. "I am sorry to bother you, Miss Register. I'm Raven, the Spa's massage therapist. Mr. Vincent wished for me to offer my services this morning. I perform a kind of therapy called Manual Lymphatic Drainage. It is very useful in dealing with any kind of swelling or injury."

Breakfast in bed, now a massage? Reanita had died and gone to high-end heaven. "I could get into that. Just give me a few minutes to dress."

Raven held up a hand. "No need. Just come as you are. The robe is fine. You would just have to undress, anyway."

"Now?"

"I have my therapy room ready for you." Raven hesitated. "Would you like for me to bring a wheelchair?"

"No wheelchair. Absolutely not."

Reanita took two hops and grabbed the crutches. Making her way around the suite on one leg was one thing, walking any distance was another.

She followed the slight woman with the waist-length black hair down the patrons' wing, onto the elevator to another long hallway on the first floor. She recognized the area.

"The workout room is way down there, right?"

Raven nodded. "Yes. My rooms aren't quite that far. Lucky for you."

Two doors down, Raven stopped. "Do you prefer the beach, the forest, or the heavens?"

Reanita chuffed. *Why did everything at Dark Island consist of a multiple choice quiz? Like the rich and famous couldn't do with just one flavor.*

"Depends. Will there be alligators?"

Raven laughed. "My therapy rooms are decorated in themes. I have three so that patrons won't feel rushed to exit after treatments."

"I see."

Reanita considered and chose the heavens. She didn't care for salt spray or sand and already she'd had enough forest wilderness to last her a lifetime.

When the therapist opened the door, Reanita stared. The walls, painted in shades of blue dotted with fluffy cumulous clouds, provided the illusion of free-floating. The massage table—thick with a sheepskin pad and white cotton sheets—stood in the middle of the room. The tile and the room-sized rug were brilliant white, as were the pristine cabinets and countertops. Low lighting, cast from two wall sconces and a white candle, filled the room with a soft ethereal glow.

"I'll let you get settled," the therapist said. "Tuck yourself beneath the sheets, face up. I prefer you not wear underclothing, but I can work around it if you feel more comfortable. You will be carefully draped at all times." She moved toward the door. "I'll knock in a few minutes and we can get started."

Raven left. The minute Reanita reclined, her body seemed to get some secret *Relax! Relax Now!* signal. Her breathing calmed. Her pulse slowed to an even thrum.

The ceiling, painted in a gradient of deepening blues, seemed to reach to infinity. Constellations created from phosphorescent stars scattered in patterns. Reanita recognized two: Aquarius, the water bearer, and Libra, the scales. She rummaged through her knowledge of astronomy. The two zodiac signs would not normally appear in the same night sky. She wondered if the placement held significance for whoever had painted the room. Her mother—a weak woman whose spirituality had consisted of a weird blend of Protestant euphemisms, astrology, and astronomy—was responsible for her knowledge of the night skies.

The therapist knocked twice then entered when Reanita answered.

"This is unreal. It actually looks as if I'm gazing into space."

Raven held a demitasse cup in one hand. "Isn't it wonderful? The other rooms are just as nice. Maybe you can choose a different one for tomorrow's treatment."

"Tomorrow?"

"The Spa package allows for one spa treatment per day. More, if you wish to add. I provide hot stone massage, Reiki energy healing work, deep tissue, Swedish, Craniosacral and neuromuscular deep tissue work."

"I don't know what half of that stuff is, but sign me up for all of it."

Raven handed Reanita the delicate china cup. "I forgot to give this to you before I left."

A strange aroma floated from the cup, a blend of licorice, lavender, and something Reanita didn't recognize. "What is it?"

"A special blend of herbal tea. It helps the body to release toxins," Raven said. "It is a tad bitter, so it is best, I think, not to sip."

Reanita could think of no clever excuse to refuse. She accepted the drink and knocked it back like a shot of tequila. She immediately wished she had a lemon to bite. Anything to cover the miasma of nastiness covering her tongue.

"You weren't kidding about the taste." Reanita shivered. "God, that is awful!"

Better hope she didn't have to pass a drug screen test when the assignment ended. No telling what kind of bells and whistles her urine would set off.

Raven handed her a bottle of spring water. "The taste fades fast. Our overseer blends all of our medicinal teas and massage lotions. He is well-versed in herbal medicine."

"Don't tell me…that Arby guy." Reanita took a swig of water and handed the bottle back to the therapist.

Raven nodded. She moved around the table and adjusted the speaker's volume on an I-pod dock. Outer space music eased into the background and blended with the tinkling of a small tabletop water fountain. Reanita watched as Raven chose two vials of amber liquid—she assumed to be oils—from a tray filled with bottles.

The therapist moved to the foot of the table and held the bottoms of Reanita's feet in the palms of her hand. Then she moved to the top of the table where she touched the crown of Reanita's head. "I am tuning into your energy field."

"Ah. Of course."

A week's worth of this New-Age mumbo jumbo, and I might need more than herbal tea to clear toxins. Reanita took a deep breath and tried to assume her best wealthy girl attitude. Heiresses were probably accustomed to all of the posturing.

"So, how long have you worked at Dark Island?" Reanita asked.

Raven lifted the sheet over one of Reanita's legs and tucked the edges carefully to provide ample coverage of the private parts at the top of the thigh. She oiled her hands, and executed one long continuous stroke from the ankle upward. "A little over four years."

"Do you like your boss?"

Raven stiffened a bit; a split-second reaction Reanita's trained eyes registered. "Mr. Vincent is a wonderful employer."

Reanita's vision blurred. She fought to focus. "Tell me about him. About this place."

Raven's answers came in short, practiced snippets. Just enough information, nothing elaborate. As little detail as possible.

What the hell? It's like she has these routine answers, or something... What is she hiding?

"It would be best for you to allow your mind to come to a place of peace and quiet," Raven said. "Allow your body to yield to the healing energy of the massage."

Reanita tried to make her mouth move. So many questions. As Raven's experienced hands continued to circle and stroke, she closed her eyes.

Then, nothing.

Raven sighed. Some patrons had questions, others not. The pay here—more than she or her husband would ever dream of making elsewhere—more than accommodated for dodging the occasional inquiries. Her daughter would go to school, to college. To a better life than she might have had.

Raven would never reveal her thoughts. She had questions, too. Many questions. But they paled in comparison to where she might have been without the help of Vincent Bedsloe III. Like the others—people cast aside by the world and trampled down to subhuman—Raven would never betray her employer.

If someone rescued you from the lip of the abyss, you did not turn around and push him in.

****

Arby nodded to the massage therapist as they passed in the hall. Did Raven ever question why a groundskeeper wore white, logo-printed scrubs and a surgical mask? Arby wondered. If she did, she kept it to herself. She was told only that each patron received a special injection of vitamins after their massage, given to enhance energy and well-being.

He opened the door a crack and hesitated. His love rested on the table inside the room. So suitable, that she had chosen the treatment space with the heavens motif. Reanita was his angel and the room's décor fitted her like none before.

Arby sat the white leather doctor's bag on the counter and removed a small syringe and vial. The liquid glowed in the low light. His years in the nursing field—before he moved onto the study of the law—taught him the importance of sterile conditions. He donned a pair of fresh surgical gloves and laid his implements on a white cloth.

Reanita rested, her breathing deep and even. The blood fern and chamomile tea had done its job. She would sleep with vivid dreams for about an hour and awaken refreshed, feeling years younger. The distillate would work its magic immediately, with more noticeable results by the end of the week.

In the four years since the Spa at Dark Island opened, Arby had never—not once—taken liberties with the patrons. The sheet drape stayed in place. He only rescued one arm for the injection and blood draw. So many beautiful women had lain on the massage tables. Tempting, but even a rat has his standards. He could tell Reanita's ample breasts weren't surgically augmented by the way they rested, soft beneath the sheet. Implants stood like round ripe casaba melons, their erect nipples pointing to the ceiling.

How Arby longed to look. He reached for the edge of the sheet. Stopped.

"No," he whispered. "If you see the Goddess, it is because of her invitation."

The sound of his lowered voice caused Reanita to moan. Sexual. Deep-throated. Arby wondered if she imagined a lover in her dreams.

No worries. The anesthesia worked. She wouldn't stir until noon.

He moved to the end of the table and lifted the corner of the sheet enough to see the wounded ankle. Deep, angry bruising. He rested his palm on the skin. Hot to the touch. Any doubts he had about providing relief evaporated. He replaced the sheet.

A Goddess should not have to suffer human indignities.

Arby lifted the glass vial and drew two cc's into the syringe, then carefully expelled a bit of trapped air from the barrel. He moved to Reanita's right side, uncovered her upper arm, and used a pre-moistened alcohol pad to clean the skin. The needle's diameter, so small it barely made a pinprick spot. He left one drop of the distillate on the skin and rubbed it in. Any sign of the injection site disappeared. She wouldn't even have a sore arm.

The needle and disposable syringe went into a small Sharps container inside the bag. He stared at the other equipment—a section of rubber tourniquet tubing and the blood donation bag and needle assembly.

Arby moved to the head of the massage table and studied Reanita's face. Moisture formed at the corners of his eyes. He dabbed a tear with one finger and looked at it in wonder. Rat boys didn't cry.

"I can't do it to you." He gently wiped aside a stray sprig of hair that had fallen over her eyes. "I *won't* do it to you."

Vincent had a way of ferreting out duplicity. Uncanny. Spooky. How would Arby explain why his beautiful heiress's blood wine did not appear in the week's stock? Arby knew the rules. He had written the original contract and signed it. Dark Island—shrouded in deep secrets—had to be protected at all costs. Especially for the permanent inhabitants, trust was paramount. A breach would result in immediate dismissal: a rat-faced boy cast from the Island Garden of Eden with his tail tucked between his legs.

When he left the room and started down the hall, he heard the sounds of the other guests gearing up for a fun day at the Spa. A low thrum echoed from the gym: Stefanie with an *f* and her starlet pupil Patrice in the fever pitch of a jazz dance and kick-boxing aerobic combo. Behind the next massage room door—in the ocean room—the faux British baritone and female murmurs of the Actor and the senator's wife. Arby pulled his digital day planner from the pocket of his scrubs.

"Ah, yes. An intimate couples' treat."

Raven providing massage at one table. The day-hire esthetician performing a facial on the other. After an hour, the two therapists would switch positions. Two hours later, two blissful, exfoliated and well-oiled patrons would emerge—no doubt after completing a little after-treatment kibitzing.

Arby had seen the same theme played out many times. The limited time span intensified the affair into a gear not usually reached off-Island. The men would return to their worldly obligations with renewed vigor. The women, he wondered and worried about, especially the wives of politicians. They basked in the social limelight and prestige of men of such noble calling, yet had to endure who-knew how much shame at the hands of their mates. Power corrupted, always. The wife—head of the hearth, keeper of future generations—was expected to paste on a smile even when her husband kept three mistresses hopping and made little attempt to cover his tracks.

What ever happened to real commitment, Arby wondered. Just one person loving that special other one, and only one.

He scrolled down to the section in his digital planner entitled *Reanita Register* and put a digital checkmark in the B-12 injection column.

****

An hour later, Reanita's eyes flew open. She blinked to clear her vision. She didn't really want to be awake. The erotic dream had seemed so real. A man with a face hidden in shadows, making wild screeching love to her in some kind of bizarre garden. She closed her eyes, hoping to regain the feeling, but it was no use. She was wide-eyed as a Shih-Tzu on speed. She hadn't felt this rested or energetic in—come to think of it, she never had.

She ripped back the sheet and bounded from the massage table. A split-second thought raced through her hyper brain at the same time her right foot hit the floor, and she braced for the inevitable gush of pain.

No pain. A little stiffness. She glanced down. For the first time since the fall, she could see the ankle bone. Maybe it was her imagination, but it seemed as if the bruise covered less territory.

"Man, that Drano massage shit really works!"

Just to make sure, she took a few steps, hopped, and flexed.

Nothing.

And she was hungry. Evil hungry. She threw on the robe and left to find the lunch buffet. They would all just have to deal with the fact she didn't have the patience to get dressed.

Chapter 8

Vincent entered the media room. The audio-isolation door snapped into its rubber seals. He sighed. Blessed peace. The special design provided the one acoustically-isolated room in the mansion where his ears found rest from the outer world's drone—a feature the installers referred to as a *noise floor*. If he concentrated, he could still pick up a few muted murmurings from the outside, but music or a DVD soundtrack would serve to envelope him with as much privacy as an eternal being might hope to gain.

The slight motion of his entrance triggered the wall sconces as they switched onto fifty-percent illumination. His preternatural vision did not require much light. He made his way down the double tier of leather theatre recliners to a polished black marble block that served as a coffee table. No coffee for him—Arby couldn't seem to morph the distillate into a decent dark roast blend—but the morning's patron vintage bottle stood ready, with a sparkling piece of crystal stemware.

The richness of the room never ceased to amaze him, not counting the technological aspects, since he had seen television from the time of its infancy. He snapped up the Crestron Control and studied the GUI—Graphic User Interface—on its screen. No matter how many times he used the room—almost every day—the initial awakening of the system was his favorite part of the movie-watching ritual.

When he pressed the icon of a movie reel, the room came alive. A set of heavy red velvet curtains parted, exposing the eight by five-foot Stewart screen, and a Runco projector lowered from the ceiling. Two smoked glass panels, flanking the room, served to dim the indicator LED light panels that were lit up like Rockefeller Center at Christmas. As soon as the projector snapped into position, the wall sconces reduced power to twenty percent.

Overhead, a fiber optic star field mounted in the ceiling glowed to life; astronomically correct except for two constellations—Aquarius and Libra—that would not appear in the same night sky. As a special touch, the installers had added a full moon, controlled by a separate power button. No matter what the time of day or external temperature, the media room always morphed to his favorite part of the evening, a pleasant sixty-eight degrees and no humidity. One touch of a button and a CD recording of North Florida midnight swamp sounds would fill the room. If he wished.

Vincent walked over to the media storage area and perused his viewing options. What would it be this morning? The second season of *Dexter* had just arrived via the Internet DVD service. Not a vampire flick, but a pretty good character-driven series featuring an odd serial killer with ethics and purpose. He had fallen in love with *First Blood,* an HBO series as close to vampire reality as humans had ever come. Sometimes, he wondered if one or more of the writers were actually real vamps.

Arby had been ecstatic when Vincent finally decided to give the popular online movie rental company a try. So many times in the past, the vampire had purchased movies on a whim, only to stop them midway and cast them into the reject pile. Now for a flat monthly fee, Vincent shopped and ordered recent releases, vintage films, and television mini-series discs. He mailed one and a replacement appeared in the incoming parcels within a couple of days. Some came with an instant-play option for a download to the media center's computer, but he preferred the actual DVD. The good ones—the ones he longed to keep and watch again—he ordered for the library. The rejects, he returned. No waste. The overseer loved the whole going-green idea, and Vincent was able to see anything he wanted at any time. Plus, he didn't have to hear Arby stress like a nagging wife over misspent Dark Island funds. The rat boy hated to flitter away cash more than Vincent hated human warfare—all that unnecessary carnage and wasted blood.

Vincent snatched out three Blu-Ray choices and a couple of CD's. Still pondering the day's distraction, he flipped through a row of jewel cases. He loaded one of the Blu-Ray discs, hit the A/B switch from the Genelec Reference Audio rig to the Paradigm Signature Series system, and headed for a recliner.

He cast aside the silk smoking jacket and sat barechested. The line of digital mirrors reflected a man who could easily be a model, all lines and carved angles with no visible body fat. Tanned to perfection, thanks to Arby's miraculous solution. Hair, spiked on top with the just enough fresh-from-the-bedroom muss to add appeal. No gray streaks. Dark, enigmatic eyes. White, even teeth—save for slightly more pointed canines. Lips stained with enough color to mimic the living.

Vincent could study his reflection all day and not tire of it. But he was a relatively new vampire of sixty years, compared to his blood sire. When he reached two hundred, three hundred, four hundred—would he change his appearance like a garden lizard, just to keep from going 'round the bend?

He pondered. Would he go with one of the old movie icons—Cary Grant? Clark Gable? Charlton Heston? Or more recent—Brad Pitt? Richard Gere? Johnny Depp? If he desired, he could appear much younger. He made a mental note to look over the twenty-something's for a body model. Of course, by the time he grew weary of his own good looks, the hottest stars of the current age would be turning to worm food and dust, and he'd have to start anew.

Like Julio. Painfully dashing, enigmatic Julio. Gone now. Buried, Vincent supposed, in some family plot on Cuba. For several years, Vincent had followed the wealthy Latino's exploits in the Miami papers, and later online. High profile. Always in attendance at the best parties, the most exclusive night clubs. Alone for a couple of years, then with some fancy young male at his side. Had he wondered what happened to Vincent, or just written him off as another nick on his bedpost? Either way, Julio ended up as all mortals. Old, then just a name scratched on the back of a photograph.

Pity about humans. The blush of life so easily faded.

Vincent tasted the morning's vintage and jerked from his musings. "Oh, no."

Another sip, just to make sure. The distinctive tang of grave illness sang from his taste buds. He picked up the bottle and checked the coded label. A wave of sadness washed over him. Julia Holt, the senator's wife. The cancer. It was back. Did she know?

The distillate could erase so many of the living flesh's aging markers: wrinkles, dark pigmentations, jowly cheeks, turkey necks, spider veins, mottled skin, thinning hair, gum recession, excess tissue around the mid-section.

It couldn't rid the cells of years of strong, pent-up emotions: Anger. Guilt. Resentment. Fear. Unfulfilled dreams and hopes.

Vincent raked his memory for recent news of Julia Holt's philandering husband. The party line had kept him at bay for a bit during the recent Presidential election: Keep it in your pants, boy. Don't bring any harmful illumination to your affiliates. Dirty laundry aired in public stinks up the whole Capital.

Julia's sadness was palpable. He noticed it the first evening. The small dalliance with Thomas buoyed her a bit, but the evil still fed from within.

His thoughts wandered to his blood sire. How did Emmaraud manage not to feel something for the humans who made up the majority of their world? Did the hardness develop over time? Did it become necessary to squelch the innate *knowing* just to survive?

Vincent had watched Emmaraud and her ancient friends; their carefree disregard for the source of their nourishment. They fed randomly for the most part, with little thought to the inner workings of their prey.

Other than Jimmy Rob and Emmaraud's first years together, the unnatural couple had stopped the wanton slaughter. Instead, they drank just enough. Thank God. The change had to be credited to his blood child. Jimmy Rob must have had some small store of ethics. It couldn't have been attributable to his wanton blood mate.

The small Dark Island cemetery held the skeletal remains of their early victims. Graves with no markers. No flowers or small gifts left beside headstones. Nameless children of the South who ended up on law enforcement's missing persons list. Assumed dead by some free-range serial killer, or so tormented by their lives as to take off without a trace. Except for Arby, no human knew the truth. Even if they did, they wouldn't believe it.

Vincent grieved for them. No one else could.

He hoped he would never become like Emmaraud, with no more regard for humans than a carnivore to a cow.

Vincent stood and walked to a small kitchen. He poured the bottle of Julia Holt's vintage down the drain and flushed the sink with water.

From the cooler, he pulled out a bottle of synthetic blood. Today, he would dine without the aftertaste of hidden pain. He pulled out one of his private collection Cuban cigars. Then he pressed *play*.

****

When Reanita bounded into the patrons' dining room, she spotted the others. Thomas and Julia sat at a table, their heads bent together. Julia traced a ripe, powdered sugar-coated strawberry around the actor's lips. He bit down. The senator's wife wrapped her mouth around the other end of the berry until their lips met in the middle. Reanita squeezed her eyes shut.

For the love of Pete. Get a room! she thought.

Patrice sat alone. She jabbed at a small salad with a fork while perusing a copy of *Cosmopolitan* magazine. Probably some article on touching your inner child.

The noon buffet held five different types of vegetable and pasta salads. One hinged sterling silver container steamed with grilled chicken cutlets topped with goat cheese and slices of garden-fresh tomatoes.

Reanita grabbed a plate, then a second for the overflow. She heaped on spoonfuls of each dish. For dessert, she chose a piece of key lime pie, a slice of chocolate torte, and two scoops of vanilla ice cream topped with crushed pecans.

Reanita stood beside the starlet's table. "Mind if I join you?"

Patrice glanced from her magazine, taking in the DEA agent's bare feet, then her robe. "Sure." Her eyes opened wide when she noticed Reanita's tray. "Wow. You must be really hungry."

Reanita slid into the chair and dug in. She was aware of the viciousness of her feeding frenzy, but didn't care who watched.

"Stefanie with an *f* is going to run you ragged. You realize that." Patrice stabbed a romaine lettuce leaf and chewed.

"Don't care." Reanita glanced up. "Besides, isn't she the a.m. trainer?"

Patrice nodded. "True. The afternoon person—I don't remember his name, he's new this year—generally does yoga and meditative type of stuff. Still, they talk. She'll be laying for you tomorrow."

Reanita jabbed the air with her fork. "Bring it on. She shows up at my door at the crack of dawn, and I will be ready for the walk from hell."

"You must've had your first B-12 shot. It always gives me a boost."

Reanita shook her head. "I don't remember getting any shot. Trust me, I hate needles. I would remember that."

One of Patrice's perfect eyebrows lifted. "Oh, you got one. Arby gives them three times during the week's stay. Usually after one of the spa treatments, from what I've heard."

"Arby? The weird little gardener guy?"

Patrice nodded. She took a sip of green tea, then added, "He's like this herbal guru. Knows all about plant extracts and stuff. I use his face cream all the time. Have it shipped to me during the year."

Someone had stuck her without her knowing it? Was that even legal? Reanita shivered. She stopped eating long enough to run her hands over her arms.

"Don't look for a mark," Patrice said. "You won't find one. I asked him once. The needle is, like, really teeny. Kind of like one that diabetics use for insulin shots."

"I still don't know how he would manage to stick me without me knowing it."

Patrice shrugged. "I guess you were really relaxed, and he's really good."

Reanita crammed a large chunk of chicken into her mouth and chewed for a few moments before she spoke. "So, you been coming here for how long?"

"This is my third year."

"Wow. You must be really familiar with everything. What do you know about Vincent Bedsloe?"

"He's a hunk and a half. I would love to..." The starlet stopped. "Fat chance. I'm pretty sure he's gay."

"You've seen him with a man?"

"Oh, no." Patrice gestured with a fork. "Nothing like that. He plays his cards too close to the chest to ever give up anything about himself. It's just—let's just say I have provided many opportunities for him to invite me up after dinner."

The starlet finally made eye contact for longer than a second. She glanced away quickly, but not before Reanita registered the pity and revulsion in her eyes. Reanita felt a flush of anger and stuffed it down. God forbid Little Miss Perfect would have to look at anything less than stunning.

"You've offered yourself up and he hasn't bitten. That automatically makes him a homosexual?"

Patrice huffed. "Way I figure. I mean, look at me."

The woman had to be the head of her own fan club. No doubt.

Reanita smirked. "Truly. What was I thinking?"

Patrice turned her attention back to the magazine and Reanita sought comfort in the one thing that would never judge her for her appearance: chocolate.

****

Lars, the production manager for PSG, consulted Vincent's computer-generated site plan and squinted across the expansive south lawn. The weird little Dark Island overseer stood beside him. Even in the escalating morning heat and humidity, the guy wore long-sleeved coveralls and a beekeeper's hat. No problem. In all the years Lars had owned the production company, he had seen just about every kind of individual. This guy was mild compared to some of the people he had met, not to mention the bizarre behaviors of party guests. He could write a freaking book.

The Spa at Dark Island gigs always paid top dollar, on time, and took no issue with his work. At least three times a year, Vincent Bedsloe hired the group, and Lars was happy to travel from the Capital city for a few days. Sure, Arby followed every move and double-checked each detail, but Lars had become accustomed to his ways. The Dark Island folks picked up the tab, and Lars made certain they were happy. It was his business to make sure the technical and electrical aspects came off without a hitch. He was a perfectionist and it paid off.

"As you can see, Mr. Bedsloe wished the main tent positioned so that the guests can come in through the entrance tent here—" Arby walked a few paces and gestured to the ground. "—and they can then flow easily through the lighted pathway into the moon garden entrance at the edge of the lawn clearing, to view the new water garden and the *piece d' résistance*—the new sculpture at the crest of the waterfall. Not a word to Mr. Bedsloe. It's a surprise for him."

Lars nodded. "You want the main tent air-conditioned, I assume?"

"As much as I would prefer it open to the night air, yes. Tuxes and formal gowns would not mix well with our humidity. It plays havoc with the women's hairstyles, too. At least initially, while they dine, we'll keep them cool. After the alcohol takes effect, it will be less of an issue. I've seen even the best-dressed gentleman dancing with his shirt off later in the evening, and the women take off their Pradas. No one seems to care at that point. Still, I must pay attention to their comfort at the start. Even with the evening breezes, it is still well into the eighties. I do want the main tent to have the Cathedral windows or clear side walls, though. Be sure to convey that fact to your tent supplier. Vincent plans a huge entrance and it is mandatory that the guests see his approach."

The production manager scribbled notes on his clipboard. "Got it. I'll position the entrance tent just off the circular drive. The main tent—" he pointed to the drawing, "will be 150 foot long by 80 foot wide." He glanced up, visualizing the layout. "I'll position the kitchen tent on the west side with the entrance facing away from the main tent. Makes for a few more steps for the servers, but I don't like the guests seeing into the work area."

Arby felt ecstatic. Someone shared his eye for details.

"Your team always does a superior job, Lars. If you have any issues," he gestured to the short-wave radio clipped to his coverall, "give me a buzz. Otherwise, contact me when your tent people have the area staked out and I'll sign off on it."

Chapter 9

Tuesday evening

Reanita stood at the edge of the lap pool, still energized. She glanced at the outside wall clock. Well past midnight. The others had long since eaten and drank themselves into oblivion. Shortly after dinner, the lovebirds flew off to the senator's wife's suite to consummate all the obvious flirting and posturing during dessert and coffee. Miss Perfect Starlet excused herself to the nightly commune with the universe, or whatever.

Reanita took a moment to appreciate the go-fer who had picked out her attire. The racer-back Speedo, in a much brighter print than she might have chosen, was a sight better than the three clips of cloth that made up the other swim costume. A costume; the way she thought of the pitiful excuse for swimwear. The skimpy suit was only good for two things: sunning and strutting. No way would it stand up to water and heaven forbid, actual swimming.

It is so good to be alone, she thought.

Dark Island provided room to spread out, but little privacy. Someone always seemed to be hovering, ready to take care of every real or imagined need. After the initial blush, Reanita found it tiresome.

The water temperature proved perfect. Cool, but not cold.

She warmed up with a couple of laps in the American crawl, then moved on to the backstroke, breast stroke, and the intense butterfly. Her pulse thrummed.

Reanita had not grown up with the sport. Other than an occasional splash in some family-oriented lake park, her childhood had not included swim meets and green chlorine-tinged hair. The public pool—opened for a short time near her family home—fell into disrepair by the time she might have contemplated formal training. Plus, the money for any kind of lessons would have seemed wasteful to her father. Why throw money at your daughter, when you could use it for a couple of drinks a day at your favorite watering hole?

The DEA agent warmed to the sport while she was in the academy. At first, she could only dog-paddle with her head sticking from the water like a turtle. A couple of the guys took pity on her. She watched their effortless strokes and copied the movements. In a couple of months, she matched their speed. Other than shooting, she found swimming the only other thing that her appearance could not hinder. In the water, every person—bat-faced or gorgeous—floated equally.

She stopped once to rest at the shallow end. The fine hairs stood up on the back of her neck. So many times, she felt as if Dark Island watched.

"You are spooking yourself, Reanita, old girl." She affected the British lilt her fellow patron Thomas so loved.

****

Arby heard the rhythmic splash of water and stopped dead. Who would be in the pool this late in the evening? Vincent disliked water. The on-Island staff wasn't allowed in the patron areas, unless one had gone against the rules.

He shook his head. The loyalty of the former-downtrodden, now well-paid staffers was something he should never question. To go against orders was tantamount to treason, and the offending party would be immediately stripped of status and escorted past the security gates.

He couldn't imagine Thomas the faux-British actor in a swimsuit, unless it was to strut around showing off his silver-streaked chest hair. Julia the senator's wife didn't strike him as the type to do laps. The starlet? Nope. He had just passed the yoga studio. Patrice was in mid-Ohm.

Arby's mind raced. Jimmy Rob? No way. The redneck vamp spawn might take a dip in a muddy swimming hole, or even a natural spring, but chlorine? Too sissified for his tastes.

He smiled and a heat rush flushed through him. Only one choice left.

Arby slipped through the screened-in pool's rear door and hid in the shadow of a potted palm. The swimmer—obviously adept at several strokes—performed lap after lap, punctuated by perfect flip-turns. Graceful. A water sprite. A beautiful, bat-faced water sprite.

He watched until her head popped from the surface at the shallow end. Rivulets of water poured down her body. Arby could see—even from the far end of the pool—her erect nipples. She pulled herself from the water in one easy motion instead of using the nearby ladder. Her small tight bottom twitched in rhythm with her steps. While her back was turned away, he used the opportunity to exit the pool atrium.

****

Jimmy Rob felt better, sitting behind the wheel of the '67 Montero Blue convertible GTO. Restored to cherry condition, the classic muscle car sported a 360 hp engine and a manual three-speed transmission, and better brakes than on the first years' models. He caressed the white vinyl seat with one hand and drove with the other.

Pontiac GTO. The Goat, he thought, *a real man's ride. Made back in the days before all the cars turned so pussy.* The kind of car that invented road rage long before the shrinks gave it a proper psycho-babble name.

He pulled into a gravel road off State Highway 27—a pig trail more than an actual driveway—and hit the brakes and accelerator simultaneously to fishtail the rear end. Loose rocks sprayed in an arch and pinged off the cars and trucks parked in the lot. Screw them if they didn't like it. He could do what he damned well pleased. It was his bar. The green and red neon sign said so: *J.R.'s Joint.*

The club had changed little in the past few years. Same concrete block walls: Stained, dark green—a color of paint so awful, it had to have been on severe markdown or free. One window, smeared with flat black paint. Flickering beer advertisement signs. Beat-up wooden door. A shingled roof, patched and re-patched, with a few spots of bare tarpaper showing through. Not a single blade of grass survived on the grounds. One dim yellow bug light—a bare bulb in a rusty fixture—cast a pool of light immediately in front of the threshold.

Just the way he wanted it. Unchanged. A mausoleum to his misspent life. His living, breathing self. Before eternity interfered.

Jimmy Rob cut the ignition and sat for a few minutes, involved in an uncommon exercise: thinking.

Just two short years ago, he had been a loyal patron of the rundown establishment—then named the Gulf Breeze Bar—a regular, hard-drinking, hard-loving Son of the South. He had bedded most of the women, even the married ones, at least once. Some several times. Sucked back cheap beer by the case and whiskey that tasted like stale swamp water. Knew every song on the juke box. Shot pool until he was so drunk he couldn't see the cue ball. Or the stick.

Had he asked to walk out right as Vincent Queer-bait Bedsloe the Freakin' III decided to take his first drink from a live, breathing donor? Hell, no!

He, Jimmy Rob Jones, was the victim in the scenario. The freakin' victim! A point he battered his blood sire with on so many occasions, that Vincent had begged for a chance to provide Jimmy Rob with whatever compensation he required to make the whole undead ordeal more bearable.

"I want my own bar," Jimmy Rob had whined. "Buy me the joint where you hunted me down like a sick cow. You owe me that much."

Like a beleaguered parent giving into a petulant child's tantrum, Vincent caved and purchased the Gulf Breeze. He handed the title and appropriate business and liquor licenses over to his blood spawn.

"Still ain't fair," Jimmy Rob mumbled as he brought his awareness back to the present and switched off the ignition. "Vincent Girlie-boy Bedsloe still owes me plenty."

He launched himself easily over the driver's side door, then kicked the rear tire so hard the shocks complained.

"That whole *got-damned* bar full of alcohol, and I can't drink a drop anymore!"

The bar's door opened. A buxom blond stumbled out. She spotted Jimmy Rob before he had a chance to duck.

"Yoo-hoo! Jimmy Rob!" The blonde lurched in his direction. "Shit-fire. I was gonna leave, but I think I might just change my mind and stay awhile."

Whiskey fumes curled through the humid night air. The woman was drunker than Cootie Brown on a bender. Matter of fact, she most likely passed Cootie's limit a good two hours back.

"Hey there, Sherry."

The blood glamour hung around her like an aura. Now, that was a little detail they needed to put in the *Idiot's Guide to Vampires*. Once he drank from a woman, or slept with her, or both, she carried a bit of him with her like a wreath of fairy dust.

What had Sherry been swilling tonight? Jimmy Rob tested her exhaled air. Couple of beers, shot of two of whiskey, several rum and Cokes. The gal was going to feel like a NASCAR pile-up, come morning. He decided to do her a favor—just for old times' sake—and drain a little off the top.

Jimmy Rob slid his arms around her waist and kissed her hard. She moaned and leaned into him.

When she came up for air, she stuck her tongue in his ear and followed up with a whispered, "You want some of this, do you baby?"

Jimmy Rob stepped back and smiled. He led her to the far, shadowy corner of the bar, behind a thick hedge. Kissed her again. Nibbled her neck. Bit down and drank until he felt her knees buckle.

He pulled back abruptly. No need to kill the gal. She'd had a hard enough life. Two younguns at home to support. Low-end job waitressing at a truck stop off I-75. Divorced twice; both, losers who had sponged off her goodness and left her with less than when they'd come, except for the kids.

Jimmy Rob decided to reward her. He felt better already, thanks to her high blood alcohol level. He pierced his bottom lip with one pointed canine tooth and dripped a few drops of vamp blood into the open wound on her neck. She moaned. The twin puncture marks faded and disappeared.

With as little effort as a buff lifeguard picking up a drowning toddler, Jimmy Rob hoisted the comatose blonde and deposited her into the front seat of a battered Camaro. She'd awaken in a couple of hours and drive home, a little less inebriated and totally clueless about the encounter.

"Little Sherry, sleep tight," he repeated a little ditty left over from childhood. "Don't let the bed bugs bite."

The notion of Sherry worrying about the miniscule nibble of a bed bug when other things far worse might interrupt her sleep, made him chuckle out loud. He was still laughing when he swung open the door to J.R.'s Joint and stepped inside.

****

"Now this one is a native hydrangea." Arby stopped in front of a clump of backlit greenery and pointed to a cluster of white blooms. "See how the blossoms differ from the shrub I just pointed out? The native variety's blooms follow a more conical pattern, where the others are spherical. And—of course you can't tell this in the low lighting—the native plant's flowers are white, whereas the cultivated cousins are pink or blue, depending on the acidity or alkalinity of the soil."

Reanita nodded. The entire stroll through the moon garden had been a running commentary on the positioning and types of vegetation. Clearly, not as random as what she might have thought, and surely not as simple. Then again, her first walk through the same area had been with the enigmatic host of Dark Island and she barely remembered even glancing at the garden.

"What's that smell?" she asked.

Arby tilted his head. "Ah, that would be night-blooming jasmine. Wonderful, isn't it?"

Arby wondered if his goddess would appreciate the bouquet of his special plants. Would she be offended by their unique odors? For the first time, he toyed with the idea of showing another human his private sanctuary. He had shared with Vincent, but he didn't count. He was a vampire. Very little repelled him.

"You know so much about gardening. You must have been in the field for years."

Arby nodded. "I have always tinkered with plants. I started out with Bonsai. Only in the past five years since coming to the Island, have I fully embraced the field."

"So, cooking is your profession, then? Or, is it herbal medicine?" Reanita purposely brushed her hip against his. The whole flirtation game seemed so foreign. But if other women—pretty women—could do it, so could she. "Honestly, I have heard snippets about you from everyone here, and I can't figure you out."

"I have played many roles."

Even drug smuggler? Reanita wondered. "I find you intriguing, Arby. Please, tell me. What kind of roles?"

He searched her face for any sign of duplicity and found none. Could she truly be interested in him? His pulse picked up the pace.

"Everything from low-end jobs like short-order cook—back during college—to nursing assistant. I received my RN degree and worked in intensive care for a few years. Then, I went back to college for my law degree."

She stopped. "You were an attorney?"

"I *am* an attorney. I still practice, though on very limited scale. Mainly on retainer for the Dark Island Corporation."

"Wow. I thought you were just—"

"A lowly groundskeeper?" Arby smiled, though she couldn't see the expression behind the dark mesh.

"I didn't mean—I'm sorry."

"No offense taken. I like to say, I am an attorney by trade and a gardener by heart."

Reanita smiled. "I like that."

Arby motioned toward the mansion. "Perhaps we might return to the house. Though I have enjoyed this respite, I have work to do. The gala won't unfold by itself, I fear. Besides, we don't want to tax your ankle."

Reanita glanced down. "Truthfully—I had forgotten all about it."

"Another lymphatic drainage session with Raven, and you'll be back to a hundred percent."

"Actually, tomorrow—or should I say later this morning—I'm down for a hot stone massage. Whatever that is."

"Delightful, that's how I would describe it. You will totally relax. It is one of our patrons' favorite and most often requested spa treatments."

They stood facing each other at the back door.

"Thank you, Arby. The swim. The walk. I feel as if I can calm down enough to sleep now."

"It was my pleasure, Reanita."

She smiled. "Rea."

Had he been anyone else—someone handsome or someone with ordinary features—Arby might have taken the opportunity to reach over and draw her close for a kiss. The hell with Dark Island rules against patronizing with the guests. Instead, he bent down, lifted the bottom of the netting, and brushed her hand with his lips.

"Rest well."

She stood for a moment with a bemused expression playing across her features. Had he overdone it with the chivalrous and chaste gesture?

"Good night, Arby."

Then she was gone. He turned away and pulled the digital planner from his pocket. Already, the garden seemed empty without her.

Chapter 10

Wednesday morning: the wee hours

The creepy sensation wouldn't leave him.
Vincent tossed the Wii remote aside. Nothing seemed to help. Not the Internet chat rooms, hanging out with the vamp-wannabes. Not the DVD reruns of the old *Dark Shadows* vampiric soap opera. Not three games of Wii bowling.
He picked up the most recent spa vintage and glanced at the coded label. *Patrice Palmer.* Starlet extraordinaire.
"I just can't face all that self-absorption tonight."
Vincent corked the bottle and returned it to the temperature-controlled wine cabinet. Patrice could wait. Surely none of her dramatic problems would be of grave importance. A fungus beneath one of her rhinestone-studded gel nails? A scuff on the toe of whatever designer shoe she was currently sporting? A millimeter of dark roots shining beneath the carefully-layered salon colors? Or, maybe her latest dressing trailer wasn't decorated to her standards?
He chose a vial of synthetic blood—no hint of human strife, just simple nourishment. Sometimes he liked it when his food didn't talk back.

He paced the spacious suite, trying to squelch thoughts of his blood sire. No use. Emmaraud Bonneville came to mind the second he let down his guard.

"All right, mommy dearest. You might as well intrude on my peace."

The Master of Dark Island gave himself over to a full-on Emmaraud session.

What would she look like when she came? She *was* coming. Of that he was sure. Julia Roberts? No, she didn't particularly like red hair. Sandra Bullock? One of his favorite actors, but not flashy enough for his blood sire. Madonna? Maybe.

And her entourage of friends? How many would show up to run rampant? Two, three, four? The thought of running herd over the miscreants made him tired, and vampires didn't generally feel weary.

What kind of car would she drive this time? A tricked-out Hummer? He shook his head. He couldn't see Emmaraud in a chunky sports utility vehicle, no matter the marketing hype or the price tag. A Porsche? Mercedes? BMW? The color wasn't a variable. Emmaraud always chose black.

To say that the vamp would sport the latest designer clothing and accessories was like saying Minnie Mouse would wear a polka-dot skirt. Nothing that didn't soar miles above the common woman's lifetime salary would touch Emmaraud's skin. She set the curve. Fashion followed her, not the other way around. When she tossed an outfit to the curb, literally, the rest of the world was just picking it up.

He did another lap of the suite.

What new pastimes? She had climbed Mt. Everest. Twice. Had suckled the blood of every remote tribe on the globe. White-water rafted. Skied. Yachted. Raced sailboats. Bungee jumped. Sky dived. Deep sea dived. Seen countless solar eclipses from whatever continent that had provided the best view at the time. She had piloted a hang-glider, a locomotive, and a Stealth bomber. The details were still unclear how she had managed the last one. At least she hadn't decided to fly a transcontinental commercial jet. Emmaraud Bonneville in charge of hundreds of human lives at several thousand feet over the ocean—now there was a thought that would keep the Pope awake at night.

For certain, she wouldn't show up with a tattoo. She had tried that once. The inks didn't jibe with vampire blood chemistry. The colors had morphed into bizarre blurred shades and it had taken several days for her to regain unblemished skin.

What had Emmaraud *not* done? Vincent pondered and came up with one answer: she had never flown on the space shuttle. Either it hadn't occurred to her, or she couldn't figure out how to get past NASA's security. She would orbit the planet at some point, probably far into the future when ships carried space passengers as easily as current jetliners shuffled tourists and tycoons.

When a woman was eternal, nothing was out of reach. Nothing was out of bounds.

Vincent slipped on a scarlet and black silk smoking jacket. Time to roam the mansion and grounds. Anything to keep his body moving and possibly squelch her from his thoughts.

The big house was quiet of human sounds. Now, the voice of the mansion spoke in creaks and low hums. As it had from the first time he awakened in its arms, the old place wrapped around him like a cocoon. He allowed his preternatural senses to engage.

Four humans remained awake in the wee hours. Raven was up with her young daughter Christina. Some kind of childhood ailment. A stomach ache? Arby was busy in his private greenhouse. The caretaker seemed to sleep as little as his employer. Many times, Vincent had urged his overseer to hire extra help for the various galas, but Arby trusted few people. The outfits he hired in—caterers, party planners, security and parking personnel—had been carefully screened. Like the staff, the hires were extremely well-paid.

Still, Arby allowed no one to aid him in the overall logistics and the endless details of Vincent's design.

Who else fought sleep?

Vincent walked past the atrium and stopped dead. Someone—or something—sat in the shadows.

Mother of all darkness. His throat constricted. *She's here.*

He picked up a distinctive human scent, mixed with a citrus-based cologne.

"Who's there?" he asked in a soft voice.

The figure stood and walked into a pool of pale moonlight.

"Julia? Are you okay?"

A heavy sigh contained sadness and something else. "Vincent. I'm sorry. I didn't mean to disturb anyone."

The vampire entered the atrium and stood in front of her. "I thought you had turned in some time ago."

"I couldn't sleep. Thomas was snoring." A slight smile flickered across her lips. "Why is it, I always manage to find men who make such absurd noises in the night?"

Vincent gestured with one hand. "I was just coming down to make a little herbal tea. Would you like to join me?"

"That would be nice."

Julia followed him to the kitchen and he motioned to a small battered wooden table.

"I rather like it in here," he said. "Seems more intimate. Do you mind?"

"I'm not high maintenance, Vincent, though my public persona might say otherwise." She took a seat at one of two oak chairs. "If I had my choice, I would prefer a small hovel far away from anything resembling society and especially politics."

Vincent poured hot water into two small tea pitchers. For Julia, he would steep chamomile tea for its restorative and calming properties. For him, one of Arby's special dried blood blends—compatible with his system, yet with the appearance of a normal brew.

"I've always admired you, Julia. From our first meeting four years ago. You possess a poise and grace few people can manage."

He placed two delicate, logo-imprinted china tea cups and saucers on the table.

"Would you like anything to eat along with your tea? A scone, perhaps?"

She waved her hand. "No, no. Tea will be fine. I haven't had much of an appetite...lately."

Vincent placed the tea service, two silver spoons and linen napkins on the table and sat down. "You do look a bit—pale. Are you—?"

"—well?" she completed his question. "No, Vincent. I am not."

"I'm a good listener, if you care to share."

"That you are." Julia raked a pale hand through her hair. "Did I ever tell you about the surgery I had some years back. For ovarian cancer?"

"I believe you were recovering on your first visit to The Dark."

"That's right. I had forgotten. I came here to rest." She sighed. "The details get so mixed up in my mind, anymore."

"The Island is good for respite and healing."

Julia seemed lost in thought for a moment. Vincent poured a cup of chamomile tea for her, then decanted the blood tea blend for himself from a second pitcher.

"It's back, Vincent."

"How? Did they not remove the offending—parts?"

"Doesn't matter. If even a tiny speck of ovarian tissue remains, it seems the devil can rear his ugly head, even years later."

"Stress can play a role, from my somewhat limited understanding."

She added a scant amount of tupelo honey to her cup and stirred. "Not like I haven't had any of that."

"What can I do, Julia?"

"You've done it, Vincent." She held up her hands. "Dark Island. This wonderful, magical place. For one week, a few precious hours, I have been just Julia. Not Julia Holt The Senator's Wife. Just Julia, the woman. For this, I am forever in your debt."

The vampire smiled and nodded.

The senator's wife took a sip of tea. "This is wonderful. I must get the name of the brand before I leave."

"Arby special orders it from a company specializing in fair trade practices. Organic, too. He's a stickler for organic."

Julia's red-rimmed eyes fixed on him. "There is one small thing you might do for me."

"Of course. Anything."

"Hang my no-good louse of a husband from his balls." She laughed—a giggle at first, then on to holding her belly and shaking.

Vincent joined in. If mirth offered any solace, then he was in.

Julia wiped the joy-tears from the corners of her eyes. "God that felt good. You must think me evil."

"Not at all." Vincent thought, *I should know. I have seen evil. You're far from it.*

She shook her head and smiled. "I just had this visual of the honorable Senator Harrison Holt, swinging by his privates from some Dark Island cypress tree. God, would the tabloids be all over that!"

"He is coming for the gala. It could be arranged." Vincent grinned.

She closed her eyes. "Don't remind me. I have to make nice with him and his politico friends. I just don't know if I have it in me."

"I'll be there to help you through it, Julia." Vincent paused and sipped. The blood tea was delicious. He'd have to remember to compliment Arby. "Back to your illness, if you don't mind talking about it. Are you undergoing treatment?"

"There will be no more chemo. Not this time. I made that decision before I came to Dark Island. I'm done, Vincent. The cancer is spreading. I have spots on my liver, my lungs, and my kidneys. Probably other places yet discovered. I'm not going through all of the crap, only to buy myself a few more months, or days, of life."

"Does your husband know?"

She huffed. "Harrison? Shift his focus away from a run for the President? No, I haven't told him anything."

"Don't you think he would want—?"

Her eyes flashed. "No. He only wants what is perfect and presentable. He'll find out soon enough when I can't appear on his arm at some Washington function. I almost look forward to my deathbed." She stopped and stared at her host. "That sounds so awful. I can't believe I just said it. I really don't want to die—yet."

The irony of the situation stung Vincent. Here, he longed for the promise of a deathbed, and this woman—this kind woman—might change her mind and forgo the Grim Reaper if she could regain health for even a few more hours.

"I am here for you, Julia. Even when you aren't on The Dark. I'll make sure you have my private cell and email address."

Julia reached over and brushed his hand with hers. If she noticed the inherent chill of his skin, she gave no indication.

"You are a true friend, Vincent Bedsloe."

True friend? True, but as fleeting as all of the human tethers he had enjoyed in the past years.

Vincent fought back tears. They would be the pink-tinged blood tears of a vampire. No need to cause alarm.

"Always, Julia."

****

A handful of dead-drunk patrons stayed on at J.R.'s Joint. Three shot a sloppy game of pool. One old gal had passed out with her head on the bar, a line of spittle forming a puddle on the faux-wood Formica. An adolescent boy stumbled from table to table in search of left-over drinks. Jimmy Rob watched him remove extinguished cigarette butts and kick back tepid watered-down alcohol. He couldn't blame the kid. He knew what it was like to be poor, underage, and desperate.

The five blood drinks Jimmy Rob had sipped in the past hours—courtesy of his stewed patrons—hadn't stopped the string of thoughts about Dark Island. Especially of Vincent and his rat-boy sidekick.

The whole deal just squeaked of stupid. Why would Rat Boy leave a successful law practice—from what Jimmy Rob had heard—to run a spa? Plus, garden and be everything for Vincent? He had always wondered if the two were queer for each other.

The thought of Rat Boy and his blood sire all cozy made Jimmy Rob swear out loud. Now, the bat-faced gal had gone and thrown a wrench into his queer-boys theory. Or, was the Rat Boy capable of waging his weenie on both sides of the fence? He sure had looked all goofy and pie-eyed at her in the garden, walking along with her hung on his arm like a clot of eel grass dripping from a boat prop.

"Jee-zus in a jumpsuit," he said aloud.

"Hey, J.R.!" Sully—one of the good ole boys—called out, "come on over and shoot a game."

J.R. wiped spilled beer from the bar and threw the dirty towel into the sink. What the hell. Might as well.

Pool used to be his passion. Close behind cars, drinking, and women. With his preternatural ability, he could smoke any player in the South. Sucked the joy from the game, when he knew no one could ever best him.

He grabbed a leather case, extracted a custom cue, and screwed it together.

"Rack 'em up, boys. Let Daddy show you how it's done."

He'd have to scale back a lot. Miss a few banked shots. Let the others feel as if they could play in his league.

"You know, buddy," His oldest friend Ray clapped a meaty hand on Jimmy Rob's shoulder. "You are just a joy to live with, these days." He glanced at the other two. "Ain't he, boys?"

"Ray—"

"I mean it. Time was, a couple of years back, you would be fightin' everything that moved by this time of night. What's up with that?"

How could he tell his best buddy—the guy he had shared more women with than anyone else in three counties, the man who had on more than one occasion held Jimmy Rob's head up when he puked the excess alcohol from his stomach, the only man who ever borrowed one of his muscle cars—how could he tell him the real reason? He didn't fight anymore—couldn't fight anymore—because he could snap Ray's thick neck easier than a blade of dried wiregrass.

Jimmy Rob applied blue chalk to his pool cue. "Ain't no big secret, Ray. The Po-Po made me take one of them anger management courses."

Ray nodded. Complete understanding. All of them knew the local law enforcement personnel on an intimate basis.

Chapter 11

Doesn't it ever cool off down here? Reanita wondered.

She glanced at the luminous numbers on her watch face. Way past midnight—nearly three o'clock—and it had to be pushing ninety degrees. Judging from the way the sweat beaded on her skin without a prayer of evaporating, the air had soaked up just about all of the moisture it could hold. How did these Southerners stand it? Maybe the mild winters held appeal, but she sure as shit would make tracks out of the place, come spring.

The DEA agent wished she really was a pampered heiress. She'd still be mired in the pillow-top mattress instead of tromping around in the saw palmettos in the dark. Luckily, the moon was only a couple of nights away from its full phase, and she could pick out the trail without risking turning on the flashlight.

She located the beach shack and pulled a set of lock picks from her pocket. Easy work. Once inside, she turned on the small flashlight and swept the narrow beam around the room. Empty!

"What did you expect?" she mumbled. "Bails of pot all nicely labeled? Zipper bags full of pills?"

A piece of plastic caught her eye and she moved to one corner for a closer look.

The bag was empty. She cussed beneath her breath, then noticed printing on one side: a warning about not handling the contents without skin protection. Dry ice; the bag had once held dry ice. She frowned.

"What the heck are they moving through here that requires dry ice?"

She drew a blank. Maybe they were importing some kind of fish or meat, something on the endangered list? She shook her head. Wild theories would get her nowhere fast. If it wasn't illegal, why all the secrecy? The middle-of-the-night delivery? The locked shed? Why couldn't they just use the set of docks further down the coast?

Another dead end, she thought.

She pitched the bag back into the corner, as close as possible to its original position. Reanita glanced down. Her sneakers had etched marks into the soft sand. She raked with the flat backside of her forearms to erase the footprints. She used her fingertips to rough up the dirt to a more natural appearance.

Reanita closed and locked the door and stood at the water's edge. What to do, now? She could go back to the wonderfully soft Egyptian cotton sheets and continue to probe the tight-lipped staff, but she hated to waste time.

Earlier, she had noticed a second path—narrower than the one leading to the coastline. What the heck? She was too hopped up on adrenaline to sleep, and she had to keep moving or the mosquitoes would tote her off and eat her somewhere else.

She found the pathway and trained the flashlight through the palmettos. The place was a rattlesnake round-up waiting to happen. No way was she turning off the light. Things jumped and ran on either side as she passed by. Something big whisked by overhead on ghostly night wings. Reanita shivered and pressed on. The trail had to lead to somewhere, and it wasn't wide enough for one of Stefanie with an *f*'s jungle safaris.

She trudged for what seemed like miles, in reality only one, until the forest abruptly stopped at a grassy clearing. She snapped off the light. Through the moon's reflected glow, she could make out the silhouette of a small building, with what appeared to be some kind of shed to one side. She picked through the tall grass and stopped to study the dwelling. A vintage travel trailer with all kinds of crap lying around. Old car bodies lined up like gravestones. The hull of an old wooden fishing boat, serving now as a garden for weeds. On closer inspection, she noted that the shed was an automotive garage. Who could possibly live here?

The low growl stopped Reanita dead. A bright floodlight snapped on and she threw her forearm over her eyes. The light blinded her for a moment before she could focus on the mangy dog with the toothy grimace. He let out a series of resonant barks. Reanita lowered her arm slowly. The mutt caught sight of Reanita's face, yelped, and ran under the trailer. She heard it whimpering.

Jimmy Rob's eyebrows shot up when he recognized the human who had dared to set foot on his property: Rat Boy's bat-faced gal. He had heard of a face that would stop a clock, but she had one that would stop a pit bull. Amazing.

The vamp stepped from the shadowed threshold of the shop. "You lost, little lady?"

Reanita managed to find her voice. Just imagining what the dog's huge jaws might have done to her, had sucked the breath right out of her.

"I—I think I might be."

Damn. The gal really did have one hell of an ugly mug. Not a bad little body, but an ugly mug—a hubba-hubba torso with a less than hubba-hubba face. Jimmy Rob took a few steps in her direction. "Not such a good notion, wandering around on Dark Island this late. All kinds of things in these woods might like to get a piece of you."

Reanita swallowed. Who was this guy? She decided to fall into the poor-little-lost-rich-girl routine.

"Um...I'm really sorry, Mister. I couldn't sleep, so I decided to take a walk. I thought I was on the same trail we always walk in the mornings. Really, I didn't mean to disturb you."

Reanita studied his attire. Ragged blue jeans, even in the heat. A plaid shirt with the arms cut out, frayed at all the edges. Bare feet. A filthy ball cap with the number 88 emblazoned on the front.

"Aw, now..." He stepped a few feet closer.

She stuffed the urge to turn tail and dash as fast as she could in any direction other than his.

When he smiled, the expression didn't make it to his eyes. "You didn't disturb me. I was just getting ready to rebuild a carburetor."

"At three in the morning?"

Jimmy Rob chuckled. "I got me a bad case of insomnia. Runs in my family."

"So, you're a mechanic? You live here all the time? Do you work here—on the Island?"

"You ask a lot of questions for a gal caught roaming the swamp in the middle of the night." He tilted his head and studied her, wondered what a bat-faced gal's blood might taste like. "Not that it is any of your business, but—yes to all your questions. I keep the limos purring like contented kittens."

Might as well make the best of the opportunity. "I see. So, you know Vincent pretty well?"

"Better than most."

"What is he like...really?"

Ah, so that was it. The bat-faced gal had a thing for his blood sire. Poor little thing. She'd be better off jumping Rat Boy.

"Not bad. Not bad. He ain't exactly your type. What did you say your name was?"

"Reanita. Reanita Register."

Jimmy Rob pulled on his chin as if he was considering. "You're one of them spa people."

"Um...yes."

"I thought they kept you people on a pretty short leash." He chuckled and took the last few steps and stood in front of her. "I best help you get on back to the mansion. Boss won't like it if one of his precious patrons gets herself all dead."

The telltale hairs stood up on Reanita's nape.

"Let's not walk back through the woods, if you don't mind," he said. "Lots of critters feed in the dark, especially in the moonlight."

He gestured to an auto she hadn't noticed at first. Classic muscle car. GTO.

"I was just about to take the *Goat* out to test a new timing setting I just done on her engine. Might as well ride along."

"I haven't seen one of these in years. Wow!" She walked around the car, admiring the lines. "My dad used to have one." She started to touch the hood, then drew her hand back. "You mind?"

Jimmy Rob shook his head. "Naw. Reckon not. What, you like old cars?"

She felt for the hood release. "Do I ever!"

"Here, let me get that for you." He raised the hood.

"Wow. Now, this is an engine!" She leaned over and studied the motor from several angles. "Don't you just hate the new ones, with all their computer crap and energy-efficient stuff? I do."

Jimmy Rob smiled. Even her face was starting to look a little better to him.

"Don't you know it!" He lowered the hood and bumped it closed. "Jump on in, sugar. I'll take you back to the mansion in style."

The thrill of a ride in the classic car almost made her forget. She was supposed to be fast asleep, not wandering around Dark Island.

"Um...I kind of got busted once before, for walking around after dark. Seems Mr. Bedsloe frowns on it. If I show up in this car, with you, they might decide to pack me off."

Jimmy Rob considered. "Good point. Let's you and I take a ride down the back roads, open her up so you can get a feel for what she can do. Then, I'll get you back in. I know the gate combo. I can take you down one of the service roads and drop you off at the edge of the gardens. Anyone spots you after that, just make up some shit about having a problem with sleep walking."

"I know! I'll tell them it's my sleeping medication. It's been known to cause amnesia and night ambulation."

"Yeah...whatever." He patted the GTO as if the automobile's side panel was the flank of a favorite quarter horse. "You just slide your little caboose into the shotgun seat and Jimmy Rob will show you what's what."

Reanita made her way around to the passenger's side and got in.

He turned the key and the car released a pent-up growl followed by the low satisfied purr of a tiger anticipating a juicy meal. He grabbed hold of the shifter and shoved it into reverse, then put her in first gear and turned down the road that led to the Dark Island Bridge, toward the main road. For a bit, he held off on accelerating. No need to fire her up too soon and bother Prissy-boy's oversensitive hearing. When he turned onto the state highway, he pushed his testosterone-driven foot on the accelerator. The tiger's purr turned into a roar.

The Redneck vampire sat in his seat like a rooster perched atop a hen house. The engine obeyed his every command, and the new timing setting was cherry. The rush was the closest thing to having an engine installed on his pecker. It was that manly.

Reanita was pinned to the bucket seat. Why did she feel like a high school freshman who had just gotten into the car with the forbidden senior class stud? How could such a hardened, police-trained woman be swooned by this? What the hell, she thought, Dark Island offers so many assaults on the human psyche, what was one more?

She nestled into the seat, relishing the G-forces. A dark country road. A man who obviously reeked of danger. Reanita's flair for risk allowed her to enjoy his night race to nowhere.

Jimmy Rob drove in silence for a while, listening to his machine, tuning in to all the sounds the car provided to offer up the diagnostic clues of its workings.

"Well, babe, what do you think of the Goat?"

"This rocks! Um—I mean," Reanita remembered: she was supposed to be playing the part of a rich heiress. "It's great. But it's no Ferrari."

"Damn right, it ain't," he defended. "This here's a real man's car."

Jimmy Rob released the shifter and put his hand on the back of Reanita's neck. The country boy's rough machismo flowed into her like Spock's mind meld. July in Florida, and she shivered.

Reanita struggled to keep her bearings, but Jimmy Rob's icy touch felt like a transfusion of lust. Her desire to gather information quickly faded as other cravings took over. "So, you take care of the cars for the mansion?" With Jimmy Rob massaging her neck in slow, deliberate circles, it was an effort to hold a thought long enough for it to make it past her lips.

He motored onto a county-maintained road that ran parallel to the Gulf. The moon was yellow-round and sent a trail of light down the water's surface, beckoning like Dorothy's Yellow Brick Road.

The city girl was awed by the moonlight. Life seemed to take on a surreal glaze. Like she moved through molasses, even as the car zipped through the night.

"Who the hell cares about that shit back on the Island?" he gave her a meaningful look.

He pulled the Goat into a parking space carved out of the underbrush, a spot where locals came to look out over the

Gulf at night. The GTO's radiator hissed steam and the engine offered up a cadence of metallic clicks.

"Why don't you slap that seat back, little lady? Make yourself more comfortable."

By this time, Reanita could only follow his directions. He kicked the drivers' side bucket seat back as far as it would go and hit the recline lever. Reanita shed her clothes the best she could, taking no regard for buttons or clasps or anything that might slow her down. She reclined, breathless, as Jimmy Rob studied her anatomy by Braille. She lost track of time as the moon dipped behind a bank of clouds.

Before the moon could reappear, Jimmy Rob rode the high country as Reanita arched upward. Cloaked in the heat of passion, she took little note of his strangely cold skin. Odd thing; he never once tried to kiss her.

She lay still, gasping for air. Jimmy Rob climbed back behind the steering wheel and adjusted the seat.

They flew the back roads until the first streaks of pale peach licked the eastern sky. Jimmy Rob—true to his word as a southern gentleman—dropped her off near the vegetable garden. He leaned over. She felt her body grow warm again. If another round was what the man required in exchange for a ride in the GTO, she would gladly consider it an even trade.

Jimmy Rob kissed Reanita full on the lips. She had never felt anything like it: a combination of being slapped by a ripe tomato and sucked up by a Hoover. He licked her earlobe, then nuzzled her neck. He bit down.

Reanita experienced the most orgasmic feeling she had ever known, better than her body's physical reaction earlier in the night. She closed her eyes and let herself bathe in the sensation. A rainbow of colors swirled behind her eyes. The flavors of a hundred blended spices tingled on her tongue. Her skin prickled. She had never wanted anything to last forever. Until now.

Jimmy Rob pulled back. He allowed a couple of drops of their mingled blood to close the twin puncture wounds.

"You better get on back to your room, little gal."

Reanita's head felt all swimmy. "Yeah. Um. Thanks for the ride." She opened the door and slid from the passenger seat.

"Anytime." He gave her a little wink and a nod, and pulled away.

She watched the red glow of his taillights until they disappeared in the early morning sea fog.

Jimmy Rob laughed as he accelerated. Sometimes, his job was just purely fun. No worries about Reanita remembering the encounter. Any of it. One good thing about the blood: his victims never recalled anything after a few minutes. Pity really. He might just come to like the bat-faced gal.

****

Reanita entered the mansion by the unlocked back door and tip-toed down the carpeted hallway. She rounded the corner and ran into Vincent.

"Miss Register?"

She blinked twice as if her gaze looked upon another reality.

"Miss Register? Rea?" Vincent waved his hand across her eyes. He cupped her elbow in his hand. "Let me help you find your way back to your suite."

"Sweet? Did you say sweet? I like sweets." Her voice; all soft and dreamy.

Vincent escorted his charge to the elevators and to the patrons' wing. It was only after he had settled Reanita beneath her covers and quietly closed the door that the difference in the heiress registered.

Reanita Register glowed with the blood glamour. And it wasn't his.

Chapter 12

Wednesday morning: at dawn

Anyone who chanced a glance at Patrice Palmer would find it hard to believe she could be the star of anything, unless it was a slasher flick.

"You look like horrors," she told her reflection.

No makeup. Mascara smudged beneath puffy eyes. Hair spiking out in every direction and soaked where she had splashed water on her face. Skin, blotchy with a greenish undertone.

She stared at the little white plastic stick perched on the edge of the sink. Plain as day. Same as the one she had stared at last week, when she had finally noticed that her period was way overdue.

No little blue cross to confuse things. Even a moron could tell what the results were; the word *pregnant* clearly spelled out the verdict.

Patrice rushed to the toilet and vomited for the third time. The taste of stomach acid made her retch again, only this time all she managed was a good case of the dry heaves.

She sank to the cool tile and buried her face in a wet washrag.

"I am *so* done. The part calls for a hot female vampire. No way they're going to fall for a pregnant vampire."

If she was a star, they might concede to just head shots when her belly started to poke out too far. Not so for someone who had yet to scratch, claw and sleep her way to the top third of the pile.

Yes, it was fashionable in Hollywood to run around town displaying a prominent baby bump. The fan rag-mags loved it! If she was a star. Which she wasn't.

"I am going to be a *has-been* before I am a *has*."

She heard an insistent, perky knock at the door and groaned. Who the—had to be Stefanie with an *f*, all geared and juiced for the morning marathon walk. *Shit.* Patrice managed to stand and fought another round of nausea. She inched to the door and opened it a crack.

"Good morning, Patrice! Time to rise and shine!"

The trainer's voice rang in her ears. No one told you that morning sickness was like the hangover from hell. And she couldn't even order up some hair-of-the-dog, alcohol-laced concoction to help her get past it.

"Um...not today. I am kind of under the weather, 'kay?"

"Oh no. Anything I can do to help you? Actually, a little exercise might make you feel better. Why don't I come back by in a few minutes and get—?"

"No. Really. Just, please. Leave me alone."

She shut the door before Stefanie with an *f* offered any more suggestions.

Patrice curled up in a fetal position on a chintz-covered chaise lounge. When did this happen? She thought back. Too many parties. Too many men. Could it have been the all-nighter she pulled right after she found out she had landed the part? She and the newly-chosen cast had hopped from one bar to another. Most of the evening, she didn't recall and couldn't really remember whether she had ended up at home in the morning. It wasn't unusual for her to wake up and not recognize the sheets.

Who was the baby's father? No way of knowing.

Only one solution, if she wanted any chance of a career. Terminate it. She hugged herself and sobbed. Other than becoming a famous actor, the only thing Patrice Palmer dreamed of was becoming a mother. The thing inside of her more than likely was no larger than a peanut, but she already found herself cupping her hands protectively over her stomach.

She pawed for the in-house phone on the cherry table beside the lounge.

Barbie's voice: "Good morning, Miss Palmer. How may I help you?"

Barbie. Perfect blonde Barbie with the flat stomach Patrice would never have again if she decided to keep the baby.

"I am kind of sick to my stomach. Do you guys have anything—like, something natural—for that?"

"Yes, Ma'am. I'm sure we can find something to help you out. Mr. Arby makes this wonderful ginger tea. I sometimes use it myself."

"Okay. Yeah. Maybe that and some saltine crackers or something?"

"I'll have Maria bring a tray right up for you."

Patrice curled up on the lounge again and rocked with her arms curled around her knees.

"My life is over. My freakin' life is over."

****

Reanita awakened with a powerful longing for grits.

She could just see them in a buttery glistening pool with two fried eggs—their yolks yellow and runny—slightly overlapping one side. A buttermilk biscuit as big as a laborer's fist perched on the edge of the plate. And a slab of country ham dripping with red-eye gravy. Yum.

For a moment, she felt disoriented. She could have been asleep for an hour or two days.

She threw the covers aside and bounded from bed. Without so much as splashing her face with cold water, she snatched on a pair of running shorts and a top.

Her athletic shoes were crusted with mud.

"That's weird."

Had she gone out the previous evening? She combed through her memory and barely recalled leaving the mansion on some nocturnal mission. But to where?

Reanita untied the laces and crammed her feet into the running shoes, sans socks.

"You're losing it, Reanita. Get a grip!"

She tied the laces, closed her eyes, and tried to recall. A path in the dark. The shed!

The dark pants she had worn lay in a crumpled pile. She dug in the pockets and found the set of lock picks. The rest of the scene appeared in her mind's eye. Frustrating: like trying to view a taped movie with a broken rewind button.

Okay, so she remembered the shed. It had been empty, save for something.

She pounded her forehead with the palm of her hand. "Think!"

A plastic bag with a warning label. Dry ice! Though what the heck dry ice meant, she didn't have a clue. What needed to be kept on ice?

The rest of the night simply refused to replay. So much jittery energy jerked through her body, she couldn't sit still, much less get her brain to function.

Exercise. She needed to burn.

She dashed from the suite and nearly collided with Stefanie with an *f*.

"Oh, Rea! I was just coming to see if you wanted to w—"

Reanita grabbed the trainer by one sleeve and jerked her toward the elevators. "Let's go."

"My, aren't we perky this morning!"

"You people have done this to me. Seriously. I hate mornings."

"It will be just us today," Stefanie with an *f* said. She punched the button for the first floor. "Patrice is not feeling well, and Julia and Thomas—well let's just say they are sleeping in."

The minute the two women stepped from the back door, Reanita jogged in place. "I feel like running. Can we?"

"Sure."

The DEA agent took off. Stefanie with an *f* fell in behind until she managed to pull alongside.

"Wow." The trainer spoke between breaths. "I've never moved quite this fast before breakfast."

"Good for you. Get that blood pumping in those designer sneakers of yours."

A large torpedo-shaped insect hit the dirt in front of them and scurried from the path.

"What the hell was that?!"

"One of those cockroaches I was warning you about," Stefanie with an *f* replied.

"Jeez, it had to be three inches long!"

Reanita didn't know what they fed their bugs in the South. Had to be some kind of nuclear waste dumpsite nearby. The roaches in Washington were healthy, but the roaches on Dark Island made the D.C. insects look as if they weren't big enough to be taken away from their mothers.

"Cockroaches can carry twenty-seven different diseases," Stefanie with an *f* said.

"Lovely statistic. I'll have to write that down. Maybe your husband should start stalking them instead of rabbits."

The morning *walk* took less than twenty minutes. By the time the two women returned, the trainer dripped with perspiration.

"Thanks for the run!" Reanita called over her shoulder.

The trainer bent double and gasped. "Sure." *Breathe. Breathe. Breathe.* "Anytime."

The DEA agent dashed straight to the patrons' dining area. The only occupant was Patrice Palmer, her head bent low over a scant plate of food.

When Reanita didn't find what she required in the sterling silver covered warming trays, she hailed one of the servers and put in an order. One thing about the folks in the kitchen: they'd serve up the devil on a garnished plate if a patron wished.

"I have a question." She sat down opposite of the starlet with a large cup of coffee.

"Huh?" The starlet peered at Reanita. Pale face. A little more than green around the gills.

Reanita studied Patrice's plate. Two small hunks of honeydew melon, a piece of dry wheat toast, a clump of scrambled eggs.

"Do you know what red-eye gravy is? I seem to have a craving for it. And, grits! I can't recall ever eating *a* grit, much less a plate full of them. And, fried eggs? I don't even like my eggs fried. The yolks ooze all over the plate. Especially if they don't cook them long enough and the white part is like Jell-O, you know?"

Patrice slammed a hand across her mouth and dashed from the room.

****

Arby thanked God and everyone else in the heavens. The statue for the water garden arrived in time. No small miracle.

The grounds crew had dissipated to their daily chores. Lars and the tent vendors were busy on the south lawn. So much remained to be done before the gala. Arby wouldn't abide any imperfection in the house or grounds, not with so many people—so many deep-pocketed people—coming to the Island. The hedges had been trimmed a month ago in order to look proper now, but Arby would recheck for dead or withered branches. The rose and flower gardens had to be stripped of spent blooms, the lighting checked for blown bulbs, the grass shorn and edged, and fresh mulch spread around the beds. Three full days left until the Blue Blood Ball. Three days filled with frenetic activity. If he could clone himself, or better yet, become a vampire, he could make it all appear effortless.

The five-foot tall statue towered over the waterfall. The pond and falls had been constructed months earlier in preparation. Hidden behind a temporary barricade deep in the moon garden. On the night of the gala, the inner courtyard would be revealed to visitors. A winding slate path, well-lit, would draw them toward the musical sound of falling water. Floodlights trained on the centerpiece would lead their gazes upward to the newest addition to the Spa at Dark Island moon garden, a slightly-abstract, yet recognizable, statue of a mosquito fashioned from scrap metal by a renowned Key West artist.

Arby stepped closer to study the detail. Amazing, how the welder had connected cogs and various industrial cast-offs to form the body, head, wings, and legs. Around the insect's neck hung a thick chain with a medallion sporting the Dark Island logo.

A rendering of the statue had been sent ahead to the catering company. Two ice sculptures, smaller versions of the metal parent, would be on display under the big party tents. The focus of the decorating scheme spaced between the patrons' tables.

Jimmy Rob interrupted Arby's statue worship. "You need me anymore, Rat Boy?"

"That will be all, Jimmy Rob. Please, thank your friend for the use of his truck and flat-bed trailer." Arby peeled off a handful of hundreds and handed them over.

The redneck vamp stuffed the cash into his pocket. "Don't forget, Rat Boy. You promised to make me up some of your special liquor, something tasting like whiskey. I ain't gonna drink that pansy wine you make for queer-boy."

"I told Vincent I would create something especially with your refined tastes in mind, and I shall."

The redneck vampire turned and left without the courtesy of a response.

Good. Go back to the oil pit you crawled out of. Arby wanted to say it aloud, but opted to think the words. Vamp hearing was acute.

After watching Jimmy Rob single-handedly hoist the statue from the trailer and place it above the falls as if he had lifted no more than a twin bed mattress, Arby chose not to tug on the redneck's ripped plaid shirttail.

The whole operation—a surprise for Vincent—had truly been a planning nightmare. The statue was too heavy to bring in by a small boat. The only choice had been delivery by semi tractor-trailer. Problem number two: the semi weighed too much to traverse the Dark Island Bridge.

Nothing a little hard cash couldn't solve. Enter Jimmy Rob and a heavy-duty pick-up with a flat-bed trailer, borrowed from one of his questionable friends. Three men managed to roll the crate onto the trailer, since Jimmy Rob couldn't step up and display his true abilities in front of the humans.

Problem three: the service road ended a good two-hundred feet from the waterfall area. Arby had failed to consider that small detail when he planned the surprise.

Jimmy Rob had shrugged, lifted the statue from the opened crate, and asked, "Where you want this thing?"

Arby watched in open-mouthed awe as the vamp strolled the last lap carrying the huge metal mosquito like a sack of marshmallows. Such amazing power, and he lived and worked with two such creatures, either of which could fold him like origami if they chose.

Vincent would love it. That's all that mattered. Though it hadn't been a guilt gift at first, Arby now thought of the statue as such. A present to cover up his series of infidelities.

The image of Reanita appeared in his mind and he lost himself in review of the scene earlier in the day.

Reanita, supine on the massage table, deeply sedated by the combination of herbal blood fern tea and hot stone massage.

He had stood over her resting body. Desire so strong, it left a sweet aftertaste on his tongue. He lifted the sheet over her affected ankle and was happy to see the last of the bruising had almost completely faded.

As he had so many times with so many patrons, he went through the sterile routine and administered the distillate. For the second time in one week, he stopped before drawing the requisite ounces of fresh blood.

He could double up on one of the other patron's contributions. Maybe Vincent wouldn't notice.

Oh, yeah. That will work. Like hoping Santa Claus won't notice Christmas. Like believing his childhood caretakers wouldn't notice how his face made the other children cringe.

Arby would suffer the consequences, whatever they were. Vincent would not have the life liquid of Reanita Register.

He packed up the kit and stood over her. Loving the way she breathed in and out with a slight high-pitched wheeze. The way the fine hairs around her mouth stood out like whiskers. Beautiful.

The blood fern tea made her eyes swing wildly behind their closed lids. Her mind, open to suggestion in its comatose state.

Arby leaned down and whispered in Reanita's right ear. "Dream of me, my love. Dream of my voice, calling you in the moonlit garden. Long for the touch of my hands."

The DEA agent moaned through her smile.

****

When Reanita awoke, she knew where she was this time. In the heavens' massage room. Relaxed. But hungry as two wild boars. The huge country breakfast was a dim memory. She'd have to cruise on down to the patrons' dining room and scare up some lunch.

The dream stayed with her. She felt the sting of arousal between her legs. And the memory of a slightly-familiar voice calling her out to play.

****

Vincent cast the emerald and gold smoking jacket aside and flopped into one of the leather lounges. Arby decanted a flute of the morning's vintage.

"Who do we have today?" Vincent asked.

Arby threw a white hand towel across his forearm and carried the glass and bottle across the suite. Vincent loved it when the overseer played wine steward.

"For this dawn, we have a California 2010 Aging Actor." He handed Vincent the cork.

Vincent sniffed and nodded. "Ah."

"You may note a slightly floral bouquet, with undertones of Colonial pomposity and overindulgence. A good, solid vintage in previous seasons, yet turning somewhat acidic and less desirable in recent times."

Vincent motioned for Arby to set the blood wine aside. He would taste it later, when his senses could be fully attuned to nuances.

"How are we coming with the final preparations? Not that I have to inquire. You always have such a firm handle on things."

The praise flowed around the overseer and landed mid-chest. No one—not until Dark Island and Vincent Bedsloe III —had ever thought to praise anything he had ever done. Not one of the slime balls he had squeaked past a prison sentence, not a single divorcee who got away with more than his or her fair share, not even a politician from the panhandle whose drunken hot tub party with a clutch of minors had landed him in jail. Arby's talents had helped the career politician walk away with a handful of payoffs and a slight slap on the hand. The publicity had actually been good for the man. Last Arby heard he would more than likely run for a national position again. Amazing.

"I do my utmost, Sir." Arby consulted his Palm Pilot. "I have double-checked with all of the factions. We are on task. The tent vendors are on-Island, and quite busy. Oh…I did manage to locate a thoroughbred black stallion for you. He will be delivered to the Dark by Friday morning."

Vincent clasped his hands together like a child who had been served chocolate cake. "Smashing!"

Arby's eyebrows knit together. "You're not going to start up with a British accent—some part of this year's costume—are you? One fake Brit on the Island is about all I can take."

"Heavens, no."

"If you don't mind the inquiry, Vincent. Why a horse?"

"The grand entrance, Arby. The grand entrance." Vincent grabbed the remote and cued the DVD. "Watch."

The video started mid-movie, at a spot where Frank Langella's Dracula astride a frothing black stallion galloped through a graveyard and maintained his balance as the animal reared and stomped around. The vampire's cape flowed like a black river in his wake.

Vincent hit the pause button. "That will be me on Saturday evening. With the outfit and my fiery steed, I will astonish and amaze our guests. Plus, it fits the gala's theme perfectly." He thought a moment, then added, "Make sure Lars has a fan positioned to make the cape flow when I stop on my mark."

"You dressed as a vampire. A bit come-as-you-are, don't you think? And, it's not even Halloween."

When Vincent laughed, the sound reverberated through the suite like surround sound, seeming to bounce from all angles at once. It was a sound Arby had grown to love. He relished the times when he could be the reason for the vampire's mirth.

"You should come as the Doctor, the Professor—oh, what was his name?" Vincent snapped his fingers. "In the Bram Stoker novel—the one who wanted to kill him so desperately?"

"Dr. Abraham Van Helsing?" Arby asked.

"Yes. Perfect!"

"Suppose I could, Sir. But only the most astute literary types might understand the connection."

"It would please me, Arby."

The overseer nodded. "I shall make it happen then." *Now he expects me to show up in a costume, too? Shit.*

Vincent switched the DVD player off. "Any more niggling details? Might I go online this morning, or perhaps make some calls?"

"Thank you for offering, Sir. I have it all under careful control." He smiled, thinking of the special surprise awaiting the vampire. He still couldn't believe he had kept the statue project beneath Vincent's radar.

"I do have a small surprise for you, Sir." Arby pulled a small white box from one of the coverall's pockets.

"Cigars?" Vincent asked. He studied the box. "Too flat. Too small. What?"

Arby gestured to the lid. "Open it and see."

Vincent removed the top to reveal several rows of molded white and dark chocolate figures. He looked closer. The confections replicated the mosquito ice-carving design for the Blue Blood Ball.

"How charming! Absolutely charming. Where did you locate these?"

Arby said, "I found an on-line vendor that could replicate anything into a candy mold. The chocolates, I made myself. Go ahead. Try one."

Vincent glanced up. "Cruel of you, Arby. You know how much I used to adore fine chocolates." He turned away. "Save them for the guests."

"You wound me, Vincent. I have made plenty of others for the gala. These are for you. Blood mixed with the essence of cocoa. My secret recipe."

Vincent spun around. "Truly?"

Arby nodded.

Vincent extracted one of the mosquitoes from its nest and popped it into his mouth. The flavor of rich dark blood chocolate washed across his tongue. He closed his eyes and moaned.

"Good, eh?"

"Oh my yes. But, how—"

"I located a source of high-quality Swiss blood. That, I mixed with cocoa powder and reduced the mixture several times. It shouldn't affect your delicate system. Plus, each of your chocolates has a special liquid blood center that will burst out when you bite down."

"Arby, you are a genius!" The vampire grabbed the little man and gave him a hug.

The caretaker stood for a moment, too stunned to react. Never, not in the five years he had known Vincent Bedsloe III, had the man ever touched him, much less shown any kind of physical affection.

Now he really felt guilty.

Vincent tilted his head and studied Arby. "Is there anything you wish to tell me? Hmm?"

Arby's thoughts flew immediately to his deception. Had the vamp noticed the conspicuous absence of the heiress's vintage? Or, could he see the image of the hidden surprise sculpture hidden in the caretaker's mind?

"Ah...so you do conceal something from me." Vincent smiled. "Not to worry, Arby. Every romance movie ever made expounds the same weary human truth."

Arby swallowed hard. "I don't know what you are talking—"

Vincent rolled his eyes, a playful gesture few ever saw. "Do you think me blind and dumb?"

"No Sir."

"Miss Register might not be everyone's spot of tea, yet I can see where you might be smitten." Vincent grinned, hoping his British reference might prod Arby to smile. The overseer seemed terribly tense.

He knows. He knows. "I don't—"

Vincent shook his head. "—want to admit your attraction to her? That, too, happens in the movies. All the time. Approach, avoid, approach, avoid. Classic." He smiled. "Don't worry, Arby. Your secret is safe with me. Though, you might consider doing more of the approach aspect. It is mid-week and she will be leaving the Island on Sunday."

"I will take that into consideration." Arby switched subjects. "You're not still pondering adding riding stables to the Island, are you?"

"It has been often requested. Certainly, we have plenty of trails."

"And rattlesnakes. I fear a patron would come to harm. Just think if one were to be thrown."

"True."

"Plus, we would need to add to the staff. Groomers, caretakers, a veterinarian willing to make Island calls."

"I'm sure if I—if we—decide to add the equine element, you can see to that. Still, I will think a bit more on it. No need to make hasty decisions."

Though Arby admired the powerful animals, horses didn't take to him. The few times he had chanced to sit in the saddle, he had either been cast off like an annoying fly or scrubbed off on the nearest tree. And stepped on. He still had a half-moon shaped scar on his left foot.

"Very good, Sir." He slid the Pilot back into his pocket. "Is there anything else? I need to call the artist about the ice carvings."

"We might have one small issue, but it is one I will address."

"Have I overlooked something?" the overseer raked through his mental notes.

Vincent sighed. "I'll have a talk with our resident redneck after dinner this evening."

"What's he done now?"

"Jimmy Rob's been dipping into the patron till again. I noticed his fresh glamour. Obviously his, since the distillate's aura would come from me."

Arby frowned. Who? Thomas and Julia were so wrapped up in each other, they barely left the mansion. He dismissed Reanita immediately. Not Jimmy Rob's type. Had to be Patrice. He nodded. Jimmy Rob would find her type too attractive to resist—like a toddler left alone with a full jar of warm chocolate chip cookies.

"Won't be the first time he's crossed the line."

Vincent sighed. "I'm just glad he plans to be off-Island during the Blue Blood Ball."

"Who did he nip? Do I need to up the distillate to the patron? You know his glamour has odd effects on humans. Their tastes take a definite turn for the common."

"Might not be a bad idea. I'd hate to see another one end up on the more seemly side of things." Vincent paused, considered his words before he continued, "Seems he has chosen Miss Register for his blood smoothie. Sorry to be the one to tell you, old boy. She seemed fine, but you might give her a bit extra in case. I'd hate for her to have a sudden, unexplained longing for cheap booze, fried food and tube tops. At least my blood son has learned a little restraint. He doesn't kill them anymore."

Arby struggled to control the rage bubbling inside. The cretin had besmirched his lady's honor! And it wasn't as if he could challenge him to a duel.

****

"How dare that mechanic monkey touch my Reanita?" Arby mumbled as he left Vincent's suite.

The overseer's mind raced. The perfect solution popped to the front.

If I can't even the score man to man, he thought. *I will call upon a force more powerful.*

Arby had used the long arm of the law to settle disputes, medicinal concoctions to battle medical injustices, and other less-than-reputable solutions to lash out against the bullies of the world. Now, he would call upon a power that could hopefully overcome the strengths of a vampiric adversary. Mother Nature.

Driven by fury and the niggling need for revenge, Arby scurried to his greenhouse.

He set to work. Poison ivy, Sumac, and poison oak grew in abundance on Dark Island. He had already experimented with hybrids. It would be mice-play to take the development of their more caustic properties one step further.

After the leaves cooked down in separate small pots, he strained the greens to remove the liquid from each—three vials of syrupy, malignant goop. Arby retrieved three bottles of the Jack Daniels blood distillate that were curing in a back locked cabinet. He broke open the seals and funneled several tablespoons of his new potions into the bottles of amber liquid. The first container got the sumac. The second, the poison oak. The third, the poison ivy. He used a red pen to mark a small number on each label. If the redneck noticed—which Arby doubted he would—the master gardener would rattle off something about quality control. In reality, the numbers would enable Arby to tell which potion, if any, hit its mark. He resealed the bottles and put them back into storage. Wouldn't Jimmy Rob be pleased that Arby thought enough of him to put a rush on his new blood-whiskey order?

Arby grinned. Nobody could ever slam his commitment to customer service.

Now, for a more immediate back-stab at the middle-school graduate.

Arby pulled on a pair of rubber gloves, found his trusty pestle and mortar, and dumped in an assortment of the poisonous leaves. His anger fueled his fevered movements, until he had reduced the mixture to a pulpy paste. He scraped every particle into a plastic lidded bowl and burped out the air.

Arby's lips curled up. The plan was perfect and flawless. As soon as the mixture had a few hours to stew in the heat, he would find an opportunity to stop by Jimmy Rob's garage and initiate part one of the payback: the injection of the noxious slime into Jimmy Rob's #10 can of Mojo Hand Cleaner—every mechanic's best friend.

Ah, and the car wax Jimmy Rob used for the limos! Easily accomplished. Arby could put a loaded syringe-full of the poisonous goop into the wax immediately. Genius, pure genius!

As he left his inner sanctuary for the evening, thoughts of the clever scheme gave Arby some modicum of solace. The meek didn't inherit the world. Arby quit believing in that maxim years ago. But he sure as hell could muck it up a bit for the strong.

Chapter 13

Wednesday afternoon

The only thing Reanita wished for—above a new Glock or maybe a new doughnut shop near her home in D.C.—was a hot shower. The afternoon session with Carlos the p.m. trainer had royally kicked her faux-heiress butt: weight training, followed by some bizarre Latin combination of kick-boxing and salsa dancing. Patrice had begged off early and Julia and Thomas barely made it past the first round of core exercises. Suppose they were getting their aerobic activity through other channels.

Just her and Carlos humping, bumping and grinding in front of the floor-to-ceiling mirrors. Hot in more ways than one.

The odd thing: Reanita wasn't tired, just sweaty. If she still felt this way by the end of the week, she could single-handedly take out most of the drug-runners on the Gulf side of Florida. Piece o' cake.

Reanita cast the damp workout clothes—in coordinating shades of pale lavender and deep purple—on the floor and noticed a fancy party invitation propped on the table by the chaise lounge.

You are cordially invited to an evening by the pool for a traditional Southern cookout. Attire: casual, swim wear suggested. Seven p.m.

Reanita's mouth watered. Finally, some plain all-American chow. The high-brow stuff had been wonderful, really. But she could sure go for a greasy cheeseburger, pile of fries and a cold beer.

A thought struck her as she adjusted the digital temperature settings for the three showerheads. *I'll have to actually wear that miserable excuse of a swimsuit.*

The one-piece was great for swimming laps, but an heiress at a pool party? No way. She'd be expected to *show out in strings*.

Reanita stepped into the center of the spacious tiled shower. Water pounded her body like a drive-through car wash.

"I will truly miss this," she said.

When she returned to D.C., Reanita would have to break down and buy a new shower head. The one she had was so encrusted with hard water deposits, only about half of the holes allowed water to pass. Dark Island's water pressure had hers beat all to hell, too.

Reanita used liquid Shea butter soap on a natural sea sponge to work her skin to a frothy lather. She ran one hand down her abdomen, opened her eyes, and stared at her stomach. The muscles seemed more defined than she remembered. Water coursed across the ripples like hard rain on a washboard dirt road. Her hands moved to the sides of her thighs. More taunt. Then, to her buttocks. Not a hint of jiggle anywhere.

"Agent Register," she mimicked the voice of her supervisor in D.C., "All of your diligent work has paid off."

Reanita squeezed a generous dollop of herbal shampoo into one palm and worked it into her scalp. Was it her imagination, or was her hair thicker and longer, too?

She shook her head. "Nah. Couldn't be."

All of the other patrons' talk about the magic of Dark Island was getting to her. Mumbo jumbo. Seaweed wraps and exotic oils. Crystals placed over her chakra energy centers, whatever they were. Some tarot card-reading psychic telling her of passion and love in her immediate future. That one had been hard to swallow and not regurgitate hysterical hiccupping laughter.

Her thoughts darkened. Here it was mid-week, and she still had no solid link between Dark Island and any alleged drug activity.

Suspicions, but a whole lot of nothin'.

Her father's words came to mind; one of his few pieces of wisdom that had actually made reasonably good sense. *Keep turning over enough rocks and eventually something slimy will crawl out.*

****

Reanita arrived fashionably late. She held the thick white logo-printed terry cloth robe together so it wouldn't gap open. Naked; that's how she felt. She had to shave her down-under to avoid looking like a cavewoman. By the next day, the razor rash would be a bitch.

The pool enclosure looked like someone had gotten vilely sick and thrown up the Bahamas. Potted palms studded with bromeliads and orchids crammed in every nook, with realistic stuffed Macaws wired to their fronds. Layers of fresh-flower leis looped around the guests' and servers' necks. So much vivid tropical print, Reanita's eyes nearly crossed. One corner contained an impromptu beach made from white sand scattered with starfish and shells.

Rows of iced drinks—mojitoes, Mango Tango dark rum daiquiris, wine coolers, and margaritas—stood ready on slabs of ice. Wooden buckets of frosty imported beer surrounded a treasure chest full of faux gold doubloons.

Jimmy Buffet meets Blackbeard the Pirate, thought the DEA agent. *With enough booze to send both of them on a bender of unequaled abandon.*

Everything on Dark Island was so over the top. Four patrons, and there was enough alcohol for a team of adolescent football players, plus their cheerleader girlfriends.

One of the servers—Reanita recognized the Hispanic woman, Maria—glided over with a tray.

"Chew would like?" the woman asked.

Reanita picked one of the mint-embellished mojitoes. She had often heard them mentioned on her favorite show, *CSI Miami*. One sip turned her into an instant fan. Hard not to love a drink that tasted like summer vacation and sugary decadence with a kick of rum.

Three mojitoes later, Reanita's terry robe came off. The other patrons stared. The Dark Island staff took furtive glances. All that feminine hard body excellence, and a face like *that*. Reanita could read their expressions. Screw them and the houseboat they rode in on.

Arby hid behind the gas grill, doing his best to catch his breath. The goddess's bathing suit left little guesswork. She was perfect, more so, than he imagined. She was a Venus de Milo, with hands.

Reanita walked over to a small side table and piled a plate high with appetizers: skewered grilled Gulf shrimp, broiled water chestnuts wrapped in bacon, baked brie with toast points, chilled dark and white chocolate-dipped strawberries and pineapple, and a type of miniature sausage in honeyed red sauce. Not your average redneck party fare, but Reanita supposed you could only go so far with tradition. Pigs-in-a-blanket and melted cheese spread over corn chips might not fly with this group.

A silver stand wrapped in ferns and orchid blossoms held the menu:

Sirloin hamburgers with choice of Swiss or cheddar cheese

Black Bean burgers, with or without cheese
Baby-back ribs with bourbon barbeque sauce
Grilled chicken tenders with pineapple and brown sugar glaze

Side items:
Seasoned corn on the cob, cooked in the shuck
Creamy southern Cole slaw
Red Potato salad
Fresh seasonal fruit salad
Baked barbequed beans

Breads:
Corn fritters with butter
Heated multi-grain hamburger buns

Dessert:
Banana pudding with meringue
Eight-layered coconut cake with Dark Island Chocolate Sauce

Drinks:
Southern sweet tea with mint
Spring water with lime
Choice of carbonated beverages

The array of condiments alone had to have cost a fortune, she thought.

Five kinds of mustard, three bowls of chilled mayonnaise blends, catsup, dill and sweet pickles, sliced jalapeno peppers, diced Vidalia onions, romaine lettuce leaves, and a plate of sliced deep-red tomatoes. Sea salt and pepper grinders, herbal spice mixtures and several bottles of hot sauce and steak sauce.

Reanita was pretty sure if she asked for mango chutney made only from fruit grown only on the west end of, say,

Cuba, the Dark Island staff could produce it before she had time to pitch a fit.

No wonder they called it The Good Life.

By the time the servers announced dinner, three out of the four patrons' eyes were starting to glaze over. Patrice—opting for the virgin version of the iced drinks—could have posed as the designated driver had the party's end accommodations been more than thirty feet away.

Reanita stood behind Patrice, in line for hot-off-the grill burgers.

"You prefer a bean burger, Miss Patrice?" a familiar voice asked the starlet.

"Perfect. You know, I am a vegan."

Reanita rolled her eyes. If Patrice Palmer was a vegan, then she was Princess Diana's twin. Unless one considered dairy, eggs, chicken, fish, steak, and an occasional slab of deli ham as part of the recommended fare.

"Yes Ma'am." Arby used a pair of tongs to position a thick bean burger on Patrice's bun.

"You forgot my cheese."

He didn't miss a beat, only waved to the two choices. Patrice chose one of each.

"How about you, Miss Reanita?"

"Oh, come now, Arby. I thought you and I had gotten past all of that formal stuff."

"Of course." He glanced around to make sure the other staffers weren't within hearing range. "Rea."

"Forget the fake shit for me. I like my meat real, red and rare."

Reanita held out her plate. Arby's hand shook as he flipped one of the sirloin burgers to warm both sides. His face burned, and he was glad for the beekeepers hat. "Cheese?"

"Hit me with everything you've got, baby."

Arby wanted to do more. He wanted to take her. Right then. Right there. Instead, he piled two slices of cheese atop a burger, waited for them to slightly melt, and moved the tower of cholesterol onto her mayonnaise-smeared open bun.

Funny little man in his long-sleeved tropic-weight shirt and pants and that screwy hat, Reanita thought as she stumbled to a nearby bistro table. *But, cute and kind of hot, in a bizarre sort of way.*

****

"The key to perfect, high drama lies in the element of surprise," the Master of Dark Island whispered. In life, as it was in his favorite daytime drama, *The Young and the Restless.*

Vincent couldn't believe the moves he had planned. No one in over fifty years—especially the patrons and staff—had seen Vincent Bedsloe III in anything other than a silk smoking jacket or Armani suit. Why now? He felt reckless. Things needed to be stirred a bit.

Could Emmaraud be prodding me from afar? He wondered.

Vincent glanced down at his pool party ensemble.

Tropic-print swim trunks—he purposely avoided spandex. Back when he was a relatively normal hot-blooded male, he had been told that he was hung like a donkey on steroids. For all the good it did him now. No need to flash his candy and make the human males feel inadequate.

Covering the swimwear—a plush black terry robe with the Dark Island logo embroidered in gold on one pocket.

And the ever-present tan in a shade any surfer dude would die for.

Vincent surveyed the pool patio. Thomas and Julia bobbed in one corner of the deep end, engrossed in a little aquatic foreplay. Patrice Palmer—dark designer glasses in place despite the decreasing daylight—reclined on a cushioned lounge chair. Reanita Register sat at one of the bistro tables, alternating chunks of coconut cake and swigs of mojito. Good thing the distillate helped to level blood glucose levels, or the heiress would later crash from an extreme sugar high and wake up with a head that felt like an over-inflated beach ball.

The servers had cleared away the last of the food. The only staffer watching over the patrons' needs was Arby. Perfect.

The vampiric host stood at the pool enclosure entrance and waited for his preternatural magnetism to rein in the humans—a trait he called *That Ole Vamp Black Magic*. One by one, they turned in his direction, even Arby, who had stopped cleaning the stainless steel gas grill.

Vincent nodded and the corners of his lips lifted with a slight smile. He walked purposely to the edge of the pool. He untied the fabric belt and slipped the terry robe from his shoulders. It fell in a dark puddle at his feet. The women gasped. Vincent noted how their lips parted and their breathing and pulses accelerated.

The digital mirrors told him several times a day: You, sir, are the epitome of the male form. Ripped abs. Dark hair and features. Muscle definition without too much bulk. Evenly bronzed skin. A smooth chest with one thatch of curly hair.

The first sight of their host sans formal attire was enough of a confection, and his next moves added the whipped cream topping. He executed a shallow dive and swam five laps. Purposeful. Powerful. Perfection. Even the challenging butterfly stroke.

Minutes later, when he gracefully pulled himself from the water, no one spoke. Arby appeared with a thick white towel. Vincent took his time drying his body.

Thomas and Julia exited the pool and walked over to where he stood. Patrice sat up and lowered her Oakley sunglasses to peek at him over the top rims. Reanita took a deep swig of mojito and stifled a belch.

The host of Dark Island asked, "I trust you have all enjoyed our little Southern cookout?"

"Um-hum." "Yeah." "Yes." "Oh, my yes," came the mingled responses.

"All good!"

Arby handed his boss a crystal glass with a double shot of blood bourbon. Vincent swirled the amber liquid around the glass and took an appreciative sip. "Please, don't let my presence interfere with your continued enjoyment."

The vamp smiled and glanced at each patron in turn. "On a normal week, I would invite you to a formal dinner on Saturday evening, a little conclusion to your stay. But the week preceding a large event is a bit different." He motioned toward Arby. "My overseer can attest to the fact: we become frenetic and rather distracted before a gala the size of the Blue Blood Ball. So many details, right Arby?"

The overseer nodded.

"Ah, but the night is young," he paused. "And I am not."

The vampire chuckled softly. The only one—other than himself—who knew the absolute truth behind the jest said nothing.

He continued, "I'd like to take this opportunity to spend a little one-on-one time with each of you."

As if on cue, the group dispersed. Vincent settled onto the chaise lounge nearest Patrice. "I really should stop to enjoy life a bit more. Don't you agree—life is to be savored?"

The starlet sighed, settled her glasses back into place, and returned her head to the pillowed cushion. "I suppose."

"Tell me about this new role—playing a temptress vampire, was it?"

"No big deal. A bit part in a B-movie."

Vincent studied her profile. The blood glamour revealed more than her voice. Flat. Very little emotion of any kind. Odd for the effervescent starlet. Stranger still was the fact that she wasn't making any move to slide one of her long legs toward his. Patrice was anything but subtle.

"Come now. You seemed positively giddy on Sunday evening. The blush can't be off the bud in such a short time, can it?"

She dismissed his question with a wave of one taloned hand. "I don't feel like talking about all of that."

Vincent's eyebrows shot up. Humans could be so exasperating at time. He made a mental note: *check the latest vintage for Miss Patrice Palmer. Something is terribly amiss.*

"Excuse me, Patrice." He rose and walked over to the bistro table. A third piece of coconut cake sat in front of Reanita Register.

"I don't have to ask if you are enjoying the food, Miss Register." He motioned to her plate.

"Must be all of the exercise, or this place." She waved her hands in a circle. "I don't usually eat sweets like this." She considered. "I have been known to polish off a doughnut or two. God, my blood sugar must be off the charts."

"Nothing wrong with a hint of sweetness in one's blood." The vampire smiled. "Has everything met with your satisfaction, Miss Register?"

"Rea." She sucked the dregs of a mojito until the straw gurgled air. "What does it take to get you people to just call me freakin' *Rea*?"

"Point made, Rea." He gestured to the empty glass. "Another?"

She blinked. Considered. The usually-sharp DEA agent's mental cogs turned in a quagmire of rum, simple sugar, and mulled mint. "Sure. What the hell. Not like I have to drive home."

Vincent lifted a finger in Arby's direction and a frosty tumbler materialized seconds later. "There you are. Enjoy."

Reanita raked a hand through her damp hair. "Stefanie with an *f* is going to flay my butt in the morning." Her words tumbled together like first-graders heading for recess.

Vincent excused himself and moved to the next table where Thomas and Julia sat.

"Mind if I join you?"

Julia patted the chair beside hers. "Please do."

"The ribs were excellent, Vincent," the senator's wife said. "I can't recall how long it has been since I've eaten such delectable barbeque."

"I'll pass the compliment to my staff. Arby makes the sauce. His own special, secret recipe that he guards like the Coca-Cola formula."

Vincent studied the couple. Their glamours mingled and formed a soft rose-tinted bubble. Hard to believe, since they had just met a few days prior.

The distillate had improved the tone of Julia's skin. The purple smudges beneath her eyes seemed less prominent. Yet, the evil conqueror deep inside gnawed at her core.

He turned to observe the actor. Had Thomas lost weight? Vincent thought back to the vintage sample he had tasted earlier. The chemical soup coursing through Thomas's arteries carried less of a taint. The blood pressure medication that left such a bitter aftertaste had been barely detectable. Cholesterol levels were sharply down. Could it be, the man might have actually followed the Dark Island Nutritional Advisor's advice and cleaned up his act since last year? Good. He wouldn't feel a smidge of guilt for promoting one of their shared vices.

"Thomas, I have a couple of cigars. Do you care to join me?" Vincent asked.

Thomas reached over and gave Julia's hand a gentle squeeze. "Do you mind, dear?"

"Not at all. I'll leave you two boys to enjoy yourselves. I'm a little tired." She stood and wrapped a towel around her damp swimsuit. "I think I'll turn in a bit early." She smiled at Vincent. "Thank you for such a delightful party."

"My pleasure, Julia."

The senator's wife leaned down and kissed Thomas on the cheek. "I'll see you...later."

The vamp and the actor watched her until she entered the mansion's rear door.

Vincent retrieved his robe and pulled two square-pressed Padrón Anniversario cigars from an inner pocket. The two aficionados didn't speak until the preliminary rituals were completed. Sweet fragrant smoke lifted into the evening sea breeze.

"Lovely woman, the senator's wife," Vincent said.

"Yes." Thomas nodded and smiled.

"Nice to have a little—discourse—away from the prying eyes of the press," the Dark Island host stated.

"Confession time, old boy." The actor took a thoughtful pull on the cigar. "Julia and I are not a new item."

Vincent waited. Delicious; the human game.

"We met a few months back at a fund-raiser for the Senator. I was one of the lucky celebrities to be invited from the Hollywood set." The last statement, uttered with a sarcastic edge.

"Ah yes. The good senator is up for re-election as I recall."

Thomas huffed. "*Good* senator? The pompous ass. He flaunts his floozies beneath my Julia's nose. He doesn't lower himself to consider her feelings."

"Pity. Power corrupts some men." Vincent took a puff. "Most, actually."

"Julia deserves so much more. If only—"

Vincent allowed a moment to pass before he asked, "I did note how very close you two seemed after such a short time."

Thomas looked wistfully toward the mansion. "It is the first time for many things." His gaze moved back to Vincent. "The problem with living one's life in the public eye—for both Julia and myself—is that there truly is no place to find shelter. Until Dark Island. A *timely coincidence*; that we had reservations for the Spa on the same week. Our relationship up to this point has been the desperate joining of two hearts via email and cell phone conversations. Moments of stolen time."

Vincent stifled the urge to smile. The actor's words sounded like a scripted monologue for a date-night Hollywood romance movie. As he listened to the aging actor's saga of star-crossed lovers, Vincent relished the taste of the fine cigar punctuated by sips of blood bourbon. Thomas's vintage might hint at the story, but not the richness of emotion. Vincent craved the feeling more than the fiction: the difference between watching a travel video and actually sensing the dirt of the ancients between his toes.

The psychic who traveled to Dark Island once a week from Cassadaga—a small Southern burg renown for its saturation of sentients—knew the same secret as did Vincent Bedsloe III. It took so little to reveal a person's innermost desires. A few well-placed questions, a gentle tug on the bridle and most humans would gladly lead the seeker in the correct direction. Any individual—preternatural or merely observant—could follow the clues and appear highly accurate with predictions and precautions.

Vincent heard the rumble of a tight powerful engine long before the vehicle pulled into the mansion's circular drive. He glanced toward Arby, who had frozen like a white-tailed deer caught in the sights of a crossbow.

A few moments passed before a woman stood at the pool enclosure's door. Vincent felt his already-chilled blood drop a few degrees. Arby sucked in a breath.

"Oh my God," Patrice Palmer whispered. "It's her—look!" The starlet's head swiveled toward Reanita and back to the woman.

Reanita squinted. *Nah. Couldn't be. Her daddy owns resorts on every planet short of Mars. Why would she come here?*

The woman flipped her waist-length platinum blonde hair. She cradled a small animal that looked like a jewel-encrusted rat. It took a second for Vincent to realize the creature was a tan Chihuahua in designer couture.

"It *is* her!" Patrice sat bolt upright and threw a questioning glance toward Vincent and Thomas.

The cigar smoke froze in curls in the damp evening air.

"Vincent, why didn't you tell me Paris Hilton was coming to The Dark?" Patrice asked.

The Master of Dark Island couldn't seem to locate sufficient air to coax his vocal cords to vibrate. His overseer found enough to utter one word.

"Emmaraud."

Chapter 14

Thursday: the wee hours of morning

Jimmy Rob recalled the first time he had laid eyes on Emmaraud Bonneville. One minute he'd been stumbling from the Gulf Breeze Bar, two sheets and a couple of comforters to the wind, just looking forward to ditch-hugging his way home in the old Chevy Malibu and falling into bed clothes and all. The beer buzz had long since given way to the raunchy-biker-babe-looks-good stage. Time to call it a night, son.

The next minute—or so it seemed, more like several hours later—he opened his eyes and tried to focus. The alcohol had mysteriously worn off. Completely. He saw Cher looking down on him. Honest to freakin' God—Cher. He thought he must've died, must've wrapped the Chevy around an oak tree and ascended, or whatever those New Age idiots called it.

The woman who stood in front of him now, had pulled up in front of his bar in a brand-spanking new black Maserati Gran Turismo—a Maserati!—looked like the tall blonde chick whose Daddy owned more high-end hotel real estate than a lucky Monopoly player. Named after a city—he tried to recall—Madrid? London? No, Paris! That was it—Paris.

Jimmy Rob didn't know shit from shinola about designer clothing, but he could tell just by looking at Emmaraud that she'd spent a pretty penny on the outfit. Bless her black heart, she tried to dress all southern-gal, but it just didn't quite fly. Even her short denim skirt probably cost more than all of the other good-old-gals made in five years of hard work. Over one shoulder, she carried a huge black leather bag with brass accents. Something inside of the fancy purse growled. Honest to God.

He did his level best to stay cool.

"Well...I'll be damned. Lookit what the dogs done drug in. When'd you blow into town, sugar?"

"Just now. I've been in Miami for a few days."

Emmaraud sat the bag down and unzipped the top. A little rat-like head shot out and barred teeth at him. The miniature dog's eyes looked red-rimmed and its upper canine teeth were twice the length he'd ever seen on a dog. Emmaraud scratched the creature between the ears. The lips uncurled, but it continued to regard him and everyone else in J.R.'s Joint with malevolence.

"Kind of ill-tempered, ain't he?"

"*She.* Diente is a little girl." Emmaraud slid onto a bar stool. "I'm famished." She ran her tongue across her lips.

Jimmy Rob tore his gaze away from the ruby-tinged lips and busied himself polishing the smudges from a glass. "I could probably rustle up something to tide you over for a bit."

She slid a hand over his. "I need more than a little something."

Good thing he healed quickly. He had a good feeling tonight was going to get freaky. Fast.

Jimmy Rob pulled an unlabeled brown beer bottle from a concealed cabinet and poured two shot glasses full. He slid one in front of Emmaraud. "Cheers." He lifted the glass and took a sip. She did the same.

"Yuck. What is this?"

"My special dark lager. You like?"

She pushed the glass aside. "You know I detest synthetics, Jimmy Rob. I want the real thing."

"Patience, baby. Patience. He tipped his head toward a middle-aged couple sitting at the end of the bar and mouthed, "What'd you think?"

Emmaraud considered the male: A little paunchy in the midsection. Male pattern baldness, but nice blue eyes. "Not bad. I could make do, I suppose. What about her?"

Jimmy Rob glanced at the woman: Petite. Good bone structure. A few laugh lines. Bleached hair showing dark at the roots. He shrugged. "When you're starving, even a bologna sandwich tastes like sirloin. They're well on their way to being out of it."

The Chihuahua curled up between them and closed her eyes.

Emmaraud tapped her black painted nails on the bar. "What do you expect me to do in the meantime, knit?"

The thought of Emmaraud Bonneville sitting in one place long enough to do something as domestic as knitting delighted him. He laughed. "I'd picture you spinning a web with silk shooting from your tight little butt before I could picture that."

She glanced around the room. "What's up with you behind the bar? You working here now?"

"I own it. Didn't you notice the sign when you walked in? J.R.'s Joint." He thumped his chest with one finger. "That's me."

"Charming." She took in the dirty paint, stained floors, and dim lighting. "I like what you've *not* done with the place." She gestured toward the jukebox. You got any Dixie Chicks? Or, no! Carrie Underwood—*Before He Cheats*? I just love that one. About how she totally trashes her cheating boyfriend's pretty little souped-up four wheel drive truck. It absolutely wrecks me."

He dug in the cash register and handed her a roll of quarters. "Knock yourself out."

Jimmy Rob watched her swivel across the room like each hip rode on its own separate suspension. Everyone in the bar watched her, even the two women. Damn, she was hot! Who could ever want another female after tangling with the likes of Emmaraud Bonneville? She could be, and was, a different woman each time she blew into town. Any time she changed her celebrity fixation, she morphed into someone new. Refreshing. Exciting. And, all of them made him hotter than a four-peckered Billy goat during mating season.

Emmaraud slammed the quarters into the machine, poked the buttons, and the metallic band started to play. She danced a few steps and turned to face him, wiggling a come-hither finger. "Dance with me."

The three good ole boys at the pool table stopped to watch. The couple at the bar ceased their conversation and tuned in to the action on the dance floor. The lone female sitting at a table rested her head in her cupped hands and fought to focus.

When he stepped up to her, Emmaraud swiveled her hips and ground into him.

"Where you been all this time?" His voice was husky with desire.

"Spain. France. All over." She closed her eyes and lifted the long blonde hair over her head with both hands.

"You know, babe." He whispered into her ear. "You teach me that shape-shifting thing you do, and I could come hang out with you more often."

She frowned. *No way.*

The last time she helped a male vampire remember how to shape shift—a talent all possessed, but few recalled the innate knowledge—he had become a horrible nuisance. Felipe. Crazy Felipe. Stalking her. Turning up everywhere she went. Finally, she had managed to pawn him off on a female vamp in France. Last she knew, the two were all codependent cozy somewhere in Provence. Good for them. Love was too complicated. And a bore.

Right now—and who knows for the next forty or a hundred years—Emmaraud had a taste for Southern Redneck. The high life in low places. The taste of fried chicken grease, hot wings, and cheap beer in the blood.

She curled her fingers through his sweat-damp hair. "Maybe later. If you're a very, very bad boy."

"So you're planning on hanging around awhile this time?"

He hated himself for missing her even as she had just arrived.

"Few days. Got some business on The Dark."

He frowned. "You're staying with the fag, then."

She pushed him away. "Oh, for Pete's sake, Jimmy Rob. Get over it. Vincent is my blood child. And, sort of a friend—long before I met you."

"Whatever."

She smiled. "Suppose I could spend a few nights with my favorite redneck boy while I'm in the States."

His bad mood evaporated. "I'll change the sheets on the air mattress."

"No need." She pulled close to him again. "You still have that fold-out couch in the garage? The smell of all that grease and oil makes me want to act up."

"I like what I'm hearing, little gal." He wrapped his arms around her small waist and held her tight against his body.

"But, I'm hungry, Jimmy Rob. Really."

"You done gone and gotten soft on me, Emmaraud? What happened to the thrill of the game?"

She pushed him away and walked toward the seated couple. "Hey there. I'm Emmaraud. Can I buy you two a round of drinks?" The vampire temptress turned on her magnetic charm. "I hate to drink alone, and my boyfriend—" she gestured toward Jimmy Rob, "—has to make sure the other customers are taken care of."

Jimmy Rob returned to his spot behind the bar. He marveled at how easily Emmaraud switched from rich heiress to backwoods Daisy Duke. No one would doubt her accent was authentic. A blood rush warmed his chest. *Boyfriend. She called me boyfriend.*

The woman offered a lopsided grin and nodded. "We can't have you feeling all lonely, can we, sugar?" She stuck out one hand. "I'm Joanie." She tipped her head toward the man. "This here is Taylor."

Emmaraud barely brushed the tips of the offered hand. "Emmaraud. Pleased to meet y'all." She glanced toward the bar. "This here is J.R. He owns this place."

The woman tapped her lips with one finger. "Emmaraud. That's a cute name. I think I used to have a perfume named that, way back."

"Yeah," the vampiress said. "My mama named me after it. It was her all-time favorite. She always kept a big old bottle on her dressing table."

Jimmy Rob shook his head. Emmaraud could lie more convincingly than a backsliding Baptist preacher caught in a hot tub full of underage coeds. The way her voice shook, she might break out in blood tears any second.

Easy, Emmaraud, he thought, *they catch sight of that, and they'll think they're witnessing a miracle.*

Joanie—full of southern female concern—reached over and rested a hand on Emmaraud's shoulder. "Oh, honey. Is your sweet mama still livin'?"

Emmaraud's gaze fell to the floor. "She's passed."

Taylor sat his beer down. "I lost my dear mama just last year. I feel your pain. I really do."

Emmaraud looked up and offered him a sympathetic nod. Kindred spirits united by cheap booze and the weird camaraderie shared by complete strangers.

What a bunch of bleeding heart human shit, the vampiress thought.

Something passed between Taylor and Emmaraud. Jimmy Rob had to give it to her. She could hook in a human male in about the same amount of time it took the Maserati to go from zero to sixty. Now, he'd have to do his part by helping Bubba-boy and his girlfriend get sufficiently soused.

Jimmy Rob popped the top on a cold can of beer and slid it across the bar to Joanie. For Taylor, a double shot of Jack Daniels. He refilled his and Emmaraud's shot glasses with the blood lager and raised one in a toast, "I say, we drink to mamas everywhere."

"Here, here!" The human couple said in unison. She took a huge noisy swill of beer. He knocked back the Jack Daniels.

Joanie reached across the bar and barely touched the still-sleeping Diente. The Chihuahua's bug-eyes popped open and she snarled.

Joanie snatched back her hand. "Oh my! I'm so sorry. I scared you, baby." To Emmaraud: "Dog's usually love me."

Emmaraud leaned down to the quivering dog and whispered in a low voice, *"no muerdos a los humanos, por favor."*

Jimmy Rob thought a moment, then came up with the Spanish to English translation: *don't bite the humans, please.* Live in Florida long enough and you pick up the second language of the state.

Then, the vampiress said to Joanie, "He's always a little irritable after we travel."

"That's too bad. I get a little carsick myself. We're not from around here either. Me'n Taylor's from down near Apopka. My step-daddy lives over just outside of Cross City, not far from here. Where'd you come in from?"

"I just got in from Alabama. Talladega. You know where that is?" Emmaraud asked.

Taylor slugged the remainder of the Jack Daniels and gladly accepted a refill from Jimmy Rob. "Shit yeah. Everyone knows where Talladega is. We go to the NASCAR race up there. That's one of the hottest races on the circuit."

Emmaraud leaned close to Taylor. "I love fast cars. All that raw power under the hood. All that…thrust."

At least that's not a lie, Jimmy Rob thought.

Emmaraud glanced across the room. "Looks like the pool table's free. Y'all wanna shoot a few?"

Joanie swung one hand through the air and almost lost her balance on the bar stool. "God, no. I just plainly suck at that game. Y'all go on. I'll sit here and nurse my beer."

"Least I can do since you're lettin' me borrow your man, is to pay for y'all's drinks." Emmaraud slipped her hand into the jean skirt's pocket, pulled out a wad of cash, and slapped it onto the bar in front of Jimmy Rob. "Keep 'em coming. My treat."

The vampiress spun around and swished toward the pool table, the shot glass of blood lager in hand. Taylor shrugged and followed after her.

She reels them in. I put 'em in the boat. Jimmy Rob sat a fresh cold beer in front of Joanie.

"She sure is a nice lady," Joanie commented. Her words tripped all over each other trying to make it past her thick tongue.

"Uh-huh."

Joanie studied Diente, once again sleeping soundly on the bar. "That little darlin' must be pure wore out. She surely sleeps a lot."

Jimmy Rob wiped the water rings from the bar. "Good thing. It's when she's awake you have to worry."

****

An hour later, the foursome stepped from the bar—the last revelers to leave. Jimmy Rob fastened the padlock on the door. He and Emmaraud exchanged knowing glances. *Party time.*

"Remember about the House Rule," Jimmy Rob said to Emmaraud in a low voice.

The vampire temptress rolled her eyes. "You are such a huge drag these days. We used to have such a blast together."

"Look." He grabbed her by one elbow and they dropped back a few steps from their new best friends. "You get to light out of here after all is said and done. I have to live with Vincent and his bitching. You know how he gets. No bodies. Drink some, but no bodies. Get it?"

"We'd better do this before they drive off." Emmaraud motioned to Taylor and Joanie. He was making an attempt to fit his key into the door of a used pick-up truck. She leaned down and puked.

"Nice." Emmaraud said. "I'm glad you get the one smelling of fresh vomit. I hate that. Maybe you should put her out of her misery."

"Never bothered me when I was human. Sure as shit won't bother me now. C'mon."

"Hey, y'all," Jimmy Rob called out. "Wait up!"

The drunk and unsuspecting couple didn't comprehend the speed of the woman and man coming toward them. In the darkness, they both felt the twin punctures on their necks, the orgasmic warmth that lasted for a few moments, and the overwhelming fatigue that followed.

A few hours later when they awakened, neither remembered why they were outside of a darkened backwoods bar in the middle of nowhere, Florida.

****

Reanita woke at two a.m. and held perfectly still as she took post-binge inventory. The room wasn't spinning. Her vision was clear. Nothing—including her head—hurt.

She flipped aside the sheets and sat up. No black twirlies. No dead-rat taste on her tongue. Nothing. Amazing.

She felt energized and ready to prowl. A deadline loomed: three more days on Dark Island. The agency would expect something in return for the healthy expenditure.

Reanita dug through the laundry bag and rescued a soiled pair of pants and T-shirt. If she was in her apartment back in D.C, she'd have plenty of ratty slug-through-the-swamp clothing. But that wouldn't fit her persona here. At least she could wear dirty designer pants. Seemed right.

No sounds came from the patrons' wing. Reanita tiptoed down the long hallway to the central staircase and descended to the first floor. She wondered where the new woman stayed. Though Vincent had finally snapped to life and introduced her as Emmaraud somebody—last name like an old car model—Studebaker? Pontiac? No, Bonneville. Weird. Even more bizarre, that she was a dead ringer for Paris Hilton, rat dog included.

Where to, tonight? She wondered. *A nice stroll through the spiders and snakes? Or would I prefer the gators? Tough call.*

When in doubt, one of her DEA buddies often said, follow your snout. A clever, rhyming way of admitting she hadn't the slightest clue how to proceed. Just move in some direction and hope she stumbled on something useful.

A few minutes later, she stood at the edge of a clearing.

"Haven't I been here before?" she wondered aloud.

Two tidbits stuck in the recesses of her brain: a big, snarky dog and some kind of spotlight. Useful information. What was going on with her memory? She shook her head to jump-start her sluggish brain. Had to be the alcohol and sugar.

Reanita followed the edge of the clearing and approached the dark dwelling from one side. She hunkered down behind a stack of some kind of bales and studied the property. Quiet, except for the ever-present slithering and scurrying noises in the woods around her. Almost too quiet.

Her nose picked up a scent. Again, familiar. She leaned close to one of the bales she had assumed to be hay. Hay, wrapped in burlap? They did things weird in the South, but that seemed a bit abnormal. Wouldn't burlap cause hay to rot in the humidity?

She slipped a small knife from her pocket, cut a short slit in the rough material, and teased out a piece of a stiff stem.

One sniff. *Shit! It's marijuana.*

Reanita's pulse accelerated. Thank God, she had finally stumbled on something.

Even a blind hog finds an acorn every now and then. Her father's drunken words echoed in her mind; ever the supportive parent, he was.

A set of powerful halogen headlights swept across the clearing and she hunkered down to avoid discovery. A sleek black sports car slid to a dusty halt within feet of her hiding spot. She heard a loud, slobbering bark.

"Shut up! Shut up, for the love of God!" A male voice snapped.

The sound of his words stirred Reanita. Her first impulse: jump and run to their source. White-hot desire. Fortunately her training kicked in, and she maintained position.

"One hell of a set of wheels there, babe."

Reanita dared to peek around one of the trussed bales. A man who had just spoken stood beside an exotic low-slung black convertible. A woman unfolded from the driver's seat—the Paris Hilton double, Emmaraud. The blonde reached inside the car and picked up the Chihuahua, cooed in its ear, and put it down on the grass. The little dog's huge ears perked up. Reanita froze. The damn rat dog was making a beeline in her direction.

Several things happened at once. A bright flood light popped on. A big, ugly mutt dog jumped from beneath the old battered Airstream trailer on cement blocks, spotted the Chihuahua, and lunged. The rat dog spun around, snarling and showing a nasty set of pointy teeth. Something about the little dog's attitude stopped the pit bull mix in mid-lunge. He sniffed the air. Whimpered. Tucked his stubby tail between his legs and dove beneath the end of the trailer.

Wow. Reanita shivered.

"Diente," Emmaraud cooed. "My poor *chica*."

The woman walked over and scooped the little dog into her arms before it could remember its original mission. Emmaraud continued to speak to the dog in what sounded like Spanish.

"What the hell kind of name is *Diente*, anyway?" the man asked.

"It is Spanish for *tooth*. Actually, her name is *Diente malo*. Means *bad tooth*."

The blonde tipped her head toward the man and they walked to a large shed behind the Airstream.

Reanita released the breath she had been holding. The tinny taste of fear lingered on her tongue.

She waited until the timed floodlight snapped off. She ducked behind a row of parked cars. Closer, she noted the distinctive scent of automotive decay: rust. Of the six car bodies, only two had windows and several were missing doors, hoods, and seats. A graveyard of sorts.

The sound of the woman's throaty laughter and the man's low moans wafted from the shed. Her neckline prickled again. Could the tiny erectile muscles at the base of her neck hairs get cramps, she wondered. If so, she was heading for a minefield of pain.

She halted and stared. The couple lay entwined on the hood of vehicle—one of the muscle cars that used to suck up pavement and fuel in unequal parts. Reanita didn't know how or when, but she was certain she had ridden in that car.

Emmaraud's long white neck arched as the man nibbled and crooned. Bile rose in Reanita's throat. She crammed her fist into her mouth to suppress a sob. The two took no note of her. She could stomp and scream, but their passion would continue to build.

A battle raged inside Reanita. The law enforcement officer, still on an adrenaline rush from finding the contraband, tried to trump the odd sensations of a broken-hearted, betrayed lover. What the hell was going on?

The jilted female won out. Reanita could watch no more. She turned and dashed madly into the high grass, with no regard for the slimy creatures that had concerned her earlier.

Chapter 15

Arby closed his eyes and sighed. At least he had two things to be thankful for: the party tents were in place and Emmaraud didn't seem to have brought any of her skanky vampire friends this time. The ratty canine had a bad case of little dog syndrome. It snarled at anyone who came within two feet and had already tried to attack Angelina's favorite feral cat. But at least it wasn't going to leave a wake of human bodies.

"What I really need is a decent night's sleep," he mumbled.

Tomorrow—Thursday—would be a frenetic day. The electricians would arrive with the generators and miles of wire. The executive bathroom trailers would be set into place. Tables and chairs delivered. Landscape and special lighting installed.

He would be as busy as a rat eating garbage after a county fair.

Sleep? Fat chance.

Every fiber in his body seemed to quiver. Someone could have easily squashed his last nerve, if he had a good one left. The last few days prior to a huge event were hectic enough, but with Emmaraud added in for a special treat, his pressure release valve was screaming. A few hours of rest would work—even a couple.

Maybe he could convince Vincent to hold off on the huge parties. Take a year off, with only the normal spa guests to worry over. A few weeks, perhaps, without spa patrons. A vacation. There was a thought. He hadn't had a break in five years, nor had Vincent. Did vampires take vacations? A mental image of his boss in a wife-beater tank top, weird flowery shorts and sandals with socks with a couple of cameras strung around his neck—the standard attire for a male Florida tourist—made him chuckle.

He walked toward the secret garden. A few stolen moments with his children might help. Their blended aromas often acted as a balm.

So far, everything had fit into place. Vincent had spent months vetting the vendors and suppliers. Most, they had worked with for many events. A few were new. Vincent took no chances and screened everyone involved. He spent hours interviewing caterers, reviewing the donor guest lists, making seating charts, tasting dishes and desserts for the menu, and sketching the design layout plans for the tents. He must have been phenomenal back in his human incarnation. Five years of intense practice since the Spa at Dark Island opened had kicked the party-planning vampire to the top tier of the Gold Medal platform. Though Arby carried out the daily details as Vincent's *gofer guy*, the overseer would never take credit for his boss's careful attention to minutiae. Nothing in Arby's experience compared. Even a scratch-and-spit divorce suit couldn't match the intensity of a Dark Island special event in the making.

As Arby stepped onto the pathway leading to the private greenhouse, a furtive movement caught his attention. He stopped. Listened. A shadow moved past. Couldn't be one of the gala workers. They all had to check in and out of the main gate to maintain security. The last of the trucks had left before the patrons' pool party.

He veered away from his route and followed the figure. When the person passed through a small pool of landscape lighting, Arby recognized her. Reanita.

Sleepwalking. She must be sleepwalking, he thought. No other explanation for it. Why would anyone roam the grounds in the dark, especially after many warnings? The sprained ankle should have been sufficient to make her take pause before further nocturnal wanderings.

It was bad to jolt a sleepwalker awake. He'd always heard that. Better to follow her, keep her safe from harm, and figure a way to gently guide her back to her suite without undue alarm.

Reanita continued on the main trail until it branched, then took the secondary path toward the far end of the island. She walked with purpose.

Where is she going? he wondered. It hit him. Jimmy Rob. *She is heading toward the redneck's lair. Jimmy Rob is using his powers to summon her!*

Not if he could help it.

Before he could intercede, Reanita crept across a clearing and hunkered down behind some kind of barrier to the south of Jimmy Rob's Airstream. The place appeared deserted. Arby released a breath. Okay, he was wrong. She had to be asleep. Maybe she had come by mistake. He stepped from the edge of the woods. A pair of bright head lights swept across his path, and he dove back into the shadows.

Arby witnessed the scene as if he watched an action flick from the front row. Jimmy Rob and Emmaraud exiting the car. The little dog sniffing toward Reanita. The mutt dog charging and retreating. Arby's first impulse: to dash across the high grass and rescue Reanita. Reason triumphed. What could he do, up against two vampires who were obviously in heat? They would rip him to rat ribbons.

Reanita held her ground. The immediate danger passed. Emmaraud and her redneck lover strolled to the shed, all over each other, the Chihuahua wiggling like a snared snake in the crook of one of Emmaraud's arms.

Arby released the breath he held. Now to intercept the sleepwalker. He stepped out again, only to witness his goddess pop up from her hiding place and trail behind the loving couple. He picked up his pace. Before he could reach the half-way point, Reanita dashed by, a few feet from him, heading in the direction of the mansion. As she passed, he heard the distinctive sound of a woman in pain; so distressed, she didn't notice him.

The overseer broke into a full-on run, took an overgrown pig-trail shortcut, and managed to make it to the mansion gardens a few minutes before she did. He calmed his breathing with an effort.

When she appeared, Arby walked into her path, saying her name in a gentle tone.

"Wha—?" Reanita frowned.

"You have been sleepwalking, my dear. Come. Let me help you back to your room."

She shook her head. Tears made zigzag lines down her cheeks. "No. No. I don't want to. I don't—"

"Let's walk then. I don't know what has you so upset, but I'll stay with you for awhile. Maybe a little stroll through the gardens will help you calm down."

****

Reanita fell into step with the funny little gardener guy. He spoke to her as if she was an injured child. She wasn't sure what he made of finding her wandering around, crying her eyes out, but she'd have to go along for a bit. She wracked her brain for some good reason for being out in the dark, again. No way would she reveal her secret to Mr. Beehive Man.

The overseer paused, seemed to be considering options.

"I have something you might find interesting." The little man motioned to a thick wall of some kind of tall stick-like plants.

Oh, for the love of Pete. Don't tell me this weird little guy is some kind of perve.

She decided to go along. No choice, really. He hadn't grilled her about her intentions yet. She was pretty sure she could take him out if he tried anything. Plus, it might provide an opportunity to gain his confidence. And possibly, find out the secrets of Dark Island.

Reanita snuffled. He handed her a linen handkerchief. As with the whole hand-kissing gesture, his offering struck her as terribly quaint and chivalrous.

She blew her nose. "Sure. Whatever."

He walked toward the thicket, then disappeared. Reanita frowned and stared. *What the hell?*

Arby stuck his hat-covered head out and motioned for her to follow. When she neared, she noticed the clever design of the vegetation cover. It reminded her of something she had seen in one of those tomb-robber action dramas—the appearance of a solid wall with a disguised opening only visible from a couple of steps away.

The blended odor of sulfurous compounds hit her as soon as she stepped through the cane break. "What is this place?"

"My secret garden." His voice came out reverent, as if he had stepped into the threshold of a cathedral.

Reanita wandered around the circle of plants. A blooming vine caught her attention and she leaned down to inspect one of the plate-sized lavender blossoms.

"Um...you might want to—" he said, too late.

She heard an odd gurgling noise. The flower quivered and spit. A wad of slime hit her on the cheek.

Arby froze. Waited for her to let loose with a string of profanity. Or scream.

Instead, Reanita laughed. "What kind of plant is this?"

"One of my special hybrids. *Mousezilla Passionata.* I call it a Spitting Lily."

She wiped the foul gel from her cheek with the handkerchief. "That is so cool!"

"Really?"

"God, yes. It's like—well, you know how a cheerleader is? All in-your-face pretty and no one can touch her because she's popular and so un-freaking-believably perfect?"

"Yes." Arby understood.

"This flower is so pretty. And to be able to do something so disgusting—it's like finding a wart on the head cheerleader, you know?"

His heart rate accelerated. "If you like that, I have another you might enjoy."

He led Reanita to the private greenhouse. She stepped inside. Her gaze wandered around the room, taking in the colors and shapes of the hybrids, his babies.

"This place stinks." She wrinkled her nose.

His spirit sagged. Too good to be true. She hated it. "All of my blooms have unusual scents."

When she looked at him, he was shocked at the unmasked awe on her face. "You did this?"

He nodded. "My specialty. Exotic hybrids. It takes a particular kind of gardener to appreciate their uniqueness. Not many do."

A camellia bloom caught her attention. She walked over, bent down and studied the flower for a moment. Strange: she felt as if she looked in a mirror. The pointed bud. The whiskers. The little stamens like beady yellow eyes. "This one...this one is so amazing. It's like the others. Beautiful, but with a weird, stinky edge. I love it!"

Arby's face flushed. No one really understood. Not like this. Vincent tolerated his hobby. Encouraged it. Unconditionally. Like a parent with a strange child whom he loved, anyway.

But Arby's goddess—the object of his every desire—got it.

"You asked me if I ever took off my hat," he said.

The tone of his voice—soft and whispery—caused Reanita to turn her attention from the remarkable bloom.

"Yeah?"

"Do you know what I named that particular camellia?"

She shook her head.

"*Reanita Japonica.*"

She tilted her head and smiled. "Oh?"

Arby reached up and removed the beekeeper's hat.

****

A print-out of the site plan in hand, Vincent confirmed the location and orientation of the tents. He walked into the twenty-by-twenty entrance tent and gave it the once-over. The enclosures were in a raw state now, more like a plain painter's canvas on an easel. The frills and embellishments that would transform them into true art would come soon.

He moved to the main tent and his gaze searched overhead. The material was taut, no holes. Arby had confirmed that fact during the daylight hours when the small openings would be easier to detect. He inspected the walls: no footprints or smudges. Any small imperfections, Lars and his crew would smooth out with strategically-placed lighting equipment and theatrical flourishes.

Vincent searched the ground for ant beds, turtle nesting holes, and depressions: a necessary task before the installation of temporary flooring and carpeting. Nothing would be worse than a guest covered in the biting fire ants so prevalent in the South.

He dictated into a digital recording device. "Check with Lars to make sure there is a solid tent wall on each side of this exit, as noted on his event sheet."

He left the main tent and headed to the kitchen *prep* tent. The forty-by-forty foot room stood ready for its transformation into a full working food preparation area. It flowed into an adjunct tent, one used for plating the food. Both enclosures had the proper solid walls to shield the guests from viewing the staff.

Next on his checklist: the marquee tented hallways which would guide the party attendees to the executive bathroom trailers. The washrooms would be delivered and set into place in the following days.

Every gala became more of a challenge. Not like in the old days when a little clever presentation and exotic appetizers sufficed. Today's jaded crowd—especially the well-healed jet-setters—expected to be astounded and amazed. In the age of special digital effects and holographic imaging, simple tricks would not provide the proper level of titillation. Vincent and Lars had to invent ways to catch their eyes. So far, the party-planning team did not disappoint. Sometimes at the eleventh hour an idea would pop into his or Lars' mind and they would scurry to make their vision a reality.

Unlike Arby, Vincent required no sleep. Yet another vampire myth. Vamps did not actually slumber. They slipped into a suspended state for as little as fifteen minutes or as long as decades. Most did so to stave off boredom. Vincent rarely closed his eyes for longer than five minutes. Too many interesting diversions! Languages to learn! Internet sites and chat rooms to stumble upon! Movies to watch! The ever-changing landscape and gardens!

His innate insomnia came in handy in the weeks and days prior to a Dark Island gala. No single human could master all of the countless details. He could, and relished it. As soon as a party passed into history, the next event loomed. Between sipping vintage blood wine, catering to spa patrons, puffing smuggled Cuban cigars, and trying to soak up life on the planet from his sanctuary on Dark Island, Vincent managed to continually plan one bash after the next. He had no clue as to how much money the charity events had gathered over the years: probably in the triple digit millions. He never stopped long enough to tally the figures.

Emmaraud's surprise visit threatened to divert his attention. He squelched the worries. When he was in full *party-rama* mode, details could not fall by the wayside. He had only one shot at a big event like the annual Blue Blood Ball. Screw it up, and the deep-pocketed contributors wouldn't return with their checkbooks in hand. People could drop dead beside him. A comet could strike the Island. Giant roaches could stalk the gardens. Even a whacked-out female could appear with a dog she had managed to turn into a vampire. The planning had to go on.

The stallion had been delivered earlier in the day. Vincent took one last look at the gala grounds and walked in the direction of the improvised corral located behind Arby's private garden area. Many animals regarded vampires with suspicion, especially horses. By the time he galloped to the entrance of the gala on Saturday evening, the steed would be accustomed to his odd chemistry. The preternatural magnetism worked on large animals; it just took a little longer to convince them than their human cousins.

From one of the closed-circuit security monitors, Vincent had watched the magnificent steed as the handlers unloaded him, skittish and high-strung, prancing and rearing, even after he was released into the corral. His coat had been brushed to a high, glossy sheen. Black as a moonless night. Mane and tail combed. The perfect vampire accessory. Vincent was in love.

As soon as he passed close to the private greenhouse, Vincent's ears picked up a weird keeling like some kind of vermin in pain. He stopped to tune in to the sound. A second noise joined the first. A series of high, guttural moans punctuated by high-pitched squeaks.

A realization dawned on Vincent. *Rat sex.*

"Oh, Sweet Jesus wept," he said to himself.

Vincent spun around and hurried toward the mansion. The equine bonding sessions would have to wait a couple of hours. The only place he could hide—the sound-proof room. He'd turn on something loud with a thumping base—maybe rap, though he generally steered clear of urban music. Anything to cover the sound of his overseer and the only person on-Island capable of making the accompanying unpleasant noise—Reanita Register.

Had he trained his hearing to the other end of the island, he would have picked up on the carnal screams of two other lovers. Luckily, he had too much on his mind to tune in.

Arby: the perfect, well-paid, loyal employee. And friend. Cut-throat attorney, handy for any of the infrequent run-ins with the state environmental protection guardians. Gourmet cook. Skilled nurse and phlebotomist. Wonderful manager.

Vincent placed few restrictions on his overseer, other than the code of silence.

In the five years since Arby had come to Dark Island, he had revived its overgrown gardens and masterminded the idea of a profitable spa, Vincent had never known of any sexual dalliances. Couldn't imagine any woman willing to attempt such.

"Good for you, my man," he said.

A wave of melancholia soaked through his cool demeanor, a longing for the touch of a lover. He reached the mansion's back entrance, listened once more to the bizarre noises coming from the gardens, and shook his head.

Tomorrow, he would politely ask his overseer if he might consider curtailing his new pastime to the daylight hours, well after the vampire was safely ensconced behind a mostly-soundproof barrier.

Chapter 16

Thursday: Morning

"Just look at this closet!" Emmaraud swept one hand down the long row of silk smoking jackets and they rocked on their velvet-flocked hangers. "Sweet Son of Lucifer, Vincent. You never change!"

Having Emmaraud Bonneville as his blood relative was not unlike entertaining a fussy mother for all eternity. One who showed up unannounced with the white gloves stuffed in her designer purse. Anxious to rearrange his life. Ready to remake him into her image of the perfect son. She never failed to remark on his attire—this, from a woman whose latest boyfriend's idea of fashion was a flannel shirt with the arms ripped out.

He'd rather drink blood from a rabid crocodile than spend one moment alone with her.

"I don't see anything wrong with—"

She spun around and faced him. Her delicate nostrils flared. "Nothing wrong? Nothing wrong!" Emmaraud sucked in enough air to deplete the Western Hemisphere and blew it out. "You're stuck in the '50s, Vincent. No...cemented and shellacked in the '50s—that would be a better way to put it. At least get some blue jeans, some fun clothing. I could take you shopping in New York. We could shift right now and be back before noon. I know designers on a first-name basis who would love to fit you for anything other than a smoking jacket."

"Why do I need all of that? I'm perfectly comfortable."

She huffed. "Style is not about comfort, Vincent. Never has been. Never will be."

"Is that why you're so irritable all the time, then?"

"Don't push me, Vincent. I've had a long night."

He smiled and nodded. "What's the matter? Did your pet redneck wear you out? You must be loosing your edge."

She frowned. Took a handful of hangers and cast them on the floor, as she did every time she came to the Dark. No doubt she would attack his underwear drawer next.

"No, I'm not losing my edge." She propped her hands on her hips. "It's Diente. Long distance shifting has such a negative effect on her."

Vincent rolled his eyes. "So it seems. Angelina—the baker who comes in during the morning—is still upset. Your damned little dog tried to maul her favorite feral cat. What were you thinking, Emmaraud, turning a poor defenseless dog?"

She sighed. "I get so attached. Then they die. None of them live long enough. I couldn't bear the thought of loosing Diente—she is *so* like me—I turned her."

"Not really fair. Turned animals never adjust."

"I know. They go a little wacky after a few decades. Still, I'll have her longer than I would otherwise."

"All about you, isn't it?" Vincent said.

She flashed a wicked grin. "Damn straight."

"Still, I would ask that you find a way to keep your little spoiled darling from annoying anyone—animal or human—while you're here."

"I'll talk to her. She doesn't listen very well. Kind of has a mind of her own."

Not unlike her owner, he thought.

She walked over and pulled out several drawers in a tall cherry wood armoire. "Don't worry, Vincent. Even if she does accidentally nick someone, she doesn't have the ability to create. She's just hungry."

"I'm hungry, too. You don't see me chasing down everything with veins."

She ignored him and grabbed a handful of intimate apparel. "Boxers? You still wear white cotton boxers, even after our previous discussions?"

He snatched the men's undergarments from her hand, shoved them back into the drawer, and closed the armoire door. "Leave my privates out of this. You wear your—whatever, butt-floss things—all you wish."

"But boxers? They're so far out they're back in! At least go with those stretchy kind…they're kind of sexy."

"Why bother? No one sees them anyway."

She tapped her chin. "When will you get over that Cuban loser, huh? We need to hook you up with a vamp boyfriend. I could bring—"

Vincent felt the familiar rage bubble inside. The reference to Julio, calculated. If he allowed, their little mother-son chat would turn into a shouting match. Emmaraud lived for it, and he'd be damned if he bought a ticket.

Vincent held up both hands. "No. Absolutely not. I forbid it. I've met some of your so-called friends. I wouldn't touch them with a ten-foot fang."

"You are such an old queen, Vincent. I don't know what I ever saw in you in the first place."

Time to change the subject. Reroute. Vincent asked, "So, why have you graced us with a visit this time? Run out of playthings across the Big Pond?"

The vampiress ignored his question, walked across the room, and threw herself onto the chaise lounge. Such a drama queen. She picked up a glossy pamphlet—one advertising a huge auction of Hollywood paraphernalia—and studied it.

"What's this?" Emmaraud asked.

"One of the studios is selling off old movie props, costumes and such. I might pick up a few items for future galas."

She looked closer. "Wow. Get a load of this. They supposedly have a replica of Cleopatra's golden chair. I knew her. She never had a chair like that."

"Back to why you decided to pop in—?"

"Actually, I'm here on business."

His eyebrow cocked. "Business? Since when does anything remotely resembling work interest you?"

She ignored the jab. "I'm thinking of converting my villas in the South of France and Spain into spas, like this one. Turn a little profit. I already have a name for the one in Spain—*El Balneario en la Villa Oscura*—The Spa at Dark Villa. Nice ring, don't you think?"

White rage seared his spirit. He closed his eyes briefly, willing the barrage of words waiting to spill forth. How could she dream of imitating his careful work? Make a mockery of his good intentions at The Dark? Use his and Arby's vision to suck life from patrons with nothing given in return? Vincent couldn't see his blood sire going out of her way to help a human, and Lucifer forbid what her blood distillate would do! Overt interference never worked with Emmaraud. Best to hang back and find subtle ways to reroute her Titanic.

"You, run a spa?" Vincent forced a laugh. "You have no clue how to go about it, Emmaraud. It is a lot of work, not all play and parties. If it wasn't for Arby, I would have a struggle. It was his idea to start with. Before we met, I was just a hermit vampire living in a run-down monstrosity of a house; one you used to like and take care of, before you lost interest and moved on."

"So I'll hire someone to manage them. Arby will share his secrets with me. I'm sure. No problem finding someone like your little rat boy to do my bidding. Not like money is an issue. Plenty of humans would jump for the chance. The world economy is in one of its little downturns."

"Ditch the comments about Arby, Emmaraud. You know I hate it when you rag on him. Besides, I can't believe you're even mentioning the world's economic concerns. What, have you been watching CNN?"

She shifted the pillows behind her back. "I do live in the world, Vincent."

"Your world." He slipped off his smoking jacket. "A bit removed from the real world of poverty, war, and pestilence." He cocked his head. "Well, you might fit in with the pestilence part of things."

The vampiress stepped close and caressed his check with one hand. The touch, icy as his own; a glacier meeting packed snow. "Must we bicker? My time with you is often short."

Hardly short enough. "Okay. Truce."

From the queen of adversity to concerned, estranged parent. Emmaraud could shift emotional gears without losing a lap.

A soft rap sounded at the suite door. Vincent turned to the sound. "Now, if you will excuse me, Emmaraud. I have my morning massage with Raven. And I really need it today."

She gathered herself and stood. "I have plans, too. Your esthetician is giving me one of those delightful sea salt rubs. Exfoliates dead skin, you know."

"Have a good time, dear. Don't let her take all of your dead skin. You'll end up a skeleton."

"Funny, Vincent. Very funny."

She opened the door and passed by the massage therapist. "Give him all you've got today, hon. He is in a positively ghastly mood."

****

The massage followed by a session in the special tanning bed worked its usual magic. The Master of Dark Island emerged relaxed, renewed, and as bronzed as the skin on a Thanksgiving turkey.

"Today is the first day of the rest of my eternal life," Vincent intoned his mantra. "I am good. I am happy. I am worthy. I like myself."

Too bad the whole late '80s self-help notion of daily affirmations seemed to have faded from popularity. Vampires needed all the positive support they could get. Especially when he would have to deal with his blood sire later, on a sensitive issue Raven had brought to his attention. Tangling with Emmaraud Bonneville twice in one morning. He didn't know if there were enough affirmations on the planet to help him.

Vincent pulled up the Blue Blood Ball file on the computer, poured a tall glass of synthetic blood wine, and sat down to review the day's activities. The checklist popped up. Today, the lighting and electrical units would be installed. His other tasks: call the caterers, check in with the deputy sheriffs who would be controlling traffic on the main road, make sure the batteries were fully charged on the Dark Island transportation carts used to shuttle the party attendees from the parking area off-Island to the entrance tent.

His private in-house phone chimed. Barbie. "Sir, the production company folks have arrived. Lars just stopped by the desk, asking for Arby. I can't seem to raise him on the walkie-talkie."

He heard his receptionist sigh.

"And there is this little horror of a dog running around here. Lars had to side-step the thing just to get to my desk."

Vincent took a deep breath. *One crisis at a time.* "I have a pretty good idea where to locate Arby. Tell Lars I'll send him to the south lawn. As to Diente; just be watchful of your ankles."

After he hung up, he dialed the private number to the caretaker's inner sanctum.

In the greenhouse, Arby woke to the sound of buzzing. For a moment, he thought a massive mosquito had somehow managed to brave his floral barriers. He looked over at Reanita—still wrapped in his overall, asleep on a make-shift pallet on the greenhouse floor.

He checked his watch. "Oh shit!"

Had he been Thomas, he might have said *oh, bloody hell!*

He picked up the wireless headset.

A smooth deep voice said, "Good morning, Arby."

"Sir."

Vincent said, "Lars is here with the electrical crew."

"Um…yeah. I…I guess I lost track of the time. So very sorry, Sir."

"Are you unwell, Arby?" he asked, amused.

The caretaker glanced down at the sleeping goddess. *Very well. Deliriously happy. Satiated. A little wiped out.* "No Sir. I'm fine. I must've overslept. All the gala planning, you know. Must've been pretty tired."

"Had to have been it. You are usually so punctual."

Arby searched for his underwear and held the phone to his ear with his shoulder as he hopped around on one foot, trying to dress. "I'll leave for the south lawn right away."

"Very good. Call me if you run into any unforeseen problems."

"Yes Sir."

"Oh, and Arby?"

"Sir?"

"My regards to Miss Register."

Busted, Arby thought. How did Vincent do that? He returned the wireless unit to its charging base and crouched down to tease his overall from Reanita's grasp. No time to dash to his suite for fresh clothes.

She opened her eyes, blinked, smiled, and stretched. "Um…what?"

He bent over and kissed her on the forehead. "I have to go to work now, my love. Stay as long as you like."

She sat up and pushed the hair from her eyes. "What time is it?"

"A tad before eight."

Reanita jumped up and searched for her clothes. "I have a massage at nine!"

Arby held her shoulders in a gentle grasp. "Relax. You have plenty of time to shower and grab a little breakfast. You've missed the morning walk, however."

She slipped on her underwear. "Oh, how sad."

Arby pulled Reanita to him and kissed her.

"When can I see you?" she asked.

The overseer sighed. "I'll be tied up till late this evening, and the next couple of days are going to be hectic."

Reanita's gaze fell to the earthen floor. "I see. No problem. I get it."

"No, no! I don't mean that as a put-off. Really. It's the gala. My schedule is crammed with details right now. But, I'll make time." He thought a moment. "Tonight, after dinner—let's see, let's make it eight o'clock. Meet me at the mansion's back door."

She smiled. "Okay."

"I have something to show you. I think you'll like it."

Reanita's chest constricted and her heart rate increased. Weird, how the man affected her, already.

****

The concept of reality television shows baffled Vincent. Humans needed to be inspired, lifted up, shown the value of true love and compassion. How would pitting them against each other and training cameras on their every move be of any lasting social benefit?

Yet, he was addicted to *Big Brother*, a reality show where a clan of people—mostly young—were cooped up in a house and forced to compete for a money prize. Juvenile. Juvenile. Juvenile. And he couldn't wait for each new season to begin.

The last episode waited on the master system, stored in its special digital home until he wished to view it. Nothing like a little mindless television to escape from party planning for a few moments. He used the Crestron control, hit the power button, waited a few minutes for the screen and projector to ready, then he punched the corresponding icon to access the stored show.

Time for the next task: sampling the recent vintage for Patrice Palmer. The looming gala shouldn't eclipse his normal spa duties.

Vincent took a sip. Frowned. Took another. A definitive blood protein stung the taste buds on the sides of his sensitive tongue; a singular protein, present only in females. One that he had only sampled a couple of times in the past five years.

"Is this the source of your dismay, Miss Palmer?" he said aloud.

The blood didn't lie. Patrice Palmer was pregnant.

Chapter 17

Vincent paused at the door to Emmaraud's suite. The sound of her raised voice—an irritated squawk—made him want to turn tail and dive back into his soundproofed media center.

He tapped twice and heard her yell, "Come in!"

After opening the door a slight crack, he asked, "Is it safe?"

Emmaraud stood by the queen-sized bed, glaring down at Diente. "Don't go there, Vincent. We're not having a good morning."

The Master of Dark Island stepped through the threshold and stared, open-mouthed, at the mound of clothing scattered like dead leaves across the bed and hardwood floor. On closer inspection, he realized the outfits were miniature.

"What gives?"

She snorted. "I can't get her majesty here—" she jabbed a finger toward the Chihuahua, who had curled up on a small antique-white canopied canine bed beneath a pink Sherpa suede blanket. "—to agree to an outfit."

At least he wasn't the only one to fall beneath Emmaraud's glaring fashionista's eyes. "What—tan fur isn't enough cover for the well-heeled, excuse the pun, rat dog?"

"Funny. Very funny." She picked up a denim skirt and lime green tank top—both doll-sized—and the four coordinating bootie shoes. "What about this, *Madre del niña pequeño problema?*"

Vincent silently translated, *Mama's little problem child.*

The little dog snarled and barked once.

"No? No!" She pitched the outfit and foot covers onto a growing pile of rejected clothing. "You can't show up tonight without a cute little outfit, Diente. I can forgive you not wanting to dress up so soon after shifting from Spain. Travel upsets you. But not this evening."

Vincent sat down on a high-backed chair. This scene beat reality TV to heck and back. "What's up this evening that requires proper canine couture?"

"Fish fry at J.R.'s Joint. Big deal, according to the owner. I wanted us to match—had the outfits all picked out and Maria ironed them—now, this."

"You had one of my staff iron dog clothes?" Vincent glanced from his blood sire to the petulant little dog.

"Diente would never show up in wrinkles, Vincent. Of course I had them ironed."

Vincent actually felt an odd kinship with the irritable Chihuahua. "I could loan her one of my smoking jackets."

"I am teetering on the edge, Vincent. The edge."

"I'm sure you and Diente can find something suitable to wear to a redneck event. Just rip up an old white T-shirt, drag it in the dirt, and wrap it around her. She'll still be overdressed."

She frowned. "Right. I'll do that."

"Where did you find all of—" he swept his hand through the air, "—this?"

"You really do live a sheltered life, Vincent. Canine attire is quite the rage. Actually, all of these are from Paris Hilton's new line by Little Lily."

"Paris Hilton designs dog clothes? Fitting, given your latest incarnation."

"Isn't it? I have had the most fun outfitting my little darling. Normally she adores this. Must be the infernal heat and humidity here. It has her positively cross."

Vincent remembered the reason behind his visit. "Speaking of cross...Raven brought an incident to my attention, earlier this morning."

Emmaraud picked up a fuzzy chew toy—designed to look like a Louis Vuitton bag—and offered it to Diente. The little dog sniffed and ignored the peace offering.

"Seems your precious pup took a nip of Raven's little daughter Christina last night," Vincent said.

Emmaraud frowned and swiped a hand through the air. "It was nothing."

"Raven and Hector—the child's father—were quite upset."

"Oh, Hades forbid! I can't see the problem, Vincent. The child was bothering Diente. She nipped her out of self-defense."

"The child is a toddler. Sweet-natured and gentle. How, pray tell, did she manage to offend a vampire Chihuahua? Hmm?"

"She tried to pet Diente. Twice."

Vincent couldn't keep the sarcasm from his voice. "Ah, yes. I could see where that might greatly upset a dog."

"I let Diente run a little, before we went to catch up with Jimmy Rob. She tends to get a little rambunctious after travel. I finally found her back behind the mansion, near the staff houses. I guess the child found her first."

"That late?"

Surely, Raven would've put the child to bed by then. Was Christina still teething? Humans tended to be cross when they cut their teeth. Maybe Raven had taken her outside to calm her down? Made no sense, but a lot of things parents did to satisfy their young made no sense. He had heard stories of fathers and mothers riding their children around aimlessly in mini-vans in the wee hours, just to get them to sleep.

The vampiress shrugged. "Whatever. So Diente bit the kid. Drew a little blood. Maybe she should learn not to pet strange animals."

"I must insist that you keep Diente on a leash. No more mishaps."

Emmaraud scowled.

"It is not enough that I have to monitor your vampire friends every time you drag them along to the Island? Now, I have to ride herd over a dog the size of a box of tissues?"

"Don't be cruel, Vincent. It's not your style."

"Maybe you're rubbing off on me."

She picked up a small mesh bag and corralled several dog toys. From the looks of it, his blood sire had spent hundreds. "You should be so lucky. Maybe it would get you out of those boring smoking jackets."

****

Arby took one last look across the south lawn. Two executive restrooms—Lars and his crew called them *honey wagons*—stood in place, lighting installed, generators hooked up, special flooring installed. Everything on Vincent's list was checked and double-checked. The tables and chairs had been delivered and stacked, awaiting placement; the black and white parquet tile dance floor had been installed. Wires were either buried or covered. His ground crew had added last-minute touches to the landscaping. Lars followed behind, installing temporary outdoor lighting.

He wondered why the Master of Dark Island still found the written spreadsheets necessary. After so many successful events, Arby could ferret out problems with little to no prompting. No matter. He didn't take any of it personally. Arby understood attention to detail.

He waved to Lars. The last of the delivery trucks had long since trundled away. The production manager stayed behind to perform his own set of inspections. He was pickier than Vincent—the reason both Arby and Vincent always hired PSG for any large event.

Arby jumped onto a golf cart and hustled to the mansion. He still had the normal spa duties. A special dessert for the patrons' evening meal. A conference with Stefanie with an *f*'s husband Scottie about the continuing rabbit problems in the vegetable garden. Distillate injections—luckily, Raven had been gracious about rescheduling the massage appointments for later in the day. He had jumped back and forth between the south lawn and the mansion all afternoon. Some days, he felt as if he changed roles so often, he suffered from multiple personalities. At least he wasn't bored.

He glanced at a Crape Myrtle branch as he passed by and stopped dead when he realized what he had seen.

"No!"

He wheeled around and grabbed the drooping limb, almost tipping over the golf cart. Curled vegetation, turning brown around the edges. He flipped one of the leaves over and studied the backside with a frown. Miniscule white dots clumped together like cooked orzo pasta.

"Blast!"

The aphids had returned. Or, they had never left. Little buggers. Of all the insect infestations, aphids proved the worst to remedy. Pesticides didn't seem to be effective long enough to justify their impact on the environment. Neem Oil worked, but had to be applied in the very early morning to avoid poisoning the bees. The best solution the gardener had come up with after weeks of trial and error: spraying diluted biodegradable dish soap on the affected trees and shrubs. The process had to be repeated often, as only one or two live aphids were all it took to start a new infestation. Next spring, he planned to release ladybugs, a natural predator of the annoying pests; suggested by some of his online gardener chat room friends. Until then, the battle was on to salvage what remained of the Crape Myrtle's blooming season.

He'd have the staff look around for nearby ant hills, and destroy them. Ants loved the sticky goop—the honeydew—excreted by the aphids, and would *nurse* any fallen eggs up the tree and back onto the leaves. Symbiotic relationships fascinated him—rattlesnakes sharing boroughs with gopher turtles, a rat-faced man and a vampire sharing a patchwork life—but this was one he could live without.

A basic fact Arby understood about nature: he could not defeat it, only slightly alter its course in his favor. A beautiful bloom, a plump red tomato, the tender leaves on his banana pepper plants: if he loved it or it tasted good to him, other agents of destruction would covet it, too. His hybrids, though, would teach the little shits. The repulsive scents would send them scurrying off to the other plants that didn't benefit from his forced evolutional traits.

He could no more rid the garden of ants than he could of aphids. Best bet was to keep them both on the run. Without his constant supervision, the Dark Island grounds would return to the same wild and neglected state as when he first came.

Arby grabbed a small digital recorder from the coverall's pocket and dictated a quick reminder.

"Don't forget to spray the Myrtles for bugs," he said in a calm voice.

The afterglow of love gone rat-wild insulated him from the normal state of high rolling boil he assumed prior to a Dark Island gala. Nothing—not even an aphid infestation—could touch him.

Nothing, he thought with a smile, *except a certain heiress.*

****

Arby stood over Reanita's sleeping form. Weariness seeped through his body like spilled blood. The low lighting and ambiance of the massage room washed over him. If only he could crawl onto the table with Reanita, curl into her arms, and rest.

The caretaker forced himself not to think about their lovemaking as he gently injected the final dose of distillate. He didn't bother to open his supply satchel for the blood collection supplies. Who was he kidding? He could not bring himself to take anything from her. Vincent had a backlog of vintage and a freezer full of synthetic blood. Fresh Cuban supplies would be delivered in a few days.

Vincent did not require Reanita.

Arby did.

Just three more days—a string of precious hours—before Reanita Register walked from his life forever.

He daydreamed. The two of them would amble into her parents' grand home, holding hands. *Father, mother,* she would say, *this is Arby, my fiancé.* The father would shake his hand; the mother would give him a welcoming hug. They would sit down to drinks, a gourmet dinner served on fine china. Champagne in crystal flutes. *Have you set a date, dear?* the mother would ask. Reanita would look at him with such unmasked love; his heart would feel near to bursting. *Soon, Mother. We don't want to wait.*

Arby's attention snapped back to reality. Like any of that could ever happen. Even if Reanita somehow wanted him in her life after Dark Island, the scene would never play out that way. Her parents would take one look at his rat-boy face and scramble for words. It was one thing to have a daughter with unusual features—she was their daughter!—but to entertain the idea of someone like Arby as a son-in-law and father to their grandchildren? No way.

Might as well face it. After Sunday, the too-brief and sweet affair with Reanita Register would live only in his memory. And his heart.

Chapter 18

Thursday evening

Vincent heard the ragged female sobs as soon as he opened the door leading from his private suite. He tilted his head to hone in on the direction and source. First floor. Patrice Palmer. He listened for a moment longer. The atrium.

"Drama. Drama. Drama," he muttered. "So much of the human experience is Drama. Drama. Drama."

His inner gay event-planner voice chided, "but you live for it, don't you Vincent?"

He often thought of writing a script for a vampiric dark soap opera. He even had a title picked out: *Evenings on Dark Island.*

He located the starlet curled into a fetal position on one of the cushioned lounges.

"Miss Patrice?" he said in a low, gentle voice. "Might I help you in some way?"

She unwound a couple of notches and scraped several damp strands of hair from her face. A line of mucus trailed from both nostrils. Eyes rimmed in bright red. Blotchy skin. Swollen lips. This, Vincent thought, was a woman who, when she cried, released herself into the role with wicked abandon.

"Oh." She looked around the room as if she had only just noticed how disheveled she might appear—so un-starlet-like.

Vincent pulled a clean linen handkerchief from his jacket pocket. She took it, blew her nose in one wet burst, and dabbed the tear tracks beneath her eyes.

"Thanks."

"You are most welcome."

His thoughts moved to his fix-all for female maladies. Sometimes, the cure for raw emotion rested in simplicity. Vincent had witnessed several meltdowns in the five years since the Spa at Dark Island first opened its ornate iron gates. Most responded to the comfort provided by a warm drink—coffee or tea—and a little kind conversation.

"I was just going to fix myself a cup of tea. Would you care to join me?"

Patrice sniffed. "Sure—but herbal, okay?"

Vincent noted the way one of her hands moved instinctively to cradle her stomach.

"Very good then."

In a few minutes, he returned with a silver tray laden with two china cups and saucers, a pot of chamomile tea, a small decanter of his blood brew and the accruements.

"Honey? Raw sugar? Milk? Lemon?" he asked.

She snuffled. "Just a little sugar."

The civilized act of decanting the hot tea—Vincent had studied the technique in detail on countless old films—seemed to lull Patrice into a greater sense of calm. She accepted the filled cup with a slight smile.

"Thanks."

"My pleasure." He settled down opposite the starlet on a rattan chair and took an appreciative sip of the blood brew.

"You must think I'm a freaking mess," she said.

"Life can be a bit messy at times. I suppose yours is no exception."

She scowled. "Men are such pigs!" Then, "Oh...sorry. That was..."

"No offense taken, my dear. I agree wholeheartedly. Men can be pigs."

She took a sip of tea. "I feel so sorry for Julia."

Vincent's eyebrow shot up. This was unexpected. Patrice Palmer worried about someone—anyone—else? Plus, he figured her outburst had been related to the blood vintage's recent revelation.

He waited. Given a little silence and a bit of patience, Patrice Palmer would reveal.

She balled up a fist and shook it in the air. "That scum sucker of a husband of her's. What a slime ball!"

"Oh—politicians can be—"

She interrupted. "Do you know what he did?"

Vincent filed through the Senator's recent alleged dealings. Graft? Corruption? Money laundering? Special interest pandering? Hard to pick just one. The list seemed endless. "I don't know if I—"

"He emailed her. Told her he had been caught in some high-rent hotel with this woman who works with his re-election campaign. The tramp had gotten mad about something and gone to the press about him and his advances. Accused him of sleeping with her—and she may be pregnant. Oh, God! What a mess!"

Vincent frowned. "My. My."

"Yeah. And he's planning this big ole press conference thingy so he can, like, publicly apologize, or serve up some line of garbage. They all do that lately. Have you noticed?"

She sat up and blew her nose again. "Jee-zus! Like, it makes it perfectly okay. Like, I'm so sorry and please forgive me and I love my wife and she's behind me all the way. What a load of crap!"

Vincent nodded. No way was he stepping in front of this steamroller.

"Now Julia has to be all, like, I love you and forgive you and poor baby, you've been under so much pressure." Her eyes flashed. "He's coming to the gala on Saturday night, you know. Making this huge, like, show of coming to be with his loving wife."

Vincent wondered if Patrice could talk without the word *like*. Could be somewhat interesting, he thought. Julia, her new lover and reticent husband all trussed up in designer clothes, shooting eye-daggers at each other over gator tail and champagne.

"I see," he said.

"Why does it all get so screwed up, Vincent? What happened to the whole love- one-person-for-your-whole-life and raise-a-family and happily-forever-after?"

He shrugged and took a sip of blood brew. Even given eternity to dissect human behavior, he was often mystified. "I assume Julia spoke with you at length about this problem, then?"

Patrice nodded. "I bumped into her coming out of the patrons' media room. She was pretty torn up."

"Where is she now? With Thomas?"

"Nope. She didn't want to see him, or any man. We talked, she calmed down a little, and then she went up to bed."

"Oh." Vincent ditched the idea of offering another cup of tea and consolation to the senator's wife. He was a vampire, but still a man.

Patrice added, almost as an afterthought, "and I'm pregnant."

Nice segue, he thought. *Never saw it coming.* "Congratulations."

He studied the glamour surrounding the starlet. Waves of maternal concern bubbled around her and swirled in iridescent spirals toward her stomach. Her unborn child: Already cherished, whether she knew it on a conscious level or not.

"Yeah. Thanks." She sipped her tea, pensive for a moment. He waited.

"What'll I do, Vincent?"

"What does your heart tell you?" He felt proud of the question; a sort of non-answer and perfect reply. Very Hollywood. Would've sounded great in a made-for-TV movie.

"I want the baby. I think." She breathed in and out. "Shit. My career will go down the toilet."

Vincent considered. "You could always say you're entering rehab. The tabloids love that sort of thing. Come here—come to Dark Island. You can lay low until after the baby arrives."

"Here? Stay here?" She tilted her head. "I could do that? You'd let me do that?" Her features switched from hopeful to helpless. "I don't think I can afford—"

Vincent rested a hand on her shoulder. "Don't concern yourself about the money. We can work something out."

"Why would you do that for me?" She narrowed her eyes. "Wait a minute. You're not one of those holy-rolly pro-lifer's, are you? You're trying to make me keep this baby. That's it, isn't it?"

Vincent sat, stunned. "No. No. Not at all. You have every right to make your decision. I am not attempting to influence you, Patrice. Merely to provide an alternative should you need sanctuary."

"Oh." Fresh tears formed in her eyes. "Thanks. You're really a great guy. I wish more men were like you." She paused, then asked. "Why haven't you ever hit on me? You gay or something?"

He smiled. "Or something."

She slapped one knee with her hand. "I knew it!" She jumped up and hugged him. "This is fantastic! I have always wanted a gay best friend."

Vincent had heard that line from another female over fifty years prior. At least this one wasn't going to bite him and drag him off to her island lair. Snatch his one chance of love from him. Ruin his human life. Not to mention being a pain in his backside from that point forward.

"Consider yourself Bested, then." He stood. "I do hate to cut this short, but I absolutely must stay somewhat on task for the gala."

She stood and stifled a yawn. "That's cool. I'm pretty wiped out. All this emotion, you know. Thanks, Vincent." She pecked him on the cheek, hopefully fast enough to not notice the chill to his skin. "G-night!"

He watched her blend into the shadows, and waited until he heard the snick of the elevator doors before he turned to leave.

****

Reanita glanced at the strange little man beside her. "May I remove your hat?"

Arby chuckled. "Guess so. That's the point of being in a screened-in room, I suppose."

She reached over and lifted off the beekeepers hat and felt the same sense of surprise and affection as she imagined a groom might feel lifting his beloved's bridal veil. The sight of his features—as familiar as her own reflection—had become comfortable in such a short period of time.

"Don't you get tired of something over your face?" she asked.

"I have grown accustomed to wearing some sort of cover. It's just easier. For me. For everyone. If you wear a mask long enough, it becomes a part of you."

Reanita empathized. Her mask was one of bravado and overachievement, but still a sort of armor. She patted her side—an automatic gesture. No gun, yet she felt at ease. His maleness posed no threat, and she felt no need to compete to prove her worth as she did with her male DEA counterparts.

Arby studied the horizon. The sun had dropped, forming a half-sphere of fiery orange with a yellow halo. He turned to look at Reanita. Her eyes reflected the sun's dying flames.

"This place is amazing," she said. "Did you have it built for the spa guests to have a spot to watch sunsets without the bugs and other creepy stuff?"

"Actually, it was a gift from Vincent a couple of years back. The only person who comes here is me." He smiled. "And now you."

She reached over and grasped one of his hands and returned her gaze to the sunset. "Oh, look! I see fins! What is that? Sharks?" Reanita pulled her legs to her chest, then forced herself to relax and unfold. Surely the aquatic predators couldn't just wiggle onto the sand, open the door, and drag her off to their base camp for dinner. Maybe they would just go after Sponge Bob Squarepants.

"Dolphins. A pod comes by here most early mornings and evenings—playing, feeding," he shot Reanita a meaningful glance, "maybe mating."

"Can you imagine trying to do...*that*, and swim at the same time?"

Arby laughed; easy with Reanita. "Suppose it's natural for them. They don't have to worry about drowning."

They sat in shared silence for a few minutes.

"What is it about Dark Island, Arby? It's so isolated. What makes you stay?"

He watched the sun dip lower until only a sliver of orange remained. The blue and purple sky rushed to lay claim as the daytime source of heat and light melted into the ocean.

"It's the one true place I can call home. I can be me."

"Lots of crazy, scary stuff running around. I know how to act in the inner city, how to take down anything that might want a piece of me, but here..."

He slipped an arm protectively around her waist and she leaned into him. So what if gargantuan roaches waited in the dark like henchmen and gators could do a forty-yard dash? Arby would not let anything eat her. He exuded a load of confidence for one so small in stature. And with no gun. How was that possible?

"Watch." He motioned to the horizon. A thin strip of illumination was all that remained of the sun. "Listen closely enough—or so the legend goes—and you can hear it sizzle as it sinks into the water."

She listened: The lap of waves, the whisper of the night breeze through the marsh grass, the faint scuttle of tiny crabs. No sizzle. No need to kill his illusion. "Yeah. Pretty cool. I can see why Vincent picked this spot to build this little screened room. It's beautiful."

"Florida mostly sucks, but parts of it are outstanding." He studied her features in the fading light. "I'm glad you like it."

"I like both of your special places. The greenhouse is fascinating. I could spend hours there. I even feel like I might like digging in the dirt. And trust me; I've never been one to dig. I kill plants in record time, back home." She held up her hands. "Black thumbs. Not a touch of green."

"Everyone is teachable. When you understand what living things need, it is easier to provide."

"Do you know what I need?"

He squeezed her body close to his. They watched the last streaks of scarlet fade to the purple of twilight. The north star—Venus—appeared. More pinpoints of light popped out until a long section of the Milky Way dusted the heavens like spilled diamond dust.

"I never get to see this in the city. Too much competition from the man-made lights." She lifted her hand and fanned it through the air. "So many stars."

Arby smiled. "I think I would've liked to have been an astronaut. Travel far, far away. See things no one else has ever seen."

"It'd be a kick to find some new life form. Something vastly different from ourselves," Reanita said.

He nodded.

"Can we stay out here all night?" Reanita asked. "I love it here. The sound of the waves. The breeze."

"Be right back." He left and returned with a large canvas bag he had lashed to the back of the ATV.

Reanita watched him unpack.

"We can't stay all night, though I would love that. But we can be comfortable for a few hours until my duties call me back." He presented the items he had unloaded, one by one. "Sleeping bags, a nice thick ground pad, sheets, pillows, and a light blanket."

"Hmm…"

He raised one finger. "Not finished. A bottle of wine. Cheese. Crackers. And chocolate."

"Chocolate! You think of everything."

His expression grew sad. "Tonight may be the one chance I get to show you how much I care about you, Reanita. I was just dreaming that it could be all night. I have to get back in a couple of hours. But, we can still make the best of the time we're here. Starting early tomorrow, my duties will suck up every available bit of time. Then, the gala…and you depart Sunday to go back to your life."

The thought of leaving Dark Island brought heaviness to her chest. "Until then, let's not waste any time."

She drew him in and kissed him. The kisses became deeper, more intense. Their union wasn't the frantic coupling of hormones beckoning to each other. Tonight, Arby and Reanita made slow, deliberate love.

Afterwards, Reanita curled into the circle of his arms and sighed. His breath grew even and deep in her ear. A low rumble caught her attention. She disentangled and sat up. A set of lights—one red, one green—skimmed across the water parallel to shore.

She poked him in one arm. He sat up and yawned.

"What's that? God, don't tell me you have UFO's down here, too."

He followed the direction of her gesture. "Probably just some fisherman out late."

"In the dark? What gives?"

The motor's noise grew faint, then stopped. From the sound, Reanita estimated the craft had cut its engine, possibly beached a short distance down the shoreline. The DEA agent inside of her longed to jump up and follow her nose. The lover wanted to go for round four with Arby.

She sighed. The lover won out.

"Don't worry." He pulled her back down and nuzzled her hair. "Boats pass by here at all times of the day and night. No big deal. It's Florida."

****

As the last pale orange streaks of sunset dusted the horizon, Vincent headed to the south lawn to give his final nod to the lighting and electrical installations. He felt alive: a stretch for one so dead.

"Party planning is in my blood," he said aloud.

He wondered if that was technically true, since the majority of his essential fluids came from sources outside of himself.

Event planning—especially the big-ticket galas— proved a high-octane profession, riddled with split-second decisions and an often complete suspension of reality. God, he loved it so! The next few days, he would be mired in his element. For a few stolen moments, he could immerse himself in the minute details and forget the troubles of the patrons, worries over the state of world affairs, and most important, shove Emmaraud to the back of his mind.

The let-down after any big gala, he suspected, felt much like it did for a kid after Christmas.

This part of the preparations fired his imagination more than any other. Light intrigued Vincent. Odd, for a creature who shunned the direct sun. Another vampire myth: that the sun's rays burned their skin.

Wrong again, blood-sucker fans, he thought.

Vincent could venture out into the harsh Florida sun. He chose not to, or to curtail his outings to as few as inhumanly possible. The gloaming—the time of day where harsh shadows traded places with soft silhouettes—appealed to his senses. Low illumination, reflected from the moon or cast from one of Arby's many solar-powered fixtures, caressed his hypersensitive skin.

The magical qualities of lighting—direct and indirect—served a party planner well. Vincent understood the basic human reaction to illumination. Working with a talented production manager like Lars, Vincent could transform an open lawn dotted with standard party tents into a wonderland for the senses.

One basic truth: the human eye would always find the brightest spot in any space. There could be armed guerilla freedom fighters with machine guns, armies of rabid bats hanging above, a body dangling from a chandelier, and snakes curling underfoot. A party guest entering a tent would gaze immediately toward a benign centerpiece, if it was properly highlighted by a concealed spotlight.

The production company—PSG—had the entire event site fired up for his inspection. As he approached, Vincent could see the interior glow of the tent; a huge luminescent spacecraft docked on the south lawn. Lars met him at the entry tent.

"Are you ready for me?" Vincent asked.

"Sure are. Everything is on, and all systems are a go." Lars led the way into the main tent.

In the center, a table marked the position for the first of two ice sculptures. Lars switched on the lighted pedestal. "This is how the ice centerpiece will be lit," he explained. "Ice is a cool medium, so to speak—it's clear and will reflect and refract any color of light. We're going with blue underlighting, so it'll look like it's glowing blue." He pointed upward. "I have spots positioned in the top of the tent to add the proper brightness to the sculpture. It will be the center of attention."

They moved on to examine the various spotlighting for the guest tables, bars, and floral display positions. Then, on to the main color wash lighting that would set the mood in the tent.

Vincent consulted the checklist as they walked to the far end of the tent to inspect the dance floor and stage area.

"Everything looks to be exactly according to plan," Vincent said.

Lars directed Vincent to a corner of the stage. "Check this out!" He hit a switch and the dance floor exploded with fog, flashing lights, and even the Dark Island logo spinning in the center of the black and white floor. It looked as if someone had released the *Saturday Night Fever* disco genie from his bottle.

"I should have kept my white shoes and thick gold neck chains," Vincent said.

The inspection moved from the main tent, where they examined the kitchen task lighting, electrical connections for the cooking and prep equipment, and the temporary landscape lighting.

Vincent was pleased. "Arby will be proud to see his handiwork so handsomely displayed. The landscape really deserves this attention."

The remainder of the checklist centered on the pathway lighting, restroom operation, and a myriad of other event logistics. Lars made notes on his clipboard for the next day's to-do list. With the plans set, Lars began to extinguish all of the lighting and shut down the generators. Darkness consumed the south lawn. Nature resumed its orchestral night serenade.

"See you tomorrow, Sir." Lars parted for some hotel time. It had been a long day, and he had to be back onsite early the following morning.

Vincent ran one finger down the spreadsheet page on his digital planner, programmed in several marks and a few notes, then headed for one of the black Dark Island golf carts. Jimmy Rob's job—his only requirement for the Blue

Blood Ball, besides being long-gone—was to assure all of the transport carts sat clean with polished seats and chrome, and with fully-charged batteries. Given the recent wanton turn of events in the redneck's life, Vincent didn't trust him to recall the elementary instructions. Best to check on them himself and take one small pebble off Arby's pile.

A sweet sound like the singing of cables in the wind caught his attention. Two voices carried on the gentle night breezes. It took a moment for Vincent to recognize the low harmonious hum. Rat love. True rat love.

"Atta boy, Arby."

He jumped into the cart and turned the key without bothering to flip the switch for the lights.

"Headlights? We don't need no stinking headlights!"

The pirated movie quote amused him so much; he laughed most of the way to the cart stables.

****

By the time Arby dragged himself to his private suite, he could barely shuffle. From sunrise with the production crew to sunset with Reanita, he had not taken a moment to properly rest. A quagmire of details needled his brain like paper wasps on a rampage.

Added to the mix: two hours spent in the mansion's kitchen with Angelina, mixing and baking the bottom butter cake layers for the gala's premier dessert—a dish Arby called *Baked Florida*. The mutant version of the classic Baked Alaska would be ultimately shaped like a mouse's head, filled with almond chocolate ice cream with a layer of meringue on top, and set on fire to awe the party-goers. No theme park officials appeared on the guest list. Even so, they would probably take the satirical gesture as a jovial tribute to the theme park that ate Central Florida. Only Arby, and perhaps Vincent, would recognize the confectionary jab.

Arby shucked the beekeeper's hat, shoes and coverall, brushed his teeth, and fell into bed. His last thoughts were of Reanita.

Chapter 19

Friday morning—the wee hours

Reanita waited until she heard the soft click of Patrice and Julia's suite doors before she slipped from her room. She paused outside of Thomas's suite. No light beneath the door and quiet as Dracula's tomb. Next door, she could make out the low murmur of blended conversation punctuated by Julia's laughter. The two lovebirds had seemed rather distant at breakfast. Reanita assumed some sort of Dark Island lovers' spat. Obviously, the sun had set on their quarrel.

Patrice's suite was quiet.

The DEA agent tiptoed down the hall and took the staircase to avoid the hum of the elevator motors. Once outside, she oriented herself to the direction of Arby's private beach cabana. She dashed between pools of white cast by the floodlights set up on the south lawn. The moon took over in a few steps and provided sufficient light for her to navigate the path. Once out of sight of the main house, she flipped on the small flashlight.

When she walked up to the cabana a few minutes later, Reanita stopped to relive the highlights of the evening with Arby. She decided to step inside the enclosure. No need to huddle in the dark and provide an all-you-can-eat buffet for the mosquitoes. The screened room provided an ample view of the Gulf, without cavorting with all the slithery stuff.

None of the Dark Island inhabitants bothered her as much as they previously had. When something brushed up against her ankle before she closed the door, terror registered, but didn't check in. If she lived in Florida, maybe all the bump-in-the-night creatures would cease to be novel. A person could become accustomed to anything, given time and proper medication.

The shimmer of moonlight across the Gulf waters lulled her to a level of calm she would have thought impossible before Dark Island.

She waited for an hour.

"Best get on back to the Ponderosa," she mumbled. "Doubt anything's going to shake loose tonight."

She rose to leave, and froze. The thrum of an outboard motor at full throttle sounded to her left. The noise increased in volume for a bit, then the whine changed pitches abruptly to a soft hum. A small craft, she judged, heading to shore in the same direction as before. Twice in such a short period of time? Her law enforcement second sense kicked in.

Reanita followed the curve of the muddy coastline for a while until she heard voices. Two male. One female. Laughter. Someone was pretty happy about something. She inched closer, careful not to create overt noise.

In the bright moon glow, she spotted the owners of the voices. The tall blonde woman—whatsername? Emmaraud?—and the redneck boyfriend. Another skinny man. Her pulse accelerated. What was with her weird attraction to the good ole boy? Too rough around the frayed flannel edges, even for her city-cop tastes. No couth. No way.

She hunkered down behind a thatch of saw palmettos and observed. The two men carried what looked like bales to an idling ATV. Emmaraud straddled the vehicle's seat, wriggling back and forth, making comments and laughing.

How many bales? Three, maybe four? Enough pot to put a gold star in Reanita's column. Along with the stack she had already found at the redneck's fancy digs, it was enough to squelch her supervisor's doubts about her abilities and the cash outlay for this assignment.

With so much product, there had to be some sort of repackaging facility—a back room, a storage unit. If she could manage to infiltrate the business end of the operation, she'd snag more than just the redneck and his moll.

Approaching him was out of the question. Something about the backwoods' bumpkin drew her like a Yankee to a pot roast. It was time she and Emmaraud had a little meeting in the ladies room.

****

Friday mid-morning

Emmaraud sensed the human female at the suite's door before she knocked.

"For the love of Ramses, why can't that damn woman leave me alone?"

At times it truly sucked being a magnetic creature.

The knock: twice.

Not the starlet. She always did the perky little five-knocks, pause, two-knocks thingy.

"Come in!" Emmaraud called out.

The demented Chihuahua hopped around in a pink taffeta skirt with matching collar, barking, snarling, and flashing teeth.

"Diente! *Ve a tú ataúd*! Go to your coffin!"

The little dog narrowed her eyes, but obeyed and returned to the little canopied bed.

"I'm not interrupting anything, am I?" Reanita asked.

Emmaraud sighed with relief. *The bat-faced chick.* "Oh, no. I'm just glad it's you instead of the prom queen from Hades."

"Prom queen?"

Emmaraud threw a pair of jeans onto the bed. To Reanita, they looked like something one might find on a homeless woman or in the reject bin at Goodwill. Not so. Emmaraud had forked over five hundred dollars and some change for tears, bleached spots, and a zipper that would only fasten halfway.

"Patrice Palmer," the vampiress answered. "Miss Pee-Pee. She's driving me batty. Every time I turn around, I practically trip over her."

"A *celeb hag*," Reanita supplied. "Likes to cling onto celebrities. Suppose you resemble Paris so much, it kicked Patrice into gear."

Reanita closed the door and took a few steps into the room. Diente opened one eye and growled.

Emmaraud shot the little dog a withering look. "Stuff it, sister. You are testing my nerves this morning."

Reanita tried the female bonding approach. "So—what you up to?"

Emmaraud motioned to the pile of clothing on the bed. "Still trying to pick out an ensemble for the party. I had something I thought would work, even had it pressed. Now, I don't think I like what Diente and I chose."

"Party? Odd, I didn't get a notice. They usually leave one on the bedside table."

The vampiress shook her head. "Not one of Vincent's fancy productions." She paused. "What does one wear to a Southern, NASCAR-themed, backwoods fish fry?"

Waders? Tube top and cut-off shorts? How the pluperfect hell am I supposed to know? Heiress or DEA agent; neither persona would have that particular information readily available.

"Umm...something casual?" Reanita offered.

Emmaraud's painted lips twitched at one corner. "You're helpful."

"Where's this fish fry?" Reanita sat down on one of the cushioned chairs, purposely as far away from Diente's canopy bed as possible.

"Friend of mine's. Jimmy Rob. Owns a little bar not too far off-Island."

Reànita sensed the opening and dove in. "Can anyone attend? I mean, not to invite myself, but—it's kind of dull around here at night, you know."

Emmaraud shrugged. "Why not? I don't think they'll have a bouncer or anything. Might not be your usual crowd, but what's wrong with soaking up a little local color while you're in Dixie?"

"This guy—you suppose he'd have any-thing…umm…better than beer or wine. Something a bit more…naughty?"

Emmaraud studied Reanita, then smiled. "I think he just might, if his price suits you."

"Money is not an issue."

Emmaraud nodded. "Good then. Consider yourself invited."

"Cool. Only, I don't know if I have anything suitable to wear, either."

Emmaraud grabbed a pair of scissors and started to hack the sleeves from a cotton shirt. Pieces of shredded material hit the bed and hardwood floor. "Just improvise. That's what Diente and I plan to do."

Reanita stood. "Think I might catch a ride with you? I flew in, so no car."

"Sure. As long as you can keep your mouth shut about my driving. That kind of crap pisses me off."

****

At times, the spells washed over Vincent like a sudden blood fever. A gush of affection for Dark Island so strong it shackled him in fear that somehow the sanctuary might fall to decay and ruin.

He loved The Dark. All of it. The mammals, birds, insects, reptiles, and amphibians. The flora: towering live

Evenings on Dark Island

oaks, pine, scrub oaks, and sabal palms. Every saw palmetto, blade of marsh grass, poison ivy vine, and invasive weed.

So much of The Dark existed as it always had. No cement parking slabs, no artificial lighting, no thriller park rides, no convenience stores. Old, old Florida. Ancient Florida. The land of the native tribes, probably the Timucuans, dead and gone before Europeans ever took an interest. Vincent's research found little to prove the natives had ever inhabited this marshy part of the northern peninsula of the Gulf Coast. Still, Vincent liked to image he walked the same paths as the earliest inhabitants, and he easily sensed the occasional unearthed Deptford pottery shard. From his research on similar pieces, he knew they possibly dated from 500 BC to 300 AD. Archeological records of that period were sparse, as were the written Spanish records. More than his *go-green* overseer, Vincent understood the true meaning of *not leaving a footprint*. The vampire knew: when eternity was his ruler, he had to be watchful of every inch.

Vincent studied the framed detailed rendering of Dark Island hanging above the media control center. He knew every cove, each small squiggle, on the coastline. Six miles long by two miles wide, the peninsula oriented slightly northwest to southeast, mimicking the mainland contours. Vincent often entertained the idea of removing the small land bridge between the Dark and Taylor County. He could create a man-made moat, complete with a drawbridge. And Dark Island would become, truly, an independent entity.

A direct hurricane hit held the potential to wipe the land clean. Fortunately, the larger named storms seldom made landfall in the area, favoring points farther north.

The thought of a forced evacuation tormented Vincent. He didn't fear for his life, but for the safety of the only place he had ever thought of as home.

Vincent trailed one finger along the line depicting the coastline and offered up a special protection mantra, one he had repeated every day for sixty years.

A tap sounded at the suite door. Vincent gave one last glance to the map and sat down at a small rosewood desk, especially designed for one of the three networked computers.

Arby stepped in. "Good morning, Sir."

"Morning." Vincent studied his overseer. "You look a bit more rested, Arby. I was concerned—"

"No need to be, Sir. My body seems to know when I've had enough. Only got a few hours, but I slept like the dead."

Vincent smiled. *I know what that's like.*

Arby paused. "Um...no offense, Sir."

Vincent waved a hand. "All well and good. What's the report this morning?"

"Big day, Sir. I'll be on the south lawn all day." Arby checked his day planner. "The glasses, plates, chargers, and silverware have already been delivered. We'll be setting up the tables and chairs. Lars and his crew will set up the kitchen gear. The black and white-tiled dance floor is down, but we still need the rest of the flooring in the main tent and walkways. They'll finish tweaking the lighting by sundown."

"I'll be there for that."

"Yes, Sir. I know that's your favorite part."

"Also, I will need the final seating assignments. Once the linens are in place tomorrow, I can double-check to make sure the placards are in the proper places."

Vincent nodded. "I will give that one last look before I sign off on it. I'll have it to you by tonight, the latest."

"That works."

"Anything else?"

Arby slipped the day planner into its coverall pocket. "Let's see...Christina is healing well from her unfortunate run-in with Diente. Really, Sir, there must be something done about that little nuisance canine. Angelina down in the kitchen is ready to shoot Diente. The little demon is determined to bite our baker's favorite cat."

Vincent sighed.

"And Maria is none to happy either. Seems, Diente relieved herself on one corner of the rug in the library. Have you ever tried to get blood urine out of an Oriental carpet? Not easy, Sir. Not easy."

"I will speak with her again, maybe this evening." Vincent said. "As if it will do any good."

Arby shook his head. "You won't catch her tonight, Sir. According to Maria, Emmaraud has had her ironing outfits since yesterday for some function, for her and that demon dog."

"Ah yes. The fish fry at Jimmy Rob's bar. How could I forget? He has one every year about this time."

"I thought he was blowing the Island for the 400 at Daytona?"

Vincent shook his head. "That's Saturday night *under the lights*. Jimmy Rob always throws some sort of cookout before one of the big NASCAR races—the nearby ones—the 500 at Daytona, the 400 at Daytona, the final one in November, last race of their season, at Homestead, Miami Speedway."

"Amazing, Vincent. You have such a grip on this NASCAR thing."

"One must know one's adversary's hobbies, Arby. In Jimmy Rob's case, I guess you could say I am just trying to keep up with where my blood child spends his time and energy. Jimmy Rob was quick to point out that I had no knowledge of the sport, so I made it a point to get online and research." Vincent tilted his head, considering the idea of parenting. "Besides, the crashes are phenomenal at times."

Arby shrugged. "Cars going in a circle really fast. Eludes me."

"It is all about strategy."

"I shudder to think what you've found online."

Vincent grinned. "I really, really want a Digger T-shirt."

"Digger, Sir?"

"A little animated groundhog character. He runs this camera on the corners of the raceway. They call it the *Digger Cam*. He pops up and down. Very cute. And interesting how you can actually see pieces of rubber flying into the air as the cars whiz past."

Arby made a mental note. "I'll make sure you get one for your blood-birthday this year."

Vincent jiggled. "Oh! And a camo-print ball cap with *Boogity, Boogity, Boogity!* printed on the front."

Arby's eyebrows scrunched together. *Which smoking jacket could possibly go with a camo-print hat?* he wondered.

"It's a catch phrase that Darrell Waltrip—D.W.—has made famous. He's one of the FOX announcers for the first part of the season. Fun kind of guy." Vincent pumped one hand in the air. "*Boogity, Boogity, Boogity! Let's go racin', boys!*"

"You worry me sometimes, Sir."

"No need. It's a phase. Not a true addiction. Now, *The Young and the Restless*? That's an addiction."

"Of course. I see the distinction."

"I suppose Jimmy Rob thinks he's performing some sort of public service by getting his friends—let's see, what does he call it—?" Vincent pulled on his chin. "Oh, yes. *Loose. Juiced. Ready for use.*"

Arby smirked. "Class act all the way." *I'll have to make sure the mechanic boy gets a bottle of his special blend of Jack Daniels before race time,* he thought.

Vincent waved a hand through the air. "Enough of that. Do you have Reanita's vintage for me this morning? I can't seem to locate it."

Arby swallowed past the lump that had formed in his throat. "Ah...umm...I'm afraid I'm somewhat remiss, Sir."

Vincent nodded. "Been a bit distracted, have you?"

Distracted. A good word for it. "I haven't had a chance to distill Reanita's blood, yet. This gala—"

"Don't stress, Arby. You make me nervous when you stress."

****

Emmaraud bustled around her suite, grabbing chew toys and stuffing them into the pocket of an oversized yellow leather hobo dog tote: seven hundred and fifty dollars, retail. A knock sounded on the door.

"What's up, Vincent?" she asked when he stepped inside. "I'm a bit pushed for time. I promised Jimmy Rob I'd help with the cheese grits."

Vincent laughed. "You? Cook? You must really have your pet redneck snowed."

She propped her hands on her hips and regarded him. "I can cook. I choose not to. What's the point? Not like I eat. Unless it's warmed blood and cookies at bedtime." She considered. "I'll have to talk to your rat-boy about a recipe for blood cookies. I could get into that."

"Arby's pretty tied up at the moment."

"Good. He needs to be tied up." She chuckled, then back-shifted to the insult aimed toward her cooking abilities. "Besides, what could be so hard about cheese grits? You take a grit or two, add cheese. Viola!"

"You've never had grits, have you?"

"Of course not. Back when I could eat, they weren't exactly the rage in ancient Egypt. Sometimes you can ask the silliest questions, Vincent."

He walked over to a chair and sat down. "We need to talk."

The vampiress rolled her eyes. She stood in front of a digital mirror and shellacked on a thick layer of deep red lipstick. "Mother of All Darkness. I've got to leave in a few minutes. Can't it wait?"

"It's about Diente. She's being quite disruptive—again."

Emmaraud added a second layer of mascara. Good thing she had preternatural strength. It would take considerable power just open her eyes.

His blood sire dabbed the excess with a tissue. "I haven't let Diente anywhere near that meddlesome human child."

"Christina is fine, and she's far from meddlesome. Sweet, sweet child. Seems your little darling is tormenting Angelina's cat to the point he won't even come from the woods long enough to eat."

"Can I help it if dogs like to chase cats? It's their nature."

"Most domesticated dogs don't make it a point to drain the cat of its lifeblood. A subtle little difference."

Emmaraud opened the carrier. When she bent down to collect the dog, Diente growled and flashed fangs.

"Be sweet, *chica*." Emmaraud crooned as she stuffed the Chihuahua inside the purse.

"Sweet?" Vincent said. "A tad out of character for that thing."

"You should get a pet, Vincent. Give you something to faun over. You spend way too much time in your *special room*—" she air-quoted with two fingers on each hand, "—just doing whatever it is you do in there. It's not natural."

"Nothing about either of us is natural."

She swatted the air. "Death is what you make of it."

"Back to Diente. She's relieving herself on the carpet in the library."

Emmaraud shrugged. "Girl has gotta go."

"So take the time from your lusty encounters with my blood son and take the dog out to pee."

Emmaraud secured the carrier's zipper. Diente squirreled around inside. The bag churned as if possessed by a captive alien bent on escape.

"How long has it been since you actually left this mansion?" she asked.

"I go out most evenings."

"No. I mean *off* the Island. As in—anywhere but here."

He tapped his chin. "Last year, I was—no, that was—maybe three? Four years? I lose track."

She reached over and caressed his cheek in an uncharacteristic gesture of concern. "It's easy to lose track of time when one has so much of it. I know."

Emmaraud the Aggravator, he could handle. Emmaraud the Empathetic left him several notches off-center.

"How many languages do you speak now, Vincent? Three? Four?"

He mentally tabbed. *English. Spanish. German. Chinese--Cantonese. Italian. French. A smattering of Portuguese.* "Six, fluently. Why?"

"What's the point of it all, if you never use them?"

"Knowledge?"

"Knowledge for knowledge's sake is a foolish waste of time, even eternal time."

She knelt down in front of him. "You could come to Spain. Help me ready the new spa. It could be so exciting, the two of us working side-by-side. We could travel to the capitals of Europe! Anywhere we fancy. I could show you things, Vincent."

"I shudder to think—"

The vampiress willed him to look directly into her eyes. "I will teach you to shift. It's not difficult. Really. Shifting is just remembering how to do something your blood already knows how to do."

"If it's so easy, why haven't you taught me?"

"I would have gladly, Vincent. I never sensed you even remotely entertained the idea of leaving this island."

"So, what's the secret?" he asked.

"Just think of where you wish to be, desire it with everything inside, and you will be there."

The Master of Dark Island chuckled. "Just click together the heels of my ruby red slippers and repeat *there's no place like home, there's no place like home* like Dorothy leaving Oz?"

"Why does everything have to be a movie reference with you?"

Vincent shrugged.

"It's what you know, right? It's *all* you know. For Lucifer's sake, Vincent. You can come and go—anywhere—at will! You just have to be willing to take the first tippy-toe steps."

Vincent managed to break his gaze from hers.

Emmaraud stood. "Just think about it. At least, just promise me you will think about it."

Vincent nodded, his eyes still averted.

Emmaraud dug in a side pocket on the oversized dog tote and located the keys to the Maserati. She took one last exasperated look at Vincent and left.

Even his human mother never spoke to Vincent the way Emmaraud did. Actually, the woman rarely talked to him at all.

Vincent stood in his blood sire's suite and focused on her lingering scent: expensive perfume and the after-glow aroma of centuries of blended blood.

"Is this your odd way of telling me you actually might care, Emmaraud?"

Later, safely ensconced in his media room, Vincent chose the perfect video to suit his dark mood: *Throw Mama from the Train.*

Chapter 20

Friday afternoon

Reanita's legs still felt a little weak. She imagined it had to be the same disjointed sensation a rookie *Starfleet* ensign felt the first time she beamed down to the surface of an alien planet from the *Starship Enterprise*: glad as hell to be in one piece, finally in her destination with a phaser set on *stun,* maybe a little sad she wore red. The scarlet-shirted ensigns were always the first to get vaporized on any *Star Trek* episode.

She managed to unfold her body from the passenger seat of the Maserati, stand, and walk a few shaky steps. Reanita accepted the first beer handed to her. Had one of the good old boys or gals offered her a lit joint, she might have defied DEA rules and taken a lung-busting toke.

The Maserati ride with Emmaraud would go down in her life experiences as unequaled by anything her superiors had thrown at her in training. The opening scenes replayed in her mind.

"Nice outfit," Emmaraud commented. "Upper tier trailer trash. You'll be a hit."

Reanita nodded. She glanced down at her hot pink designer T-shirt, one she had ripped to expose her midriff. Tight white Bermuda shorts. Running shoes. No socks.

"Thanks, I—"

Emmaraud checked her lipstick in the lighted vanity mirror, then gestured to the seatbelt. "Fasten up. Florida law."

Reanita complied.

"Ready?" One of Emmaraud's perfectly plucked eyebrows arched upward.

"Sure. I—"

The vampiress slammed the car into gear, hit the accelerator, and the Maserati rocketed from the mansion's circular drive. Reanita's head snapped backward until it met the headrest. She felt the muscles in her neck tighten.

A thought flashed through her mind: *This must be how the astronauts feel during take-off.*

The rest of the ride—mercifully short in time and distance—was a nauseating panorama of pine trees and palmettos whizzing by in a green and brown blur. Reanita fully expected the Maserati to grab the wind, gain altitude, and maybe do a few three-sixty rolls in midair. She had a brief flashback to her childhood and her then-sober father, edging the GTO to full throttle with his right forearm held across her body like a fleshy safety restraint.

I'm dying, Reanita thought. *My life is passing before my eyes. And I don't even like parades.*

Emmaraud and the Maserati fused together into one pounding instrument of wild-ass crazy speed. Five miles down a narrow pitted and patched county road, the driver decreased velocity as suddenly as she had accelerated, and they fishtailed into a gravel parking lot. Rocks spit from the tires, pinged the sides of several parked vehicles, and ricocheted off a cement block building painted the ugliest shade of green Reanita had ever seen.

"We're here!" Emmaraud opened the door, dragged the yellow dog carrier from behind the seat, and got out, all before Reanita managed to remember to breathe.

The slam of the driver's side door snapped Reanita to awareness.

Emmaraud stuck her head through the opened window on Reanita's side. "You going to just sit there or what?"

If the *or what* option included stumbling out, kissing the dirt, and puking, Reanita could go for it without hesitation.

The DEA agent shook her head to clear the recent memory. Later, she could dissect it and offer up prayers to whatever God had helped her remain alive.

She glanced around the party grounds—half of the gravel parking lot in front of J.R.'s Joint, cordoned off by a dirty cotton rope suspended between two poles mired in cement-filled tires. Laced from the top of the poles to the corner of the building, a string of homemade party lights cast a festive glow—fast-food collectable cups hung upside down with Christmas bulbs jammed inside

Other than Emmaraud, the only person Reanita recognized was her lunatic chauffeur's hunky boyfriend. She felt heat rise to her cheeks and wondered, again, why the man caused such an unwarranted reaction.

"Well...Look who's decided to come slummin'! It's the little heiress." Jimmy Rob strolled over and slapped Reanita playfully on one shoulder.

"Um...I..."

"Jimmy Rob's the name. We've never been formally introduced. You spa rats don't really get to mingle with the hired help. I've seen you around, though. I keep up the limos for Vincent." He pointed to a group of men and women clustered around a barrel keg. "Help yourself to a brewski. I'm gonna be frying up some fish here, pretty soon. You rich folks eat fish, don't you?"

"Yes."

"Hey, everyone!" Jimmy Rob called out. "This here is *Ree-a-nee-ter*. Y'all make sure she has a good time. Show her what we've got." He leaned over so close, Reanita could smell his scent—an arousing blend of sweat, machine oil, and something else.

Jimmy Rob spoke into to her ear. "Vincent ain't the only one here who can pitch a throw-down. You've come to the right place. We know how to party, if you get my drift."

Reanita nodded.

"All right then." He turned away and yelled across the lot to a bearded man standing next to two metal bins hooked up to propane tanks, "Start the engine, boys! Let's go racing!"

The NASCAR battle cry caused a ripple of catcalls and whoops. Reanita noted the logos on T-shirts, tank tops, and ball caps. Different numbers—5, 14, 20, 24, 18, 48, 88. She chided herself for not taking the time to Google NASCAR stats before she left the mansion, to match the numbers with the drivers. Could have provided some conversation starters.

Reanita sipped from a plastic cup of beer and checked out the party décor. Clearly, far removed from anything Vincent Bedsloe III might plan. Four tables stood at one end of the gravel lot; made from oil drums topped with sheets of plywood. Yellow plastic tablecloths covered most of the raw wood, but the splintered edges gaped like rows of gator teeth. Paper cups and plates, napkins, and plastic utensils huddled on the end of one table next to a jug filled with a dark liquid. Reanita guessed it to be sweet tea, the official dinner drink of the South. So sugary, it would make her fillings ache for hours.

Two sealed plastic containers held cakes, one light and one dark. To the side, stood a large hub cap turned upside down and filled with moon pies. A large ice chest had been shoved beneath one table, probably filled with bowls of something mayonnaise-based. The South seemed to be lubricated with the stuff.

The DEA agent's gaze moved to the side of the building where two used sofas stood. No doubt, they would be put to good use before the night was over. Reanita could imagine the smorgasbord of biological specimens embedded in the dingy tweed fibers. A Crime Scene Investigator could have a field day.

Must be the VIP section, she thought. *The only thing this place is missing is a trash fire.*

A back door banged open and two men carried out aluminum pans filled with fish and some kind of mystery meat, mounds of cut potatoes, and a large bowl of batter.

Everyone around her drank as if the Government might ban alcohol by midnight. Reanita made it a point to sip the beer. The trick: to act loaded while remaining sober enough to ferret out the truth about Dark Island's clandestine drug dealings.

Emmaraud opened the dog carrier and Diente hopped out. The little dog's eyes twinkled. Reanita could've sworn the Chihuahua smiled.

"*No muerdas a los humanos. Saben asquerosos,*" Emmaraud said in a low voice.

Reanita knew a little Spanish, but her translation made no sense. *Don't bite the humans. They don't taste good.*

Diente dashed through the crowd, snarling and yipping in a high pitch, then disappeared into the woods.

"Um...don't you want to go after your little dog?" Reanita asked.

Emmaraud glanced once toward the thicket of saw palmettos and shook her head. "Diente can take care of herself. No worries."

****

Emmaraud thought about food and blood as she stirred a mound of shredded cheddar cheese into a pot of cooked grits. The whole mess looked like a congealed gelatinous porridge, now turning bright orange.

Food, like alcohol, gave the owner's blood texture, depth. After so many centuries of roaming the planet, the vampiress could tell a human's diet and home region as well as any linguist could detect a dialect and accent. Sicilian: the bite of ripe tomatoes, olive oil, fresh basil and oregano, garlic, and vino. French: dependant on the region, but with a heavier feel on the tongue. Rich sauces, wines, blended spices. Mexican: the ever-present sting of chili pepper, cilantro, and cumin. American: a bit harder to pin down. Such a melting-pot mixture of bubbling blood! The Deep South? Easy. Fat. Lots of it: pork, beef, chicken. Everything from the vegetables cooked with hog jowls to desserts laden with sugar and real butter and cream.

Emmaraud reviewed the evening's menu. Fish cooked in hot grease. French-fried potatoes. Hushpuppies—little deep-fried clots of dough. Coleslaw and potato salad swimming in mayonnaise. Biscuits slathered with sweet cream butter. Cakes. Pies. Cookies. Brownies. And an R. C. Cola.

Her mouth watered. Not for food, but for the life liquid of the plumpest, most well-fed sons and daughters of Dixie.

Emmaraud considered. Added another double handful of cheese to the grits pot and stirred. What were a few more grams of lard, give or take?

****

To murder a few hours, Vincent retreated to the media room and chose a handful of classic vampire videos: *Love at First Bite*, *Buffy the Vampire Slayer* and *Blacula*. The screen and projector were already in place from earlier in the day. Vincent settled down and decanted a flute of vintage from the final patron: Reanita Register. The idea of sipping the bat-faced woman's blood gave him a shiver.

"How terribly politically incorrect of you, Vincent," he said. "She can't help how she looks anymore than you can help being undead."

Time to set aside personal beauty biases and complete his role as the Spa at Dark Island's host.

The first sip stunned him. The blood, unmistakably a male's. He picked up the bottle and reviewed the coded sticker. No mistake; the vintage was clearly marked with the heiress's identifying number.

Strange.

Arby had never mislabeled a bottle of patron vintage in five years. Vincent did a rough calculation: over one thousand bottles. Why now? Had he pushed his overseer too hard? Had the Blue Blood Ball sent Arby careening?

Vincent took a slow drink and allowed the blood to flow around his tongue and coat the inside of his mouth. He closed his eyes, and the blood gave up its secrets.

A mixture of sadness, desperation, and pain. Old pain: the deep ache of loneliness and abandonment. This was a person who had been turned away from basic nurturing, many times.

Vincent sensed powerful, hidden emotions bubbling beneath the surface. Love: strong, urgent and sexual. The kind of love a person might do anything to preserve and shelter. In slightly contrasting notes, a second tang of love; this one had mellowed with age like a fine wine carefully sealed and stored. True, devoted, protective, and secure. The sort of love a human might feel toward a brother, or a life-long friend.

Something unsettling rested beneath the first blush. He took a third sip. Vincent allowed the stronger emotions to step aside, like the parting of a thick, prickly hedge. Behind, he found a splinter of discord. A carefully concealed deceit.

Vincent felt the blood tears form at the corners of his eyes and did nothing to staunch their flow. A wave of sadness flowed over him, and he fought to control his breathing. For the first time in as long as he had known his trusted overseer and friend, Vincent felt the sting of deception.

The blood vintage was Arby's.

****

One of Jimmy Rob's buddies wiped the grease from his mouth. "Ain't you and your missus gonna eat?"

Jimmy Rob shook his head. "You know how it is, son. I'm so tired of lookin' at food by the time I'm done cookin', I can barely stand the smell of it. And her—?" he motioned toward Emmaraud. "How you reckon she stays so damn skinny, huh?"

Jimmy Rob took a loud swill from his mug of blood brew. "I'll just drink my supper." He chuckled and glanced toward Emmaraud. "I'll get in a few bites, later on."

Emmaraud closed her eyes and shook her head. *Redneck humor. Got to love it.*

Reanita leaned back from the table in a folding aluminum chair; a stuffed piglet ready for slaughter. To her surprise, the fried fish had been delectable, perfectly seasoned and crisp. The home fries went down well with a generous dollop of catsup. She crunched on home-canned dill pickles, ate two helpings of potato salad and cole slaw. Sucked down sweet tea. Wolfed down doughboys and biscuits with butter. Totally enjoyed the fried meat, until one of the women answered her inquiry as to its origin.

The fish is either bream or catfish. Can't tell you about the meat, now. Don't really know which is which, hon. Jimmy Rob kilt it all, fresh—like he always does. Could be possum, rabbit, or rattlesnake. It all tastes kinda like chicken to me, once it's fried up all nice and crispy.

She had chewed the meat for a while until she figured no one would notice her spitting it into her napkin. If every strange and exotic meat tasted like chicken, why not just eat chicken and save the suspense?

The desserts had added another layer of fat-plumped lethargy. Reanita accepted a thick slice of lemon layered cake and a slab of chocolate cake big enough for two to share. She couldn't find it in her heart to resist three of the best brownies she had ever tasted. Something about the slightly crunchy texture reminded her of the treats she had eaten the first night at the mansion. Some kind of Southern mystery herb? She'd have to remember to ask for the recipe. She even managed to find room for a thick slice of a gooey rich dessert someone called Mississippi Mud Pie.

Jimmy Rob stood behind her and rested his hands on her shoulders. Heat rushed down her body and landed in her privates. Had she been anywhere near menopause age, she would have called it a hot flash.

"You told Emmaraud you wanted to do a little partying, gal?" he asked in a low voice.

She nodded.

"Come with me."

She managed to lift her food-swollen body from the chair and lumbered behind him. Inside, she followed him to a cramped room behind the bar.

Two men looked up from where they sat. A table held several plastic baggies filled with small amounts of pot. Reanita scanned the packages. No more than two, three ounces, tops. Not the huge operation she had hoped for.

"You want to try a little of our special blend before you buy, I assume...smart city gal like yourself wouldn't just take it on good faith." Jimmy Rob handed her a tightly-rolled joint and pulled a lighter from his jeans pocket.

Reanita accepted and held the joint between her lips. Jimmy Rob fired up the lighter. She took a tentative puff, held the smoke in her mouth for a few moments, then made a show of exhaling.

"Nice." She smiled and pulled a roll of twenties from her shorts pocket.

Jimmy Rob held up a hand. "No, no. I wouldn't think of taking your money. First bag is on the house. You like—you know where to find me. I can hook you up." He smiled. "Now, I know you flew in and all. Wouldn't want you to risk taking it back on the plane with you. We can work something out, a way to get all you want delivered right to your front door."

"Really. I must insist on paying you—"

One of the men—the one with the greenest teeth Reanita had ever seen—nodded and said, "I told you she was a cop. Ethel told me right off, soon as she walked up."

A stab of fear curdled the half-digested fat in Reanita's stomach. "Cop? Me?"

"My wife Ethel has a second sense about the *poleese*. Says y'all all walk the same way, like you got a corn cob shoved up your ass. And your arms kinda bow out at the waist. Sign of someone what's used to wearing a gun strapped to her waist."

Reanita's mind whirled. "No way. I don't know what you mean. I—"

The second man, the bearded one who had lorded over the fish fryers, added, "Yep. Makes good sense. You have to pay us, don't you? Can't just take the pot. Wouldn't be a drug deal then would it? Not if we don't accept cash money for it."

The correct angle, the perfect answer to get her out of this mess—an obvious set-up—struck Reanita.

"Okay, so if I *am* a cop, why would I ride here with his—" she pointed to Jimmy Rob, "—girlfriend? Huh? And, God as my witness, I don't freakin' own a gun."

"Bet you have one of them recordin' wires," Greenteeth ventured.

"Right. You see one spot on this outfit where I could hide one? Well, do you?" She held up both hands and turned in a slow circle. Reanita didn't know if she had inhaled a little of the marijuana, but she felt herself calm down and fall into the offended heiress roll with ease. "Not like I'm from here and know the damned rules! Up north, if I didn't break out a roll of money, I would be killed on the spot. How the hell am I supposed to know you're just being all Southern and friendly?"

The two men eyed each other. Jimmy Rob nodded.

"You know, I don't need your pot," she said. "I can get anything I want when I get home. I thought it might be fun to try out what you had to offer. But hey, it's okay by me. My money will spend just as well up North."

Jimmy Rob narrowed his eyes to slits. "Wait a minute. I thought you was from Tex-ass."

Reanita's heart skipped a beat. "I am…I was…that is…my daddy lives out there. I live up near D.C. Up North."

The well-aimed comment about the division between certain parts of the country hit home. No matter that the Civil War—known by many Southerners as *The War of Northern Aggression*—was years past, a lot of folks still harbored a certain amount of attitude.

"Aw…now, little gal. No need to let you go back home with a bad taste in your mouth. We'll take your money if you insist." Green-teeth shoved two bags—each filled with about a finger's circumference of product—across the table. "Just to show there's no ill will on our part, we'll throw in a second bag on the house. How's zat?"

Reanita threw the thick roll of cash on the table and picked up the bags. "I'd say; my opinion of Southern hospitality just climbed up a few notches."

Green-teeth thumbed through the money and smiled. "You're a generous little gal. I'll give you that. I might just change my opinion of Yankees."

By the time the party ended in the wee hours of the morning, Reanita had made a group of new best friends. Two of the women went so far as to write down their prized family casserole recipes for her, plus exchanging email addresses. Reanita promised to find both of them on Facebook and sign them on as friends.

At one point, Diente trotted from the edge of the swamp. Her little designer outfit was torn in several places and only two of the skull-printed doggie booties remained on her muddy feet. Her snout was red with fresh blood.

"Looks like your little *She-wow-wow* tangled with something," Ethel said to Emmaraud.

"Poor little thing," Sherry, the bleached blonde said.

"Save your sorrow for whatever she ran into." Emmaraud picked up Diente. "*Has estropeado el vestido pequeño.*"

Reanita tried to make her mind focus long enough to translate. Something about the dog spoiling its dress?

Emmaraud stuffed Diente into the yellow carrier and sat it on the top of one of the tables. The bag pitched and rolled like something possessed.

Reanita might not have made it any closer to the huge drug operation, but she really had the heiress role under control. She talked NASCAR with the boys. One of them gave her a Jimmie Johnson—number 48!—baseball cap. All with no help from excess beer consumption or marijuana; or so she thought until Ethel made a comment.

"You sure do like my brownies, don't you, honey? I'd ease up a little on them, though. You'll get a case of the munchies that will last you until a week from Sunday. I put a whole bag of pot in this batch."

Chapter 21

Friday night

Vincent pulled his golf cart to the entrance of the main tent on the south lawn. Lars sat on a folding chair, a blank stare of fatigue on his face. He rose as Vincent slid from the cart.

"Nice evening, isn't it?" Vincent asked.

"I think the weather—if it holds out—will be perfect for the event."

The two exchanged small talk while they waited for the third participant involved in the final inspection. In a few minutes, a second golf cart rumbled up at full speed; Arby running late and trying to make up for lost time. Very unusual for the caretaker.

With clipboards and PDA's in hand, the three started the walk-through. No time for idle chit-chat or humor now. They were set to scrutinize all the event logistics to insure a perfect show: table placements, glass and plate counts, linens, lighting setup, wireless mics and sound system, air conditioning, potted foliage, electrical circuits required for the coffee bar.

No stone was left unturned. All three of the professionals knew: there would be no second chance to be flawless. Everything had to be right when the guests arrived.

The pressure of holding such a large event seemed more oppressive than the Florida humidity in July.

"Looks as if we've covered all the bases," Vincent said. "Lars, you know to have the staff wipe down all the chairs before the covers go on tomorrow, and have the bartenders completely unloaded and ready for set-up by three p.m. Floral should be in by ten a.m. to start the centerpieces. The ice carvings don't come in 'till six p.m., so they are fresh. You getting all this, Arby?"

"Umm...yes, Sir," Arby answered without looking up from his clipboard.

Vincent spread his arms wide, the cheerleader spurring on the team. "Well, let's make a party!"

Lars ran a hand through his hair. He looked as if he hadn't slept in days. "I'll bid you guys goodnight. I'm trashed, man." He left to power down all of the systems for the night, and Vincent and Arby walked back to the entrance of the tent.

Vincent studied his overseer. The long hours showed on Arby's face, his features more drawn and rat-like with exhaustion. During the walk-through, Arby had made limited eye contact and answered Vincent's questions with succinct replies devoid of the usual banter. The beekeeper's hat couldn't hide Arby's reticence. Betrayal: the polar opposite of friendship.

"Is there something wrong, Arby?" Vincent asked.

"I'm concerned about the gator tail, Sir. The supplier has had the flu. He generally delivers two days prior to an event."

"I'm certain he will work it out. He hasn't let us down before." Vincent searched for words. "You seem somewhat...distracted."

"Actually, I need to show you something." Arby glanced at the darkening skies. The moon—just rising above the treetops—was a shade shy of full. Perfect. "I considered waiting on this until the gala, but I want you to be alone for this."

Vincent steeled himself. "Alone for—?"

"Come with me, Sir."

Arby walked from the main tent, past the freshly-landscaped entrance to the executive restrooms, and down a lit pathway leading to the moon garden.

Several feet into the gardens, Vincent stopped. "Do I hear water running?"

Arby motioned to an illuminated wrought iron archway, placed a few hours prior. A thick layer of fragrant mulch concealed the disturbed soil where a row of shrubs once stood. The overseer reached into his coverall pocket and extracted a thin remote control. With a press of a button, he signaled power to a series of low white lights. A winding pathway appeared.

"I don't recall—" Vincent started.

"Please." Arby motioned for his boss to proceed.

Three switchbacks through thick foliage led Vincent to a clearing. The scent of moisture. The music of a waterfall. When he stepped into the circular pool of low lights, the Master of Dark Island hesitated.

"What is this?"

Arby punched a second button. LED lights concealed in the rocks illuminated the pond and waterfall.

Vincent clasped his hands together. "You've added a water element to the moon garden. How enchanting! And just in time for the gala."

Arby's finger poised over a third button. "Yes. But that's not all. This, I ordered especially for you." He pointed toward the rear of the waterfall. "Watch."

Arby pressed a button and several colored LED lights popped on, turning the water blood red. Vincent gasped.

"Now, for the crowning glory—" Arby selected a button. A red spotlight cast an eerie light on the tall mosquito statue at the crest of the falls.

"For me? You did this for me?"

"Yes." Arby said. "Actually, *I* didn't do it. I just planned the water element and lighting. An artist in Key

West created the statue using your design renderings for the ice carvings."

Vincent circled the pond, viewing the statue from all angles. The intense red light played on the curves and lines of the giant insect, making it at once malevolent and comical.

"Delightful! But what's the occasion? My blood birthday is coming up in October, but we generally don't celebrate it, and my human birth date is at the end of January."

"It was meant as a gesture of my respect for you, Sir. And...our friendship."

The catch in Arby's voice caused Vincent to turn away from the extraordinary statue and face his overseer.

"Is there something...else, Arby?"

The caretaker met Vincent's gaze without flinching or looking away. "Don't drink the final vintage, Sir."

"Why?"

"It doesn't belong to Reanita Register. The blood is mine."

Vincent took a deep breath, held it a few moments, then exhaled. The truth was out, but he didn't feel free.

"A bit late for that, Arby."

"You...you've already—?"

Vincent nodded. The two men stood in silence for a moment.

"You know the rules, Arby. Do you offer an explanation?"

Arby's words came out in a barely-audible whisper. "I love her."

Hollywood often played on the theme of friendship versus amour. How the best buddy was often cast aside for the blush of new love. Vincent had seen the scenario in countless films and sitcoms. Still, it stung in real life.

"I suppose you didn't trust me to—"

Arby held up both hands. "No. No. That has nothing to do with it. I trust you explicitly."

Obviously not, Vincent thought. "Then, why?"

"I couldn't bear the thought of sharing her. Not with you. Not with anyone."

"I see." Vincent walked around the pond to allow his thoughts to settle. He returned in a few moments and faced his caretaker.

"Our relationship has been built upon trust, Arby. This is quite serious, your breach of that contract."

"I realize that, Sir."

"My rules are very clear. Have been from the beginning of our business partnership."

Business partnership; the sterility of Vincent's words stung Arby.

"I shall hand over my letter of resignation, Sir, effective immediately after the gala. Hector is a good man. I will make sure to leave your gardens in capable hands, and to arrange for the smooth transfer of the spa's management."

With that, the overseer hung his head and walked away.

****

Patrice Palmer wondered if she would ever sleep again.

The prescription she always depended on to knock her into sweet oblivion was packed away in the bottom of her suitcase. Just in case she got desperate and decided she had to have one, the extra time spent digging the plastic bottle from beneath layers of clothing might just make her stop and think *why* she had to quit, cold turkey. Alcohol wasn't a great plan either, so a glass of wine to help her relax was out of the question. Yoga helped her to center, but it didn't turn off her brain in the wee hours.

The whole impending motherhood thing—if that's what she decided to stick with—was turning out to be pretty intense. Eat right. Get sleep. No drugs. No drinking. And those were the ones she could come up with off the top of her head. No telling how many favorite things would be off-limits when she got home and consulted a doctor. No wonder pregnant women seemed so crabby. Other than being fat and hormonal and all.

Patrice kicked off the covers and sat up. Exercise. She was reasonably sure no one would take issue with that. Even in her hardiest party days, she had always worked out after an all-nighter. The kid on board would just have to put up with the extra sloshing around.

She checked the diamond watch on her bedside table. Four a.m. The impending evening was huge: the whole reason she had spent such a chunk of change to come to The Dark on one of the most expensive weeks of the year, and bought a gown that clung to her like warm grape jelly. Not to mention costing her a fortune. Plus the shoes, clutch, and jewelry. Good thing the movie part loomed in the future. She was a couple of steps shy of living in a cheap hotel.

The Blue Blood Ball: time for Patrice Palmer to shine and schmooze. A huge gala with plenty of opportunities to see and be seen. Surely, photographers would be around to snap shots of her rubbing body parts with the rich and over-educated. If she could just work herself into a state of exhaustion, maybe she could get some beauty sleep. Either that or she'd have to apply a pound of under-eye concealer.

Patrice threw on a shorts outfit and a pair of walking shoes, and wrapped her hair into a quick up-do. No one would be around to see her, anyway. Not at this hour.

The lights were dimmed in the workout area. Silent, and kind of creepy. She flipped a switch and a bank of overhead fixtures popped on. Better. She chose a treadmill and jumped aboard. Music from her I-pod helped her to not feel so alone and abandoned. But she had to admit, not really *so* alone as she had always felt. Odd, that she somehow sensed the presence of a second *something*—a kind of blank, knowing awareness—already gaining ground inside of her body. For sure, the longer the pregnancy continued, or she allowed it to continue, the stronger the feeling of intimacy would grow.

What kind of mother would she be? Patrice figured it wouldn't be too hard to be better than her own. Sheila—*Sheee-lahhh*—her mom always said it all drawn-out and breathless. From the time Patrice was a gangly teenager, Sheila passed them off as siblings. *We're sisters. Don't we look just like twins?* Like she was ashamed to have a kid, or she couldn't pull off being just barely over her twenty if she admitted to being a parent. Not like having a daughter slowed Sheila down. Parenthood added a slight complication, or an accessory to add to an outfit, depending on the situation. Similar to owning a dog to look like you gave a shit about animals. Her father? Anyone's guess. Just some man who wandered into Sheila's orbit long enough to leave a trail of little swimmers.

Patrice sighed. All this time, she thought she was so not-Sheila.

She could be different. She would.

A half-hour sped by. Her legs warmed to the repetitive movements and endorphins worked their magic. Patrice felt better than she had in days. Something caught her attention. She snapped her head to face the workout room's entrance, smiled, and waved.

"Hey!" She pointed to the adjacent machine. "Come on and join me!"

The Master of Dark Island threw a clean white face towel onto a bench and programmed a routine into the digital panel at the head of the treadmill.

"You're up early…or is it late?" Vincent asked.

Patrice popped the I-pod speaker buds from her ears. "Does it matter? Either way, and I'm a freak."

He smiled, mounted the machine and started to walk at a warm-up pace. "Can't sleep?"

She shook her head. "Nope. Not like I can just knock on doors for someone to chat with. Julia and Thomas are asleep. And I think I heard Reanita come in, too. Everyone in my wing is out like a light. What about you?"

"I'm a little restless." Vincent meant the statement. Sleep wasn't something a vampire longed for. Rest—the lack of concerns—was. The tumultuous emotions caused by the exchange with Arby sat on his shoulders like a heavy winter overcoat. Even time in the beloved media room had not helped.

Patrice dialed back the speed on her machine and matched his pace. "Guess it's the gala thing, huh? Must be a huge amount of work."

He nodded. "It is. Arby has it under control."

"Hmm...he seems like a good guy. A little weird, but good." She walked for a minute, before asking, "Vincent? Your offer to let me stay here for awhile. Were you for real?"

"Certainly."

"I think I'd like that."

Vincent nodded. "I take it you've decided to keep the baby?"

One of her hands left the treadmill's handle and rested on her stomach. "Yeah. I think so."

"It will all work out, Patrice. Things have a way of falling into place."

She offered a warm smile. "Thanks for being my friend, Vincent." She walked a few paces, then said, "I didn't really think about much of anything before I came to The Dark this time. I realized something."

"An epiphany? I have been known to have one myself, from time to time."

"I don't know what that is." Patrice's eyebrows knit together briefly, then relaxed. "Anyway, I realized I don't have any true friends in Hollywood."

"Oh, come now. I've seen countless pictures of you out and about with your peers."

"Not really friends, Vincent. We just drink and hop bars. One long party after another." She turned her head to face him. "I've had more real conversations here—with you, with Julia—than I have ever had back there."

"I'm sure if you think, you can say that someone...."

She interrupted, "No one. In my life—in my whole freaking miserable life—I can count my friends on one hand. Maybe on a couple of fingers. And that was back before I left home to be—," she smirked, "—rich and famous."

"What happened to them? Are you still in touch?"

She huffed. "No. I just kind of let them fall away. Never really missed them, to be honest. Or I got pissed because one of them maybe said some little thing I thought wasn't what I wanted to hear, or did something—"

"—that you felt betrayed you," he supplied.

She nodded. "That's it. Like, I was so high and mighty and so sure I was *it*, you know? Like, I never did anything wrong, and they did *everything* wrong."

Vincent picked up his pace. "Easy to judge."

"Right. Like that whole find a stick in your eye and a board in theirs, or something...you know, it's in the *Bible*."

Vincent smiled. "Very insightful of you, Patrice."

"What, like, you think I can't have deep stuff going on in my head? Just because I look hot and all?"

"No, no. I didn't mean any slight."

She waved a hand through the air. "I should know you wouldn't be like that. All *I'm so much better than you* and *I never do anything wrong.* You're pretty cool, Vincent." She smiled. "I think me and the kiddo are pretty lucky to have you as a BFF."

Best Friend Forever, he translated the acrostic. Compared to *his* eternity, Patrice couldn't fathom the meaning of forever.

Chapter 22

Jimmy Rob drove as if the GTO was stuck in the no-passing zone behind a lumbering school bus. Thirty miles an hour. Only there was no school bus at three a.m., and no one would've given a hoot if he straddled the middle dividing line and booked it as fast as the muscle car could fly.

Why speed? The old man was so near death, the buzzards were circling and calling for reinforcements.

Waste of gas, he thought. *Waste of my not-so-precious time. I wouldn't piss up his ass if his guts were on fire.*

The only reason Jimmy Rob responded to the call was his sister Roberta—Bert for short. His only link to a past he'd like to forget. Bert—the one human who truly understood what it had been like growing up in that house.

Jimmy Rob was new to eternity. One aspect had only recently dawned on him. In a few decades—less, for some family members—Jimmy Rob would cease to be encumbered by close blood relatives. *Woo-hoo.*

A sorry lot; the majority of them. Spineless. Shiftless. Socially bankrupt. Other than Bert, he couldn't think of one who had amounted to much. None of them paid their bills on time, if at all. Most of his kin enjoyed the hospitality of the State of Florida penal system. Probably looked on incarceration as a steady meal ticket and dependable shelter. Cousins married cousins, and their offspring didn't look quite right. Parents beat their kids, or slept with them. *Keeping it in the family*, his father called it, back before the old man found God and got all preachy.

Jimmy Rob figured he had turned out pretty good. All things considered.

Just minutes before he and Emmaraud planned to take a little double-sip from one of the drunken revelers, his oldest friend Ray had come stumbling up to him. "Your sister called. Your old man's on his death bed. Bert's pretty upset. Hopes you'll come."

Poor, sweet gullible Bert. So like their mama, God rest her soul. Somehow, the old evangelist had managed to suck her in. Again. How many times had the geezer knocked on Death's Door? Jimmy Rob had lost count. Seemed like the Grim Reaper would grow weary of all the commotion and yank his daddy to the other side.

The house looked the same as it had when he walked out at age fifteen. Clapboard siding stained with dirt. Roof patched with so many types of shingles, it looked like a crazy quilt. No adornment of any kind, except for the two overgrown azalea bushes on either side of the cement steps. Might as well have a sign that read: *Poor White Trash*.

Not that his daddy couldn't afford to fix up the place, had he managed any of the cash he weaseled from repentant sinners over the past ten years of tent-campaigning for Jesus. *Pass the plate and please the preacher. You'll be a shoe-in at the Pearly Gates. Come on up here and I will lay my hands on you and heal!*

Jimmy Rob knew there had to be good, honest people who really looked to God to help them live better lives. His daddy wasn't one of them. A parasite, stuck on the artery of the church. If his son poured a pound of salt on his daddy, would the old preacher shrivel up and die like a garden slug?

Bert met him at the door and hugged him hard. "Jimmy Rob."

He felt the blood tears gather and forced them down. The last human he wanted to freak out was his sister. "Where is the old fool?"

Bert dabbed the corners of her eyes with a crumpled tissue. "He's really bad off this time, Jimmy Rob. This might be it."

He reached up and pushed a hank of hair from his sister's red-rimmed eyes. "He's too mean to die. Hell is full and Heaven don't want him."

"I know how you feel, bubba. I've had to really work to find a place in my heart, a way to forgive him."

"He doesn't deserve your forgiveness, Bert. You, of all people."

She sighed. Jimmy Rob noticed the age lines on her face. How life had beaten the corners of her lips into a permanent frown. How her once-lustrous brown hair had faded to a mousy gray.

"Just go in for a few minutes, Jimmy Rob. If you don't, you might regret not being able to speak to him one last time. Make peace. If you can. I have."

When he stepped into the darkened bedroom, Jimmy Rob forced himself to concentrate on the underlying scent of mildew. The overpowering smell of death permeated the air.

"Who's there? Who's that?" his father's voice called out.

"Jimmy Rob."

"Son? My son?" the figure tried to rise slightly, then fell back onto the mound of pillows. "You've come to me. My prayers have been answered."

"I'm here. What do you want, old man?"

A bony hand rose from beneath the sheets and beckoned. "Come near."

Jimmy Rob shuffled to the side of the bed. Fear nibbled at his stomach. Just as it had when he was a small boy.

"I've heard the call, my son. The Lord is waiting for me."

Jimmy Rob huffed. "Unless you're talking about the Lord of Darkness, I doubt it."

The room simmered in gloom, save for a sliver of light from a hall fixture. Jimmy Rob's preternatural vision picked out every subtle nuance of his father's withered features.

The cadaverous hand jabbed at him. "You're going to burn in Hell for all eternity! You have to change your evil ways!"

Jimmy Rob laughed. "You want Hell? I've seen Hell, old man. I can send you there right now."

For a moment, the vampire considered clamping down on his father's sinewy throat. Tasting all of the perversion of the years. The hypocrisy. Draining him of the last of his lifeblood. Maybe turning him so he would never know the peace of death.

He thought of spending eternity, knowing his father still roamed the earth. A powerful, preternatural being incapable of feeling nothing but demented lust and the need for others' worship. If anyone could play the role of the Antichrist—

"You blaspheme! Lucifer lives in you!" The old man's body shook.

Jimmy Rob backed away from the bedside.

"Go on to your reward. It's waiting for you, Daddy. Just close your eyes and let it happen. I'm sure you'll end up in the right place."

Jimmy Rob spun around and left the room. Behind him, he could hear his father quoting scripture after scripture. Good words on bad lips.

Bert waited in the cramped living room on a broken-down sofa. She stood when he walked by. "Jimmy Rob! Jimmy Rob! Wait up!"

He stepped outside onto the rotting wooden porch and forced his breathing to settle.

"I'm sorry." Tears made dusty tracks down his sister's cheeks. "I thought—"

"I love you, Bert. I do. But some things, words will never make right."

She wiped her eyes. "The service...do you want me to...?"

Jimmy Rob shook his head. "Anything you want of his—not that there's much of anything left—is yours."

"You will come to the funeral, won't you?"

He pulled the keys to the GTO from his pocket and leaned over to kiss his sister's cheek. "Don't look for me, Bert."

****

Reanita woke with a powerful need to see Arby. A little of the party's fuzziness still lingered around the edges, but she felt, for the most part, normal. With all the beer she had consumed—far from the one social drink she had planned—and the mound of marijuana-laced brownies, Reanita was amazed at her sobriety. God help if she had to pee in a cup anytime soon. The drug panel would scream *cannabis sativa.*

She glanced at the clock. Five a.m. She couldn't have slept more than a couple of hours at best. Had to give it to them; the rednecks really knew how to throw a party. She recalled hearing story after story about NASCAR drivers and races past. How Richard Petty was the all-time king of winners. How Kyle Bush was a bit of a bad boy that everyone loved to hate, but admired all the same.

Reanita didn't trust some of her memories. She had seen both Emmaraud and Jimmy Rob doing some kind of weird necking on the sofa, and not with each other. Must've been a hickey-making contest. Both of them seemed pretty intent on sucking on their partner's neck. She wondered if the woman and man would wake up and wonder what the heck had attacked them the night before. Perhaps it was a southern tradition—like a badge of honor.

Reanita splashed water on her face, brushed the fuzz from her teeth, and threw on clothes and shoes. Arby could take a few minutes of his time from the gala preparations. Surely, this early in the morning, he wouldn't be tied up.

She found the entrance to the inner garden with no trouble. A dim light shone in the greenhouse. Surprised that the building was unlocked, she opened the door and walked inside. No Arby. She took a moment to admire the plants—especially the Camellia named in her honor—before stepping outside.

Reanita walked around the circular inner garden, touching the plants as if greeting old friends. She could get used to coming here. An odd leafy branch jutted from the cane break. She walked over and inspected the foliage: dark green and sparsely hairy on the upper surface, paler and more densely hairy below, hand-shaped, with five to nine finger-like leaflets with jagged margins and prominent veins. The DEA agent recognized the illegal plant. She parted the thick woody cane stems and stared at the tall bushy plants they concealed.

"Oh, Arby..."

****

In Jimmy Rob's opinion, one truly wonderful trait of Emmaraud Bonneville—other than she was hot—was how swiftly she could get ready to go somewhere. As long as she didn't have to coordinate outfits with the little ankle-biter, the vampiress could pull her look together in a flash.

Jimmy Rob roared to a stop in front of the Airstream and blasted the horn. "Let's go, woman!"

Emmaraud materialized by the driver's side. "You're in a pleasant mood. Went well with your father, I take it."

"I don't want to talk about it. We need to hit the road. We've got a three-hour ride to Daytona, depending on traffic."

"Let me drive. We can take the Maserati."

Jimmy Rob thought back to the last time he'd been a passenger in one of Emmaraud's sports cars. A semi-tractor trailer had collided with a mini-van on I-4, and traffic was backed up for miles. Some wise-ass in the car next to theirs made some kind of lewd sexual remark aimed at the vampiress. Next thing Jimmy Rob knew, Emmaraud was out of the car holding the dude in mid-air by the neck. It got ugly. By the time Jimmy Rob managed to corral her, three people had broken parts, four cars were overturned, and sirens blasted in the distance. Good thing she could shift the two of them to the next county post haste.

She still stewed over the fact they had deserted a perfectly good Ferrari.

Jimmy Rob flashed his most enigmatic smile. "Babe, not to downplay your abilities, but I'd rather handle this one. You know how you get in heavy traffic."

"I make one little mistake and you hold it against me forever." She crossed her arms over her chest. "Let's just shift over. We can get there in a matter of minutes."

He ran his hands lovingly around the Goat's steering wheel. "Much as I like to have the car with me, I reckon we could do that. That damn dog going with us?"

Emmaraud's gaze scanned the clearing. "She's Devil-Knows-Where. I couldn't get her to wear the cute little Jimmie Johnson collar I bought online. She was in one of her moods. She'll come crawling back around dawn and find somewhere to sleep."

"I ain't never seen that little dog when she wasn't in a mood." Jimmy Rob vaulted from the GTO's driver's seat without bothering with the door. "Lemme change into my other Dale Earnhardt, Jr. shirt. I got catsup on this one. And I'll grab that bottle of blood brew Jack Daniels the rat-boy brought by last night."

"Ugh." Emmaraud shivered. "Don't bring it on my account. I'm not one for whiskey. I'll just take my blood fresh from the crowd. I'm sure someone there will be drinking what I like."

Jimmy Rob called over his shoulder as he walked to the Airstream, "More for me, then."

A few minutes later, the happy couple stood hand in hand in the shadow of a hulking customized bus in one corner of the Lake Lloyd premium RV camping lot, located in the center of the infield of the Daytona International Speedway. Prime real estate: first-class, waterfront sites with views of Lake Lloyd and the famed Superstretch.

Emmaraud smoothed her short denim skirt. The hot pink Jimmie Johnson #48 rhinestone tank top and tight skirt showed off her curves. She checked the time on the Jimmie Johnson #48 Ladies Allure watch—white leather strap, mother-of-pearl face printed with Jimmie J's signature, and rhinestones studded around the edges.

"Wasn't that better than wasting time on the highway?" she asked.

"Damn straight. I really got to get you to teach me how to do that shifting deal."

Like Hell, she thought. The vampiress pulled a tube of Kiss of the Harlot red lipstick from a small Louis Vuitton bag and applied a fresh coat.

"Let's go catch a quick snack before everyone starts gearing up," she said in a low voice. "I read online, there're six different camping lots. Bound to be a few drunken stragglers tailgating somewhere around this place. And I want to go shopping as soon as the vendors open up."

Jimmy Rob followed in Emmaraud's fragrant wake. If anyone could rustle up blood breakfast, she could.

Chapter 23

Saturday morning: early

Regardless of the fact that the Blue Blood Ball preparations had revved up to a high hum, life inside the mansion rolled along on schedule. At 6:30, Reanita heard Stefanie with an *f*'s distinctive perky knock. She groaned, rolled over, and pulled the sheet over her head. The knocking continued.

"For the love of—" Reanita snatched off the covers, stumbled to the door, and yanked it open.

Stefanie with an *f* did a little step in place. "Morning, Rea! Time for our last little WBB!"

The a.m. trainer bounced from one foot to the other, a trick Reanita once thought part of a warm-up routine. After a week with Stefanie with an *f*, she knew otherwise. The chick didn't need to warm up. She never allowed herself to cool down.

"Do you put Tabasco in your Twinkies, or what?" Reanita asked.

Stefanie with an *f* laughed. "You are *so* funny. Isn't she just the funniest, you guys?"

Reanita tilted her head to look behind the a.m. trainer. The rest of the patrons didn't look too thrilled. Julia and Thomas had an aura of gloom hanging over them in place of the normal newly-bed flush. Patrice seemed a little perkier, though pale, like she might just dart off to throw up at any moment.

"Come on, Rea," the starlet said. "Do us all a favor and get dressed."

Reanita frowned. "It's Saturday. The Big Day. Don't you have to, I'da know, go set up tables or something? With the big hoopla tonight, I figured we wouldn't be out marching around the swamp at the crack of dawn."

The a.m. trainer shook her head. "We pride ourselves, here at The Spa at Dark Island, with providing a continuing high level of patron service and training, as if this was a normal week. No slacking here."

Reanita took note of the trainer's outfit. Baby blue this morning. Matched down to the shorts, socks, and the stripe on her shoes. No mixing of brand names, either. Unreal.

Got to admire the chick, Reanita thought. *She's got the party line down. But am I really any different? I live, eat, sleep, and crap law enforcement—or I did until I came to The Dark.*

"What about that stupid menace of a dog?" Reanita asked. "Kind of hard to get all into nature with that little freak nipping at your heels."

"Not a *problemo*," Stefanie with an *f* said. "Scotty has somehow managed to train Diente to guard the gardens for rabbits. Weird thing: Diente doesn't like normal doggie treats. Scotty is using bits of raw beef. Even then, she just chews the blood out of them and spits out the rest."

The trainer shrugged. "My husband has actually started to like that little dog. He built a special tiny guard hut for Diente, kind of like one you see at a border crossing. Crazy thing is—Diente scares the fur off the squirrels and moles, too. Even makes the deer think twice about nibbling the lettuce." The trainer grinned. "Diente's not that bad. She just craves attention. I guess every creature needs a niche."

Reanita threw up her hands. "All right, Sparky. You lead the little happy entourage out of here and I'll get dressed and meet you at the trail head."

She closed the door and leaned her forehead against the cool wood for a moment. Odd thing: she didn't feel exhausted. She should have. She'd had slept fewer consecutive hours in the last week than she had ever missed in her life.

Reanita slapped cold water on her face and grabbed the first shirt and shorts in the drawer. She had just tied her shoes when someone knocked on the door. Forced health maintenance was beginning to wear on her last nerve.

"Look, Stefanie with an *f*—" she yanked the door open, prepared to launch into a tirade.

Arby stepped back. "I'm sorry, Rea. I'm…umm…"

"Oh, hey! C'mon in!" She grabbed her lover by the arm and pulled him inside, snatching off his hat with one hand.

Reanita kissed Arby hard. "I've missed you."

"Me, too. I mean, you, too. I mean—"

They sucked together. Reanita backed toward the bed, pulling Arby along, managing to partially strip off her shirt. Before they could fall into a mass of tangled limbs, Arby pushed back.

"I can't," he said between gasps. "I—we—can't." Arby allowed his breathing to settle. "I'm really, really crazed this morning. You wouldn't believe."

Reanita pulled her shirt back into place. "Right."

"Really, Rea. I'm on my way for the morning report to Vincent. I'm supposed to be there—" he glanced at his watch "—now."

She smirked. "Don't let me hold you up."

"I stopped by to ask if you'd like to meet later. I can give you a private tour of the south lawn before it gets really nutty."

Reanita nodded. "Sure. Besides, I really need to talk to you about something."

He pulled on the beekeeper's hat. "I'll come for you, say around four? We won't have long, but you can hang with me while I go through the final walk-through."

Love makes people into complete freaks, she thought. *All clingy and desperate. So not me. No wonder people kill each other over it. It's making me crazy.*

"You go ahead." She gave him a quick hug. "I have a hot play date with gators, snakes, and mosquitoes."

****

Vincent viewed the Looney Tunes cartoon again. *Transylvania 6-5000*, his all-time favorite, where Bugs Bunny makes a wrong turn, ends up in Transylvania and spends the night at the spooky castle of Count Bloodcount. Vincent had watched the short clip hundreds of times, and it still made him laugh out loud.

So many questions ran through his mind whenever he viewed the old cartoons. Why had they been banned as too violent? Even when a character fell thousands of feet, he still got up and walked away—looked like an accordion, but still managed to move. No heads rolled. No blood splattered. Sure, they conked each other over the head and stars swirled around them for a few frames. But nothing like the realistic blood and guts he could see on any network, practically at any time of the day or night.

Why didn't people say wonderful words like *egad* and *idgit*? Perfect words, and such fun. Good thing Yosemite Sam had come along years before anger management therapy. Pepé Le Pew would be considered a rapist at worst, a stalker at best. Foghorn Leghorn wasn't politically correct, with his southern swagger and mistreatment of Miss Prissy the Hen and the Barnyard Dawg. Bugs Bunny would be considered a sociopath. And Marvin the Martian? He'd greatly offend homosexuals with his swishy voice and mannerisms, for sure.

Vincent worried about the future of mankind. Everything seemed so complicated anymore. So many things were changing. Some for the good as people tried to be more conscious of their effect on each other and the planet. Still, the wars raged and humans found more ways to expound their differences than explore their commonalities.

Vincent heard his overseer's knock. Arby entered.

"Good morning, Sir."

"Good morning, Arby."

The caretaker consulted his checklist. "We're on schedule. The frou-frou team is on-Island."

Vincent's spirits sank. Was this to be it, then? Formality, as if they were two former lovers who could barely stand to be in the same room?

"Good. Good. The gator tail, did it arrive?"

Arby shook his head. "Not yet, Sir. I did hear from the man's daughter. She plans on delivering the order this afternoon. He is in the hospital in Gainesville. They think he might have that H1N1 flu."

"Oh my. If you will, find out his room number. I'll order a gift basket."

Arby scribbled a note. "Very good, Sir."

"Where are we with everything?"

"The frou-frou team is going over the décor as we speak. I briefed them on how the linens should be placed on the tables. They're going to be laying out all of the table settings. The caterer has already inventoried the chargers, plates, silver, and glassware. When they finish that, they are going to start on the chair covers. I've left a copy of the design detail to refer to as needed. The florist will be here shortly. They built the centerpieces last night and have them stored in the walk-in cooler. The ice sculptures will arrive around five p.m. to minimize the melting."

"All good." Vincent asked, "And my horse?"

"The groomer assures me the stallion has been bathed and combed to a high sheen, Sir. The handler is trained in animal massage, so she plans to work on the horse a few hours ahead of your ride, just to calm him down."

"Not too calm, Arby. I don't want to look like I'm on a broken-down tourist trail-ride horse. He's quite spirited, enough to rear when I ask it of him."

"The handler is aware of your plans, Sir. I spoke with her this morning, first thing."

"What would I do without you, Arby?" Vincent asked.

The question suspended time for a few beats. Neither the human nor the vampire spoke until Arby broke eye contact and glanced at the widescreen.

"Watching cartoons this morning, Sir?"

A wistful expression washed across Vincent's face. "*Transylvania 6-5000.* Remember it?"

"I do." Arby's spirit felt sore, as if too many emotions had been beaten down. For some reason, his mind went right to the Mighty Mouse theme song. *Here I come to save the day!* He could use a superhero about now, even a mouse in a cape and tights.

Vincent hit the play button and Count Bloodcount, playing the perfect vampiric hotel host, escorted Bugs Bunny into one of the castle's bedchambers. "My favorite line is coming up. Listen."

Rest is good for the blood, the cartoon vampire told Bugs.

Arby smiled. "That line, if I recall correctly, struck us both. The Spa at Dark Island came into being because of it."

"Your idea, Arby. An inspiration that saved me from an eternity of isolation." Vincent sighed. "And look where it has taken us. Five years later, and we run a successful upscale retreat."

"Like any good idea, it spreads forth into the world. To Spain, then to France, if Emmaraud actually moves forward as planned," the caretaker said.

"In a few decades, there could be Dark Island-styled resorts around the world. No use in defying Emmaraud.

Might as well get used to the franchise idea. Like a McDonald's on every corner."

Arby added, "T-shirts. Key chains. Maybe some kind of official mascot?"

Vincent chuckled. "A bat? A piranha? No, my favorite little blood-sucker...a mosquito."

The men laughed as the cartoon concluded. Bugs Bunny, as always, came out unscathed.

"Anything else, Sir?"

"No, Arby. I know you have everything under control, as you always have."

"Very well, Sir. Enjoy your morning massage. If you need me, I will have the radio with me at all times."

After the overseer left, Vincent stood in the media room. Through the sound-proof walls and floor, he could still make out the hum of activity, a higher-pitched frequency than a normal Saturday. By mid-morning, over fifty workers would bee-hive around the mansion and south lawn.

In their midst, a small man in a white, crisply-pressed coverall and beekeeper's hat would keep perfect order.

****

Patrice Palmer stood in front of a full-length cheval mirror and studied her reflection. Front. Back. Sides. Firm arms, legs, apple-shaped bottom and tight stomach.

Good. No baby bump yet. The clingy pale blue gown didn't allow for a spare ounce.

"Take a good, long look," Patrice directed to her reflection. "You will never be this fabulous again."

How could all of this happen to her, when she had mapped her life out so carefully? Paved like the red carpet to the Oscar's. A few years playing the beautiful, damaged, or tragic heroine. On to the all-knowing mother or auntie—still beautiful. Finally, to rich, full-bodied elderly characters spewing pearls of wisdom and pithy humor.

She would defy Hollywood and resist the plastic surgeon's knife. Add lines to her face that would add lines to her scripts. Like Katherine Hepburn and Jessica Tandy: actors whose faces weren't shy of showing the etchings of all the emotions they had modeled over the years.

Patrice's obituary—when death did come at a full age—would appear across the globe. Pages of tributes and quotations from her famous friends. Pictures from every age, every film.

The starlet paused. She'd have to look into purchasing a cemetery plot as soon as she returned to California. So many years in the future, the prime real estate might be taken. A quiet spot. A place to spend eternity in peace, yet accessible enough for the throngs of grieving fans.

The dream crashed. Her life as she had planned had ended. She might have well been a drive-by shooting victim. Picked off the porch by a random chance bullet. A starlet on a stainless steel table, a tag tied to her toe.

"Enough of that!" she shoved the gloom aside, removed the gown, and returned it to a flocked hanger. She ran one hand across the silky material. Soft, like a newborn baby's downy hair.

Tonight, she would bask one last time in the peripheral halo of fame. What of tomorrow? She stretched to recall a famous line from *Gone with the Wind*. Green-eyed beauty Vivian Leigh—what did she say? Something like...*I can't think about that right now. If I do, I'll go crazy. I'll think about that tomorrow.*

She turned to face the mirror again. "I have plenty, plenty of years left. I have all the time in the world to figure things out. It's not like I'm going to die today."

Patrice Palmer shivered.

****

Vincent slathered *Vamp Tan in a Can* liberally over his skin and crawled into the tanning bed. Raven's soothing touch and melodic voice had performed its usual magic. His blood might run a few degrees cooler than his human counterparts, but he had more than enough endorphins to warm his sore spirit.

He thought about pain as he reclined. Another vampire myth: that his sort could feel physical pain. All of the fictitious scenes with vampires writhing and crying out amused him. As he watched the enactments of misery in countless films, Vincent often wished for some kind of buzzer, or better, a gong, to clang when the writers got it wrong. Watch the vampire go up in flames and contort with the unbearable searing of his undead flesh! *Gong!* See the horrid expression of agony as the vampire shrieks with the rising sun! *Gong!* Experience the vampire's contortions as the wooden stake drives deeply into his black heart! *Gong, Gong, Gong!*

Vincent felt only mild discomfort, and for a short time. A vague memory of pain. A deep cut might sting initially, but the magic of the blood sealed the wound instantly. Within seconds, any trace of a disturbance would vanish. He understood troubled young people with the burning need to cut their skin. Just to feel something. Something to let them know they were alive, or to relieve the pressure of living.

If Vincent wasn't alive, then pain couldn't help.

He thought of love. How long had it been since Vincent Bedsloe III had felt the passion and desperation of love? The memories of human attachments had faded like wallpaper too long in the sun. Grayed outlines of feelings like a taste on the back of his tongue. Was it sweet, bitter? Not enough of the essence of Julio remained to discern.

Arby loves Reanita enough to betray my trust, my rules. Vincent allowed the thought to settle.

Love and hate powered the human psyche. Too much of either created a dangerous imbalance. Every character in every movie Vincent watched was motivated by the polar-opposite emotions. Men, and women, did things and said things far removed from their personal code of ethics. War. Murder. But, also great feats of heroism and compassion.

Humans were complex at times. He should know. He used to be one.

Would he break the rules for someone he held dearer than blood? If so, could he forgive a friend for doing the same? And was his loyalty to one he thought of as a friend the same as love? Might he go against his own code to protect a friend? He thought of Arby. The one human who really knew him. The answer came quickly, and it startled him. *Yes, he could kill for Arby.*

The pondering was taking a toll on the endorphins. Vincent pushed the questions aside and made his mind go still for a brief moment.

Emmaraud and her last diatribe about the ease of shifting popped to the top of his mental queue. *Shifting.* Couldn't be that simple, or Jimmy Rob would already be doing it. Unless, like Vincent, he was under the same assumption that Emmaraud held the only key.

Her words replayed in his mind: *Just think of where you wish to be, desire it with everything inside, and you will be there.*

Vincent pictured his private spot on Dark Island. In his mind's eye, he saw the deep cypress woods. Smelled the mixture of decaying vegetation and salt air. Imagined himself sitting down on the water-finder tree, his feet connected to the damp earth. With every fiber, the vampire put himself in the spot.

For a beat, nothing happened. Then, he felt a swimmy sensation. A lightness. Disconnected from the heaviness of his body. When he opened his eyes, Vincent blinked a few times to assure himself of the reality. He sat on the bent trunk of the water-finder tree, bathed in the thin beams of light that filtered through the overhead cypress branches. In *his* spot.

He looked down and laughed.
Naked.

Suppose when one shifted, it might be best to wear clothing. Good thing he hadn't concentrated his efforts on the south lawn. He laughed again. Imagine the expressions on the party workers' faces when the naked Master of Dark Island popped in for an impromptu inspection.

Vincent sat for a few minutes, relishing the tranquility of the swamp. A doe stepped from a palmetto thicket and stared, before flipping her white tail into the air and bounding away. The vampire closed his eyes and breathed deeply.

He could travel anywhere on the Earth—anywhere!—and return as easily to this spot. The thought gave Vincent great comfort.

Chapter 24

Saturday afternoon

Arby strolled with Reanita's arm draped over his. The activity on the south lawn reminded him of an animated movie he had once seen in some middle-school science class: a huge blood clot formed after a cut, with cells rushing in from all directions and generalized inflammation swelling to a fever pitch.

Golf carts whizzed past, transporting workers and materials: flowers, ice, cases of bartending supplies. Security officers planned the flow of the off-Island parking area and circular drive in front of the mansion. Caterers carted in vans full of food and scurried around with plates, silverware and glasses for the table settings. The band unloaded equipment. A handful of groundskeepers scouted the lawn for any lingering ant hills. One final misting from the irrigation system assured the fresh appearance of the surrounding gardens. The honey wagons were inspected for sufficient disposable hand towels and toilet paper. Through the crowd—like an army of avenging white blood cells—Lars and his cast of experts patrolled for any last-minute problems.

"Wow. I never realized how much work this might be," Reanita commented.

One of the caterers careened by with a box of stemmed glasses.

"If we do it right, it will look effortless to guests." Arby pointed to the entrance to the moon garden. "I have something cool to show you."

The air temperature seemed to dip noticeably as they entered the water garden. Reanita circled the monstrous mosquito sculpture.

"This is…something else," she said.

"I suppose blood-sucking insect art is an acquired taste," Arby said. "It pleased Vincent. That's all that matters to me. That…and you."

Reanita turned from the waterfall and faced Arby. "I'm not what I seem."

"Many people aren't."

"Really—I—"

The radio hooked to Arby's coverall buzzed, and the caretaker listened to the caller. "I'm so sorry, Rea. The woman just arrived with the gator tail. Finally. I have to meet with her, give her a check."

"Arby, I really need to talk to—"

He grasped her hands. "After the gala. After all of this madness. I promise we'll talk. I won't let you leave Dark Island to go back to your glamorous life without having one last chance, a few more hours…"

He lifted the beekeeper's hat and leaned in to give her a gentle kiss. "I love you," he whispered.

Reanita stared at him, but offered no reply.

"Now." He wiped a tear from her cheek. "Shouldn't you go rest up? I can't wait to see you in your gown. You'll be the most beautiful woman on Dark Island tonight."

Reanita watched the overseer disappear down the winding pathway through the foliage. She sat down on a rock near the pond's edge and stared at the misty spray of the falls. Her tears fell like drops of blood and blended into the rippling water.

****

Jimmy Rob had never seen anyone take to a thing like Emmaraud had taken to NASCAR. Fueled by a few pre-race blood cocktails—courtesy of a clutch of all-nighters in the Orange Tent Camping Lot—the two vampires glowed with exuberance. Jimmy Rob suspended his *drink-no-male's-blood* rule, but figured it was okay since Wayne, Fred, and Little Ricky—from up in the panhandle of Florida, Jackson County—were kindred NASCAR spirits, full *of* spirits. He topped their blood samples off with half a bottle of the rat-boy's whiskey. Not bad stuff.

Those were some good ole boys, Jimmy Rob thought. *Regular ole down-home folks.*

He wouldn't have minded swapping racing stats with the trio until minutes before the 400. Emmaraud had other ideas. She made a bat-line directly to the souvenir row/ fan walk off the 4th turn—a NASCAR devotee's wet dream. Trailer after trailer of anything imaginable—clothing, jewelry, flags, key chains, cups. Even a doorstop made from a dried cow pile would have flown off the shelves if it was printed with the number and colors of a beloved driver.

As soon as the haulers—the semi-trucks used for transporting the traveling shops-on-wheels—opened their side panels for business, Emmaraud descended on the Jimmie Johnson merchandise. If it had a number 48 on it, she toted it off. Emmaraud even bought the damn little fang-dog a present: a Jimmie Johnson #48 pet jersey.

The vampiress dragged Jimmy Rob from one seller to the next. Finally, they made it to the vendor for his number-one driver—Dale Earnhardt, Jr., *Little E, Junebug.* He got two new ball caps out of the shopping spree—one, a digital camo-print National Guard Dale, Jr., the other, a black cap with the phrase *Real Men Work in the Pits* printed across the front and a small American flag decal on one side. He found a sharp pair of khaki pants in his size, good for the handful of times he might want to dress up a little. And a new T-shirt with Dale Jr.'s smiling face superimposed over the number 88 car. *Whoo-wee!*

The vampiress went all-out, renting two headsets and hand-held closed-circuit televisions for the race. Not only would they see the action—in real-time and on the tiny screen—Emmaraud could tune to the designated frequency and hear Jimmie J's chatter over her headset and Jimmy Rob could listen to Dale, Jr. on his. The only thing that could be any better would be to meet the man in person. Fat chance, but he could dream big. Never hurt to dream big.

Jimmy Rob took all the shopping in stride, toting bags like a pack mule on a backwoods camp-out. He didn't complain one time; a feat Emmaraud rewarded, later in the morning in some fellow's deluxe, tricked-out R.V. How she managed that, he didn't know, and didn't ask. Emmaraud had a way of getting what she wanted—no matter what. The circus-like atmosphere, blood rush, and the building energy of the crowd had made the two of them higher than Georgia pines. Emmaraud banged him like a loose storm shutter in a hurricane.

After the marathon shopping spree and hot-rod sex, Jimmy Rob marveled at Emmaraud's ancient magnetism. She turned her glamour to full-on razzle-dazzle. Combined with the fact she was a dead ringer for the billionaire hotelier's daughter, her orbit pulled in men, and a few photographers, from all angles. In minutes, the two of them sported pit passes. Changing into long pants and closed-toe shoes—required down in the pit area—Jimmy Rob felt like a kid at Christmas. Not his childhood—he'd never gotten shit from Santa or anyone else—but the holiday fests he'd always heard about, where a boy gets what he longs for the most.

Emmaraud sashayed in front of him. He admired her tight rear, packed like two ripe honeydew melons in a new pair of blue jeans with a rhinestone #48 shimmering on one rear pocket. She wore a tight white Jimmie J. T-shirt with the bottom tied up to show off her midriff and the collar ripped to reveal plenty of cleavage. Every man they passed took a second look. Most, a third. A few got punched in the arm or knocked in the head by their offended womenfolk.

The two vampires strolled through the fan zone and listened to the chatter between the commoners and a scattering of pit crew members. For a boy from the backwoods of Taylor County, it was like walking into a dream: a NASCAR beehive swarming with plain folks who spoke his language. Testosterone flavored the air, mixed with sweat, motor oil, grease, and engine exhaust. Jimmy Rob floated through the crowd; a kid in a meandering theme park filled with automotive confections.

"This is lame," Emmaraud said after a few minutes. "I want to see Jimmie J. and his car."

"Won't happen, Emmaraud. This close to the race, the cars are probably impounded. No one, but no one touches them after that. They don't want anyone fooling with the engines. No unfair advantages."

"We'll see about that."

She oozed over to one of Jimmie Johnson's crew, a handsome dark-haired young man with a winning smile and an obviously easy way with the fans. Emmaraud turned on her glamour. The crowd parted. She trained her wattage directly on the young man. Poor sap. He never knew what hit him. Only that it did and he would've gladly swallowed a gallon of 122-rated octane racing fuel, just to feel the white-hot spotlight of Emmaraud's attention.

"I'll just bet you can let us back there to see Jimmie J…and that amazing car. I would just love—" she swiveled her hips. "—to crawl up under the hood with you."

The man's Adam's apple bobbed up and down like a cork signaling a fish on the line. "Sorry, Ma'am. I can't show you the car. It's in impound. Locked up and secure. They'll bring 'em onto the track and line them up a couple of hours before the race, but they'll be surrounded by NASCAR officials—the guys in the white uniforms."

Emmaraud looped a hank of blonde hair around one finger and twirled it into a ringlet. "I am so disappointed. I told my brother here—" she motioned to Jimmy Rob. "—that you looked like the kind of fellow who might be able to pull some strings for us." She leaned over and said in a low tone, "I'm a huge fan of Jimmie J's and my brother just eats, drinks, and sleeps Dale, Jr. It would mean the world if we could just see one of the cars and maybe catch a glance of the drivers." Her face morphed into a mask of anticipatory grief. "My brother Jimmy Rob, he looks fine, but he ain't. He don't have much longer, if you know what I mean." She mouthed the dreaded word *cancer*.

"I'm real sorry to hear that. I had a cousin died of that, just a few months back. Left two little kids behind." The crew member—*Kevin,* embroidered in script across one shirt pocket—looked from Emmaraud to Jimmy Rob, and back. "I thought you was...you look like that rich gal, whatshername?" He held up one finger. "Hang on a sec. Y'all stay right here."

"Your *brother?*" Jimmy Rob asked after the pit crew member left. "I don't think you'd do to your brother what you just did to me back in that R.V."

"Like that would concern you, given your family history. Shut up and play along."

The crew member returned in a couple of minutes and motioned for them to follow. Jimmy Rob trailed behind the couple—his vampire girlfriend with her arm looped in Kevin the crew-member's arm, her head bent toward his, intent on every word the man said. *Sucker*.

"I can't show y'all the race car, Miss Emmaraud. But I can show you the back-up car." He led them to one of the hauler semi-trailers parked behind pit row. An elevator lowered the race car, and the three of them huddled around the opened hood. The way Emmaraud looked at the poor guy as he talked about the cast-iron V-8, 358 cubic inch engine made Jimmy Rob wonder if she might just invite him to lay her back on the engine and have a go, right then and there.

Kevin the crew team member gave the two the five-dollar tour. Described everything from the frame and roll cage to the five-point driver's harness system, and the gages and collapsible steering wheel. He covered details that made Jimmy Rob salivate. Compression ratios, torque, induction, suspension, brakes, wheels, and tire tread width.

"How fast you reckon it will go?" Emmaraud's eyes sparkled.

"Two hundred miles per hour," Kevin said.

Jimmy Rob tuned out the crew member's babble when the man described the men of the pit crew and their jobs. The Jack Man. Gas Man. Catch Can Man. Tire Changers. Tire Carriers. The *Over-the-wall Crew:* seven athletes who could jump the wall, change all four tires, and get twenty-two gallons of gas into the car in about fifteen seconds of the most chaotic, most skillful dance in any sport on the planet. It looked like a free-for-all with everyone charging around the race car like a bunch of wild boars. In reality, a successful pit was the result of long hours of practice and superior mechanical skills.

Emmaraud's not-so-subtle body language urged Kevin the crew member onward. He reviewed the meaning behind the set of flags used by the official flag person in the tower: green, yellow, red, blue with yellow, black, white, black with white, yellow with red, and checkered. He went over the driver's safety equipment from helmet construction to the fire-retardant driving suit, gloves, socks, and shoes, to the HANS device, a semi-hard collar worn to reduce head and neck injuries. The man moved on to describe the points scoring system for the thirty-six Cup races.

Freakin' NASCAR 101, Jimmy Rob thought. He could've just bought her one of the glossy books that covered it all, saved the man some brain cells.

Around them, the inner sanctum swarmed with the hard-working men and women behind the scenes of the NASCAR experience. Members of the press wandered around, snapping pictures and talking with the drivers and crew. Barbeque grills dotted the area, and the scent of cooking food filled the air as the crews catered to their drivers' pre-race needs. To Jimmy Rob, it looked like a little city set up within the guarded inner sanctuary behind pit row.

Emmaraud ran her hand across the crew member's cheek and leaned in to plant a kiss. Kevin looked as if he had been hit with a stun gun. His face froze into a goofy lopsided grin.

A voice sounded from over Jimmy Rob's left shoulder. He turned to see Jimmie Johnson standing behind them. Emmaraud expanded her glamour to encompass the man.

Kevin introduced the two vampires to the famous NASCAR driver. Jimmy Rob thought of a million things he wanted to say, but nothing made it from his mouth, only a mumbled, *pleased to meet cha.*

Emmaraud made up for his lack, and the object of her admiration graciously answered her questions and maintained a respectful distance. The man had obviously had plenty of practice with over-zealous female fans. Even after he excused himself, Emmaraud continued to mix with Jimmie Johnson's crew, her glamour drawing them in as they took valuable time to share war stories and tales of races past.

My people. My people, Jimmy Rob repeated in his mind. *These are my people.* These people were his *family.* Had been since he was a little boy. The only sense of belonging came when he was at the racetrack amidst the sights and smells of NASCAR.

Jimmy Rob froze. He spotted his idol. Dale Earnhardt, Jr. The man! Son of the legendary *Intimidator.* Did the son know just how lucky he was, to have had a daddy like Dale, Sr.?

He couldn't move his feet. Wanted to. Wanted to walk over and strike up a conversation with the man. Dale, Jr. had the reputation as being a nice kind of fellow. The kind of guy you could shoot the shit with.

Dale, Jr. disappeared into the crowd. The moment was lost. Chance of a lifetime, missed.

What would my life had been like if Dale, Sr. had been my daddy? Maybe, I could'a been somebody. Maybe I would've been right here, pacing around in a fancy fireproof suit, just itching to start the race.

Just being back at the famed Daytona International Speedway evoked a profound sadness. The last time Jimmy Rob had attended a race—the 2001 Daytona 500—he watched Ralph Dale Earnhardt, Sr. crash into the wall on turn four of the final lap. The crowd held its breath, seemed like. The crash looked minor, and not nearly as dramatic as his famous 1996 wreck at Talladega, when his car had been pelted several times in the roof and windshield as it slid across the track. Jimmy Rob waited for the man to pop out of the damaged race car as he'd done countless times before. But he didn't. He died from a fracture at the base of his skull. And Jimmy Rob damn near felt like he had died that infamous day, too.

The Intimidator. Ironhead. The Man in Black. Known for his aggressive style. Seven time Winston Cup Champion. 1998 Daytona 500 winner. Sprint All-Star Race winner, three times. IROC champion, four times. Numerous awards and kudos.

Nothing could stop *The Intimidator.* But, it had. And Jimmy Rob could not come back to the Speedway for a long time. Until now.

Following Dale, Sr.'s death—bringing the total to six in less than two years—NASCAR focused on safety, requiring the use of the HANS head-restraint device, safer barriers at all oval tracks, new rules for seat belt and seat inspections, and the development of a next-generation car built with driver security in mind: *the Car of Tomorrow.*

The Intimidator and the others left a legacy: not only of talent and courage, but of protection for their fellow drivers.

Emmaraud appeared beside him, and he broke away from the memories. Her glamour shone with such intensity, he was amazed the humans couldn't see it rippling off her in waves.

"I want to do this! I can do this!" she bounced up and down.

Dread stabbed at him. "Now, Emmaraud. How fair would that be?"

Vampires had no learning curve. No trial and error. If they did something incorrectly at first, the next time was perfect. Any learning curve morphed into a short, straight line between point A—*not a clue*—to point B—*expert*. Jimmy Rob had never met a human who could compete.

She shrugged off his comment. "So, I'd win. But wouldn't it be fun? I would have them take off those silly restrictor plates, of course. They just slow you down."

Restrictor plates, he knew, were devices installed at the intake of the engine to limit the power output of the motor, hence slowing the acceleration and overall top speed. Primarily, NASCAR's Sprint Cup and Nationwide Series used the restrictor plates at Daytona and Talladega Speedways.

"What do you know about that? Restrictors are put in for a good reason. To slow the race down a couple of notches. These cars can get to going too fast. Over two hundred, and the tires pretty much leave the pavement. Not good. The restrictor plates are pretty damned important at tracks like this one and the one at Talladega. Without them, there'd be more really bad crashes."

"Who's afraid of a little crash or two? Isn't that what these humans come to see? Besides, it's not like a crash could kill *me*."

Jimmy Rob frowned. "Wouldn't be so good on the other drivers. The humans."

She flipped one hand in the air. "There are a zillion of them, Jimmy Rob. And more trying to climb up the ranks."

He wanted to throttle the vampiress. The sanctity of NASCAR was threatened. And not by lack of safety devices or engine restrictor plates.

The carnage! Jimmy Rob thought of a driver bumping Emmaraud's race car, spinning it into a wall. Her spewing from the window in a full-on blood rage. Cars flying into the stands. Innocent humans dying.

"No! No way! You can't do it, Emmaraud."

She propped her hands on her slender hips. "Since when do you think you can tell me what to do?"

"Right now. I sure as hell am telling you. Our kind can't compete with humans. They will lose, for one thing. It's their game. Their victories." He swept his hand around in a circle. "All these guys, they been dreaming and working on this since they were little boys driving go-carts and four-wheelers. I will not let you take that away from any of them!"

He backed up and punted before she could figure a way to rip out his lungs and use them for laundry bags. "What kind of challenge would it be, Emmaraud? After one race, you'd smoke 'em all. No challenge in that, no fun."

She stuck out her lower lip. "You are such a spoil sport."

He let go of the breath he held for a beat. He had stood up to Emmaraud Bonneville, and nothing had exploded. No one had gone flying through the air. When he got home, he planned to take a permanent marker and make a big black note of this date on his girly calendar. The day he backed Emmaraud Bonneville down.

The vampiress' eyes lit up. "Then, we'll race each other!"

"What?"

"Build a track. In Spain. I have plenty of land. Our own private speedway! I know plenty of vamps who will lunge at the chance to learn racing. Against each other, so we don't kill off any of your precious humans." Emmaraud tapped him on the shoulder. "You, by the way, didn't seem to mind killing off a few when we first met. Remember?"

"Some people need killing. That's beside my point."

She rolled her eyes. "Seems the same to me. Dead is dead."

Jimmy Rob ignored her invitation to argue. "I've always wanted to race. It'd take the element of crash-death out of the picture, for sure. And it'd boil down to the talent and strategy of the driver and pit crew, the quality of the car...and balls!"

"Hey, easy on the *balls* comments. I have a bigger set than you and every man here put together."

"Good point." Jimmy Rob decided not to push the issue. Sometimes, Emmaraud could get downright hateful about the whole women's lib thing.

Emmaraud grinned. "We could call it BASCAR—the Blood Association of Stock Car Auto Racing."

Chapter 25

Saturday evening: the Blue Blood Ball

Vincent took one last look at the local weather radar. A few offshore storms. Nothing to worry over. One large system to the east passed inland, bringing cooler air. Perfect for the party. An unusually balmy seventy-eight degrees on a July evening. The citronella lanterns, suspended from wire Shepherd's hooks around the south lawn periphery, would deter his hungry blood-sucking insect friends from crashing the party.

From the suite's windows that faced the front gardens, he watched the steady stream of limos and customized Dark Island motorized carts disembark clots of well-dressed dinner guests. Not a blue-light-special shopper in the bunch, he'd venture to guess. Some—the newbies—might wonder why the host of the Blue Blood Ball wasn't there to greet them. The veterans knew: Vincent Bedsloe III always made a grand entrance after the initial teaser appetizers and ample amounts of libation had been consumed.

And what a grand selection of food and beverages they would have. Vincent mentally reviewed the menu, delighting in the faint memory of the taste of food. Initially, the *pass-arounds*—the platters of gator tail, grouper fingers, and bacon-wrapped water chestnuts. Delectable little teasers of the culinary treats to come, served to the milling crowd as they sipped cocktails or wine while awaiting the invitation into the main tent.

The plated, sit-down meal would follow; no all-you-can-eat, trough-style food bar for this bunch. First, an organic spring greens and cucumber salad with balsamic vinaigrette. Then, Apalachicola Oysters Rockefeller followed by a creamy Florida Lobster Bisque. The main course, a tender filet mignon and succulent quail combo, served with wild rice pilaf and asparagus with hollandaise sauce. For the bread lovers, an assortment of freshly-baked rolls and sweet cream butter. Of course, Vincent had planned for every contingency. A roasted vegetable medley over whole wheat penne pasta would be available for the true vegetarians in the group.

The dessert course—Dark Island sweets were legend—would consist of Arby's special Baked Florida and a Key Lime Pie so tart and divine, guests would be talking about it for months.

The Master of Dark Island closed his eyes and moaned. If only he could experience the seduction of food.

Vincent checked his reflection in the newly-installed holographic 3-D imager: a step up from the digital mirrors. From any angle, the Master of Dark Island was perfect. Black Armani tuxedo. Shoes polished to a high gloss. Sparkling ruby cufflinks. But, the *piéce de résistance*? A full-length black cape lined in red satin. No well-dressed blood-sucker would be caught undead without it.

He smiled and allowed his lips to curl enough to show off his sharp canine teeth. The humans would marvel. *Surely, he had them custom-made by a local dentist, and glued into place,* they might whisper. *They look so real!* Vincent touched one razor-sharp edge. Pity he didn't use them to actually bite anything.

In a half-hour, the private phone buzzed. Everything was on time. A bell-ringer had circulated around the lawn filled with guests mingling and drinking, announcing dinner in the main tent.

Arby's voice: "Ready for you in ten minutes, Sir."

Vincent took one last look at his three-dimensional image and spun around. He lifted a wall sconce and a bookshelf pivoted, revealing a hidden stairway that led to an underground exit from the mansion. Not that he ever needed to hide, but the gothic flair of having the passageway seemed appropriate for an old showplace owned by a vampire. The trainer waited with the stallion, an animal he had grown fond of in a short time. Vlad—named after the legendary Vlad the Impaler—would be staying on at Dark Island after the gala. Plans for the expansive stables awaited on Vincent's computer.

By the time Vincent sat in the saddle, the party guests were seated in the main tent. The wine stewards milled around the room. The lights were lowered. On cue from the overseer standing in the shadows watching for Vincent to appear, a voice announced: "Ladies and Gentlemen. Your attention please. The Master of Dark Island has arrived!"

Vlad galloped through the gardens and onto the circular drive, stopping as rehearsed in the spotlights. Vincent reined in hard and the animal reared, pawing the air and snorting. The vampire clung to his broad back as if the two were one being. Vlad danced in place, his front hoofs clattering on the pavement, his nostrils flaring. Vincent patted the animal's sleek black shoulder and spoke endearments. The animal's ears perked forward. He calmed and stood still as Vincent dismounted. A handler took the reins and led the horse away.

The Master of Dark Island turned to face the tent. Lars hit the special FX fans stationed in the greenery. Vincent's cape billowed in the lights, revealing the red lining that flashed like a river of blood. With the bold look of a God, he entered the tent.

Vincent ended his parade in the spotlights at the center of the tent and stood next to the main floral display featuring a four-foot ice sculpture of a mosquito. He looked up and surveyed his appreciative audience. Two hundred people, seated eight to a round table, watched his every move. A good number—former spa patrons—shone with the faint halo of his blood distillate's glamour. Vincent smiled. He was among many old friends.

This moment. This time in the spotlight. Vincent reveled in it! He loved it! The applause flowed into him like a pint of his best Cuban blood.

Play it, he thought. *Play it!*

Vincent was so on fire he had to look down to see if his feet were still on the ground. He grabbed a wireless mic staged in the floral and said, "Thank you all for coming. You have been so kind to the Hemophiliac Association. I do hope this evening expresses our appreciation."

Vincent continued the kudos while his event planner's eye evaluated the service staff, the table settings, floral, lighting, the other men's suits, and the linens. Upon finishing the *obligatorys*, Vincent extended his invitation to the guests to enjoy all the treats that the Blue Blood Ball had to offer for as long as they wished.

"And...Oh yes, you must visit the glorious addition to the Moon Garden here at Dark Island. The very capable Arby Brown has blessed me with a new garden sculpture set in a waterfall. It is extraordinary!" Vincent raised a glass of distillate especially placed for him and toasted the evening. "So my friends, enjoy!"

With that, Vincent put the down the mic and began to mingle with his adoring guests. Lars signaled to dim the lights to dinner level and hit the background music. The din of small talk filled the room, and the staff served up the salad course. The votives on the tables flickered on the faces of the patrons as they discussed nothing, and the standard aroma of the southern evening event, citronella, wafted thru the tent.

Arby—clad for the evening in a camo-printed tuxedo and beekeeper hat—observed the whole entrance extravaganza from Lars' control station.

Lars finally sat down, released a breath, and looked at Arby. "This rocket has been launched."

Arby pated the production engineer's shoulder, gave him a thumbs up, and disappeared into the perimeter of the gala grounds.

****

"Where did you get these tickets? From some guy on a street corner?" Emmaraud frowned as she looked down the backstretch of the Daytona Speedway.

"I got 'em from a fella who hangs out at the bar. He and his old lady couldn't come. I think her mama took a bad turn. Got a good deal on them. Beggars can't be choosers. Most of these folks have had their tickets well over a year in advance."

Emmaraud pointed to the Megatron monitor. The drivers—waving from flashy chauffeured Corvettes—were being shown off to the cheering crowd on the opposite side of the racetrack. "They're not even going to drive by these stands! Way to go, Jimmy Rob. I get us behind the pits to meet the drivers and you have us sitting in the worst seats in the whole damn speedway."

He pointed to the first and second rows beneath them. "Not the worst. We're pretty high up. Them down there's the worst. Those folks end up lookin' like they've been in a tornado. All the debris and bits of tire rubber fly all over them."

The Tiny Lund section—about mid-track of the 3400-foot Superstretch—had a decent view of turns three and four. Not the pits. Would he have preferred to be smack dab in the middle of the front stretch where he could watch all the pit action? Sure. But, just being here was meat enough. The rest would have been gravy. Most of his life, he'd had to settle for no gravy. He got used to it.

He handed Emmaraud a set of green earplugs. "You better put these in. It gets pretty loud, with the crowd noise and the cars. My ears rang for a week last time, and that was back when I was human. Might not be a great experience with hearing like what we got now."

"How am I supposed to listen to Jimmie J. through this headset if I got foam crammed in my ears?" She shoved the earplugs into a front jeans pocket.

He shrugged. "Got a point there, Emmaraud."

Jimmy Rob glanced down the backstretch and reviewed the stats on the track. A 2.5 mile Trioval, with 32 degree banking in turns one through four, 18 degrees in the Trioval, and 3 degrees in the backstretch. The Daytona 400 race: 160 laps, 400 miles.

"You have that goofy look on your face again," Emmaraud said. "Snap out of it and tell me what happens now."

"Somebody will sing the national anthem. Then, they'll be a fly-over in a bit, after the drivers are introduced. I love that part. I could come just to watch that. Then, some fella will say, *Gentleman, start your engines!*"

"And they start racing then?"

Jimmy Rob shook his head. "They do a couple of what they call parade laps first. Watch and see, Emmaraud. Just watch and see."

To have been on the planet since before the birth of Christ, the vampiress had as much patience as a two-year old. Probably less.

"Good thing we got these little closed circuit dealies, and that monitor shows us what's going on. Otherwise, I'd be really pissed. You know how I get when I get pissed."

"No, I wouldn't have a clue."

Later, when the line-up of race cars passed by behind the pacer car, the crowd stood at its feet. Jimmy Rob felt the blood rush of energy flowing from the humans around them. The scent of the racing fuel, a strong aroma like denatured alcohol, filled his nose. The perfume of NASCAR.

"Why do they do that squirrelly driving?" Emmaraud asked. The cars—lined up two deep—trailed the pace car and weaved back and forth in line.

"They're warming up the tires. Watch for the pace car to turn off its lights. You know it's coming then."

A roar arose from the front stretch as the pace car left the pack. The official waved the green flag.

"Whoo-wee!" Emmaraud jumped up and down. She balled up her fist and looked for something to pelt. Jimmy Rob volunteered his shoulder to keep the humans around him from ending up in the hospital.

A woman in her late sixties—fried blonde hair, pancake make-up, hot pants, from her attire, clearly a Dale, Jr. fan—held up her shirt and flashed her naked chest each time the #88 car whizzed past. If she kept it up, everyone around her would see her melons two hundred times.

Jimmy Rob noticed a tattooed #8 in faded blue over the woman's left breast. Since Dale, Jr. had recently changed his racing number, Jimmy Rob wondered if the woman would add the second eight, and to which side. Humans were such fun.

At times, the concept of eternity hit Jimmy Rob like someone had slammed a car hood over his head. Not one of the new light-framed ones, either. One of those heavy jobs like the one on the *Goat*.

In such a short time, the now-fresh young male faces of his idolized drivers would disappear, replaced by others who had dreamed of sitting behind the wheels of bright-colored cars stamped with sponsors' logos. In a hundred years, would the cars still even have wheels? Or maybe skim along on air currents, fueled by some kind of yet-to-be-discovered energy cell? At this pinpoint in time, Jimmy Rob still felt as if he belonged—just another good old boy fan. A pea-shade-shy of human.

With a few centuries behind him, might he act just like Emmaraud Bonneville? Like every human pastime held a burst of amusement before it, too, faded into timeless oblivion?

Jimmy Rob shuddered. Sometimes he had deep thoughts. If he waited a bit, they would leave him be. He needed a stiff blood drink. He glanced around the crowd. One group a couple of rows back seemed to be particularly pickled. All five twenty-something boys could barely stand. One kept waving to Lake Lloyd, yelling out, *Where are the boats? Where are the got-damned boats!*

A ripple of odd twitchiness came over him, as if he itched from the inside out. He glanced down at his hands. They had turned a brilliant shade of orange since the morning. What in the hell had gotten into him? He thought back. Nothing out of the ordinary back on the Island. He had waxed two of the limos with some new concoction Arby had given him. He shook his head. *Nah.* Could it be something in the blood drinks from the previous night? Nothing had bothered him before, and he had sipped from some pretty questionable donors. *Nah.* Vincent always told him the sun really didn't hurt vampires, but maybe he was special. They'd been roaming around in the harsh Florida sun for hours. Then, why come it hadn't affected Emmaraud? *I'm just more sensitive.* He nodded. *Gotta be it.*

Jimmy Rob shivered. The itchy sensation came in waves. In the stands behind him, the boy continued to bellow about boats. Jimmy Rob wouldn't have to look too far to find a cure for what ailed him. He'd have to invite the fellows for a drink later.

Two hours into the race, Emmaraud turned to him. "We have to shift back to the Island."

"What?" he yelled back.

"I have a surprise planned for the gala."

Jimmy Rob strained to talk over the crowd and engine noise. "I promised fruity-boy I wouldn't crash his little tea party."

"Okay. But I didn't."

"He'll be pissed."

"When has that ever bothered you?"

Jimmy Rob scowled. "What the hell, Emmaraud. We'll miss the finish!"

She grabbed his hand and dragged him from their row. "I'll get you back in plenty of time to see the checkered flag and all that *burning the tires* shit. I promise. Only, we have to go now."

****

Vincent sensed the vampires before he saw them. From across the main tent, Arby sucked in a startled breath. The guests, unaware, *oohed* and *ahhed* over the flaming Baked Florida desserts that seemed to float around the enclosure, held high by the servers.

Emmaraud was resplendent in a gown of pale blue. Jimmy Rob, cleaned up and in a tux, still managed to emit a trailer-trash aura. The old adage about not being able to make a silk purse from a sow's ear ran through Vincent's mind. His blood son's hands were a strange shade of orange. Had to be a story behind that. Vincent glanced toward Arby. His caretaker wore a sly grin.

Diente, cradled in one of the vampiress' arms, sported a sky blue party frock with matching velvet bows attached to her head. The girly outfit didn't match the little Chihuahua's ill-tempered expression.

Heads swiveled around the room. Vincent heard the name of a famous hotelier's daughter whispered from multiple lips.

No folks. Sorry to disappoint you, Vincent thought. *This pseudo-heiress would rather see you stone-cold on a marble slab in some crypt than all comfy on a pillow-top mattress in a fancy hotel room.*

Vincent managed to paste on a smile. He walked over to the party-crashing couple and grasped Emmaraud's hand as if he greeted a long-lost favorite cousin.

"What are you doing here?" He spoke in a low voice into one of her sapphire-decorated ears. "You promised."

"Oh, Vincent. How very ungracious of you. You really think I'd miss your little party?"

Jimmy Rob eyed a vapid blonde sitting at the table next to where they stood, and wondered if her blood would be as sweet as her blank expression.

"Don't get any ideas, Jimmy Rob," Vincent said through clenched teeth.

Emmaraud brushed one hand across Jimmy Rob's cheek. "He'll behave. Not to worry."

"So you've made your grand entrance," Vincent said. "Why not do all the warm-blooded creatures a favor and make your grand exit?"

"You are such an ungrateful child. I came back especially to give you a little surprise." Before Vincent could respond, the vampiress clapped her hands twice.

A vintage Volkswagen painted like a ladybug screeched to a halt outside the tent, in the exact spot Vincent had appeared on horseback earlier in the evening. A troupe of little people tumbled out, dressed in mosquito costumes. They skipped, somersaulted, and ran into the tent and buzzed in circles around the seated guests.

"Aren't they just the cutest little vampires?" Emmaraud asked. "I turned them at a fair outside of Lisbon. I plan to use them at my spa."

Vincent stared, his mouth agape. No words could describe the scene: a munchkin *Cirque de Soleil*, complete with wings and fangs. Diente barked and twirled in circles in their midst, adding another layer of bizarre. All commenced to dancing around in the spotlights trained on the frozen mosquito sculptures.

"Don't look so stunned, Vincent. They agreed not to bite your precious party guests. Aren't the little buggy outfits adorable? I thought they would fit in perfectly with your theme."

"This is wrong on so many levels, Emmaraud. I don't even know where to begin."

Vincent gasped. One of the costumed players circled around a beautiful brunette, showing teeth.

Vincent turned to his blood sire. "Emmaraud, get them out of here! I want them off The Dark! Now!"

She frowned. "You are such a bore."

Somehow, the professional servers had managed to complete the dessert course through the melee. Unaware of the dangerous nature of the little bloodsuckers that juggled the silverware and performed back-flips around the tent, the gala guests laughed and applauded as they dug into the Baked Florida dessert.

"See?" Emmaraud said. "They're a hit. They call themselves *El Circo Oscuro*, The Dark Circus."

Vincent forced his voice to remain low and calm. "Off. The. Island. Now."

Emmaraud twisted her lips into a pout. "Can't they stay a bit longer? I promised to take them to Disney World tomorrow. They'll be terribly disappointed."

"Zap them to the dark side of the moon and pretend it's a thrill ride. I don't care. Just—"

The vampiress sighed. "All right. All right. Pull your cotton boxers from your crack."

"Jimmy Rob is wearing off on you, Emmaraud." Vincent shook his head.

"You don't know the half of it." She turned her attention to the bedlam and clapped three times. The little players glanced her way, then trundled from the tent. They crammed back into the VW. The car rumbled, backfired a couple of times, and took off in a puff of smoke and burned rubber.

The guests applauded and laughed.

"You'll thank me for this later, Vincent. This will be one Blue Blood Ball they'll never forget."

Vincent took a deep breath and exhaled. "Where are they going, just in case I need to alert the law enforcement officers off-Island?"

Emmaraud swatted a hand through the air. "I telepathed the leader. They know how to shift, so I'll meet up with them at my place on South Beach tomorrow. I want to go to

Disney, too. And you know Jimmy Rob is dying to go. I can't believe you've never been."

Vincent smirked. The Magic Kingdom would never be the same.

The Master of Dark Island became aware of another brewing problem. Reanita—seated at the table with Julia and the Senator—and Jimmy Rob's gazes were locked together. Reanita's cheeks flushed with blood. Arby noticed it and stepped between the two. Jimmy Rob's eyes narrowed.

"Drop it." Vincent warned in a low voice. "You don't really want her, and now is not the place or time. Let her be."

Jimmy Rob glared at Arby, then at his blood sire. He stepped back. Vincent allowed his pulse to calm. One thing the guests didn't need for entertainment was a bitch-slapping contest between two vampires.

The Master of Dark Island lifted his nose and sniffed. "Do you smell that?"

Jimmy Rob and Emmaraud sampled the night air.

"What?" Emmaraud asked. "The browned meringue on the Baked Florida, or the wood smoke?"

"Wood smoke." Vincent's pulse quickened.

The lightening. Given the recent storm, the scent of smoke was an evil portend.

"I'll step outside and shift. Take a look around," Emmaraud offered. She walked from the tent and returned less than a minute later. She wiggled her finger, motioning for Vincent, Jimmy Rob, and Arby to follow her outside.

The vampiress kept her voice low. "I've a bit of bad news, Vincent. Seems your island is on fire."

Chapter 26

"All right then," Vincent said.

Arby stared at his boss. How could he manage such a state of calm?

"What part of the Island, Emmaraud? How fast is it moving?" Vincent asked.

Emmaraud thought for a moment. "It's at the tip, pretty far off, past the docks. But it's gaining ground fast."

Vincent lifted his head and studied the tree tops. "Luckily, there is little wind."

"We have to get the guests off-Island," Arby stated.

Vincent nodded. "Yes." He glanced around the group. "Arby, contact security, alert them that we will be evacuating immediately." He looked at the circular drive, to the line of parked cars and modified golf carts. "We'll load up all four of the limos with as many as possible. I want every vehicle capable of moving, taking people off-Island."

Arby grabbed his radio. "The production team and caterers have vans."

"Radio Lars. Have him round up his workers, the wait staff, barkeepers, and caterers. Tell them to leave the equipment. Anything that might be destroyed, I will pay to replace. Priority: get the humans to safety. Have him get his people off, then return with the empty vans to help get the guests out of here. Call Barbie and alert the Dark Island staffers. We'll need everyone down here to help."

****

On the other side of the south lawn, Lars listened to Arby's terse message and broke into a run. The production manager commandeered the caterers to gather their crew, fill their trucks, and immediately leave the island. He motioned for his audio tech to start up the rental truck, while one of the lighting techs flung open the back door. A second tech jumped into the back and started pulling bartenders and other staff into the truck as fast as he could. Lars took off in the direction of the auxiliary tents.

When the production staffers had crammed in as many bodies as possible, the tech slammed the back door and motioned for the driver. "Go! Go! Go!" he yelled.

As the truck sped off, the tech left to locate Lars and found him in the kitchen tent disconnecting the propane tanks.

"Here," Lars called out, "help me load these!"

The two men slung tanks into the company van. Lars grabbed his laptop from the control station, and they jumped into the van and sped toward the main gate.

"As soon as I get these tanks off-Island, I'm coming back to help Vincent get the guests out. Not their usual fancy ride, but I'll bet none of them will turn it down tonight."

****

Vincent turned to Emmaraud and Jimmy Rob. "You two, position yourselves at the back two corners of the main tent. I'll make the announcement. I need you to use your glamour to reinforce mine, to help keep the humans calm."

Emmaraud spoke up, "Humans can be like cattle when they're panicked. I was at this soccer match one time—"

Vincent held up a hand. "Save the anecdotes for later." He glanced around the small group. "Everyone understands what to do?"

Arby nodded and walked a few feet into the darkened edge of the garden to make calls without alerting the guests. Jimmy Rob and Emmaraud exchanged excited glances. Vincent noticed their glamours undulating as they fell in behind him.

The Master of Dark Island—resplendent in his flowing vampire cape—ramped up his glamour and walked into the main tent to the dance floor microphone and motioned to the technician to bring the lighting up to full.

"Honored guests. May I have your attention, please?"

The tone of his voice flowed like honeyed blood around the large enclosure. The clatter of utensils quieted. Conversations ceased. Everyone looked at the dashing figure beneath the blue-tinged spotlight.

"I am sorry to call this delightful evening to an end at such an early hour, but I must."

A low murmur of voices hummed around the room. Vincent pushed a wave of calming glamour outward.

"The recent storm a few miles from our lovely Island has ignited a brush fire at the far end of The Dark. As a precaution, we will be moving everyone off-Island. I ask for your orderly exodus. We have time and vehicles to accommodate everyone."

All lies, thought Vincent. *It will be just short of a miracle.*

The Master of Dark Island motioned for the table nearest to him. They stood and filed toward the main door as if they had just been asked to join a leisurely stroll through the moon garden. Vincent continued to send a wash of glamour across the room. He noted Emmaraud and Jimmy Rob doing the same from the back corners. Everything went smoothly until the line-up reached the table where Senator Harrison Holt and Julia Holt sat.

The Senator grabbed his wife's elbow and yanked. "C'mon. Let's go."

Julia stood and blinked as if she had been drugged. She turned her head to locate Thomas at the next table.

Vincent noticed the raw hatred flash in her eyes when she turned to face her husband.

"No."

The Senator wrapped his arm around her midsection and spoke to her as if he addressed a simple-minded child. "Come, Julia. Come with me. Let's—"

Vincent watched the scenario with interest. The glamour energy snapped and popped around Julia as if she had forcibly cast it aside.

The Senator's wife glared at him. "I'm not leaving with you, Harrison."

He leaned down and spoke through clenched teeth, still managing to maintain a semblance of a smile for the benefit of the crowd. "Don't cause a scene, Julia. Not here, for God's sake."

She turned and called, "Thomas!"

The actor left his table and crossed the short distance. Julia turned back to face her husband. "I'm not going anywhere with you, you lying bastard. You miserable excuse for a man!"

Two of the media photographers snapped to attention and grabbed for their cameras.

Vincent left his post by the front entrance and approached the stand-off. "We should talk about this outside, please."

Julia shook off the Senator's grasp and stepped toward Thomas. He nodded and offered his arm. They walked out first, followed by the still-smiling senator.

The next table stood and joined the line awaiting vehicles. Vincent stepped outside and joined the three feuding humans.

"To assure your safety, I suggest you three settle your differences off-Island." Vincent motioned toward the line-up of limos and carts.

Julia glared at Senator Holt. "You can go, Harrison. I'm riding with Thomas."

"What the hell is going on here, Julia?" He spotted a cameraman and flashed a toothy grin.

"You can ride back to your precious Capitol alone." She crossed her arms over her chest and stuck out her chin.

Vincent resisted the urge to cheer *bravo!*

"Now is not the time for theatrics, Julia. I have re-election coming."

"Screw your re-election, you asshole!" She yelled. "Screw your whole female campaign staff! You seem to be really good at that."

The Senator spun around and darted to one of the Dark Island golf carts. He shoved the staffer from the driver's seat, commandeered the cart, and drove off. The photographers snapped pictures of scenario: the line of people waiting for transport, the valet rolling around on the pavement, Vincent's shocked expression.

"Save your own ass, Senator Holt!" Julia called out as he disappeared down the driveway. "You always have!"

Vincent ushered Thomas and Julia to the next cart in line. "Take care of her, Thomas," he said to the actor. Then, to Julia, "and you—"

Julia held a finger tip to Vincent's lips. "I'll be in touch. Don't worry about me." She gave him a warm hug and joined her lover. Several of the other guests filed into the cart before it pulled away.

In a short time, the main tent and grounds stood empty. Off-Island, security and the local law enforcement officers coordinated the departing guests, moving them in the opposite direction of the smoke and fire dangers and setting up road blocks to prevent anyone from reentering the area.

****

Arby snapped the radio onto his belt. "Security reports all the guests are accounted for, and the production staff, caterers, and servers. Everyone is off-Island. The wind has picked up a bit, and the fire has jumped to the mainland toward the north end of the Island. Trucks are coming in to fight it. The bridge is still open, for now. So far, no casualties. But the woods are so dry; it may take some time to bring it under control."

Vincent released a breath. "That just leaves us."

The vampire looked around the small group gathered in the mansion's foyer. "I'll take the last limo load off, with all of you."

"We're staying here," Raven stated. Her husband Hector stood beside her with little Christina in his arms.

Barbie said, "I'm not leaving either."

Stefanie with an *f* and Scotty nodded. "In for a penny, in for a pound," the a.m. trainer said.

Scotty held Diente and stroked the little dog's head. Amazing.

Maria, Carlos, and Elena exchanged glances. "We no leave *chew, Señor* Vincent," Maria said.

Angelina, still in her cook's apron, wiped the flour from her hands. "I will stay, also."

Vincent held up his hands. "You overwhelm me with your loyalty, but—"

"No buts, Vincent," Raven said. "You're the reason most of us are here and not in some hovel scraping by."

Arby felt as if he might cry. Reanita, standing by his side, squeezed his hand.

"We should be okay," the caretaker said. "The watering system for the gardens is on. The grounds are already pretty moist, since we watered everything down right before the gala. Even if we lose power, the generators are sufficient to keep the pumps running. This might be the only part of Dark Island not destroyed."

Jimmy Rob leaned over and whispered into Emmaraud's ear, "If we shift now, we can still make it back to Daytona before the race is over."

"Shush." She looked from Jimmy Rob to Vincent. "Hey, where's the starlet chick that kept following me around like a sick puppy? I didn't see her leaving the Island."

Barbie spoke up, "I can't believe I forgot about her! She went up to her suite not long ago. A little before everything went all nutso. Said she didn't feel well. She looked pretty pale, come to think of it. Maybe she just has one of her migraines."

"I'll go check on her," Arby said. He gave Reanita's hand a quick squeeze. He glanced toward the elevators, thought about the possibility of a power outage, and took the staircase.

Vincent nodded and turned toward the group. "As long as all of you know, I will do whatever it takes to keep you safe. You are welcome to remain at the mansion. Any second thoughts?"

The members of the small group shook their heads.

In a few minutes, Arby reappeared and bustled down the stairs. "Vincent! You'd best come with me."

Vincent followed his overseer to the patrons' wing on the second floor.

When they entered Patrice's suite, Arby motioned toward the bed. "This is how I found her. She's unresponsive. Either she's over-medicated, or worse. We'll need to contact the authorities and figure a way to get her off-Island to the nearest hospital."

Vincent tuned into Patrice Palmer's glamour. *Alive, but just barely.* He probed deeper. The reality of the starlet's condition sunk in. One or both of the aneurisms had burst. A small portion of her brain struggled to maintain her breathing and blood pressure. Basic life functions.

Emmaraud and Jimmy Rob appeared in the room.

"She don't look so hot," Jimmy Rob commented.

Arby reached for his radio. "I'll call the County EMS."

Emmaraud grabbed his hand. "Wait. Let's think this thing through. Vincent, you've had her blood, right? What's her deal?"

Vincent reached down and tenderly pushed back a hank of sweat-drenched hair from Patrice's forehead. "She had two weak spots in the arteries deep in her brain."

Arby stared. "A stroke? You think?"

Arby fumbled in his coverall pocket for the penlight he always carried. Old nursing habits died hard. He lifted one eyelid, then the other, flashing the beam of concentrated light into the starlet's eyes. "Shit." He backed away. "Pupils are unresponsive. One is clearly blown. We need to get her to a hospital ER as soon as possible. I still don't know—"

Emmaraud shook her head. "Even if I grab her up and we shift right now, will she survive?"

Vincent allowed the sad truth to filter in. "I might not have the medical diagnostic equipment to show empirical evidence, but I assure you her brain is flooded with blood. I don't sense any of what I know to be Patrice Palmer. What is there—" he motioned to the bed. "—is a barely-alive husk."

"They could put her on life support," Arby said.

"And then what?" Emmaraud asked. "They take her off and she dies anyway?"

Arby's expression remained blank. "Not instantly. But within a few hours, yes. The basic functions keeping her body alive will gradually fail."

Emmaraud turned to her blood child. "What good would it do, Vincent? It will only shine a horrible light on Dark Island. A death here at the Spa. Not good for you, or me. Or any of us."

Vincent stared at his blood sire. "Just let her die, Emmaraud? What then, throw her body into the ocean?"

Arby couldn't fathom the vampiress' lack of feeling. "God, that's cold. Even for you."

Vincent added, "There's another consideration. She's pregnant."

They all stared down at the comatose starlet.

"She was so excited." Vincent's voice cracked. "So excited about being a mother. I told her she could stay here on the Island…"

Emmaraud grasped Vincent's hand. "We have to turn her, Vincent."

The Master of Dark Island studied his blood sire's face. "What?"

"No matter how hard you or anyone tries to save her, she's already gone. If she stops breathing, the baby dies, too. We have to turn her." Emmaraud looked down at the comatose starlet. "In a way, I've grown somewhat accustomed to her worshiping my every move. Every time I turned around, I practically tripped over her. It might be a pity to let her die."

"Not like you spent an abundance of quality time with her, Emmaraud. What? A minute here, a minute there? You're going to take her on as one of your little pet projects?" Vincent frowned. "You'll grow tired of her, and the child, in a few years. What then?"

Emmaraud rolled her eyes. "C'mon, Vincent. She'll be one of us. She can take care of herself. Don't we all grow deathly weary of each other, anyway?"

Jimmy Rob finally spoke, "Wait a minute. I thought you told me vampires couldn't hatch out younguns."

Emmaraud nodded. "I did. Two vampires cannot produce an offspring."

"Like hybrid plants," Arby mumbled. "No viable seeds capable of reproduction."

"Would her unborn human child survive the change?" Vincent asked.

Emmaraud shrugged. "Hard to predict. I have heard of others. I suppose it depends on how far along the pregnancy is, or maybe the mother's initial health. One thing's

Evenings on Dark Island

for sure, Vincent. Patrice and her baby are dead if we don't. You must turn Patrice Palmer."

Vincent's face contorted; a wash of emotions, sadness, and mild distaste. "I can't...bite a female."

"Oh, for the love of—" Emmaraud said.

Vincent pointed to his blood sire. "*You* turn her."

"Me?" Emmaraud pointed to herself. "I don't bite women either."

Jimmy Rob puffed his chest out. "Who's your daddy! Lemme do it."

Vincent and Emmaraud's heads snapped in the third vampire's direction. They said in unison, "No!"

"Well, hell! Why not? You—" he pointed to Vincent, "are too fruity to do it, and you—" he wiggled his finger in the vampiress' direction, "aren't fruity enough!"

Emmaraud propped her hands on her hips. "Only one solution. Vincent, you and I both have to do this."

"What?" Vincent and Jimmy Rob said.

Emmaraud nodded. "That way, it won't be as weird for either of us."

Arby cradled Patrice's hand and probed the wrist for a pulse.

"Look at it this way, Vincent." Emmaraud said." The kid—if it survives—will be your grandchild, and mine." She smiled like a used car salesman trying to unload a clunker.

Jimmy Rob raised his hands. "Whoa, Nellie. That's way too weird. That'd be like a mama and a son having a...grandbaby?" His features screwed up as he tried to contemplate the contorted relationship. "That is just too freakin' twisted. Besides, you don't even much like each other."

Arby gently lowered Patrice's hand and felt around for the carotid pulse on one side of the starlet's pale neck. "I don't care which one of you does it, or all three! But it best happen soon. Her heart rate is all over the place, and not very strong."

Vincent held up one hand. "Okay. Stop. Here's what we'll do. Jimmy Rob and Emmaraud will do this together."

"That could work." Emmaraud smiled over at Jimmy Rob. "You ready to be a granddaddy?"

Jimmy Rob figured he'd skipped the hard part—being a father. Probably the part he'd more than likely screw up. "I'm sittin' on go."

Vincent sighed. "I wouldn't be a very good role model, anyway."

Emmaraud stepped over to her blood child and hugged him. "Of course you would, Vincent. You can be his Godfather."

Godfather, Vincent thought. It had a nice ring. He imagined himself as the spiritual head of a big, loyal family. The leader of all. "I would be honored."

Vincent and Arby backed away from the bedside and allowed the two vampires to step into place on opposite sides of Patrice.

"Do it," Vincent said. "Do it quickly, before we lose both of them."

Jimmy Rob and Emmaraud exchanged knowing glances. He reached over and held one of the vampiress' hands. Both of them reached down and grasped Patrice's limp hands. They butted heads a couple of times like bespectacled preteens bumping noses on a first kiss, then figured a way for both to access a carotid artery. With as much tenderness as two preternatural predators could muster, Jimmy Rob and Emmaraud bit down on Patrice Palmer's neck.

Chapter 27

Arby stood for a few moments, trying to absorb the scene he had just witnessed.

Patrice Palmer, back from the dead. Or, better stated: forward *with* the dead. Jimmy Rob whining about missing the last laps at Daytona. Emmaraud promising to get the three of them there in time for the finish, then off to Miami to meet up with the happy troupe of miniature vampires. A quick shift to Orlando and Disney World, everyone!

The last thing Arby saw was the three vampires—the ancient one, the redneck, and the new convert—holding onto Emmaraud's hands. Patrice Palmer glanced from Jimmy Rob to the vampiress like a child happy to be going on vacation with her doting parents.

To everyone's surprise, Emmaraud morphed into a raven-haired beauty.

"What gives?" Jimmy Rob asked. "Who the hell are you, now?"

"Myself. This—" the vampiress let go of Jimmy Rob and Patrice and slid her hands up and down her slender body. "—is the real me."

Vincent's eyebrows arched. "You're stunning. Why would you ever want to look like another human, when your real persona is so beautiful, so exotic?"

"I get bored," she answered.

Clearly of middle-Eastern lineage, the vampiress—with her dark hair and ebony eyes and skin the color of coffee latte—could have been an Egyptian queen. She glanced down at the pale blue gown, shook her head, and changed the material to a deep sapphire, a shade more flattering to her coloration.

Emmaraud shrugged. "I haven't been myself for a few hundred years."

She winked. The three blood amigos shimmered, faded, and disappeared.

After Jimmy Rob, Emmaraud, and the newly-turned Patrice Palmer vanished, Vincent left the room. The immediate crop of crises was past. He seriously required down time in a sound-proof haven, and a chance to check the remote security cameras at the garden's periphery to assure the fire had remained at bay.

When Arby stepped into the hall, Reanita appeared from behind the door to her suite. From her stunned expression, he knew. She had seen. All of it.

"We probably should talk," Arby said.

"Yeah."

Arby led the way from the mansion to the inner garden. The scent of scorched earth and wood smoke burned his eyes, and he prayed his plant children were unharmed.

When they stepped into the greenhouse, Arby closed his eyes and gave thanks to whatever greater power had saved his careful work. For a few minutes, he walked up and down the aisles, offering waves of telepathic praise and soothing vibrations. Where so many of their kin had died horrible deaths all around Dark Island, the lucky few on the garden grounds and inner sanctum flourished. Arby felt hopeful, until he turned and saw the expression on Reanita's face.

One of Jimmy Rob's favorite expressions flashed through his mind: *Gonna be hell to pay for this.*

Neither seemed anxious to speak first. Finally, Reanita cleared her throat.

"I have something to tell you, then I have questions."

Arby nodded.

"I'm not who I seem. I—"

"Neither am I, Rea."

She held up a hand. "Just let me get through this, okay?" She took a deep breath. "My name is not Reanita Register. It is Reanita Runkle. And I'm not a rich oil-baron's daughter from Texas. I'm a DEA agent from Washington, D.C."

She motioned to the gown. "I don't wear designer clothes. Hell, I don't even own a pair of shoes worth more than forty dollars, tops."

Arby felt his legs weaken, and he lowered himself onto the edge of a wooden bench.

She continued, "I came to Dark Island to uncover alleged drug activities along the coastline of this area. And I found what I was looking for."

Surprise painted his features. "You did?"

"Time to come clean, Arby. The late night shipments? The obvious opulence of this place? C'mon…"

"Whatever you think you saw—I can explain. But, it's going to be a little odd."

She huffed. "Odd? Odd! I just witnessed two whatever-they-are's bite down on a woman's neck. A woman who was obviously pretty near death, from what I overheard. Can't really call it murder, 'cause I saw her bound out of bed a few minutes later like she had been born again at a tent revival. Not to mention, another woman who changed from a blonde heiress to freakin' Cleopatra right in front of my eyes." Her eyebrows crimped together. "Who *are* you people? Or *what* are you people?"

Arby took a deep breath and released it slowly. "I am R.B. Brown. I am everything I told you—attorney, registered nurse, master gardener. I have not misrepresented myself or lied to you about my personal details."

"Left a lot of stuff out."

"Yes. I did. Out of loyalty and a legally-binding agreement with Vincent Bedsloe III."

Arby started at the beginning, from the first time he and Vincent met. Proceeded forward to the revival of Dark Island, to the Spa, to the present. Reanita soaked it in with little reaction, even the most bizarre parts.

"What about the clandestine shipments, Arby? I saw you hiding boxes in that little shed."

"Vincent has a taste for Cuban—blood, cigars. In that respect, I do dance on the fringe of the law. He pays dearly for the supplies and no one is hurt. Many in Cuba depend on the money."

"Explains that, but what about Jimmy Rob? The bales of marijuana sitting in his yard? What about those?"

Arby blinked. "I don't know what you're talking about, Reanita."

"Right. Huge amounts of drugs floating in here under your nose, and you have no clue?"

He shook his head. "It does not surprise me. But no, neither Vincent nor I would condone or permit such behavior. Jimmy Rob has been…difficult to control."

Did she remember the redneck's bite? Arby wondered.

Reanita continued, "I saw the other one—the woman, Emmaraud—with him on the shore. She's in on it, too."

"You must understand, Rea. Emmaraud operates on a different level. And that's putting it mildly. I can take this up with Vincent. Sometimes, they will listen to him. Certainly, not to me."

Arby stood and took a couple of steps toward her. "What do we do now? You…me…"

"I don't have a clue."

"I do love you, Reanita."

Tears shimmered in her eyes. "I love you, too."

"So you'll leave and go back to D.C.—"

Reanita laughed. "And tell my superiors what? I was on this exclusive Island and it was wonderful. I got a massage every day. I ate the best food. Wore designer clothes. Had facials and mud wraps. Swam laps. Drank my weight in wine and champagne. Worked out on top-of-the-line equipment. Rode in a Maserati—driven by a vampire chick—to a redneck dive where I ate pot-laced brownies and listened to NASCAR stats until my head nearly exploded. Attended a gala where everyone there but me contributed no less than—what?—ten thousand dollars just to eat?"

"Actually, at least ten times more. The Blue Blood Ball truly deserves its name."

"And I thought the price tag for a week at the Spa was high. Shit. I can't even wrap my mind around that kind of disposable income."

He shrugged. "Nor can I."

"Oh, and that's not all, you guys. The head man? He's a vampire who used to be a gay party planner. There's a redneck vampire who loves muscle cars, and another one—really, really old from what I've been told—who looks just like Paris Hilton, down to the well-dressed dog. Only, don't count on her staying that way. She likes to switch her appearances like we change underwear, and I saw that with my own eyes. So don't expect her to look the same every time."

Reanita paced as she ranted. "I'll tell my boss that I had the dirt on the drugs. Saw stacks of pot piled head-high. Only—oops—it burned up in the huge fire that wiped out everything on Dark Island except for the house and gardens. How convenient."

She paused. "Did I leave anything out?"

Arby considered telling her about the distillate and the paltry amounts of patrons' blood in the freezer, awaiting distillation. If there was any chance for the Spa at Dark Island's rebirth, that part of the puzzle had to remain lost under the couch cushions.

"I think you summed it up well."

She ran one hand through her hair. "I do have two more issues to address."

"Bring them on."

"May sound silly, but it's been bugging me. The two constellations on the massage room ceiling—?"

Arby nodded. "Libra and Aquarius."

"Right. They don't share the same night sky."

Arby smiled. "Didn't know you knew so much about astronomy."

She lifted her hands and tilted her head.

"Vincent's two birth months," he answered. "Aquarius, for his human birth on January 25th. The Water-Bearer: The sign of one whose purpose is to understand life's mysteries. Libra, for his vampire birth on October 3rd. The sign of balance: of a diplomat, of fairness. Vincent Bedsloe is the noblest creature I have ever known."

"He must eat a lot of birthday cake."

Arby smiled. "Not really. I haven't figured a way to make food that Vincent can process. I'm working on it. He misses that most of all, I think."

Reanita thought back to the first dinner party. "He drinks wine."

"Blood wine. Blood tea. Blood brandy."

Reanita nodded. "Of course."

"He smokes cigars, too," she pointed out.

"The one thing he can enjoy without my modifications," Arby said. "You said two issues—?"

"Hard for me to keep on track, when every answer is so bizarre." She tapped her chin. "Oh, yeah…about your little hidden plants."

Arby's face fell. "You found my special herbs."

"I did. Pretty well disguised with the cane break, but I have an eye, and nose, for that sort of thing."

"Guess you'll have something to report to headquarters after all."

"They would laugh me out of the Capitol. I came to uncover a huge covert smuggling operation along the Florida coast and found a couple of healthy marijuana plants? Get real."

"I use it in cooking, Reanita. On occasion, when a patron visits us after chemotherapy, it stimulates the appetite. Leads to a sense of well-being."

"Shit, don't tell me you laced the brownies, too." She crossed her arms over her chest. "I'm zero for two. What a joke of a drug agent *I* am. You and Jimmy Rob and his coven of rednecks have that recipe down."

He rolled his eyes. "I do admit to a bit of leeway on that particular use. A small amount of pot in a brownie or two—it's harmless and helps the new patrons relax into the spa atmosphere." He paused. "You can turn me in, Reanita. I am guilty of growing an illegal substance. But I assure you, I have never allowed any of my private stock off-Island."

"Get rid of it, Arby. Get rid of it, and I will pretend I never saw it."

"That will make you go back to Washington empty-handed," he said.

"I can report my observations. Maybe they'll help round up a few minor smugglers. I'm not going to make them happy, so why offer up a couple of plants? That would almost be worse than returning with nothing." She paused. "What good would it do, really? You'd end up in jail with murderers, rapists, and hardened career criminals. The prisons are packed. I'd rather save a spot for someone deserving of the state's hospitality."

"I thank you, Rea. I know it goes against the core of your training. I assure you, the plants will be destroyed immediately."

Arby decided to side-step reason. He reached over and caressed her cheek with one hand. "It's good, you not being some rich oil baron's daughter. I might have a chance of talking you into staying."

"Here?" She looked around, as if the noxious plants held the answer.

The looming possibility of his one true love finding a home elsewhere caused a pressure mid-sternum. "You could live with me, Reanita. As my wife. Here, there. What does it matter, as long as we are together?"

She leaned in and kissed him. For a few minutes, any past deceit forgotten.

"I need time, Arby. Time to think. Time to get my shit together."

Arby felt uplifted. At least she would think about it. "Take it, then. I will wait for you."

Reanita considered. What kept her in the nation's capitol, really? If she never set foot in her neighborhood, her apartment, would anyone sense the loss? Maybe they might comment on not seeing her, as if an unsightly eyesore had been razed to the ground. But to leave law enforcement? It was as necessary to her as breathing; her gun as much a part of her as her arms.

"I could put in for a transfer."

Arby squeezed her hand. "Just, might I ask the small favor—if you do decide to come back to me—make that transfer anywhere but Orlando. I don't think I could take all of the theme parks."

Chapter 28

Sunday evening

Arby leaned down and admired the perfect peppermint pink and red-striped blossom of *Reanita Japonica*.

"You are a beauty. I thank the heavens you survived."

A furtive movement behind him startled the gardener. He snapped upright.

"Vincent." Arby released his breath. "If I live to be five hundred, I still won't grow accustomed to the way you just appear out of thin air."

"Interesting human figure of speech, living to be five hundred. Do you really suppose a fabled creature exists, one that might actually live to such a grand old age?"

The two men—one human, one vampire—smiled.

"I figured I would find you here," Vincent said. "Just another evening on Dark Island."

"It's the first time I've had the chance to check on my hybrids since the fire, other than a perfunctory inventory. I'm so lucky they survived."

Vincent touched the perfect blossom. "Fortunate that we were able to get the guests and gala workers moved to safety. That scene shall haunt me…"

"It's all over the Internet, Sir. The online early editions of the papers—the *Miami Herald*, the *Orlando Sentinel*, the *Tallahassee Democrat*. You made *Entertainment Tonight*, too. They're calling you the *Vampire Hero* and the *Monster with a Heart*." Arby added, "Because of your costume, you see."

"I know. I've been online. The forums and blogs are abuzz, too. Isn't it ironic? The media finally tells an absolute truth—about the vampire part. But, hero?" Vincent shook his head.

"Front page stuff, Vincent. I have no doubt the story will appear above the fold in many Sunday printed editions. A picture of you ushering guests into a cart and driving them, personally, to safety."

"I was never in danger, Arby. None of the vampires were. Only the humans. I couldn't allow them to perish on my watch." He shrugged. "Besides, you all took part in the evacuation. You, Stefanie with an *f*, Scotty, Hector, Maria, Elena, Angelina, Barbie, Raven. Lars and the production team members. Without all of us flying out of here in anything with an engine and wheels, things might have turned out differently."

Arby nodded. "I was surprised at Emmaraud and Jimmy Rob. The Maserati didn't hold many at a time and the GTO—well it was good of them to pitch in."

"Might take several therapy sessions for the guests who hitched a ride with Emmaraud." Vincent chuckled. "Don't give those two a lot of credit for their personal sacrifices. Mainly, they used the rescue efforts to spirit the muscle car and Maserati off-Island to the parking lot at Jimmy Rob's bar. Their motives weren't altruistic. Jimmy Rob threw that strange mounted fish, the pit bull, and a few of his prized tools in the back seat. I suppose those things and the car were the belongings he valued most."

"Still...," Arby said. "People got off the Island because of their efforts."

"True." Vincent nodded. "The pictures of Senator Holt and his altercation with Julia are pretty hot, too. It didn't sit well with the attending media, when he took off in a golf cart with no cares about the others waiting to be transported off-Island."

"He'll bounce back, Vincent. He's a career politician. Give him a few hours and he'll put some kind of spin on it, make it sound as if he did everyone a favor. It's an election year."

"How could I forget? He suggested a sizeable campaign donation every time I passed by their table." Vincent shook his head. "Seems your fire break around the gardens and mansion worked. That and your careful attention to frequent watering." Vincent touched the leaf of a tender blood fern, one Arby had managed to root from cuttings from Vincent's special spot deep in the Dark Island swamp. He supposed the trees and ground would be now laid barren, blackened by the fire. He had not had the heart to check.

"It would be wise for us to plan a series of plowed fire breaks, for the future," the caretaker suggested.

"Arby, I made a grave error in not listening to your earlier council. For my part in our recent problems, and our estrangement, I offer my apology."

"I broke the rules, Sir."

"Rules." Vincent meandered between the rows of plants, gently touching a leaf, a tender shoot. "Yes. You did. But it was wrong for me to expect you to choose between your loyalty to me—to Dark Island—and Reanita. If only you had come to me…"

"I didn't. I'm sorry, Vincent. Truly, I am." Arby plucked a fading leaf from an overhanging thorny vine. "I was afraid. Afraid of losing her. Afraid of never feeling that way again."

"And you worried that I might take her from you, Arby?"

"The people whose blood you drink; in a way, a part of each belongs to you. I can almost feel the pull toward you, myself. I never did before you—"

"Drank from you," Vincent supplied.

Arby nodded.

"We've both been in error, Arby. So many gray areas. So little real communication."

They faced each other. Vincent finally broke the silence.

"One thing the fire showed me—no matter how much or how little time any of us have, there is never a reason to desert a good friend." Vincent held out one hand. "I am asking for your forgiveness, Arby. You have mine."

The caretaker hesitated for a moment, then reached out and shook his employer's hand. Cold, preternatural flesh to warm, human flesh. The effect to Arby: like grasping a hand formed of alabaster.

"What do we do now? How do we get past—" Arby circled his arms in the air to encompass the scalded whole of Dark Island. "—this?"

"I've given it careful consideration, Arby. First, you agree to stay on; to continue your careful care of the gardens, and of the Island."

"I find it hard to imagine my life elsewhere, Sir."

"Time to drop the formality, don't you think? I propose a full partnership. Business, of course."

"Us?"

"Who better to oversee the resurrection of Dark Island from the ashes than the two beings who most love her?" Vincent asked. "Like the Phoenix on our logo. Rising from the flames, more beautiful than before."

"Nature has a way of renewing herself, Vincent. Dark Island will be as lush as before. It will take time, but it will happen."

Vincent offered a slight smile. "Time is something I have in abundance."

The vampire studied his overseer for a moment. "With you here, watching over her for us, our Island will be reborn. I have ultimate faith, to place her in your hands."

"You sound as if you are not going to be here. Are you leaving?"

Vincent pulled a printed computer-generated picture from his jacket and handed it to Arby.

Arby studied the page and glanced up. "Transylvania?"

"I'm going away on a holiday, Arby. Long overdo. Emmaraud—no matter how self-absorbed she is—was right. Dark Island has been my prison since I lost Julio, not just my sanctuary."

"I don't believe it, but I think it's fantastic. You should take a few days and go somewhere. I can make the travel arrangements."

"No need. I've learned to shift. Been practicing a bit. Earlier this evening, I popped over to Orlando—"

"Don't tell me…?"

"Sorry, Arby. I just wanted to check in and make sure the terrible threesome and that mob of little vampires hadn't stormed the entrance castle and taken hostages. Thought about dropping by a gift shop and buying you one of those cute little mouse hats."

"You didn't!"

Vincent grinned. "I changed my mind."

"Thanks." Arby thought of Jimmy Rob. The familiar burn ignited deep inside.

Vincent noticed the shift in his caretaker's aura. "You need to find a way to let it go, Arby—your distaste for Jimmy Rob. It can only end up poorly for you."

"How did you—?"

"Anger and jealously color your energy a foul shade of pea green. Not very attractive."

"I guess I can't hide anything from you now. You'll always be poking around in my head."

Vincent sighed. "Not the case, my friend. I only use the power when I am concerned for your—or any human's—well-being." He paused. "I don't think Jimmy Rob will bother you, or Reanita. He's distraught about losing his trailer and workshop, and Emmaraud plans on keeping him busy in Spain. Something about a race track and every automotive tool he has ever dreamed of."

"He has that dive of a bar. I can't imagine him deserting it."

"He asked his friend Ray to take over the day-to-day operation. I'm sure Jimmy Rob and Emmaraud will shift back from time to time to check on things."

Arby's lips drew into a thin line. "Oh. Joy."

"He doesn't know how to shift by himself yet. Seems my blood sire is holding out on him. But, that won't last. The way Emmaraud tires of things—especially if they don't directly benefit her—she will let him in on her guarded secret soon. There's Patrice for her to consider, too. Our little vampiress starlet is buzzing about the endless possibilities of an eternal acting career after the baby comes, so I know she'll want to shift to Hollywood. I can't see Emmaraud hauling Jimmy Rob and Patrice back and forth across the globe like some kind of vampiric soccer mom. She'll eventually break down and teach them to amuse themselves."

"Again. Joy, joy. Patrice doesn't concern me, but I'll have to worry about him popping in, and when you're not around."

"I will be only a thought away, Arby."

"Good." The caretaker smiled and nodded. "What about Diente? Emmaraud just kind of ran off and deserted that little dog."

"I spoke with my blood sire on Diente's behalf. She agreed that the Chihuahua might be happier here on Dark Island. Now that Emmaraud has tired of the Paris Hilton charade, she finds no need for the accessories."

"Scotty likes Diente. He's used bits of bloody raw meat to train her to stalk rabbits. Kind of creepy. Nevertheless...Diente guards the garden against anything intent on eating my plants. That makes me happy, and it keeps the little monster occupied."

"Everything and everyone needs a purpose," Vincent said.

"But—" Vincent waved a hand through the air. "I digress from my travelogue. I figured I would pop over and visit the heartland of the vampire fable. Trace the ancient footsteps of *Vlad Terpes, Vlad the Impaler, Vlad III, Prince of Wallachia*: the man behind Stoker's *Dracula*. I'd like to see Bran Castle, the Carpathian Mountains. Take in the sights and scents of Central Romania. Afterwards, once I get past the turmoil of her recent visit, I may stop by Emmaraud's new spa and see what she's so excited about. She'll need some guidance so the whole deal doesn't turn nightmarish for the human patrons. Plus she knows little of business organization."

"You'll be gone for some time, then."

"Yes." Vincent's expression softened. "I also want to visit Cuba. I have a certain *friend* who's buried there. I wish to find his resting spot and pay my respects."

"Cuba? Do you think that safe? The political atmosphere..."

"You forget, my friend. I can blend most anywhere. Don't concern yourself. A month, two, three. I can come back and check in with you periodically." Vincent paused. "I think it's time we gave the mansion a face lift. New furnishings mixed with some we don't wish to part with. Maybe, a fresh coat of paint. Refresh. Renew. It will be fun to renovate the old place. With you and the staff here handling things, I can roam the globe for just the right treasures."

"You wish to reopen the Spa eventually, then?"

"Well, of course! Our absence will only make all of those aging Hollywood hearts grow fonder." Vincent smiled. "Besides, it's not just you and me in this, Arby. A lot of

Evenings on Dark Island

good, faithful people depend on Dark Island for their homes, their livelihoods."

Arby nodded. "Good point."

"You'll stay then?"

Arby smiled. "Yes."

"Good. It's settled." Vincent clapped Arby on one shoulder. "You draw up the paperwork, and we'll make the partnership legal."

"What about the stallion? Do you wish—?"

"I know you aren't overly fond of horses, Arby. But, I have become quite fond of Vlad. Be sure to hire the handler full-time during the day. He can train Hector to attend to any needs when the handler is off-Island. I've contacted a builder about plans for the stables. He promises to move on the construction immediately."

"Very well."

"I'll leave you to your work." Vincent said. He pivoted to leave, then turned around. "Reanita—do you think she'll return?"

"I don't know. I hope so."

"Me, too."

Vincent spoke in a soft voice. "My time away will give you an opportunity to think, Arby. About the gift of the blood. Whether or not you wish to be reborn into my kinship. If you decide you want to receive the gift, I shall make it so, upon my return. There is Reanita to consider."

Arby nodded.

"I'd like for you to think about removing your hat, too. Dark Island has chosen you—as it has the others who live here permanently. In as much, she has provided the roots for us to flourish, yet we always have a place that welcomes us home. If I can gain the courage to leave my sanctuary, you can crawl from behind your mask." Vincent paused before he added, "your journey will be as initially unsettling as my own."

Arby considered the vampire's words.

"Oh, and Arby?" Vincent added. "You might cut back a bit on the cheese."

The caretaker didn't reply immediately. Dumbstruck! How could a true friend make a veiled remark aimed at his rat-faced appearance?

"Excuse me?"

Arby shoved the absurd notion aside when he recalled one important fact: Vincent had tasted the blood vintage. Arby no longer had any secrets. He knew—better than anyone—about the stagnant cesspool of pain, left from past insults. Besides, Vincent didn't have an unkind bone in his undead body.

Vincent said, "Your cholesterol is a bit elevated."

"I'll pay more attention to my diet. Thank you."

Dressed in doggie-sized military dessert fatigues, Diente marched into the secret garden and stopped to stare at the two men. She yapped, "*Ola!*" and continued on her patrol.

Vincent and Arby laughed.

"That is going to take a little getting used to," Arby said. "Is it just me, or did it sound as if that rat dog just said *hello* in Spanish?"

Vincent nodded. He pulled a Cuban cigar from his smoking jacket's pocket. "Scotty has done wonders with the little rat dog. She's not as aggressive since he has started feeding her a regular diet of beef blood puréed with a bit of chopped sirloin. He's attempting to teach her to bark a few basic words."

"Suppose I'll have to brush up on my Spanish, just in case I need to curse her in a language she'll understand."

Vincent's expression softened. "Do you realize—just a little over a week ago, you and I stood in this exact spot, having one of our talks? So many things have changed, yet remain the same."

The Master of Dark Island smiled, his dark eyes sparkling in the low light. "Life and death. They are both *so* circular."

THE END